T. J. Lustig was born in   .
He went to school in Bishop's Stortford before
going on to study English Literature at York University
and then at Cambridge, where he is now completing a
doctoral thesis on the uncanny. He was naïve enough
to think that the writing of *Doubled Up*, his first
novel, would act as a tonic, a febrifuge and
perhaps even as an anthelmintic.

DOUBLED UP

or

MY LIFE
AS THE BACK END
OF A PANTOMIME HORSE

T. J. Lustig

published by Pan Books

First published 1990 by Fourth Estate Ltd
This Picador edition published 1992 by Pan Books Ltd,
a division of Pan Macmillan Limited,
Cavaye Place, London SW10 9PG

1 3 5 7 9 8 6 4 2

© T. J. Lustig 1990

ISBN 0 330 31827 6

Printed in England by Clays Ltd, St Ives plc

Contents

BOOK I: THE CIRCUS

BOOK II: THE CITY

FOR A.B.

Know'st thou but how the stone doth enter in
The bladder's cave, and never break the skin?
Know'st thou how blood, which to the heart doth flow,
Doth from one ventricle to th' other go?
And for the putrid stuff, which thou dost spit,
Know'st thou how thy lungs have attracted it?
There are no passages, so that there is
(For aught thou know'st) piercing of substances.

DONNE: *Of the Progress of the Soul*

'Bitzer,' said Mr Gradgrind, broken down, and
miserably submissive to him, 'have you a heart?'

'The circulation, Sir,' returned Bitzer,
smiling at the oddity of the question, 'couldn't be
carried on without one. No man, Sir, acquainted
with the facts established by Harvey relating to the
circulation of the blood, can doubt that I have a
heart.'

DICKENS: *Hard Times*

Book I

THE CIRCUS

1

I Find an Author

THE END of the twisted cable; a light burning to its feeble close, opening the curtain of the dark.

Martha comes into my room in the evening with rug and medicine. She is a good listener. Once, she told me what an interesting gentleman I was, how many stories I had. She said that my life had been like a fairy-tale. But Martha is an old woman who has led a life of kitchens and saucepans and soups and cakes.

The heaviness in my lungs comes over me and the fever again and I am no longer myself, lost amidst the stagery of a dream. Long, long dream lost to light. I rally for some reason, in obedience to some command – some stay of execution – in the black London spring. Even the sparrows are stained by the city. They have learned that I only feed them at night, when the others are sleeping and the streets are empty.

During my convalescence in the early months of 1919 I began to read again. In the evenings Martha would place the stand by my chair and arrange the lamp to throw its pool of light across the page. I travelled in my mind. I conjured scenes of distant lands and revisited places I had never been. Mérimée, Hoffmann, the *Arabian Nights*: a language of incantation in which, if we believe, the marvellous leaps from the page and burns itself into our hearts. But the books fell from my hand; I found that I had lost my faith. I was sitting idly by the fire one night when an image staler than those to which I had become accustomed sprang from nowhere into my mind. Stripped of the play of any picturesque light it did not glitter but glowed dully like a fading coal. Yet this banal picture, which included even a faint and not unhomely smell of cabbage soup, nevertheless arrested me, made me turn my eyes inward from the flickering flame of fantasy.

A missing corner-stone, chipped away by frost or lost in some collision long before I arrived: the outside wall of my childhood home. All at once a

5

great procession of long familiar but forgotten things broke through the many veils I had hung between myself and the past.

To please Martha and perhaps you as well I shall tell my story. My hands ache too much in these dark winters to write so I must advertise for a secretary and dictate. Perhaps also for Lady Magenta. And for Aramind? Yes, for her too; for all the ghosts.

I placed by the first post an advertisement in *The Times*:

GENTLEMAN
SEEKS SERVICES OF A
COMPETENT AMANUENSIS
Apply to Mr Jack Spellman
Bartholomew Square

I then waited the results of this enquiry, which appeared in the issue of 14 March.

Over the next week I interviewed perhaps half a dozen applicants for the position. These were my conditions: the work to be carried out three hours nightly, excepting Sunday and one other day to be negotiated; the week's material to be typed and presented to me on Saturday evening; a generous salary, with allowances for stationery. The memoir was to be printed at my expense and according to my directions.

I was disappointed with the applicants. Although most competent, I felt either that they were merely copyists or that they wanted to assume my authorial role. What I needed – the image became definite before me – was a ghost writer who remained anonymous and established my own solidity.

I have found him! He came to me last night, as soundlessly as the ghost I had imagined. For some reason he was amused by this analogy, which I shared with him. He is an uncertain-looking young man but I think he will be perfect for my purposes. He showed specimens of his writing by hand and by a Remington machine both satisfactory. His dictation speed was adequate and I engaged him for a probationary period of one month.

The Ghost was evidently nervous and so, after showing him to an armchair, I suggested that we should open a bottle of claret to celebrate our joint venture. After my life to some extent finished, I told him, ignoring his polite gesture of deprecation, after my life finished and my travels were over I settled in this house in London. All that was left was my wealth and my books and I determined to populate my life with these, to wander in my mind's eye. I whiled away the empty hours with literature but after a while I found it empty because it invented solid things to

6

occupy a land of shadows. Then it occurred to me that I could engage another to write my own life. Perhaps through the pen of another person I could find the history that eluded me.

And so the Ghost is to begin writing me tomorrow, after a glass of sherry, at nine o'clock in the evening. In the warmth of the room my remembering voice will hypnotize itself; its sound will be accompanied by the discreet scratching of the recording pencil.

Following the customary method, I will begin at the beginning.

2

I Lose a Legacy

I WAS christened Jacek Adam Spellman: Jacek for my mother because it is the given name of her fathers; Adam for my own father and also for Mickiewicz, who died in the year of his marriage. Spellman once again for my father, old nibbler, old gobbler, slurper of broths. I was Jake to Claire Grey and Jacques to Sir Rodney, Jacko to Wilf and Knave to Mortimer Croop but mostly I was plain Jack. There are so many names, so many names to remember. But I am anticipating myself.

I was conceived in York during December 1863. The event occurred a short distance outside the city walls, in the shadow of Clifford's Tower. My father, a cabinet-maker, left York with my mother in the September of 1864 for London. I came into the world, so I have been given to believe, on a roadside south of Grantham. I was delivered in a sense already dressed, for, like David Copperfield, I was born with a caul. Whether this protective but suffocating amnion meant that I, like he, was destined to be unhappy and to see ghosts, I leave the reader to determine. Perhaps on one occasion it saved me from drowning. But that was later, much later.

My earliest memories are of my father's workshop in the cellar of the house in Canonbury, where we lived at 14 Regis Street. I would open the door to the cellar and step from the hallway with its smell of boiled cabbage onto the narrow stairs. From below wafted up the cooler smell of wood and the sounds of my father at work. He was making tables, bookcases and boxes. This was his domain; it never felt as though it was part of the house. I was fascinated by the many forms of broken wood to be found here, although as yet I had no words for them: shavings from lathe or plane, sawdust, chippings, slivers and splinters. The workroom connected with the shop: the house was built on a hill and at the back the cellar gave onto a small street. 'Adam Spellman,' the sign said, although I could not read it: white letters on black ground.

When I was very small, I remember that I returned to the workshop one day after having been sent out on some errand by my father. I was holding something in my hand. A bottle of milk from the little shop across the road? Some tobacco? I forget. I stood at the door and watched my father at work. It must have been summer since he was not wearing a shirt. As he drove his saw into a plank I could see the muscles in his back moving. My ears were filled with the rhythmic noise of his labour and I suddenly felt dizzy. I put my hand out to steady myself against the wall but I almost fell and for a moment I had the impression that my arm had passed through solid brick. When I looked at the wall, however, I realized – with some disappointment – that I was no ghost. I had merely tried to lean against the missing corner-stone. It was missing but it still had a name. How could that be?

And then I remember looking up out of the dark gorge of the street. The sky was very bright, almost too bright to look at. Clouds raced across it faster even than the model yachts on the lake at Clissold Park.

Old ravener, guardian of the hoard, consumer of the lion's share, eater of select cuts and nibbler of choice titbits, gobbler of brawn, slurper of soup. As heavy and compact as a bull-terrier my father enters the room, hands in his waistcoat pockets, preoccupied with his gut. He grunts with complacent hunger: the day's work is done. His hands tremble from his labours, lending a misleadingly feverish appearance to his eating. When he puts his teacup down it rattles in the saucer. He contains the overboiled potatoes served him by the maid as solidly as one of his own barrels; you can almost hear them dropping to the bottom.

'And after the day's work, Adam saw that it was good, and he ate, and the veil of the temple was rent in twain.' My father conflates stories as usual: it is a habit he developed to annoy my mother. He belches. Old repaster.

Upstairs my mother lies as she has done since our arrival in London seven years ago. Her gaunt face is almost as white as her pillow, her hair is combed and spread out. She is counting her rosary, mumbling prayers in Polish, fretting to my father. She thinks the house is falling in. She thinks the debt collector is hammering at the door. She thinks the tide of our affairs is turning, that we are a doomed family. The upper storey is my mother's domain. She is always in bed except once a year, at Christmas, when she reluctantly consents to be carried downstairs to watch us eat. My mother never eats. Sarah, the maid, thinks that my mother moves around in the dead of night.

'Things have moved,' says Sarah knowingly. 'Your mother is not what she seems. She counts the candles in the cupboards. Underneath she is as strong as a horse.' Sarah taps her nose and whispers down at me. 'She feasts in secret. Crusts, biscuits, pieces of dripping. How else could she live for seven years? On air?'

I nod in agreement, although it seems to me that my mother would be perfectly capable of living on air if she wanted to.

9

In spite of what may have been her secret stores of nourishment, my mother becomes drier, gaunter and more querulous as the months pass. She accuses my father of burning too many candles and, more seriously, of stealing her inheritance. He tells her that she is confused and stops seeing her.

Yes, the first floor is my mother's domain. Her spirit lurks here amongst the dark furniture, the polished banisters and the dying plants.

I am nine years old. It is Christmas and I am sitting near the fire in the front room. My father has carried my mother downstairs as he does every year. They are still not talking to each other but I am aware that they are both looking at me. I am playing with my presents. There is a horse made of wood with moving parts. It is painted green and gold and on its back sits a blue and red hussar, also with moving parts. He is slim, proud and elegant, and one day I want to be like him.

Suddenly my mother sits up stiffly and glares at my father. 'You've painted that toy in a Russian uniform!'

My father smiles. 'Nonsense.'

'It's true!'

My father loses his temper. 'And what then? Wasn't the Czar the father of your nation of ineffectuals?'

My mother falls back in her chair, shocked. 'He was a usurper!' she hisses.

My other present was a hollow china tiger. I think that my father must have bought it in a curiosity shop. It did not move, but there were shimmering stones set into the eye sockets which sparkled as I turned it in the light. If you tapped it with your finger nail, it made a funny noise like a teacup but muffled.

I was ten years old. My toy hussar had become so dirty that I decided to wash him in the basin. Unfortunately his dyes came out in the water and turned it purple. One day I accidentally snapped off his sabre. He did nothing to retaliate, however, and from that moment I lost faith in him. I do not remember what happened to the tiger; I suppose he was broken or lost.

I was eleven years old and had become my father's apprentice. He had been away all morning, buying tools and timber for a commission to supply fourteen boxes ornamented with rare veneers in a previously specified design. I had swept the workshop before lunch and was climbing the stairs when I saw, through a large crack at the base of the cellar door, my father's legs and the legs of our new maid, Claire Grey, whom I loved although she was three years older.

I do not know what prompted my stealth, yet for some reason I mounted the remainder of the steps in silence and applied my eye to the aperture.

10

My father and Claire were standing very close together and they were oddly quiet. As I watched, Claire leaned back against a table which had been made by my father. She smiled up into his face and he placed his hand on the lower part of her stomach. She giggled: 'You're tickling.'

My father bent to whisper something in her ear and slowly he raised her dress and she stiffened but then his hand began to rub her stomach and her legs relaxed and he whispered to her again. It was then that I remember feeling for the first time, as a hidden watcher, a mysterious stiffening in my organ of generation. The scene was framed like a picture as my father's hand rubbed Claire's exposed stomach. He put two of his fingers inside her and she gave out a strangled panting noise. After a moment my father unbuttoned his trousers with his free hand and moved between Claire's legs. She wriggled as if she wanted to escape. Her stifled laughter had a note of fear in it but then my father's back flexed and she inhaled sharply. His back flexed again and there was the same frightened intake of breath. Then she hooked one of her legs over his hip and they were no longer my father and Claire but parts of a great, insensible machine shaking itself apart in an abandoned factory. At last my father's back convulsed and he made the only sound to escape him during these minutes:

'Uh.'

All was silent for a moment and then my father stepped backwards and buttoned up his fly. Claire pulled her dress down. My father turned and, before I could escape, opened the door of the cellar, almost tripping over me. For a second we looked at each other and then he called out to Claire: 'You may serve lunch now, Miss Grey.'

That night in the attic room where both Claire and I slept, I lay in bed as she undressed in the dark and got into her own bed on the other side of the room.

'Jake, Jake,' she whispered across to me a few minutes later. I stumbled across the cold room and slipped between her sheets. There was an unusual smell in the bed: the smell of my father's seed, the smell that had accompanied my conception.

I lay with my back to Claire and slowly, as she stroked my forehead and whispered to me, I extended my right leg backwards until it touched both of hers. To my surprise she shifted in the bed and allowed me to extend my leg further backwards until it met and touched the damp hair between her legs. After a while, with even greater surprise and now pleasure, I noticed that Claire's breathing had the same unsteady break in it that I had remarked that afternoon. Again my member stiffened, pressing against the coarse material of my night-shirt. Soon, without manual assistance, I had discharged perhaps a quarter of a teaspoonful of seed

11

onto the bed linen. I returned to my bed and immediately fell into a deep sleep.

The next morning I arose with trembling limbs. All night my dreams had been haunted and I had seemed to wander, alone and lost, down the long dreary reaches of desire. I do not know why I was so confused by my disorientation: sperm is no more than a liquid and sperm spilled is no more than liquid spilled and a body is only a temporary collocation of moving parts.

A few days later my mother died during the night in the room below mine. When my father told me the news I wondered why I had not heard her last struggle for life. I was taken to see her later that day. She lay on her best sheets with a candle burning at each corner of the bed and I remember thinking that such unnecessary expense would have infuriated her. Incense burned in the room but underneath this aromatic disguise lingered unmentionably the smell of death, the last blocked breath.

The funeral was accomplished without undue emotion or delay. My father held himself firm and upright in the meagre afternoon light as rain spattered the Kensal Green graveside.

It did not seem long before Claire Grey showed unmistakable signs of being pregnant. This fact, however, was never mentioned. My father drank his soup and dropped overboiled potatoes into his maw as Claire moved with increasing corpulence around the table.

During these months, my father seemed to enter upon a decline. With increasing frequency he would pause in his planing to gasp with pain and clutch himself between the legs. As Claire grew bigger with child, a mysterious and perhaps retributive cancer flourished deep inside my father, forcing its way along the obscure pathways of his body like a hostile but invisible army.

My father died in July 1876. A few days later Claire brought two dead children into the world: one male, one female. She sank quickly under the injuries they had unconsciously inflicted on her viscera in their futile struggle for life and space.

My father's last will and testament was read to me as I sat at the dining-room table dressed in black. Gradually the creditors accumulated around the door and I was given to understand that my father's estate was swallowed up in debts. Somebody mentioned a man called Sir Rodney Rouncewell. Many a time, without understanding, I had heard my father's imprecations against this figure. Sir Rodney, it seemed, was owed rent on the Regis Street property and also a large sum advanced to my father for the purchase of certain tropical woods to be used in the construction of a series of fourteen boxes commissioned by the Siriso Trading Company.

I did not meet Sir Rodney at this time but his solicitors were merciless in the recovery of the debt. Rouncewell robbed me of the few pennies of my patrimony and at the age of eleven I was therefore left entirely without means of support.

3

I Leave Home

NOT WISHING to be forcibly adopted I determined some days after my father's burial to leave my familiar surroundings and try to find a job. I did not know London but I was aware that it surrounded me for miles in every direction. I packed a bag and gathered together the small amount of money which had escaped the eyes of the creditors. Having locked the front door and closed the gate I stood in the street and said farewell to the house with the missing corner-stone.

I slept that night in a boarding-house towards Greenwich. The next day I became a messenger-boy for a shipping company. My master, one Christopher Desert, sat all day in the clearing-house on the wharf like a vast maggot smoking black tobacco. He drooled and one of his eyelids drooped. At the end of my first week, as part of some crude ceremony of initiation, he and his henchmen formed a ring around me and I was pushed from one to the other until the walls of the building began to spin and their laughing faces became blurred.

This dizzy haze colours my memory of the first cargo I set eyes on. Christopher Desert gave me some forms to take to a man named Henry Wickham on board the *Duke of Devonshire*. The ship was to carry the first shipment of rubber seedlings to be smuggled out of Brazil and was to sail for Colombo that evening. Failing to find the state rooms, I became completely lost in the darkened hold of the ship. At one point I stumbled against a chest and, lifting the lid, saw pale stems twisting in moss and dark earth.

The next four years I ran from dock to dock and from ship to ship clutching bills of lading, indentures and certificates of insurance. In retrospect it seems that I had no time to think. All day I ran through the voracious, littered city, past grain stores and slaughterhouses, across scrubbed decks and cobbled quays, under the great and ever-changing sky, in the dark and multifarious streets.

I first realized during these early years that I was marked out in a most peculiar way. Since it is so germane to the progress of my life, I feel it necessary to enlighten you, Mr Secretary, concerning my genital defor-

14

mity. A large birthmark, raised a little from the general surface and of a dark red hue, entirely covered my testicles and copulatory organ.

I used to run the occasional errand for a weighty prostitute of middle years named Amelia, who lived in the room below mine. In the early afternoon I would bring her a large chop in sauce from a nearby eating house, accompanied by a quart of porter. Over these months I had, of course, fallen most completely in love with this sea of creamy flesh.

Arising from her bed of purchased pleasure, she would stand blinking and naked in the light of early afternoon as I stood at the door, chop on plate, obedient to her whim. Slowly she would scratch her gigantic pubis with its flaming red hair. Crouching over her pot, she would release a stream of urine from her massy thighs as she smiled up at me and wished me good day. I was fascinated by her quiet bulk and waxen skin.

During these years I incurred many a beating for lateness from Christopher Desert. As I watched Amelia wash herself I became incapable of leaving. I would pour her thick urine away and bring steaming water in a ewer. Later, I watched as she uncoiled and combed her red tresses with a strangely small and delicate hand. During this operation she would gaze out of the window and hum softly to herself.

I have discovered that in my dictation I am able most successfully to forget the Secretary's scratching presence. He neither helps nor hinders as I draw back the floodgates of memory; he fades most satisfactorily away into impalpability so that now I am able to commence with augmented confidence this narration of the germinal event of my life. There is nothing to divert me from the stinking streets where the bodies of women were traded amongst the sparrows and the soot.

I was dismissed from my job for tending poor bruised and beaten Amelia: a customer had been somewhat more violent than usual. All afternoon I stayed with her, applying cold compresses to her sealed eye. When I went down to the wharf to explain my absence, Christopher Desert raised himself to his full height, spat viciously on the floor and released me from my duties.

I returned to Amelia's dim and shuttered room where she lay asleep, mumbling occasionally, on her creaking bed. Her breasts, freed from their usual lace and whalebone corsetage, slumped across her splayed arms. Their surface was marked with shiny striations; the nipples were great red eyes gazing disconsolately at opposite corners of the ceiling.

She stirred and awoke as my fascinated fingers hesitantly touched her breast. Yawning, she asked me how old I was. I was fifteen.

'You look younger,' she said, 'but you are not too young. I suppose it is time, Jack. Is it time to be a man?' Her closed eye wept a thick tear onto her cheek. 'Come to bed, lovey, where it's warm.'

I was confused and uneasy but she took my hand: 'Take off your britches Jack and let me hold you. I'll show you something, something you'll like all your life. Something that drives all you poor men.'

In the half-light I removed my trousers and, covering myself, approached the edge of Amelia's bed.

'Let me light the lamp, lovey: I want to see what I'm going to put inside me.'

Amelia turned up the gaslight and prized my protective hands apart. My erect member sprang out like some absurd child's toy.

'Oh, Jack,' she said, after a pause in which her face worked with untranslatable emotion. 'Oh Jack, it's disgusting. I've never seen anything so horrible.' She turned away and began to sob into her pillow: 'I feel sick.'

For some reason I pulled a blanket over my head, unable to believe what had happened. Amelia refused to say another word to me and so, baffled and shivering, I pulled on my clothes and left. I felt like some sort of monster.

At some point, I crossed the river and entered unfamiliar streets. The city which had once seemed to surround me became paltry and intermittent. I was sick to the heart; I did not know where to turn. I was capable only of continuing, of walking onwards without destination.

It was black bleak night. I was, so I surmised, in Kent. A country road stretched up the hill before me. The moon emerged from behind a veil of clouds but, content in her flawless circularity, she looked down expressionlessly on my linearity.

Much later I fell to the ground exhausted and my body was one with earth and gnarled root. I tried to hide myself that none should see me. But somewhere in the darkness was a dim light and music like a dancer turning, turning.

4

Magic, or Orthography?

I WAS ill; I had a fever. For days I hung suspended in a chattering void. Sometimes I was back at Regis Street, sometimes I was in the clearing-house with Christopher Desert who had swollen to gigantic proportions and was in league with Sir Rodney. At other times a kindly hand and a coarse cloth wiped my face and fragments of song sounded in my ears. On occasions I seemed to myself to return to the clarity of consciousness, woken by the flap, as I thought, of canvas in the breeze and a humming as of the air across taut cord. I was on a ship, then, pitching beneath the deck of some ship. I had put out from the Thameside markets: crated in the hold, I sailed across an empty sea to be traded in some obscure port. In the dimness my nostrils sensed spices and strange scents. Then, clearer of mind, I would awake again in lantern light and looking upwards see a vault of multicoloured canvas and a wooden pole: the support, surely, of a tent. Perhaps I had already been sold and was even now beginning my life in the deserts beyond Cairo. A fierce heat dried my tongue and the smooth hand and coarse cloth returned. I had no power to find the face that owned this hand: I had gone astray in a wandering wonder. All this was more real to me than I can say, more real by far than the phantasmagoria which surrounds, crazily, our waking moments and saner hours.

Very gradually, the ceaseless babble that sounded in my ears resolved itself into various voices. Once isolated, the voices even acquired names. Mortimer Croop spoke first and loudest with a viciousness born of power. First and loudest spoke the man who owned the tent and the two who lived inside. As his voice rang out I conjured up a picture of a purple face with turgid limbs. He said that the circus was a family and that I was an adopted child for whom the family would provide a home. I was young; when fit I would not be without vigour. The knave could be useful; the knave would be cheap. Croop's hand grasped mine: my stay was sanctioned by the master.

Next, in later hours of the night, spoke the great Zanzare, the magician and prestidigitator. He talked of the past, of the fine old days that were gone. As the level of the bottle fell he ordered tapers to be lit and held forth to the shadows of his lost powers. His tongue flicked memories from one side of the tent to the other. Yes, in Novara, in Milano; in the thirties, in the forties, yes, then the people believed. They came to see magic with the innocence of children. And because they were pure of heart, they saw it: magic, before their very eyes. Afterwards, they took mysteries home with them to their villages and when the long nights came they were still delighted with the wonders they had seen. All Italy dreamed feverishly and in its curious nooks, in villages where cypresses cast deep shadows and the angelus sounded across misty fields, the reign of magic was not yet done. Zanzare put a rough but healing hand on my forehead and sprinkled some fluid upon my sheets which made me breathe more easily.

Last of all spoke quietly, because she had least power, the beautiful Aramind. She spread out her night-black hair and lit another taper as the great Zanzare burbled his nostalgia in a corner. And Aramind, the dancer with almond eyes, spoke of her life in the circus and of how her dance was trapped. Soon the dance would slough off her body like useless skin, she would crumple with emptiness and the dance would turn and turn elsewhere.

Zanzare leaned unsteadily across my bed in the early morning.

'Young man,' he said with whisky on his breath, 'young man, the costume is true, the mask is true, my wig is real, my dentures are real teeth, people's outsides tell more tales than their insides. Young man,' he said, 'there's more to surfaces than meets the eye.'

He staggered a little, but then his dark eyes found my own. 'Your name?' he asked, with such authority that I was awe stricken.

'Jack Spellman, if you please, your honour.'

'Spellman,' he mused, 'Spellman. Which choice did you make?'

'Sir?'

'Which path will you take? Magic, or orthography?'

'I'm sorry, sir. I don't –'

'– Understand, Spellman? Never mind.' He smiled down at me. 'That's as good a start as any.' He continued his observation of me for some time. At last his lips began to move again; he was telling me how I came to be convalescing in a circus: 'You lay shivering in the darkness, on a lonely road, and my daughter found you. Alfredo, our strongman, Alfredo Hagsproat gathered you without effort into his arms and brought you to our tent. That was seven nights ago. My daughter, she has been good to you. She says you have a good face.'

Zanzare interrupted my stammered thanks to give me new clothes and to instruct me to wander at will around the circus meadow. I put them on hurriedly and went out into the day. Clowns tumbled in the grass outside the main tent. I went inside and my feet trod for the first time the nostalgic sawdust of the ring. Looking around, I saw the strongman who had brought me in from that cold night lift great weights with one hand. Above him, in the dimness, tightrope walkers and trapezists practised on the uncertain cord. In a different part of the circus, lions and tigers snored in their cages and I saw a wolf chained to a stake. One of the keepers persuaded me to clean out the stall of a sedentary but foul-tempered camel. At midday and into the early afternoon awakening men with muscled chests washed themselves at pails and young women sped past in flimsy white.

Near the main gate I saw a small funeral procession and, standing to one side, heard a member of the cortège whisper: 'Poor Bill Stephens. Cholera, the doctor said.'

'Still, he died near the ring he loved,' another man replied as the gathering of people moved away across the grass.

I returned to Zanzare's tent. Inside, in the darkness, Aramind was brewing tea over a low flame. Together we leafed through an album which contained her father's collection of engravings and newspaper clippings. Philip Astley, the first man to stand on a horse's back as it galloped in a circle, was pictured with his favourite stallion, Bucephalus. There was an illustration too of Antonio Franconi, who took over Astley's Amphitheatre in Paris after the Revolution and established the French circus.

Zanzare entered the tent and gazed down on us expressionlessly. 'Will you like the life then?' he asked me as he poured himself a tumbler of whisky. I must have seemed naïvely enthusiastic for he answered my reply laconically: 'Its smells and sights are new.' He lay down on his bed and told me that Mortimer Croop wished to see me. I exchanged glances with Aramind. Gradually, Zanzare fell into a light sleep and we returned to the perusal of the album. Aramind shyly pointed out to me a daguerreotype of herself, aged eight, in the costume of a ballerina. Her arms arched gracefully forwards, her hands were clasped and one chubby leg was extended behind her. There was an expression of intense concentration upon her face but the photograph could not convey the tremor of the infant dancer as she tried to match her body to the thought of the dance. It was then that I realized that Aramind's dance was far older than Zanzare's magic. His trickery required the sophistication of belief but her art only the memory that belongs to every eye as it watches light play and colour flash and form shift and spin. But she told me that Zanzare mocked her simplicity and used her dances to fill the gaps in his act.

That evening, after I had eaten, I called on the mighty Mortimer.

5

The Textual Burden

I KNOCKED, in a darkness shot through by the gleam of distant torches, on the thickly painted and richly decorated door of Mortimer Croop's horse-drawn caravan.

'Enter,' called a voice within.

Climbing the steps and opening the door, I found myself in an interior stranger by far than even the perfumed tent of the great Zanzare. Behind a table at the far end of the caravan reclined the engorged bulk of Croop, proprietor of the Magnificent Mortimer's Travelling Circus. A dwarf whom I had not seen before and who was not wearing the costume of a clown stood beside the table, grinning at me with decaying teeth and pouring his master a glass of beer. Between them, on the table, lay a fresh deck of cards, dice and two piles of sovereigns. Croop's pile was somewhat smaller than the dwarf's but in his lap was a leather pouch filled, I imagined, with reserve currency. A large hook was fixed into the ceiling, and a glazed ham hung from it. Beneath the ham, in the middle of the caravan, stood a small table bearing a vase of dead flowers. A single lantern, turned up high, stood between Croop and the dwarf, casting its light upwards on their oily hair and unshaven faces. On the table lay a half-consumed fowl, its internal cavity spilling a darkly roasted apple and an onion. Mortimer Croop held one of the bird's legs in his fist and, as he watched me, chewed it absently. The stuffed heads of other creatures loomed from wooden plaques upon the walls: a grinning monkey, a crocodile with a pike in its jaws. In one corner was a small cupboard packed to overflowing with the largest selection of preserves I had ever seen. On another shelf lay a meat pie and a fruit-cake, both partially consumed. I attributed the smell of decay which permeated the caravan to a coal-scuttle from which protruded various bones, feathers and fish skeletons: one with a clouded but recriminatory eye.

Mortimer Croop deposited the half-eaten leg upon the table and rose slowly to his feet. The dwarf retired to the darkest corner and sat down on a small stool, his ravaged teeth still gleaming with amusement. Breathing heavily, Croop negotiated the dining-table and stood before me.

'Well, my young knave: you seem to have made a good recovery.'

'Yes, sir,' I replied.

Croop hesitated, as though shrinking delicately from an unpleasant task. 'The problem, young man, is one of mouths and money.'

'Yes, sir,' I said again, without as yet having the faintest idea of his meaning.

'You, my little knave, are from my point of view – I ask your forgiveness for my bluntness (I am a blunt but not a brutal man) – You, I say,' he poked a finger almost the thickness of his chicken leg into my chest to emphasize his point, 'are but a mouth. And, *mon petit valet*, mine is the money that puts food in your voracious but pretty little knavish mouth, nutriment in this flat young stomach.' He prodded me violently in my belly and seemed expansive, even garrulous. Suddenly he sprang at me: 'What do you say to that then?'

'I must agree with you, sir,' I said, although I had not been aware of any voracity on my part. 'You are very kind. I am fifteen. I am ready to work for my daily bread.'

'Ready to work, eh?' Croop bent his visage upon me. 'But do you have the back for it?'

The dwarf laughed from his corner and Croop glanced across at him: 'Shall we perform the test?' The dwarf was beside himself with cruel enthusiasm. 'Bring me the books then!' shouted Croop: 'Let us see what the springy-legged knave is made of.'

Outside, in the drizzling night, Croop hung the lantern from the door. I stood on the damp grass as he slowly descended the steps and began to pace out a circle around me. A moment later, the dwarf emerged from the caravan. In his long, sinewy arms he was carrying a pile of books which had been tied together with twine.

'Bend over, Jack Spellman, and meet your fate!' commanded Croop magisterially. I made my obeisance. 'Further, knave! Let your back be horizontal.' He turned to the dwarf. 'He is well grown, is he not, Pesto, for his age?'

Pesto muttered a '*si maestro*' and placed the books on my extended spine.

'Hold them, Jack Spellman, seize them, balance them and walk!'

Putting my arms behind me, I clasped my burden firmly. It was heavy, although not painfully so, and I managed to stagger a circuit around the appraising Croop and the prancing Pesto without much difficulty or embarrassment

'Again!' shouted Croop, and again I tottered my round.

This game, which I did not in the least comprehend, continued perhaps half an hour, at the end of which time I was mightily exhausted. Then

Croop commanded me to rise, which I did with aching vertebrae, handing back my freight of atlases and dictionaries to Pesto. We went back into the caravan and Croop clapped me on the shoulder as I preceded him up the steps. Once inside, he offered me the half-consumed leg of his chicken, which I politely refused, and a glass of Madeira wine, which I accepted.

'Well, my dear Pesto,' said Croop, addressing his minion and ignoring me as I stood before him, periodically sipping from the modest and dusty glass I had been given. 'What thinkest thou, wisest if not smallest of Italian fools?'

Across Pesto's face passed in rapid dumbshow a succession of contra-dictory expressions ranging from awe to horror and from admiration to contempt. These were intended, I speculated, to impart no opinion at all but merely to express deference to his master's conclusions, which came, slowly, in the usual florid phrases.

'The knave is of course, it must be frankly admitted – as I hope you will agree, Pesto – of precious little value in comparison with the inestimable Stephens, Bill of that ilk, the strong-backed Saxon who carried with such steadiness the burdens that fortune and the fickleness of fate placed upon his ready shoulders.' Pesto nodded furiously. 'He has not,' Croop contin-ued with his hand eloquently outstretched, 'he has not, let us agree at once, an ounce of Stephens's courage, tenacity or resolve. He has not, to put the matter in a nutshell, an inch of his talent. And I say to you at once, Pesto, in spite of your justified protestations,' (Pesto had not moved a muscle in disagreement) 'your unkind but wisely pragmatic dissension, that the lad could surely – ah – surely –' Croop stared into space. Then, with a shrug, he accepted the inevitable. 'Yes, my dear Pesto: you are, as always, correct. This Spellman is not worth a fraction of Stephens's – shall we say, to cut a corner – of Stephens's wage?'

Pesto listened with rapt attention. His silence seemed to spur Croop on to further floods of rhetoric:

'Yet, cruel Pesto, I beg to plead on the lad's behalf. He is young and unknowing in our affairs but he can learn our little game, can learn to stagger, begging indulgent laughter, around our sawdust ring. Pesto: I beg of you to exercise your organ of compassion! Surely we might pay this orphaned knave his keep, if in return he agreed, although so woefully inadequate, to replace the irreplaceable and imitate the inimitable: if in short he were to become the second Stephens, the bereaved Patchkey's other half, the player of the back end of our delightful but at present so curtailed pantomime horse.'

Pesto nodded himself into a paroxysm of servile agreement and, leaping from his stool, crossed the confined and cluttered space to shake me by the hand. Mortimer Croop returned to his chicken leg and, licking his lips, smiled indulgently on the fictional accord he had staged between Pesto and myself.

Mock confidentiality was a habit with Croop and as he showed me to the door that night, he bent once more to whisper in my ear: 'It will be hard work and long hours for little pay, my poor little knave. It will be a rough course to run. But what can I do with Pesto as my counsellor? He is a circus man, you see: born and bred with the cruelty of the circus. What else can I do to offer you protection and support?' He squeezed my arm and his voice resumed its usual resonance. 'Life, dear boy, is a cruel mistress and places many undesirable things in our path which we should rather avoid. We must face our fate, however, and do as we can the task which life allots us. Do not shirk the challenge, Spellman! Give us back the life we have so kindly given you!'

I turned at the bottom of the caravan steps and looked up at Croop. As yet I had uttered no words of assent. But he must have taken my silence for compliance, for he threw out these words as I walked away: 'I will have the suit ready for you by tomorrow and then you must practise and practise again to be laughed at.'

Jack Spellman: born with so peculiar a mark, once apprentice joiner, latterly London messenger, had become in the strangeness of his fate, the back end of a pantomime horse!

Outside in the darkness, against a backcloth of tattered clouds, a wind whistled through the great skeletal structures of the circus. The looming gantries, the great rib-cages of half-erected tents, the poles, scaffolds and stages: all were silent, motionless and deserted. Not quite silent, however, for there was a wind that whistled; nor yet motionless, for somewhere a piece of canvas flapped; nor even abandoned, for here and there amongst the half-constructed edifices slept the occasional circus worker.

6
The Horse Suit

NEXT MORNING, as Croop had promised, I found that my new costume had been left in a package outside Zanzare's tent. As I unwrapped the parcel, Aramind stood beside me and watched the sun rise over the copse at the end of the long grey meadow.

'So they have trapped you too have they, Jack Spellman? Will Croop take you where he goes to sell you?'

I turned towards her and breathed in her scent. 'Oh, Aramind,' I said, 'don't be sad. How can a dance imprison you?'

Aramind shrugged and went back inside the tent to wake her father. I turned my attention to my new garb, which was certainly the most uncanny piece of clothing that I had ever seen. Its voluminous bulk was made up of dozens of stretched squirrel pelts, lined on the inside with felt. The skins were sewn together with gut although here and there a seam gaped a little. The smell of ill-cured fur mingled with a sulphurous odour, perhaps of fumigation. Beneath these lingered still, unfortunately, the stench of Bill Stephens's dying diarrhoeic flow. Behind even the smell of Stephens's death, however, lingered that of years of his life, a life spent staggering and prancing in torchlight: the smell of his feet, his armpits, the grease from his scalp.

I took off my shoes and my borrowed coat and stepped for the first time into this incarnation of folly, this thing that from now on would be both my tool and my uniform. Despite the unsavoury nature of my legacy, I almost at once felt comfortable inside it: my feet slid smoothly along the legs and found good purchase on the inner soles, which were externally shaped like exaggerated hooves. The portion of the suit which was supported by my hips fitted snugly and was padded with horse hair. The whole was lent strength and form by insewn whalebone ribbing which gave the exterior the appearance of a horse's flanks and belly. My tail, naturally, was of horse hair. The costume reached to my armpits and fitted inner straps enabled me to hang it from my shoulders in order to walk around without my partner. Along the outer rim a series of brass buttons were evidently designed to connect me to Wilf Patchkey, the front end of the pantomime horse. I was somewhat surprised that no attempt had been made to hide these buttons: the makers had apparently rather chosen to announce the seam and proclaim the illusory nature of the pantomime horse rather than strive for an impossible verisimilitude.

All in all, I was not displeased with the costume and I strutted for a while, with some pride, in front of Aramind's silver mirror. After an hour or so I became inured to the aromas recorded in the fabric memory of my horse-suit. I even managed to persuade myself that in time my own more bearable smells would usurp those which now I traced. I may as well say at once, however, that this was never to be the case: throughout the ten years of my life as a pantomime horse I was never once to prepare myself for a performance without being powerfully reminded of my predecessor.

I appear perhaps, Mr Secretary, to be a man somewhat obsessed by the earthier aspects of human physicality. But shit and sweat are innocent, if relentlessly durable things.

Since I was expected to maintain the rear end of the pantomime horse in good condition, I made a visit that morning to the costumier's shed in order to procure needle and thread. Here, amongst masks and cloaks and leopard-skin suits, I found a woman engaged in a violent argument with the circus joiner. Noticing my presence, this man departed with curses, jostling me against the wall as he did so. The woman wiped away her tears and introduced herself, cheerfully enough, as Gertrude Desmoulins. I stated the object of my visit and, from a nearby box, she took needles and a spool of flaxen thread to give to me:

'Alors, vous êtes le cheval manqué, hein?'

I retreated in some confusion to the door. As I left, she called out after me: 'Mon pauvre petit chevalier!'

Outside, the strengthening rays of the sun had already begun to melt the frosty grass and wreaths of mist rose into the air. In a few moments more, still wearing my costume, I was lifting the flap of Wilf Patchkey's tent in response to his mumbled welcome. He lay outstretched upon a filthy blanket, a pale hand tugging reflectively at his nipple. My presence did not in the least disturb him and for some moments I was at a loss for what to do or say. Wilf saved me from my awkwardness by gesturing to a plume of steam which issued from his kettle: perhaps I could make something to drink. I obeyed, although my grotesquely overpadded clothing made me clumsy in my movements.

After a few sips of his well-sugared tea, Wilf's aloofness vanished and within a few minutes I had forgotten his nakedness. He sat cross-legged on his mattress, laughing and chattering, coughing and smoking. Before dressing he took his penis between thumb and forefinger and flapped it regretfully against his belly.

"'Tis too small, Jacko. 'Tis a tiny thing, lost amongst me hairies. And yet there's such life in it, Jacko, such a spring force!'

In the main tent later that morning, Wilf and I buttoned our costumes together and for the first time I stood doubled up, waiting to learn my trade. Shortly after we became so unnaturally connected, I inhaled for the first time the smell of Wilf's minute but powerfully fragrant genitals and I realized that Stephens must also have suffered, as I did now, from the rankness of his partner. All this was indeed a feast of many smells, a panorama of perfumes and a scene of scents. They come back to me even as I speak and in my pauses I inhale the past.

Wilf and I circled unsteadily in the ring as he issued muffled advice and instructions from the depths of his papier mâché skull.

'No, Jacko, hold my hips!

'No, no: hold the *hips*! Then you know how I move. The waist is useless, Jacko, I ain't got one. Feel the way my hips move: which leg's out, which leg's in. You've got to know what I'm going to do before I do it. Bill Stephens was a natural – and obliging.

'Phew! It's hot in here. Whoa, Jacko! Follow the hips! You're supposed to be the funny end, you know. You're the ragged tail-end of the procession.

'Characters, Jacko! The pantomime horse, he's got two. I'm the elegant one. You're the one who lets me down and shows me up for what I am.

'No: faster, *faster!* We've got to outrun the clowns. We should be almost as quick as the real horses!

'It's better, Jacko. But you've gone all normal now you've got used to bending your back. You've got to embroider, make things go wrong, make them funny. The back end of the pantomime horse is the bit that makes people laugh.

'Jacko, Jacko! You've got to pretend to be out of control but all the time you know exactly what I'm doing. And then, like pretending to be drunk, you stagger and swerve. So the punters know you're a human being and not a horse's arse.

'You've got to succeed at failing, Jacko. I lead: you meander around behind me – don't pull too much or the buttons burst.

'Can't you understand it? Don't you know what you're doing? You're beneath the clowns, Jacko. Even the clowns can make fun of the back end of a pantomime horse! Never kick the clowns, never dodge them: you're the one that's always tripped and trapped.

'Two animals, Jacko: two animals in a pantomime horse! Everybody knows that. Now the head end, he's as proud as a proper horse and that's ridiculous in whalebone and squirrel skin but the back end is the real, absurd soul of the pantomime horse – and the pantomime horse is the soul of the circus.

'We're two peas in a pod, two halves of a walnut!'

Such was my initiation into life as the back end of a pantomime horse. The silence of the tent that morning, the heat and the sweat, all this was the prelude to a muffled decade in a stifling prison of skin. Around me but unseen: a great and expectant human hush, the roaring silence of children's wonder; the staring of their small, dark, aged eyes.

7

Elliptical

I F YOUR pencil is at the ready, Mr Secretary and your glass freshly charged, I would like to ponder for a few paragraphs some misconceptions about the nature of the circus. Perhaps, however, I have already perpetrated one of these by referring to its 'nature'.

First, a memory from nowhere in particular: Zanzare in his booth near the entrance to Mortimer Croop's Travelling Circus. In his dark cloak, gaunt of face and very romantic, he stands behind a wooden casket from which protrude, at opposite ends, the feet and head of an apprehensive volunteer. Zanzare holds a saw which, as I watch, he fits into a groove across the lid of the coffin. The audience is gleeful but the wife and family of the victim are plainly distressed. They know it is a joke but they are not laughing.

What was this circus in which I would spend ten years of my life? A place of clichés and archtypes, certainly: the avaricious proprietor, the melancholy clown, the deceptive lure of costumes and cosmetics, all this and a hundred more hackneyed baubles.

People say that the circus brings back our childhood and the faculty of wonder which we still possessed as children. All life then was a circus. The world of things span round like a frantic merry-go-round and it was always a holiday. As adults we still look forward to attending the circus on carnival days.

Let us say, then, that the circus is outside our normal lives. It disrupts the order we preserve so rigorously from day to day. If normality implies sanity, then the circus is a temporary madness. It is a drunken interval in sobriety, a passionate affair which rends the moral fabric. It is wealth in the midst of poverty, a poem in the long bleak prose of our lives. Sitting in the audience or wandering with the crowds from stall to stall, our sense of individuality is submerged by that of community. The circus is not a rational place for we expect to find magic here and, what is more, we know that magic to be a sham. Nevertheless we all agree, as we clap our hands at the end of each act, to take the lie for a while as truth. Many of us, as we leave the circus and bend our steps homeward, find that our pockets have been picked and these thefts are another important feature of the mask. Back in our tenements and terraced houses, despite the evident artificiality of the circus, we fondly associate it with a state of nature. 'In the city,' we say, 'things are fixed and tied down. There are always plenty of signposts so that we never lose our way, but the circus moves constantly, as if it hovered a few feet above the ground.'

These are convenient enough fictions and it only remains to ask why, when we are outside the city, the sense of communal belonging strikes us for the first time. It is not only that the circus contains all of normal life and more besides, it is almost as if the city can only be affirmed beyond its walls. Strengthened by parody, perhaps; made visible, as if through a magic lantern, by the light of desire.

Yes, the city exists most of all when we have left it to visit the circus. An uncanny paradox? Certainly. The circus is an uncanny place where we pay to entertain the fantasy that illusions have a real presence. With all these feints it is perhaps hardly surprising that the circus gives birth to feelings both of loss and of familiarity. For a couple of hours it seems that the subordinate contains the primary and has even, in addition, an ineffable excess which escapes me like an imagined perfume, a ghostly flower, an ascending bird.

I am running rings around myself, I know. Looking across at the Secretary I see his brows crease in irritation at my inability to frame a line of argument. 'This is not a history,' he is thinking, 'this is all circular.' I know that he wants to keep his ins and outs, his ups and downs intact and to separate flesh from word. Too bad, I am enjoying spinning threads around myself like the blind Chinese worm.

'How can the secondary contain the primary?' you ask, amused by my lack of logic. 'How is it that the drunkenness of the circus is sobriety and more, that madness is reason in excess?' But don't you have to admit that, whilst two follows one, it also contains what preceded it?

Like a vortex the circus swallows the material world and like a miser hoards it. Like a museum the circus fills itself with a multitude of representations in comparison to which the outside world seems bare and thin. The circus is also like a market but it is not filled with commodities in the usual sense. People take nothing away from the circus; its trade is performed in the attendance.

The circus is a sump where the world o_ nings gathers in a higher density than usual. When stuff attains a certain mass it begins to generate an uncanny life, movement in the shadows glimpsed out of the corners of our eyes.

Let me push the argument over the edge. My literal descriptions of the circus can only be parabolic versions of the city – and vice versa. The Secretary is shaking his head now like a bank manager refusing credit. He cannot be tired since it is only ten o'clock but there is something in his attitude beyond mere disagreement. He is perhaps too critical, too curious. Once we ask what animates the puppet we still its flush of life and in our hands it becomes once more a dead thing.

' *"I never saw any wax-work ma'am," said Nell. "Is it funnier than Punch?"*
"Funnier!" said Mrs Jarley in a shrill voice. "It is not funny at all." '

I CAN STILL remember Aramind's voice as she read to me from the twenty-seventh chapter of *The Old Curiosity Shop*. It was a clear cold Sunday in early March and we had taken a walk from the circus encampment near Rochester to Istead Rise on the lower slopes of the Downs. We sat in the churchyard for an hour, sheltered from the wind by a thick yew hedge. Four miles away, beyond the grey smudge of Gravesend, I could just discern the sails of the barges and wherries which tacked slowly upriver laden with coal or grain. I lost track of the story, but the quiet voice still sounded in my ears . . .

. . . these audiences were of a very superior description, including a great many young ladies' boarding schools, whose favour Mrs Jarley had been at great pains to conciliate, by altering the face and costume of Mr Grimaldi as clown to represent Mr Lindley Murray as he appeared when engaged in the composition of his English Grammar, and turning a murderess of great renown into Mrs Hannah More.

This habit of reading aloud had started quite by chance at the end of January when, leafing one evening through Zanzare's scrap-books, we came across a clipping, dated 1839, from an edition of the *Humorist*. It was a review of Dickens's *Memoirs of Joseph Grimaldi*, which had been published in the previous year. A phrase or two of the article comes to me even now.

Grimaldi was a household word; it was the short for fun, whim, trick and atrocity – that is, clown-atrocity, crimes that delight us.

The circus led myself and Aramind to Grimaldi and Grimaldi led us by a brief transition to Dickens. Dickens led in turn, by a more gradual evolution, to the formulation of Aramind's project: she wanted to educate me. During our free hours in the evenings or on Sundays – even during breaks in rehearsal – she would read to me. She also took every opportunity to encourage me to read out loud. Sometimes she succeeded and I stumbled for a while through the text but more often I would excuse myself and beg her to take the book, for I loved to lay my head in her lap and listen to her voice. Throughout February we progressed steadily through Boz's edition of the *Memoirs* and Thomas Dibdin's *History of the Stage*. Aramind gave both these books to me as a Christmas present in 1889 and I have them before me now, Mr Secretary. The former book is a first edition, with illustrations by Cruikshank. I turn the pages as I speak and they seem to call up the past. But what a strange history they tell!

After his retirement from the stage, Grimaldi dictated his memoirs to Thomas Egerton Wilks, a hack journalist. Theirs was an unfortunate collaboration. Grimaldi was well-known for his rambling yarns and Wilks was a plodding stenographer incapable of editing his master's narrative. He failed to verify the great performer's anecdotes and, worse still, excised the single feature of Grimaldi's story that lent it, if not order, then spontaneity: the clown's voice.

Understandably dissatisfied, the publishers handed the bulky manuscript to Dickens and instructed him to make it readable. Whilst engaged on *Oliver Twist*, therefore, and having finished *Pickwick Papers*, Dickens dictated a new and leaner version of the memoir to his father.

As Aramind read aloud the passage from the Introduction, the idea for my education came to her. She said later that it was the expression on my face which had prompted her, my evident absorption in the little theatre,

> *where, amid the smell of sawdust and orange-peel, sweeter far than violets to youthful noses, the first play being over, the lovers united, the ghost appeased, the baron killed, and everything made comfortable and pleasant – the pantomime itself began! What words can describe the deep gloom of the opening scene, where a crafty magician holding a young lady in bondage was discovered, studying an enchanted book to the soft music of a gong! – or in what terms can we express the thrill of ecstasy with which, his magic power opposed by superior art, we behold the monster himself converted into Clown! What mattered it that the stage was three yards wide, and four deep? We never saw it. We had no eyes, ears, or corporeal senses, but for the pantomime.*

I think that Aramind and I already understood the place of the circus in Dickens's mind although I for one had no words for it at the time. The circus always stood for the same thing: for magic and a childlike wonder in which the senses, powerfully stimulated, blended into each other. It was an ecstatic interior both strange and secure.

'Ghosts appeased!' whispered Aramind to me as her father turned in his sleep.

'Barons killed!' I hissed in response, and we began to giggle.

'Crafty magicians!' She looked with mock fear over her shoulder.

I leaned towards her: 'Young ladies in bondage!'

Another voice broke in: 'Monsters converted into clowns!' Zanzare was watching us disapprovingly. Our reading was over for that night.

We found other opportunities, however, to discover Joseph Grimaldi. From Dibdin we learned of his grandfather, Giuseppe 'Iron Legs', who had acquired his singular nickname after having executed a mighty spring on stage at the apogee of which he had struck and shattered a chandelier, sending a shard of glass into the lap of the Turkish ambassador, much to this gentleman's dismay and the crowd's delight.

Grimaldi's father, the son of 'Iron Legs', was an even more interesting case. A native of Genoa and a dancing-master, he was also, incongruously, the dentist-in-waiting to Queen Charlotte. There was an unconfirmed story which circulated about him. It was alleged that on one occasion he had borrowed a large sum of money to arrange for the performance of a remarkable new dance. On the opening night a full theatre discovered that his dance was rather an old one: he had fled to England with his advance. It was rumoured that he had beaten both his wives and given the second syphilis. Dickens, of course, omitted these latter details but he provided others which amply rewarded my and Aramind's attention. Apparently, the younger Giuseppe Grimaldi had once purchased,

a small quantity of ground at Lambeth . . . part of which was laid out as a garden; he entered into possession of it in the very depth of a most inclement winter, but he was so impatient to ascertain how this garden would look in full bloom, that, finding it quite impossible to wait till the coming of spring and summer gradually developed its beauties, he had it at once decorated with an immense quantity of artificial flowers, and the branches of all the trees bent beneath the weight of the most luxuriant foliage, and the most abundant crops of fruit, all, it is needless to say, artificial also.

I was to wonder later whether a trace of the younger Giuseppe was not to be found in Mr and Mrs Plornish of *Little Dorrit*, the residents of Bleeding Heart Yard who decorate one wall of their abode in the semblance of a thatched rural retreat, complete with painted sunflowers and hollyhocks.

Giuseppe Grimaldi the younger, Dickens informed us (this time, I think, in my voice – but I have the marked page before me now) was a 'morbidly sensitive and melancholy being.' He,

> *entertained a horror of death almost indescribable. He was in the habit of wandering about churchyards and burying places for hours together, and would speculate on the diseases of which the person had died; figure their death-beds, and wonder how many of them had been buried alive in a fit or a trance; a possibility which he shuddered to think of, and which haunted him both through life and at its close. Such an effect had this fear upon his mind, that he left express directions in his will that, before his coffin should be fastened down, his head should be severed from his body, and the operation was actually performed in the presence of several persons.*

I suppose that Aramind and I might have recognized in the younger Giuseppe's attitude to mortality nothing more than the performer's very natural desire to stage his last end. At the time it seemed to us that, more than anything else, Giuseppe Grimaldi's funerary injunctions echoed his previous roles: Orpheus perhaps, or King Charles I. At any rate his obsession with death filtered into circus lore for it was he who invented the clown's skeleton scene which survived in a vestigial form even into the performances of the eighties.

It is Joey Grimaldi, Giuseppe's son, however, to whom credit must go above all others. It was he who transformed Pantaloon's servant, the rustic Pierrot of *commedia dell'arte,* into the figure familiar to us today. He was the father of the modern pantomime, the quintessence of clown. Wearing a bald-pate or blue-crested wig with rouged triangles on his cheeks, his face whitened with bismuth paste, Grimaldi was a homely magician. He could make a coach out of four enormous cheeses. During a performance of *Harlequin and the Walter Kelps* at the Sadler's Wells Theatre during the Easter of 1806 he created a man out of vegetables procured in Covent Garden Market. With candlesticks, coal scuttles, horseshoes, a tippet and muff he became in a trice the travesty of a hussar. Occasionally he would perform in 'serious' roles: his gravedigger scene from *Hamlet* was much admired for its gloomy intensity.

Grimaldi's friend Jack Bologna was another exponent of magic. He added some rudimentary chemistry to his conjuring tricks and set himself up as a modern alchemist. In order to earn money during Lent when the pantomime was not shown he gave an evening's one-man show at the Lyceum complete with conjuring tricks, a series of 'Phantascopia' and a hydraulic exhibition. Hydraulics and the pantomime? A strange combination perhaps, but remember the circus strongman Belzoni who travelled to Egypt in order to persuade the government to sanction a scheme for raising the waters of the Nile. Once there with the quixotry which typifies the circus performer, he turned archaeologist and at one point dragged a colossal stone bust of Rameses II to the banks of the Nile at the rate of four hundred yards a day for seventeen days. But that comes later . . .

Joey Grimaldi was a consummate athlete and contortionist. It ruined his health and in later life made him prone to muscular seizures of crippling intensity. In his heyday, however, he twisted and turned, scampered and stole. He could guzzle whole strings of sausages. Whilst he was digesting his performances he was a keen amateur of butterflies and developed a particular passion for the Dartford Blue. On one occasion he made three successive return journeys between Drury Lane and Dartford (all on foot and on successive nights) in order to collect a number of perfect specimens of these creatures as a gift for one of his patrons. At one point, however – Dickens dwelt at some length on this – Grimaldi almost became something more than a clown, became almost a healer.

Great excitement and curiosity were occasioned as the intelligence ran from mouth to mouth that a deaf and dumb man had come to speak and hear, all owing to the cleverness of Joey Grimaldi.

It is only appropriate that the man who saw in the circus the transcendence of the senses should ascribe to Grimaldi the ability to miraculously liberate those caged and baffled faculties. This is not a history of the circus, however, and I cannot allow the memoirs of another to obtrude upon my own.

Aramind had finished her chapter. We were still sitting in the churchyard at Istead Rise. The evening was drawing in, my head was in her lap and still I watched the distant ships upon the Thames. Aramind touched my shoulder and pointed down the road, where in the distance but drawing nearer at a furious pace were two tall-stilts walkers from the circus. They passed by without noticing us, their long legs flying, their striped trousers flapping, the sound of their wooden feet a rhythmic clatter on the road, their enormous shadows lengthening behind them.

9

A Pair of Lovers

I T IS Sunday. The first full week of dictation has passed and promptly, at nine o'clock yesterday evening, the Secretary arrived and was shown in by Martha. He carried in a small briefcase his transcription in the alien script of the Remington machine. He seemed tired as he crossed the room to hand me the sheaf of papers.

The rain continues. The Secretary's typescript appears satisfactory. Yet there is so much in it which I cannot recall having said. Perhaps this is because I was only partly conscious as I spoke. A trance came over me and I felt as if I was muttering spells, counting over the brightly coloured yet broken memories like the beads of a rosary.

It was the middle of March and our supplies of food were almost exhausted. Like awakening sleepers people stretched their slack bodies and began again their rehearsals and exercises. The more inert amongst us were dragged protesting from our beds at dawn by the florid Mortimer Croop or Pesto, his minion. Unused equipment was taken from storage, washed, repaired and oiled.

One wet morning Croop instructed us all to foregather in the joiner's shed. As I walked over, I noticed that the leaves had fallen from the beech hedges and buds now sprouted like minuscule cigars. Blanched earthworms floated in the puddles.

In the hut Croop strutted upon a makeshift stage. Aramind had already warned me that Mortimer Croop's 'spring speech' would be second in verbosity only to the oration which usually followed the last night of the season.

'Friends!' he began in martial tones, inflating his chest as we shifted from foot to foot in the chill morning. 'Friends! The miasmatic marshes bid us begone. We have outstayed our welcome with Rochester's rustics. Our pockets are empty; our fodder is nearly out. The ribs of our animals can be seen through their lacklustre coats. Friends, we must earn more money. Money is life! New life! Today, as we arranged last November, our hibernating fellow travellers will join us once more and this small circus kernel, this winter nut will swell its shell to bursting. We leave tomorrow for Sittingbourne. And then Faversham and Canterbury! Broadstairs and Deal!'

Ridiculously, Croop pranced a little on his podium and rubbed his hands with monetary glee. Tossing back a non-existent cloak and putting his hand to an imaginary sabre, he preened before us a moment and was gone, revealing in his wake the grinning mask of his diminutive companion.

The winter circus had been but a shadow of what it was to become. Throughout the day new caravans and waggons arrived, punctual to the date which Croop had set months before whilst I was still, in London, a messenger amongst the ships and stevedores and spilling foreign crates. The migrants settled themselves for the night in untrodden parts of the field.

I returned to Zanzare's tent in the evening. The meadow was deserted; the new arrivals were renewing their acquaintance with the old residents in Rochester's crowded inns. As I lifted the flap of the tent there again, as ever, was the trapped Aramind, quietly crying. I knelt beside her and took her cold hand in mine. We said nothing. Her father, half asleep, muttered occasionally, petulantly, from his camp bed. Then Aramind raised her eyes to mine. She told me.

Zanzare had been talking to Croop. Her father had been angry, she had heard him. He could no longer tolerate my presence and feared for his daughter's purity. I would have to find new quarters.

'He cannot bear the sight of you, Jack. It is making him ill.' Aramind stretched out her hand toward me but then withdrew it as if she had suddenly thought better of the gesture.

'What can I do? Where can I go?'

'You must take your things and go to Croop. He has promised my father to find somewhere for you to lay your head.'

'But no longer in your lap.' As if it would restore what I wanted, I began to cry.

Aramind waited whilst I gave vent to my emotion and when I had stopped she delivered the heaviest blow. 'We are not to meet, never, not ever alone.' Then she leant across to me and spoke quietly. 'Except – perhaps – in secret. But we must never be caught for then my father would –' Zanzare moved suddenly in his sleep and her words were interrupted.

Over the next decade I saw Aramind only occasionally as she told fortunes from the tarot cards in the conjuror's booth near the main tent or, even more infrequently, danced by herself at a great distance. Our gaze would overcome the intervening space and something would pass between us which could have been knowledge, some genuine exchange: could have been. But no longer would I hear her voice as I watched the ships tacking slowly upriver and no longer would Zanzare rise between us like a ghost with a rum bottle.

That evening I flung my horse-suit over my shoulder and picking up a bag which contained the minimal possessions I had accumulated over the past three months, I made a call on Mortimer Croop. The master was absent but he had left instructions with Pesto who, feverishly energetic, dragged me by the hand to a far-flung part of the meadow which had not, before today, been occupied. A painted caravan stood before us and nearby a chestnut mare tore mouthfuls of new grass and watched us with uncomprehending eyes. I turned around to find that Pesto had vanished. For a moment I thought that I caught a glimpse of his possessed body leaping across a guy rope far, impossibly far away. I was left to conclude that the caravan was to be my new home and, gathering my courage, I knocked on the door.

Mimi and Bessie – I was only ever to know them by their first names – flung the door wide and met me in a peal of co-ordinated laughter. An intensity and a mutuality seemed to wash over me with the lamplight that silhouetted their forms as they stood hip to hip, thigh against thigh, smiling down on me.

'This must be the lad Croop mentioned,' said the taller of the two.

'Ooh!' squeaked the smaller, 'not bad for fifteen.'

Her companion laughed voluptuously. 'Are you fifteen, little lad?' Before I could reply her tone suddenly altered. 'Fifteen, callow youth?'

I was allocated a corner at one end of the caravan. Mimi and Bessie began to remove the discarded clothing which had accumulated on the spare palliasse. I noticed that as they did this, knowing that I, in my awkwardness, could only stand and watch, they took every opportunity to brush against each other, to reach across each other for distant scarves and slips. They then took their possessions behind a paper screen at the far end of the caravan and began to whisper to each other.

I sat on the palliasse with my possessions beside me, not knowing what to do. A few minutes later Mimi emerged from behind the screen with dishevelled hair. She pointed to my horse-suit. 'You can hang that there. There, on that peg, on that nail, you fool!' A smothered giggle could be heard from behind the screen. Obediently I hung my costume from the designated hook and returned to the mattress. Standing before a mirror and attending to her hair, Mimi brusquely told me what was available for my use: a wash-bowl, a plate and a set of cutlery.

'And will he want his porridge made for him in the morning?'

I said that I would be most grateful.

'In that case he'll have to find himself a slavey won't he?' Mimi turned towards me and began to take off her night-gown. 'Turn the lamp down, Bessie. I don't want to shock the lad.' The light died yet the stigmata of Mimi's nipples remained with me in the dark and surfaced in my dreams.

Mimi was twenty-three years of age, a bareback rider at the peak of her career. Her authoritative manner and sharp tongue commanded respect wherever she went. The muscles of her thighs swept in a gleaming arc from knee to hip and the veins stood out on her forearms. Over the years to come I was to hear her choke back tears in the dark. Her injury was unnameable, irremediable; I never knew what it was. When others were present, however, the spectacle of her self-control was awesome.

Mimi flaunted her nakedness before me. She quickly learned to taunt me with her body, moving it close but keeping it out of reach, thus demonstrating her self-possession. She showed no self-consciousness as she moved about the caravan. My eyes and my glance, she thus indicated, had no power: I did not exist. Occasionally she would stand before me and insult me for a voyeur as she ran her hands across her breasts. 'That's where you always look,' she would say, 'you men with your absurd cocks who know nothing of women, their pleasures.' By touching herself in front of me Mimi hid herself. She was clothed by her insults and covered by her gestures. Nevertheless, she was a most effective torment. I longed for her and was fascinated by her strength, the more fascinated the more that was given only to be denied. She mocked the thermometer of which I was so ashamed but her mockery could never stop it rising.

Bessie, a trapezist and tightrope walker, was younger than Mimi: perhaps eighteen. Her quietness calmed Mimi's rages, but although Bessie submitted to her stronger companion it was she who controlled the fine balance between them.

Awakening sometimes in the night, I would see Mimi kneeling at the end of the bed to kiss Bessie's feet, fingers twisting air, the arch of a long throat wordlessly murmuring. Once again I was a spectator at the lovemaking of others, a watcher of something beyond mere circus. When I first met Mimi and Bessie their affair was still young and I could not but watch as intimacy flowered, as new secrets were shared, new commitments made and new pleasures enjoyed. I felt like a spectre at the feast.

10

Life in the Horse

THE NEXT day was filled with the sound of hammers and winches and the complaining wheels of carts. As I walked about the field the dimensions of the circus changed before my eyes. The fixtures vanished and the solid surfaces melted away, were stacked and covered with tarpaulin. Rectangles of etiolated grass appeared as if the ground had made a map to record our passing. The animals mewled and grunted, paced their cages, kicked the doors of their stalls. Early that afternoon a line of caravans snaked its way along the Dover road. My life as the back end of a pantomime horse had begun.

Over the spring months that followed I was to wonder on many occasions why I consented to remain under the roof – to speak metaphorically – of the circus. I had been better paid as a messenger boy, although in the circus at least I was given food and a bed – miserable as the food was, tormented as the bed so often was. The enforced separation between myself and Aramind could only be a reason the more for leaving, but I must admit that even a distant glimpse of her made my life more bearable and even compelled me to remain.

The spring brought in me no thaw. Spring succeeded spring and then once more it was spring again but I still thought of the organ that beat within as a bluish adamantine lump. Once more we moved westwards along the southern coast of England, making occasional forays to the larger inland towns. Life, like a steady clock, ticked away with the utmost regularity: the sea on our left, the land on our right; the arrival, the departure. Despite superficial difference of place, our performance was always and ever the same: the same masks and jokes, the same grimaces on the faces of the clowns and, within the pantomime horse, always the same trips and stumbles to the same roar of laughter in the same portion of that ring which, it is supposed, is a circuit of wonder and delight.

In the back end of the pantomime horse, with my legs splayed and my hands on Wilf Patchkey's hips, wonder and delight was another country. In these years I came to know intimately Wilf's peculiar odour, which far exceeded mere transitory uncleanliness and had in fact been accumulated over many unwashed years. I understood, too, why even now the smell of my predecessor Bill Stephens remained: inside the thickness of felt and squirrel skin, amongst the torches and the warmth of crowds, sweat poured from our bodies. At the end of each performance, after we had unbuttoned our respective halves, I was forced to spread my costume before the fire to dry. Wilf, however, had no patience with such niceties. He merely doffed his papier mâché head, cast it into a corner and collapsed naked onto his filthy sheets. He would flap his minute penis against his belly with an infuriating *plip*.

At moments, however, for no apparent reason, the ice would thaw for a while and something that was not of this life and its regularities would penetrate me to the core. What, in the realm of the everyday, fell into the categories of the mundanely beautiful or ugly became, of a sudden, most extraordinarily and strangely beautiful or ugly. Such feelings, however, were momentary. I spent most of my time immured in the pungent blindness of a textile prison.

At Beachy Head, I remember, I stood at the edge of the cliff as tattered clouds whipped across the sky. A sense of a vastness too austere to be benign and too distant to be benevolent overcame me. Tears of awe came into my eyes and I looked far away across the silver waters to where ocean met sky along an indistinct horizon. I looked downwards from the heights upon the wheeling sea birds and faintly heard their peevish but poignant cries. I saw beyond them to the fragile lighthouse and the rocky, wrack-strewn beach.

Another time, I took a purge for the worm and passed one of arm's length in a watery stool. It lay writhing in my bile, my blood mingled perhaps with its own. I wondered whether it was terrified by its loss of the warm secrecy of my digestive tract, its forcible expulsion into the hard world of light. Perhaps I had been, to it, a sort of pantomime horse: absurd, even vile, but necessary to life; a tool of the trade as well as a protective costume.

At some indeterminate time in this procession of months, Wilf Patch-key dragged me furtively into the cramped darkness of an unoccupied lumber room and made me a proposal. It began I know not quite how, I think with a ''Tis too small, Jacko,' his endless lament. He explained that his unfamiliarity with sheets conjugal, copulatory or – at a pinch – adulterous arose, not from his unique perfume ('They love it, Jacko, they love the smell of earth on a man, the rough touch') but from his congenital deficiency. In a trice he had downed his breeches and, to my inordinate surprise, seized my hand and invited me to touch it, to feel it, to measure its modest length and, if I wished (he accommodatingly bade me feel free to do so) to more intimately and precisely compare respective sizes. Such a contest would doubtless have been intriguing but, withdrawing my hand gently so as not to appear unkind, I managed to avoid uncovering the source of my shame although Wilf's long fingers and lustrous eyes hovered and flitted around the region of my disfigured appendage. It was then that Wilf put it to me that I might occasionally 'oblige' him.

That evening, as we cavorted and pranced to the cruel but innocent laughter of the audience, I discovered that with some difficulty and, presumably, a slight loss of symmetry in the external appearance of the pantomime horse, I was able to extend my arm between Wilf's splayed, dancing legs and to grasp at first gently but then with increasing confidence his amorously upspringing part. This seemed if anything to enhance the energy and the fervour of his performance so that I had only to hold his penis in my hand for his leaps and gyrations to provide the necessary stimulus. From time to time, as we staggered our way in the hot blackness around the ring, protected from the gaze of a thousand eyes only by the skins of a hundred dead squirrels, Wilf would encourage me with urgent whispers:

'Harder Jacko! Seize the nettle!

'That's good. You have me now.

'Oh Jacko! Harder!

'There's such life in it! Such wanting!'

This inner performance became a ritual conducted almost nightly and sometimes more than once during the evening. With the aid of a tailor at Exeter, Wilf and I were able to stiffen with whalebone ribbing the right hand flank of the horse, where the absence of my arm created a noticeable depression. We also discovered that by moving the buttons and so somewhat shortening the length of the horse we were able to accomplish our masturbatory feats in greater comfort and with far less danger of injury. It even seemed that the crowd laughed the harder at this more curtailed and foreshortened equine parody. My only objection to the arrangement was the tenacity of Wilf's odour. The hand that milked his single teat became permanently ingrained with his smell. I hesitated to mention this to Wilf for fear of hurting his feelings. Instead, if hygiene was demanded, I used my other hand.

The only hiatus in this comfortable arrangement occurred a few years later, in 1885. I remember that Aramind's twenty-first birthday was approaching and for some time I had been wanting to buy her a present. I had thought of some small piece of jewellery but I entirely lacked resources and did not know what to do. I had almost reconciled myself to the fact that I would have to give her a bunch of flowers when I was approached in the most surprising fashion by Alf Hagsproat, the circus strongman.

Late one night I was returning to the caravan from an inn on the outskirts of Bury St Edmunds where I had been celebrating the final night of our stay – a more than usually successful one – with Wilf. I said good night and turned my steps across the field. As I passed the joiner's workshop, however, I was seized firmly from behind. A hand covered my mouth. I was lifted from the ground and carried into the workshop, where I was flung onto a trestle table. I could hear heavy breathing behind me and smell alcohol, but I was still too stunned to respond in even the most pitifully defensive way to what was being performed upon me. Before I could gather breath or leap for a door my breeches were torn off and a heavy hand on my back pinned me down, wriggle as I would. I stared in front of me and saw a large tin of grease into which at that moment a hand was plunged. To my shock I discovered that my by now quivering rectum was being clumsily anointed. Turning my head I found myself looking straight into the glazed eyes of the normally gentle Alf. I noticed to my horror that, trouserless, he was smearing grease over his gigantic phallus.

The pain was intense. I felt myself split apart and ground by a vast weight into the splinters and shavings on the trestle table, brutally penetrated to an inner depth beyond belief. He worked me long and hard. Once, towards the climax, he lifted me from the table and held me in the air, the better to thrust inside me. My cries, tears and protestations seemed only to intensify the fury of his passion. I felt the feverish liquid injected deep within me and, defiled and impotent, I was cast down on the table. The weight was lifted, the sword drawn from my gaping wound and, as liquid spilled from my anal canal, I passed out of consciousness.

When I awoke it was dawn. I wiped myself as best I could with some wood shavings. The great bruise inside me began to throb and spread. Stiffly, I put on my torn trousers and hobbled back across the tober to my caravan. As I opened the door, Mimi's head – all dark hair and pale throat – was visible to one side of the Japanese screen. Quietly, in the dawn, she was being loved by Bessie. She turned her head towards me.

'Where've you been? Big Alf's been hunting for you everywhere.'

Bessie giggled from out of sight: 'He's got a crush on you.'

I collapsed on the palliasse and fell into a sleep broken only by images of the intimacy that Mimi and Bessie projected after their bodies were tired, on the magic-lantern screen of their dreams.

11

A Ring and a Riddle

I COULD not walk for a week and could not stagger as the back end of the pantomime horse for some days more. I thus deprived not only myself but also Wilf of employment. Yet he never complained of this and tried his best to be cheerful company. At each new town we visited he would search out some apparently efficacious unguent and present it to me with a dog-like fidelity as a thing of inestimable worth. He was also fiercely jealous of my violator. Even Mimi and Bessie showed a consideration for me that had been lacking before. They allowed me to do nothing for myself and for a while I became a sort of doll or living plaything in their hands. I felt freed from the responsibility of acting out my own destiny; I had become that most joyous of beings, an insensate thing.

Aramind's birthday passed but owing to my injury I found no opportunity to congratulate her. A few days later I too became twenty-one and that evening a small celebration, with beer and biscuits, was held in the caravan. My wounds had almost healed and I had entered that moment in a sickness when both nurse and patient conspire to prolong the stable pleasures of illness a little longer.

My friends' faces were golden in the lanternlight. Wilf, Mimi, Bessie and I shared stories of our past lives and of the winding roads which had brought us together. We were all surprised by an early visit from Mortimer Croop. Stooping in the confined space, he magnanimously bestowed on me with empurpled fingers 'a small gift of money – finest ever of presents – to commemorate your anniversary and which I hope will be of the highest usefulness to you'. Croop moved aside to make his departure revealing, as always, the squat and hugely amused Pestine presence. A sudden thrill ran through me for here, in travesty, I saw Aesop's parable of the eagle and the wren.

Croop's birthday gift amounted to approximately half of my lost wages and with great difficulty I eventually succeeded in persuading Wilf Patchkey to allow me to divide this windfall between us.

At about nine o'clock, after a lapse of conversation that had lasted a minute or two and during which I had begun to wonder why Wilf, Mimi and Bessie were exchanging such significant glances, there was a heavy knock at the door of the caravan. Mimi and Bessie immediately gathered up their shawls and disappeared outside without allowing me to see, through the briefly opened door, who it was that had called. I had expected no other guests and in the normal run we were rarely disturbed since we always stationed ourselves on the further edges of the circus encampment.

Wilf knelt before me, the embers of his eyes fanned to an intense brightness as if by the action of a pair of psychic bellows. 'Just remember Jacko old lad, me old mate, should you ever want, I can stick something thin and cold between the ribs one rainy night and leave him for carrion. Remember that, Jacko: he'll make nor sound nor struggle, split and down like a sack of wheat.'

Guessing at the identity of my visitor, I replied that I bridled at murder on account of the talk it set off. With a nod and a 'Just remember, Jacko,' Wilf too had gone.

A second knock, loud but somehow full of respect, rattled the teacups on the ormolu dresser.

I had thought of Alf Hagsproat over the preceding days with unmixed hatred. Perhaps I had needed the strength of this ill will in order to recover from both my physical injuries and those more unseen that sprang from my objectification. For I had been forced to become an object to gratify another. I had been a mere prosthesis enabling Alf Hagsproat for those fierce minutes to close the arc which normally divides fact from fantasy. Used and consumed, I had wriggled on the pin like a fluttering insect. Now I was a depleted version of the pantomime horse: a rag doll clothed and fed by others.

In a way which I will never be able to explain, Alf's appearance immediately dispelled my hatred and revived, with a surge, my sense of individuality. Alf had reverted to his old self and I could not but accept this self as the genuine one and the other as an aberration extreme in violence in proportion to the actual extremity of his gentleness. He gazed down on me from his great height and his eyes were alive with the play of kindness, contrition, fear and self-recrimination. He lowered himself slowly to the ground. There was silence for some time, and he toyed awkwardly with a tassel on the rug. Then the huge shoulders heaved and tears poured down his cheeks.

'Oh Jackie, I rue the day I was born with such strength: it lives inside me like another being.' He tugged and tugged again at the tassel. 'I have prayed to God for some injury, Jackie, some avenging angel to maim me. I wish I was a child again. They should have left me on a mountain, Jackie. I wish I had the soft body of a worm that you could tread on me.'

His sentences tumbled out and I tried to control the tremor in my voice as I replied. 'Alf,' I said, 'you were another man then. He was not you any more that I am you or Croop is. What happened is not between you and me. Let us forget the past.'

He stretched out his huge hand and held my own so much smaller one in it. 'But Jack,' he protested, 'Jackie. I can't forget the past: I lusted after you. More than any woman and it says that man shall not lie down with man.' With a great effort, he gathered his broken feelings and looked at me directly, frankly. 'I must make some recompense, Jack.' I made some deprecatory gesture, but Alf would have none of it. 'No Jack: don't do that. Don't reject it because I try to balance things up. It's good of you but don't do it.'

Alf reached into an inner pocket and brought forth a soft leather bag with silken draw-strings. 'I have nothing else Jack, but I think this will do. I made it myself from the gold of Australia and the opal of Australia. Made it for a woman, Jack: the one who was to be my wife.' He squeezed the bag and an expression of distant sadness came into his face. 'But she left me though I loved her. My love was not enough.' Once more he settled himself and fixed his purpose before him. 'I vowed that one day I would give this ring away and ask nothing in return. I vowed to give it not to a woman but to a man: a man who, one day, I might be in the extremity of debt towards. It is for you, Jack Spellman.'

All my protestations were useless. We passed the leather bag backwards and forwards between us as if it were a glowing coal. My denials and Alf's affirmations interwove themselves like threads of smoke, becoming ever more complex and eloquent. The exchange of this small brown bag took on, from moment to moment, added significance until it seemed almost alive. It was as if our feelings were outside us and visible in it.

Eventually I relented; my objections were overcome one by one and at last, with a sigh of relief as if he had undergone some rite of purification, Alf turned the lantern down low. 'Give me your hand, sweet Jackie who I hurt so badly. Yes, I thought so: you have her hands, her fingers. Close your eyes.'

He slipped the warm weight onto the smallest finger of my left hand. Even then it seemed to gall the flesh. 'Close your eyes Jackie, until I am gone. All is well between us now and quite healed up. Do what you wish with this ring: sell it, throw it away, give it to a beggar or a lover. It is yours and my interest in it is finished. The past is abolished and my debt discharged.'

Alf Hagsproat's voice had taken on an incantatory tone. When I opened my eyes he had gone. After some minutes, Mimi, Bessie and Wilf returned. Together we examined my gift. Set within a slim ring of fine old gold was the most beautiful stone that I had ever seen. It was like the eye of a Hindoo or Egyptian idol, like the petrified visual orb of a great cat. It had nothing in it of glitter and sparkle, only of nebulous depths that shifted as you turned it in the light. In one mood it was a pearl, in another a drop of blood. Sometimes it seemed cool, sometimes as if a mysterious heat was trapped within. We all gazed on it in silence for a very long time.

I should have thrown it away, I should have sold it or given it to a beggar. It was to play its part in the two most horrible hurts I ever sustained.

It was then that Wilf announced the climax to my birthday evening. Somehow he had managed to persuade the great Zanzare to tell my fortune. This was remarkable, for it was well-known in the circus that Zanzare never prophesied the future for those he knew. 'The seer,' he would loftily say if pressed, 'is always neglected in his own country.'

The door opened again and Zanzare came silently into the expectant hush of our ring, wrapped in the dark cloak of his trade. It was by now quite late but he had evidently been moderate in his drinking and appeared almost sober. He was like a dispossessed or exiled ruler, worn down and a little threadbare. His faculties were gradually beginning to wander but he still possessed a spark of the old authority and more than a casual access to hidden knowledge. He sat with his back to us and, turning the lantern down, looked into its flickering flame. Slowly and with a distant, almost unearthly moan which baffles my annotation, he began.

'Where is he? I search for him. Show me the way, O you who fix the laws of chance.

'Jacek Spellman, born not of conjunction but of separation . . . I see a road and a great white room with a woman moving to and fro. And I see a horseman and a tiger and a lawless desire seen and a hole. I see two dead children. There is a great deal of death . . . '

Zanzare fell into inarticulate murmurings but otherwise complete silence reigned in the caravan. I did not look at the others. My eyes were fixed on the magician's narrow shoulders and the black strands of hair which fell upon them. After some minutes he began to speak again in recognizable words.

'I have found my way again but you are lost in crowds, alone and frightened. A blazing red woman. There is another redness, which is hidden. The dancer, the root, a lighthouse, a worm, wood shavings . . . It is dissolving into things, so many things that I cannot tell. But I have seen all this that was Jacek Spellman.'

All that had been said was true and yet what fascinated me more was the obscurity of this rhetoric. With its stuttering inarticulacy it seemed as if it had been freshly lifted from the ineffable like a great fish with glittering scales. It was all sing-song nonsense. Yet oddly its meanderings saved it.

Each humble twist and turn of speech brought forth the past from silence. I had tried to forget my previous life but it had come back with all its sordid clarity. That Zanzare knew these details was, perhaps, remarkable but what was still more astonishing was his voice, which by some trick beyond magic presented the words and made them almost materialize as physical shapes in the confined space. I knew for the first time the sense of autobiography: that voice which seemed to come from nowhere could have been my own.

Stranger was to follow. Zanzare flung powder into the flame and for a moment we were illuminated by a preternatural purple light without smell or smoke. Then he spread his cloaked arms wide, like a vast raven, and again we heard that distant moan: a sound less human I had never heard.

'Come then, unfixed phantoms of desire that write what is to be. Turn the pages that I may read them and take some fragments back to where my body is. Spell Spellman for me . . . A ring will not do you harm. There is fire somewhere I cannot see, and purple or cherry, I cannot tell which. One of noble birth. Others too, but shadowy. A great theatre and a living statue but no life, a great deal of death. There will be letters from the dead and writing inside the dead but the reasons are obscure, they turn the pages so fast and I snatch what I can, indebted to them even for these scraps . . . I see a dumbshow or charade seen through an eye; one who licks his lips, another stretched out in a misery she loves. Osiris . . . There are brothers here and Spellman is the last. The pages turn again and there are crabs on a living corpse, boxes full of things and a tooth – a horse's tooth . . . Another river, colder. A boat. At dawn. The Thames. Somewhere here a heart that longs for the peace of vastness. I see another man towards the end yet sought at the beginning who haunts you although you own him, who is weak although you are his plaything, a living puppet . . . One tries to bring the things to life but it cannot be done. They will not allow it . . .'

Zanzare fell quiet. He was no longer possessed by the words. When he left us without a farewell we all noticed that his face was very white. None of us had seen him like this before. Elegant in his booth, he usually limited himself to unweaving the spells that lurked in everyday objects: apples, coins, pieces of string and coloured paper. The magic of a spoon would live for a few moments in his hands. This voice was entirely different; it came from unknown territory. Normally, Zanzare mastered his performance. On this occasion the slick patter had abandoned him and his disjoined words rode and mastered him.

Later, much later that night, as I lay on my palliasse turning over Zanzare's words from nowhere, I felt a presence near me, a warm breath on my cheek. It was Aramind and she had come to wish me well. We

48

pressed our foreheads together and had no need of talk. Our thoughts moved with ease through the barriers of skin and bone. Before she went I pressed into her hand the opal ring: 'Happy birthday.' She took the gift and then was gone.

12

Men and Women – Mostly Men

S IX WEEKS after this incident the circus established its winter quarters in Canterbury and gave its last performance of the season. A few days later, as in previous years, it had become a shadow of its old self. Most of the hands and many of the performers had left to find work until the spring. Perhaps only twenty tents and caravans remained in the long meadow which descended gently to the banks of the Stour.

It was a bare, bleak autumn afternoon and there was nobody in the caravan when I returned. I had been in town: wasting my money, as usual, on books. I took them from my pockets – *David Copperfield*, *Great Expectations* – and laid them aside to boil some water.

I had illuminated the lantern and was reading about ghosts and cauls in its light when my attention was distracted by something which lay beside me on the palliasse. It was one of Mimi's shawls. I continued reading for some time but I was no longer thinking about the words on the page. Slowly my sensations became concentrated in my hand and particularly in the fingers which stroked the silk surface of the mantle and ran, with a gentle pressure, along its creases and undulations. I closed the book and held the shawl close to me. Standing up, I flung it around my shoulders and allowed its folds to fall around me. Holding it tight around my throat, I buried my nose in the shimmering material. It smelt of Mimi.

I was awakened from this reverie when my ear lobe was seized by two strong fingers. Mimi had entered the caravan without my having noticed her. She dragged me towards the door and pushed me through it so that I stumbled down the steps and fell on the wet grass.

'You bastard,' she said between clenched teeth, 'don't ever let me catch you touching my clothes again.'

Humiliated, I wriggled away. When I heard the door of the caravan slam shut behind me, I got up and began to walk in the opposite direction with the vague idea of finding somewhere to wait until I judged that Mimi's temper might have cooled. I had not gone far, however, when I came upon another domestic disturbance. The door of a shed was flung open and, projected by an unseen hand, an object flew through the air to land at my feet. I looked at it in consternation: it was a human head. A second glance reassured me that I had not been the witness to an execution, for on the grass lay a wax representation of King Charles I complete with a wig, in the characteristic style, which had become detached in mid-flight and now lay at a few yards' distance.

The circus joiner appeared in the doorway of the shed. He was clutching in his arms a hairless male torso, also made of wax, which he unceremoniously deposited on the ground before retreating once more inside the shed. An assortment of artificial legs and arms began to fly through the air and in a short while the immediate area took on the appearance of the scene of a minor massacre. All this time from within the caravan I could hear the low sound of sobbing. The owner of this voice was expelled last of all and she struggled no more than had the manikins. Before slamming the door, the joiner shouted down at her:

'Don't come back you withered slut!'

I now recognized this woman as Gertrude Desmoulins, the circus costumier who, during the season, also maintained a booth at the edge of the circus which was devoted to the exhibition of her own waxworks. Approaching, I knelt beside her on the grass, surrounded by the broken effigies, and asked if I could help. Controlling her sobbing, she rose to her feet. We gathered up the dismembered fragments of her trade and, watched by the joiner from a small window, removed them to the machinist's shed where there was a dry corner to store them. Gertrude thanked me and, now apparently recovered, invited me back to her caravan for a glass of brandy to fortify us after our recent experience. Having nothing else to do and with domestic problems of my own, I readily complied.

''E is a rigid, inflexible man,' she said of the joiner as she uncorked the bottle. ''Is will! 'E is a tyrant, 'e want everything: 'is food, 'is pound of flesh, 'is little fuck. And 'e steal from me.' She looked at me with barely controlled outrage: 'You men! Are you all like 'im?'

I felt distinctly uncomfortable since theft, in a manner, had been precisely the cause of the disagreement between myself and Mimi. But Gertrude answered her own question. 'Oh, you are not so bad perhaps. That is what you were going to say, isn't it? But nevertheless you are a man: one of those Englishmen whose 'ome is 'is castle and who plays the despot in 'is wife's boudoir.'

Gertrude poured more brandy. Then, leaning back in her chair, she said with aphoristic incisiveness: 'Men are lines and women circles. Like the genitals: a male line, a female circle.'

Later in the evening, as I was preparing to return to Mimi's caravan and make my apologies, she returned to her theme: 'With the line you men inherit the earth. But woman, she *is* the 'ole round earth.'

That night, on my palliasse, I continued to think of what Gertrude had said. The circle that women were, what was that? A whole or a hole, a void or a fullness? And that line which described men, was that a fiction or some system of inheritance? All the categories and oppositions began to spin round in my head: was the circus a woman and the city a man? Was it possible to think myself out of the prison of my manhood and understand what it was to be a woman? Perhaps not, for the veil of flesh, though delicate, is more impenetrable than distance or material obstacles. Even the gods defer to Tiresias and he is himself cursed with blindness for his knowledge.

I was not Tiresias; I had not struck the intertwined snakes with my staff but nevertheless I did think of myself as a species of hermaphrodite. My marked genitalia separated me from simple masculinity and although it was known only to me, my difference was written between my legs. I was excluded from the sexual circuit whose joyous sensuality was perhaps a hollow plaster cast, a shadow projected by my dreams – men's dreams.

I knew men's dreams and their desire. With me, it began as an irritation below my scarlet deformity. It was always localized, directed towards an end and I hated its frankness, the straightforwardness of its uncontrolled disclosure. The organ in question seemed to have been formed by a deity who wished to amuse herself throughout eternity by the value which would be placed upon a boneless insignificance. A scrap of flesh would be Power and Right, Law and Truth, the Creative Principle, the very Key of Mastery and Dominion. What grandeur was focused on this limp four inches – which majestically extends in excess of another two inches during moments of well-directed chafing!

I rubbed myself and hated it – not as a sin, for this would only be to submit to the rod of Law and Truth – but for its banality, its linearity. Desire was trapped in the impoverishment of need. It sought only itself, time after time, with a parrot-like precision. To expedite emission, pictures passed before the inner eye which dissolved at the crisis when the brain vacated itself and transmitted a modest shiver of energy like melting ice or dying fire along the backbone. At the base of that brief line, another briefer line quivered for a moment before expelling a loop of thinnish, whitish, brackish liquid.

Beyond the bedsheets male desire meets a larger but equally impoverished landscape: that of the male soul, snug in its cities with its paper wills and contracts, its reason, its logic, its triumphs, its ends. In the city of men, to avoid infection, fantasies are placed beyond the walls. Expelled, the objects of desire which we have ourselves conjured up become desirable. Circuses, women: forgetting enables us to think that they are real. And here is the largest rent in the fabric: desire wishes to consume itself, to finish itself off. It wants, not to have, but to have had.

I try on these dark nights, Mr Secretary, to imagine how it might be for women. I try, knowing that I am already failing, to work my thoughts into that other place which lies beyond the point at which I can think them . . .

. . . A loss of direction which is not meaningless but beyond meanings. A jewel that is not an ornament but an essence. A cosmetic that does not paint surfaces so much as speak depth. A body not thoughtless but never pointing, never probing. Sights smelt, sounds in wandering tasted, touches heard. Beyond pain or pleasure again and again until everything is washed away by the surge of a great green wave, everything except the slow drip of water from the lifted blade of an oar . . .

Deviate as I will, I cannot circumnavigate the myths. I can disrupt their complacency and their respectable certainty of their own origins but this is a minor revolution, only a little bomb-throwing. Despite my subterfuges, the words, in ways beyond my ken, seem to have their own allegiances. I cannot imagine myself out of the fantasy; however far I go, I am still a man dreaming. Is it something in these mercenary words or in this stained city? Or is my enemy closer still? Can it be the Secretary? Must I suspect him of allowing, whilst I sleep, the words to make themselves up again so that they acquire a secure residence on the page and push those other, imagined words out beyond the margins, where I can almost hear, as if through a pane of glass, their urgent, reproachful tapping?

13

South and North

ANOTHER WEEK gone by, a week of the narrative of my life passed for ever and put down on paper. The Secretary came the night before last bearing another bundle of Remington scythings. And now another week begins and there is another swath to cut.

The word *travel* springs from the same root as the word *travail*: the medieval *trepalium*, which is an instrument of torture involving three stakes. To think of travel, therefore, as joyous and carefree motion is a fantasy of the modern city. The city projects the romance of the gypsy and the tinker: the winding road at sunset, healthful nights beneath hedges, the begged crust, the weatherbeaten face, the twinkling eye. Needless to say, the reality was not so painless.

We spent four or five days in each place, sometimes less, sometimes – if trade was good – a little more. The ritual of arrival and departure was performed so frequently that one had no need to think. As I hauled upon the rope or packed away the canvas, I often thought of myself as a machine. People see the life of the circus as full of change and variety. Let me assure you that after ten years – even after ten months – it became a pattern of the utmost monotony.

I found the towns of southern England (excepting only London, whose messy energy seduced and fascinated me) dull, static and seemingly condemned to labour for ever under an antiquated order. Despite what the historians now tell us, the countryside had at that time been little affected by the advent of steam. One saw, certainly, trains and agricultural engines but there were none of the mines and factories so visible in the landscape of the north. The circus floated like a particoloured bubble between the neat hedges and across the smooth downlands of the southern counties.

As we proceeded northwards, however, an imperceptible change began to take effect. The north was a revelation to me. In Manchester, for example, our mean lodgings were palaces compared to the cramped hovels of the urban poor. Men lay drunk in the mud of space, not worthy to be called a street, that wound between the shacks barely a stone's throw from the great civic thoroughfares. I saw children maimed by the looms whose harsh clatter sounded along every street. The mills ground on by day and night, eroding away the flesh, re-inventing humanity as a timed and punctual cog. At Sheffield, the factory chimneys sent showers of sparks into a poisoned night and I saw the men who worked in this pandemonium to produce a metal hard enough to inflict the injuries of which this society was capable. Everything was ordered: the great machines worked in time, spoons of lava poured down the flumes, glowing lumps of steel were lifted and set aside to cool. Occasionally one of these faceless men would meet with an unfortunate accident. But all was ordered and set to its proper time: the next Sunday his workmates would follow the coffin which contained his mutilated corpse to the churchyard, where he would be buried beside other operatives who had met, in all likelihood, similar fates. In York, the point of my conception, I saw the glassworks where men blew with all their force down the hollow rods and that malleable thing was spun into a restricted range of shapes, each one no different from the last. Other men ground and polished the cooled product, cut the pre-ordained patterns into it with diamond-tipped steel and coughed their lives away in the dusty air. The Minster represented the glory of a dead religion, for the religion of spirit had been superseded by a stronger: the religion of things, identical things produced in the heaving clatter of the new churches.

If the age was changing the face of the land and of the people who lived on it, its effects were felt equally in the circus, so permeable was it to the city, so much an expression of the city. For what was Mortimer Croop but an industrialist, a man of capital? Admittedly his factory was an unusual one but its systems and orders were in kind no different to those of any mill or workshop. Croop's products were intangible but their effect was the same as all those other mass-produced mementoes and memorabilia of the day. The circus – like a charming paperweight – made life bearable, made one forget the life that had been lost in its production. Croop sold what people wanted and desired. He satisfied neither grand passions nor basic needs but something in between: the desire to escape for a few hours, to be amused, to be happy. Conveniently for Croop, his products could be traded to the end of every road in the land. The factory carried itself to its consumers and we, the performers, were the goods on sale. Every evening at the ticket office and in the booths, thousands of small coins were gathered together and, later that night, two or three hundred sallow slaves went home with empty pockets. The next morning Croop carried the coins in canvas bags to the bank. Reserving and depositing the owner's due, some of this money would eventually be re-distributed amongst us. On wage day we would all queue up outside Croop's caravan. One by one we would enter and receive our little packets and Pesto would tick off our names on the list. For some reason, the distribution of money always made Croop philosophical. 'Unhappiness is our security,' he told me once as he placed the packet in my hand. 'Misery gives us a steady market.'

15

A Hollow Dream

I T W A S a strange decade and I have tried to give you, Mr Secretary, and you, dear reader, some fragmentary impression of its passage and of how its glitter is all but lost to me as it turns and disappears in my wake. It is time to resume my narrative, which comes clearly to me as I speak. There is something soothing in the scratching of the Recorder's pen which drags it from me gently, like a child tugging at its mother's skirt.

I had one particular dream repeatedly at this time. A dream? Or was it merely an image which sprang to mind in the last moments before sleep? Mimi and Bessie lay draped across each other in the darkness behind the Japanese screen. As wakefulness dwindled, my eyes seemed to turn downwards and inwards and – I could see into my own body. It was hollow: there was nothing inside except the inner surface of my garments. I could see the material of my shirt and the stitches which held the buttons on, my undergarments and, at a seemingly great distance, the insides of my own socks. The vision would either awaken me, leaving me without sleep through the long night or, less frequently, compel me to wander in my dreams as the fixed eye in an empty body, so that I only found myself when I awoke the next day.

I spent a great deal of time thinking about Mimi and Bessie. Except during the period of my injury a couple of years previously Bessie had seemed indifferent to my presence and Mimi positively hostile to it. Perhaps this was because I was in excess of the sum they made together. Mimi and Bessie thought of nobody but each other: to them, the other was the whole world. Confident in her reliance on Mimi, Bessie had nothing against the world but merely set herself apart from it and chose to forget it. Mimi, on the other hand, had an active hatred for a world that once had hurt her. Unfortunately for me, I was that thing which became identified in Mimi's mind with the world. I was chosen as the victim of her slow revenge.

Yet even during the miserable times that were to come, I could never hate either Bessie or Mimi. I needed too much whatever it was that emerged, almost tangibly, from their interactions. And – whatever it was – it had nothing to do with marriage and seemed even to exceed desire. They loved each other beyond flesh and bone and there was a certain poignancy in their attempts to transcend the barriers of the body, the dams of skin and muscle and face and fibre. Forcing themselves onto each other beyond limits in a frenzied collision of all that separated them, their failure was forever renewed.

For some reason I pictured them occasionally in my mind's eye as elderly women. Side by side, they sat together behind the counter of a sweetshop. Neither touching nor talking they would still be vital to each other and quite literally so, for it seemed to me that unlike anybody else I have ever known, they had found in the other the source of their own life. By joining forces and forgetting the world they had abandoned the abyss which separates circus from city, men from women. The world outside the caravan threatened them and even as they threatened me I worried for their safety; but I knew from the very beginning that even if they could never merge into one person they would never part.

16

Insult and Injury

A S I lay on my mattress in the long nights Mimi would emerge from behind the Japanese screen, her skin pale blue in the light of stars. I could sense that she was trembling although I was never, afterwards, able to decide whether this fibrillation of the limbs was caused by rage, fear, or merely the cold. Then, with the splayed footsteps of the gymnast, Mimi would approach my bed. She was balanced at these times, I always felt, on the back of an imaginary horse and she walked with grace along its shifting spine.

Mimi crossed the caravan on this first occasion and now stood close beside me, her form emerging more clearly from the shadows. I turned my head towards her and felt devoid of questions and answers, threadless in the maze. The air was thick with images and intentions like insects in the hour before a summer storm. I became aware that I had no power over Mimi: her dreams were stronger and perhaps crueller than my own.

There was never, from that first moment, the faintest possibility of eluding the tremendous force of the ritual which Mimi was performing. Yet even though Mimi had the power to subordinate me, this did not mean that the ritual therefore belonged to her. Indeed, at these times she was like a somnambulist or automaton making by her movements obeisance to some higher power and fulfilling to the letter the terms of its decree.

I suddenly sensed a cessation to Mimi's trembling. She had gained access to the cold control of her performance and her limbs were free. Slowly but without gentleness, she pulled away the blankets that covered me and exposed my upper body to the faint light which shone through the uncurtained window. The down on her arms brushed against my chest. With something approaching weariness, she straddled and knelt above me without touching any part of my body. At last she rolled my blankets completely away. My shame sprang upwards in pitiful glory and touched her thigh. Her hips heaved: not, I noticed in deepening curiosity, with anything approaching arousal but, quite definitely, in disgust and avoidance. Her response, I felt, was directed towards the male organ *per se*: she had not, like Amelia of old, been horrified by my particular deformity. Indeed I rather think that she had not even noticed it.

After some time and with infinite slowness, Mimi bent her lips to my ear and, to my intense surprise, murmured in a voice thick with hate: 'Sewer.'

How had it been possible for me to misread so completely her purpose? It seemed that desire was the only ritual familiar to my mind but there are, of course, other and darker celebrations: exorcisms, sacrifices, rites of passage. Perhaps the strangest thing of all was the way in which I allowed myself to become a symbol.

Mimi spoke again: 'Filthy gutter swimming with city shit!' Without any reluctance I became at this moment nothing but a sore bleeding death into clear water. I saw cankered fish rising to the surface before being borne away, with their furred scales, on the current. The blood drained from my penis until it lay, filled with loathing, on my stomach.

Mimi had still not finished with me. Numbly I awaited my fate as she rose to her feet. On this and future occasions, the ritual demanded that she cover her breasts with her right arm and her vulva with her left hand. It always happened like this: she stood above me and rested her vacant eyes on mine. She never once looked at my body. It was an object of no interest to her. Strangely this produced a timid recrudescence of my manhood. My marked genitals no longer counted; they did not differentiate me. Rather, I was the same: invested in that community of phalli by having to pay the price owed by man. I merely represented all those other fleshy lengths which, on violent nights, had insulted Mimi beyond all limits.

On the third finger of Mimi's left hand a silver droplet of liquid appeared, paused, fell through the shadows onto my stomach. It was immediately followed by other drops and then the full straight stream of her contumely. A pool formed between my hips and began to run off at the sides of my stomach. Still somnambulant, Mimi allowed the last trickle to pass from her loins before returning to embrace the faintly snoring Bessie behind the Japanese screen.

Rituals, like obscenities and caresses, become debased by repetition. After my first ordeal I was humiliated beyond measure but gradually, on successive occasions, the sheer force of usage began to undermine the rite. Is this once again the hallmark of a desire which is motivated by a desire within itself to overreach, collapse and die? In any case, by an unconscious turn of thought, humiliation itself allowed desire to return and debasement, far from removing pleasure, became within me its single point of origin. The ability to transform pain into joy may not in itself be a cause for self-recrimination but I have to say that this transformation was no living movement: no, it was a dead, an automatic shift. I could not help but turn things my way. This, of course, was precisely the characteristic which Mimi had singled out for punishment.

Within three months, then, Mimi's nocturnal torture no longer restrained my cowed but still sappy penis. She redoubled her insults but it was not enough: the denial of pleasure now constituted my pleasure. In a matter of weeks the mere piling up of obscenities only allowed me the freedom to revel in my filth. Each coprophilism dropped like honey on my nakedness. Each malodorous curse was a lewd, familiar tongue. For the only time in my life, words produced in me the extremity of bliss. If only writing could always do this! Such a thing would be far beyond the stray page which sets off tears or laughter.

The ritual was disintegrating under its own momentum and, although we never referred to it aloud, there was recrimination for what I was in every glance of Mimi's. She wanted me to be humiliated by my pleasure and therefore stop my pleasure. I gained pleasure from humiliation and thus she was forced to punish and humble me even more. From this I derived more pleasure. It was a spiral: Mimi's desires could only fail but the difficulty was that their failure was also my failure since failing to be completely humiliated, I was thus cut off from complete pleasure.

Let me put it another way. Mimi wanted to punish the punished person. Punishing me created the need to punish me more. She must have been infuriated by the fact that utter loss was now the fulfilment of my desire and ultimate success was forever out of reach since I only fell in love with what was meted out to me.

Let us go on in nausea to tell the end of this pathetic farce. It was in my eighth year of the circus. I was a young man of twenty-four. My singular organ of reproduction had retained its uncanny purple cicatrice. Although squarer of jaw now and heavier of frame, I knew that I had not changed at all. I felt like an insect which had slept an age in amber.

She came, then, Mimi, in this the eighth year of my life as the back end of a pantomime horse, she came with the loathing in her heart that I had learned to love and a scheme to circumvent the infarction of ritual. Standing over me prior to micturition, she incanted as usual the foulnesses I adored. With my eyes closed in abandonment I prepared myself for the urinary baptism. I wanted to drown like a worm in a puddle. Before my begging member had had the chance to rise to the nothing it wanted to meet, however, I felt with surprise Mimi's hands upon me. Something cool and smooth was slipped, without concern for my possible discomfort, over my phallus. I think it was the careless way she did it that produced in me a tremendous excitation. Goaded by her abuse I became rapidly inflamed. With erection, however, came simultaneously the awareness of a painful cramp. Looking down, I observed that Mimi had placed a strong glass phial of the appropriate size and shape over my penis. Cramped and confined, I writhed in agony as Mimi pissed fluently and with great satisfaction into my face. With one hand I attempted to remove the phial but unfortunately my engorgement had already blocked its aperture and my continuing turgidity prevented any possibility of egress. Mimi had caught me in a vicious circle: the humiliation which caused my manly pleasure would be the very thing which unmanned me. I could not fail to be aroused by the danger I was in and, as the seconds passed, this danger was increasingly of castration, of the rupture of veins.

Content with the trap that she had set, Mimi returned to her bed behind the screen. The blood beat in my head and many-coloured spots danced, with inappropriate jollity, before my eyes. Whether by genuine deformation or by the refraction of the glass, my penis appeared to have occupied all possible space, ballooning out into the phial but horribly constricted at its neck. Naked, I flung myself out of the door of the caravan and ran to the workshop where poor dear Alf had buggered me. My wild feet scrunched on the wood shavings as I turned about for help, for any idea to liberate me from my prison. My penis, which was still erect, was now beginning to blacken. As I circled the shed it bounced and banged between my legs, weighed down by the heavy phial. The pain was becoming unbearable.

At last I lay my agony on the trestle table and, with a prayer on my lips, closed eyes and a hammer in my hand, I executed my deliverance with a sharp blow. The hammer bounced off the phial leaving neither mark nor crack upon its surface. Again I tried, with greater force: again without success. I now felt that I had only a few seconds remaining before the bursting point. With a scream and the full force of my arm, I brought the hammer down for the final time. The phial flew apart in a thousand scattered shards. My relief, however, was short-lived for, as it broke, the phial had cut me deeply in several places and, as soon as circulation was restored, blood burst from the wounds. I seized a rag and, tearing it into strips, wrapped myself round and round until the spreading stain was completely absorbed.

I returned to my palliasse that night in some discomfort. Deep in my perverse soul I had enjoyed my humiliation more than ever before.

17

What was Lost in the Dark

THE SECRETARY has been uncomfortable with the last week's dictation: it all started with the incident of the scarf. I told him last night that from now on I would be more reserved. This seemed to please him as he sat there deforming the white with his twisted black loops. Perhaps he thought that after the divagation of the phial I intended to return to more straightforwardly autobiographical themes. The Recording Pencil believes, I think, that a memoir should properly concern itself with the evolution, within a single and even possibly unremarkable soul, of the moral virtues; the development of an ethical system out of the disordered flow of lived experience. But this is not a proper memoir. I am not concerned with the many ways in which a person can turn a blind eye to appearance, can plump for the deceptive solidity of theme and progress. Zanzare had told me that there was more to surfaces than met the eye.

Words can never do justice to these things unless we make them stray from home; otherwise they become narratives, they fall into generic traps. This is neither erotica nor pornography nor even the ravings of a deviant mind but the unvarnished and literal truth. If nothing else would serve to reassure you then let me tell you how hard it is to lie to the Recorder: he looks so hurt, as if I had poured him an inferior brandy.

The bonds which restrained me and from which I derived such pleasure were undoubtedly perverse. I enjoyed my own absence; my flesh tingled in the knowledge that I had become a trope. Yet throughout my humiliation I remained, despite the skewing of the ritual, true to my middle name: incontrovertibly and irreducibly Adam. I reserved the power to exchange my debasement for a wealth of pleasure.

Within two months my wounds had healed. Fortunately, I had managed to avoid infection and after the bruising had subsided my stained member retained only the pale traceries of its laceration. At twenty-four years of age I felt, naïvely, that I had explored the furthest reaches of desire, that I had seen the place where love met and fused with hate. I was mistaken of course, and had calibrated but a single dynamic of the machine of desire. Something escaped me; there was something else which is hidden from me to this day. I had been put in my place and tied down. The old fib of phallic power, the myth of the magic wand and the rod of law: all this had long gone. But however much I wanted to suffer in silence, my organ of generation still spoke for me in our renewed rites. It spoke but it was not answered. Nothing called out to the homeless nothing which I extruded.

With frequent practice and with the stimulus of Mimi's vituperation I became able to attain the sharp sweetness, the pause and flow of bliss without the absurdity of ejaculation. But still my prick rose into the air, pallidly gesturing my need to transcend earth, to escape into cloud and sky.

Within a year, I had gone further. Utterly alone in my coming now, I was not only dry but flaccid. Mimi was blind and deaf to my delight. Never had I endured such pleasure: the greater the loss, the more the ice seared me in my wanton delight. My humiliation satisfied without satiating me. The chafing of bodies against each other could never have given me this; mere fleshly commingling would soon have palled.

Mimi and I lived under a spell. By day we were as curt to each other as we had always been but at night we put on different masks and forgot the parts we played.

There was one more thing to be taken away. Somehow Mimi still knew that she had not deprived me of the dissolving utterness. And so she came then, one night, in the dreams which we now shared. I seemed to awake naked and thought I found myself on my hands and knees. The priestess stood behind me and although I could not see her, I knew that she was smiling. My time at last had come: she was to finish and free me, to perform, gently, the savage act. She hated me but she was my friend and her curse was my only salvation. My skin was cold and colder musk and myrrh were sprinkled on it. I was the pig and I was ready to be sliced. I found myself trembling with longing. My limp prick awaited release. Her thumb and forefinger encircled it, and now the time had come to enter a new stage. Another life was coming, coming soon to be over. Finger and thumb around the legendary, the lost, the predicative thing: the gleam of the blade. My desire contained a fear that had always been there and would soon be gone, two good strokes and I would no longer be the thing I was not. I would lose loss and no longer want want, would lose the mechanism, the flesh and the mastery which all unwillingly I had inherited. There would be nothing between my legs but an O swallowing all laws, replacing the I.

A scream on the altar: the final loss was a bounteous plenitude. Gelded . . . gilt with glory . . .

64

18

Disenchantment

So HERE we are, Mr Secretary, in the spring – the latening spring – of this year of Our Lord nineteen hundred and nineteen. And what do we do? Like the alchemists of old or with the narrow-mindedness of monks at their manuscripts, we scribble away, late at night, in a cramped hand, in a silence broken only by the hissing of coals on the fire. And we lament, or commemorate, or attempt, for some reason we do not understand, to revive the last century, a century of death unutterably dead.

Why? Well, it's all a fake of course, me pretending that it means something, that it makes a difference. I am only fulfilling the conditions of her will, dear departed Lady Magenta.

The skin of the beloved which haunts you; the letters which kept coming but have now stopped.

Without that bleak purpose there would be no other, only the distant muted smell of cabbage, the scrunch of wood shavings beneath the foot: those old familiarities which are now so strange and with which I once purported to beguile away the time. But I suppose that I might as well tell winter's tales and gabble away the life to come.

Sometime during the last week, however, the purpose went out of it and I find myself worn down, Mr Secretary, quite worn down by it and disenchanted. The rest of this, if it comes, will be a commentary more on my stubbornness than on my life. There is no voice any more, no song. Even if the voice and the song were just sounds I saw before me, at least they turned prettily and vibrated with life. Now, night after night, as your strength grows, Mr Pencil, mine has depleted. You are bleeding me for a wage, fastening into me and finding a purchase and dragging more and more out. You do not like what you find very much, I know.

Night after night, I find myself recalling horrors – the farthing-cheap horrors which are worst of all – looking back to the roots and nethermost recesses of misery. I narrate as though it happened, of course, as though I had a standpoint and it a genealogy, as though it wasn't just a bastard born of loneliness. It is all before me again and I can never escape, never escape being the king of it, determining it, bringing it back to the uncaring gaze. I used to be so fascinated by desire. Strange. Now, like the circus, it seems a

65

cheap betrayal. Having made a home for ourselves in magic, Mimi and I discovered that it quickly lost its strangeness. We were still a man and a woman and nothing had changed. Perhaps our maps had deluded us. In any case, the ritual came to an end.

Is all this just a series of lies, Mr Secretary? Could it ever have been really true? Or do the lies contain the truths? Or – more pointedly still – is this a sophistication we can well afford, three solid floors above the mud, sipping my finest brandy?

You might say that none of this happened except in my dreams or as it happens now, so to speak, in my discourse. There would be a certain truth in this. With its stagery, its transient surfaces, the circus is like a dream of our normal lives, odd, but replete with familiar associations. It is a style of speech, a turn of phrase, a properties department of fictional effects.

Why, then, do I offer this attempt to conjure vestiges, to call on scraps of magic inherited from God knows where? It is a weak magic too because it cannot help us. Is it Zanzare's olden days, the burbled nostalgia for wonder? 'In Novara, in Milano, in the thirties, in the forties.' I don't know. It lurks and looms, this frayed magic, it tries to weave itself crosswise into our warp. It is like a despised minor relative, excluded from the family group, who beckons from outside the circle of warm light. We no longer care about the pattern it can help us to make up.

Why do I miss those threads? Why do I never talk of that plain and unfigured textile screen, the everyday? Because I do not believe in it and, like everything else, it needs belief in order to exist. 'What of the world and its problems?' cries the Pencil. 'No more of your mystical meanderings, Mr Spellman, if you please, and something of the moral life if you will, something of duty, evolution, salvation. Enough of your louring surfaces! They do not nourish me.'

We bend our heads once more over our work and the Pencil draws his salary and drinks my brandy. He has finished his probationary month and I have told him that I am happy to continue his employment. Week after week the text opens and unfolds in my voice and his hands. It is like a flower whose petals arch back, like cats stretching before they go out to hunt. The pages turn, back and back, and we begin to expect some scented core. Urbanely in this florists, in this hothouse, we stoop to breathe in the proffered bloom which, in its leached soil, has proliferated beyond all reasonable expectation.

It is a disappointment: there is no perfume and no colour. All that we find are the silvered traceries of worms and the bitemarks of parasitic insects. Another has been before us and stolen our pure bliss. Our hearts ache for what is not. This ache, at any rate, tells us that we too, in some way, survive.

19

The History of Wax

I HAVE already introduced you to Gertrude Desmoulins and described her expulsion at the hands of the circus joiner. And now here she comes again, walking towards me across the tober, her skirts billowing in the breeze, her arms folded over her breast against the cold. She stands before me, smiling. Can she see me? Today, tomorrow? She has written some more of *The History of Wax* and would like to read it to me.

But I am running away with myself.

The Frenchwoman's waxen images, which constituted, or so it seemed, another, frozen circus in the booth at the edge of the meadow, impressed me deeply at the time despite their technical crudity. They represented famous criminals, mythological figures, historical and political person-ages. There was a model of Grimaldi as Pierrot, Charles Darwin as an ape and, as you may remember – it had been repaired by now – King Charles I at the scaffold.

Perhaps one afternoon a month in these years I would take tea with Gertrude in her caravan. She was, I suppose, the chink in the armour of my isolation and I quickly became accustomed to the teasing manner which had so abashed me on the occasion of our first meeting. She would tell me stories of France, of the Paris Commune and, which interested me perhaps more than anything else, stories of wax and the modellers of wax. *La cire* she called it, avoiding the harsher Germanic term. Even today, I think of it as *la cire*, with its softness and malleability. Wax has too hard and alien a sound.

'I am a *figure de cire* modelled from Marie Tussaud, a simulacrum of her, a little doll, a voodoo doll of Mme Tussaud,' she said one day to me, quite composedly. There was no point in arguing that she seemed to me to be a figure of the most literal flesh and blood. Her opinion was emphatic, unshakeable and final: she was a living waxwork, an ageing Olympia forged at lower temperatures by some lesser Spalanzani.

As she talked that afternoon, it became apparent that there was indeed a remarkable coincidence between Marie Tussaud's career and her own, led on a lower and later plane. She had been born in the year that Mme

Tussaud died, 1850. She had also been born a Swiss, although in Geneva and not, as Marie, in Berne. Both had married Frenchmen, from whom both had become estranged after half a dozen years. They had first learned their skills as modellers of *la cire* from their respective uncles, both of whom were doctors. Marie Tussaud's uncle, John Christopher Curtius, had produced a series of finely detailed anatomical models which, for reasons history does not relate, had caught the eye of the visiting Prince de Conti. Later, in Paris, where he had been invited by the Prince, Curtius opened his '*Caverne des Grands Voleurs*' in the Boulevard du Temple. It became a great popular attraction immediately. So much did these images, it seems, fascinate the citizens of Paris that, on 12 July 1789 as the masses, infuriated by Necker's dismissal, raided the arsenal, a mob entered the *Caverne* and, possessing itself of Necker's bust, paraded through the capital in a peculiar fusion of theatre and history, of totemism and revolt.

'*Les figures de cire* are found on the streets,' said Gertrude, 'there are no such things in the Louvre.'

Marie Tussaud modelled the leaders and victims of the Revolution, and so, during the months of the Paris Commune in April and May, 1871, did Gertrude. She felt that the brief days of the Commune were in themselves a waxwork or simulacrum, a revival of the performances of 1848 and 1789.

Both Gertrude and Marie were briefly imprisoned and both left Paris in secrecy shortly afterwards. Filling her packing cases with torsos and spare heads, Marie moved to London where her manikins were greeted with instant acclamation. They were placed on permanent exhibition in Baker Street during 1833, although they have now been moved by her great-grandson John Theodore to quarters on the Marylebone Road. Gertrude, however, did not meet with similar good fortune. When she arrived in London in 1872, she discovered that the appetite for *la cire* had somewhat declined: Tussaud had cornered the market in the capital and waxworks remained an object of fascination only in the provinces. It was also true, as Gertrude herself clear-sightedly realized, that her figures were sadly inferior to those of her elder mistress. Alone in England, she went through a difficult period at this time. Yet Gertrude's fortunes took a slight turn for the better when, in 1878, she became attached to Mortimer Croop's Travelling Circus.

Gertrude Desmoulins was no Phidias of fat. She had some claim, I think, to be regarded as the historian of her art. She was engaged, sporadically and with immense difficulty owing to the scarcity of material, in writing the history of *la cire* – if something so strange and malleable, neither solid nor liquid, can be said to have a history. Nevertheless, from year to year and conversation to conversation, her work grew more voluminous, if not more finished and acquired, in her hands, an ever greater degree of detail which seemed inversely related to the ever declining firmness of its structure.

Her Preface, so far as I can remember, was to be a sort of paean to wax, a celebration of its properties, of all that rendered it a medium at least as flexible as clay. Why, then, was '*la pauvre cire*' so despised in contrast to its aristocratic but earthy elder brother? Not only could it, like clay, be cut and shaped with facility in ordinary temperatures, it had, unlike clay, another property: at a low heat in a crucible or even an old saucepan, the substance would turn magically into a limpid fluid, enabling it to be poured into moulds. Unlike clay, too, *la cire* could take many pigments and colouring matters with ease. Wax could be turned into many other things but clay spoke only of its origin and was always itself. Every other conversation I had with Gertrude produced some new nugget concerning *la cire*.

'During their funeral rites, the Egyptians made wax figures of the gods and left them, with other offerings, alongside the bodies of the dead. In the sealed chambers of the tombs *la cire*, like the seeds to nourish a future life which were also left, did not deteriorate.

'The Greeks gave wax dolls to their children. Waxen images took on magical properties during religious ceremonies and amongst adults it was customary on these occasions to make votive offerings of these little figurines.'

Gertrude talked too of the Sigillarii, whose wax statuettes and models of fruit were traditionally purchased during the final days of the Saturnalian feast:

'Some of these small forms – a pomegranate, a figure of Dionysus – were discovered in crannies in the earth and in ruined chimneys at Pompeii and Herculaneum. They had remained miraculously intact in the midst of an environment which must have been most perilous to their fragile forms. The furious lava had passed them by and now they lie, waiting to be picked up, in ovens centuries cold. Whilst flesh was transformed into ash and adipocere, mere wax remained unchanged.'

There were other stories as well, tales of medieval legends and superstitions, South American totems and African taboos. Gertrude's history of wax proceeded in this fashion until it reached the eighteenth century. When Josiah Wedgwood translated so carefully the relief figures of Joseph Flaxman into pottery, eventually issuing the highly esteemed and mass produced Jasper Ware, *la cire* at last seemed to have been stripped of all its magic.

Incidentally, Josiah Wedgwood's son, Thomas, published in June 1802 a paper entitled *An Account of a method of copying paintings upon glass and of making profiles by the agency of light upon nitrate of silver, with observations by H. Davy*. You may find the article, Mr Secretary, in the *Journal* of the Royal Institution. It belongs, however, to a later age and is quite a different story altogether.

20

What was Found in the Daylight

SOMETHING WAS going wrong in the circus. Something had been going wrong for a long time, perhaps even from the beginning, but few of us had noticed it before and so it had not mattered. Every now and then, but with increasing frequency, a slight snagging or rending occurred. It was like ice cracking beneath its own weight or the butcher's disarticulation of meat joints. Most of the time the circus seemed all that it had been and I was lulled by my satisfied expectations. At other times, however, one could almost hear the creaking of the coming avalanche.

People, for instance; the very people who remembered and kept time. One day you would see them standing in the circus meadow, toying with a guy rope or looking at a tool in their hands. Their faces! – it terrified me. They all had the same expression of glazed amnesia. Looking at the rope or the hammer they seemed to have entirely forgotten what they were doing. This was not so bad but gradually, over months – over years – these people, the regular, the normal people, began to forget that they had forgotten. Their frowns softened into a bland vacancy and, like broken automata, they furiously set to work on tasks which had either already been done or did not in the circumstances need doing. The knot would be tied, retied and then loosened; the rope had only needed to be coiled and stowed. There was nothing on the faces now: not even the knowledge of a lack. On some days these inappropriate labours would accumulate like a drift of snow. As soon as the circus had arrived in a new town, the empty ones would begin to dismantle things as though they expected to be leaving. They never blustered when informed of their mistakes: instead, for a while, they willingly turned their attention to the new imperatives. But then these commands, too, clouded over and they wandered away at random until a large group of them could be seen walking in differing orbits around the circus meadow. Their faces were calm, almost beatific: they showed none of the anxiety that usually accompanies disorientation.

Other disturbing things also began to happen in these days: little tickings of the beetle, slight slippages behind the wainscot. The circus was gradually becoming depleted. Singly or in pairs, but never more than two

71

at a time, people were quietly leaving in the night. They made no farewells and left no explanations. Even the hangers-on who lasted perhaps a night, perhaps a month, the duration of some affair or fond fantasy, seemed to remain for briefer periods as though they sensed that there could be no long sojourn here. Croop was forced to call in a succession of joiners and smiths from the cities we visited. One day I was told that Gertrude Desmoulins had vanished without trace. My aloof and elegant friend had failed even to collect the wages due to her.

Stranger still, some of the circus animals began to go missing. A conspiracy between Croop and the cook to supplement our miserable rations was at first suspected. Croop ignored the accusations but the cook denied them vehemently and no evidence of their guilt was ever found. I myself thought that the implication of some concern for our nutritional welfare on the part of Croop made the rumour hard to credit. Neverthe-less, a llama went missing in Grimsby and, a month later in Norwich, a camel likewise disappeared. The other animals grew tetchy and lack-lustre. Even Zanzare's buck rabbit became lean and ceased to service his does. Zanzare too seemed to have entered on a decline. His simpler tricks were prone to failure: objects vanished but then refused to reappear. The old conjuror's professional patter remained intact but on several occa-sions he was forced to play, comically, the part of a charlatan and even, once or twice, to employ Aramind's dancing to cover his disgrace.

Croop grew more miserly from week to week. Exhorting us to greater efforts for smaller returns, he accelerated the pace of the second half of my last season with an energy born of desperation, a fury of activity which seemed always on the point of collapsing into lethargy and indifference. There was a drain-hole somewhere into which all our energy was disappearing. Each new venue was less profitable than the last, less accommodating, good only for the briefest stay. For this reason our procession southwards down the eastern half of England in the tenth year of my life as the back end of a pantomime horse was more rapid. We were but a few days short of Canterbury and were running unashamedly for cover now, running headlong towards the end of the season.

On the second of November, 1889, I awoke in the grey dawn. My limbs ached and there was a buzzing in my head. I could hear no sounds of life outside but this did not surprise me as we had all been late to bed the night before: such things happened frequently now. Almost always the erection of the circus was only completed in darkness and by lantern light.

I decided to walk a little in the meadows to warm myself and, locating my least dirty shirt, I dressed hurriedly. Before leaving the caravan, an impulse made me approach the Japanese screen behind which Mimi and

Bessie slept. I stood indecisively for a moment, swallowing with anticipation. Quietly, I stepped forward. At last I could see them without their being conscious of my presence. They were both older, both content in their sleep. Mimi's hand cradled and covered Bessie's. As I stepped from the threshold of the caravan onto the damp grass I was smiling.

At the bottom of the meadow I climbed a wall and, leaping across a small stream, found myself on the edge of a beech wood. A blackbird cocked an eye at me and then shrilled away into the trees. Aimlessly, I followed the path of its flight and, looking up into the boughs of a large tree, found myself, in turn, nervously and flickeringly watched by a squirrel.

A few minutes later I came upon a small gorge and scrambled to the bottom, where a brook wound a thick plait of brackish water into a shallow pool. A few late sand-martins looked out from their nests in the cliff wall. They would soon take flight for Africa, for the delta of the Nile. At the base of the cliff were larger rabbit burrows and the lair, perhaps, of a fox.

Some way upstream, where alders grew and beech trees overarched my head, I noticed a deeper darkness than usual, high up in the cliff, behind a gorse bush. Climbing up, I carefully parted the covering branches and found that I had discovered a small cave. It was almost five feet high and perhaps four feet wide. I heaved myself cautiously inside and moved forward in the darkness. Steadying myself with one hand against the friable chalk wall, I extended my other hand in front of me. It met only cool air.

Turning again to the mouth of the cave, I looked out across the gorge and into the woods beyond. For the first time in many years I experienced what I can only, ineptly, describe as the Robinson Crusoe feeling. I seemed to be alone in the world, protected from starvation or violent death only by pocket-knife and length of string. I felt unbearably free and for a second, passionately, I wanted to restore, in however rude and degenerate a form, the world I had lost. I had the impulse, for example to scoop alcoves in the wall of the cave where candles could be set. Time seemed to have slowed down and afterwards I would be able to give no intelligent estimate of how long I had spent, thus pondering, in the cave.

It was then, as my eyes wandered lazily across the morning prospect, that I noticed the grotesque figure of Pesto. Squat and self-contained, he stood on the opposite side of the gorge looking directly towards me. In no other human circumstance had I ever received, at such a distance, from one who stood so still, such an impression of fevered energy. Looking more closely, however, I noticed that Pesto was not, in fact, still at all. His whole frame trembled; his hands, which hung at his sides, jerked spasmodically. His eyes darted in all directions but always returned to the entrance of the cave, at which point a sudden contortion would seize his mouth, twisting it for an instant into something between a grin and a snarl.

I had always disliked Pesto but I have never, since, been able to account for the way in which I was now frozen in an absolute cataplexy. Outside the circus, Pesto was a different being: he was not under any control. I felt strongly that if he discovered me, he would be capable of killing me. Yet all this time, perhaps because I had not moved by an inch, or because of the darkness of the cave's interior from the outer light, Pesto did not appear to have seen me.

Suddenly, he turned on his heels and went back a little way into the wood. I took this opportunity to retreat some way further into the darkness. I felt more secure in my new position and was still able to survey the scene. When Pesto dragged a large black box with brass hinges and hasps to the edge of the gorge, I became immediately certain that he considered himself alone. Lifting the box with astonishing ease upon his shoulder, he began to descend the precipitous slope. As he disappeared from my view I noticed that he made no noise and did not put a foot wrong. I somehow guessed that Pesto had business to perform in this cave. Unless I managed to escape immediately or discover a hiding place within, my presence would soon be detected. It was now too late to emerge discreetly from the mouth of the cave. Putting both hands in front of me, therefore, I stumbled into the darkness. Even now I thought I could hear his panting behind me.

But my hands encountered only a dead end. My fingers flew hopelessly across the crumbling chalk and found – yes – near to the ground – the relief! – an aperture, a break in the forbidding surface. Crouching, I forced my body into this cleft and within a few seconds knew myself to be in a tiny annexe created perhaps, during the winter months, by the splitting of ice and the wearing of water. The air was cold and damp; it was muddy beneath my feet. I knelt on the ground and, peering out of the cleft, gazed intently at the bright entrance to the cave.

Within a few further seconds the veil of greenery was spread by two sinewy and very familiar hands. As I had imagined, the sound of stertorous breathing was heard. The black box was flung through the mouth of the cave in an ecstasy of something like joy. Pesto followed. His barrel-like body for a moment blocked out the light. He turned and, seating himself at the entrance, dangled his legs nonchalantly over the lip of the gorge, recovering his breath and from time to time whistling unidentifiable fragments of song. Every now and then he would slap the black box at his side and giggle to himself.

After some minutes Pesto arose and, fishing in his pocket, extracted a large bunch of keys. Selecting one, he opened the box and took out a small collapsible shovel which he proceeded to assemble. But I hardly watched this operation because, astonishingly, the black box was full of money. Gold and silver coins formed a matrix which was studded by larger medallions, antique intaglios, pendants and necklaces. There were paper bills: banker's orders, promissory notes or IOUs ; miniature portraits, cameos in mother-of-pearl, silhouettes in ebony, a roll of shimmering silk. I almost exclaimed from my vantage point when I saw, in their cut and rough forms, amber, coral, amethyst, ruby, pearl, carnelian, agate, emerald, jade, chrysolite, lapis lazuli and malachite. There was an ermine stole and many old brooches. Amongst all this wealth, strange to say, were objects valueless, perhaps, to all but Pesto, who seemed as fascinated by Brummagem things, by ribbons and fripperies, as by the rest of the hoard.

Pesto began to dig. As the soil flew rhythmically and the blade of his shovel sliced the soft earth of the cave's floor, he started to talk to himself in a dreamy voice. I can do no more here than to attempt, however inadequately, to transcribe that voice. The peculiar, fearful muttering brings back, so clearly can I hear it even now, the very picture, the very scene, even the clammy prickling of my skin.

' . . . A hoard of spices from the Land of Green Ginger. I followed him through the fish meal yard and we came out near broad Humber's grey-green back.

'The lace, the damask, the silks kept safe and dry with the friend whose mouth is shut.

'Pesto has been subtle and quiet. Pesto waited, gnawing at the roots. In crannies he hides his wealth. He banks with nook-shotten nature.

'Bleed them dry, Pesto: impoverish them slowly. Little bits of sleight-of-hand, little drops of blood, slowly filch it from its circuit. Keep it shiny: don't let the greed of others wear it down, the legitimate bastards with their rummaging fingers.

'I bury the bezants quiet and pretend to forget. But I remember so well, the coinstore places and hoard corners. Twenty guineas, bright as an afternoon, in a locked box at Rochester. Thirteen pieces of good gold by the seventh post on Gravesend jetty, left incorruptible where the tide uncovers it but twice a year. Good true yellow-boys! And the brooches and the Caesar coins under the altar in the ruined abbey. I heard the moaning ghosts as I defiled their sacred place. The big stone in the midst of the midden on London Fields, where the poor boys play each day, not dreaming of the wealth beneath their muddy feet. Mints in the ossuary and the charnel house, guilders in the crypt, sovereigns Norwich way in privy pit. The man who saw me is no more: bone amongst bones. Thousands of marked coins and hidden purses. The first guinea of all in the bole of the tree. And so much more on Old Stourbridge Common where the pale undergraduate watches the sun with eyes that do not blink.'

This, apparently, was Pesto's long litany of his hidden wealth. He crooned it out as if at prayer. Then, throwing his shovel aside, he placed the open box in the hole he had made. His outstretched hands hovered over the coins as though they were the embers of a fire, as though he could warm himself in their dull gleam. I shivered.

I do not know what happened next but I assume that I must have fallen prey to the exhaustion that follows enchantment. In my stupor, I had somehow worked myself deeper into the cleft where I had concealed myself from Pesto. I came to consciousness with a strong impression that I had been watched throughout my sleep even in this most secret place. In the distance, beyond the ellipse formed by the outline of my fissure, the westering sun now stood dead centre in the nearly circular mouth of the cave. It was perhaps three o'clock in the afternoon. I extricated myself from the cranny with great difficulty and stood once more in the main chamber of the cave. There was barely a trace of Pesto's work: he had been so cunning with his shovel and his switch of bracken that for a moment I thought I must have been dreaming. It was then that I saw the small red spark which lay on the ground like a splinter of the dying sun. I bent to pick it up. It was the girasol ring which Alf had given me and which I had passed on to Aramind several years previously.

Circumspectly parting the gorse branches which concealed the entrance to the cave, I stepped once more, and as if for the first time, into the world of things. I immediately realized that my rebirth was only a fairy-tale: for why had the opal ring – the old life itself – returned to me in so strange a place? Why had Aramind parted with it? In what obscure way had Pesto come into possession of it?

Suddenly, partially, I knew. Clapping my hand to my forehead, I staggered and lost my balance. The afternoon spun round me as I crashed to the bed of the clough and once more passed out of consciousness.

21

All Souls' Night

I AWOKE at dusk. The last calls of birds, now accustomed to my motionless presence, sounded from nearby trees. I sat up and realized, with a giddy swim, that I must have struck my head in falling. Rising unsteadily to my feet, I walked on, having quite forgotten how I had reached this place. I continued to ascend the valley, following the stream to its source. In retrospect, I realize that I was walking in exactly the opposite direction from the circus. My career as the back end of a pantomime horse had vanished. Ten years of my life had been torn away in an instant like a chapter censored from a novel.

The pace and rhythm of my footsteps quite overcame and numbed me. After perhaps an hour my mind began to clear. I knew, in the gathering dusk, that I must return, but I found that I had negligently wandered from the natural track described by the gorge and was now quite lost. Looking around me, I felt surrounded and outwitted by the rustling carpet of leaves. I would soon need, amongst the thickening shadows, some fiery brand to eclipse the dark but I had only the feeble ember of the opal in my pocket.

I was suddenly overcome by the feeling that my wish for light had turned into fact. It was almost as if I had myself determined what should happen next. For there, some way off into the trees, sparks of light shone fitfully like early stars. I began to approach these glimmers with great care, fearful that Pesto might still be lurking in the woods. Having silently advanced until I stood concealed behind the trunk of an oak tree, I peeped for the first time from close quarters in the direction of the lights.

In front of me was a clearing and almost in the centre of this space stood a most peculiar conical structure covered with turf. It was over five feet in height and from the top issued a thin plume of blue woodsmoke. Nearby, branches and twigs were neatly stacked in piles of varying lengths. Between myself and the mound stood a man who, every now and then, cast damp earth onto the sides of his topsy-turvy structure with a long-handled shovel, thereby blocking all apertures save the one in its roof. Each time he scattered earth into the crevices between the turves, a jet of smoke was stifled and a spark died. There was still light enough to see and I observed that the man was tall, with broad shoulders and long black hair which curled beneath a wide-brimmed hat. He wore a bottle-green corduroy jacket and his baggy trousers were of coarse, durable material. On the ground lay a leather satchel.

As the lights died, the man leaned on his shovel and, without turning round, said softly: 'What spirit is it then that led you wrong? Or are you yourself a wraith that haunts the trackless woods?'

'I was not misled, sir,' I replied after a pause in which I recovered from my astonishment at the acuity of his hearing, 'and nor am I a phantom. I fell down a cliff and I think I have lost my bearings.'

The man did not respond to my statement or offer to put me right. I felt no fear as I approached more closely, only surprise when I first saw his face. He was much older than his easy movements and the colour of his hair had suggested. I gestured to the mound in front of us: 'Please excuse my inquisitiveness, but what are you doing?'

He fixed me with his grey eyes. 'This pile, you mean? It arouses your curiosity, does it? Well, it is nothing romantic: merely a charcoal-burner's fire.'

'Oh,' I replied, 'I have never seen such a thing. I was brought up in the city, you see.'

'You are lost in the country.'

'Yes. I am not familiar with the ways here.' I looked around the clearing and then blurted out impulsively: 'I'm Spellman, sir. What is your name?'

Once again the charcoal-burner did not respond in any way. Instead he turned to his hidden fire and patted the turves with the flat of his spade. 'They are simple enough things,' he said gravely, continuing to answer my first question, 'but you must keep the fire cool and slow, a little lingering life. I use the mud to keep it damp overnight. You must keep it smothered. Flames is burning and burning is ash, not charcoal.'

My eyes drooped and, thrown off balance, I staggered. The charcoal-burner quickly supported me. Two eyes that seemed darker now looked down into mine and a voice, his voice, said: 'You won't be getting back to your city tonight, I fear.'

He sat me down against the trunk of a tree. After cleaning and honing his spade in the last of the light, he crouched and put his whetting-stone into the leather satchel. He took out a box of matches, lit his lantern and hung it from a hook at the end of his spade. The surrounding trees seemed to sway a little in the play of light. The charcoal burner helped me to rise to my feet and took me companionably by the arm. I was too tired to speak but he was not offended by my silence and kept up the conversation for both of us as we started along a winding path.

'I have been a charcoal-burner for seven seasons, imitating in small space great nature's metamorphoses, the aeon-slow conversion of vegetation into coal. It is an insecure trade. Strangers are felling the woods wholesale these days. Over there, towards Harrietsham, for higher pastures. And there, Doddington way: oak and elm and ash for skiffs and wherries. Also in Stockbury and Oad Street for the Chatham paper mills. It is unhomely around here now. But I was always a stranger. Pedlar, chapman, furze-cutter, waterman: a foreigner everywhere. Sometime a poacher but never the gamekeeper.

'Once round here, there was a future which was born out of the past. There was some sort of ground to build on, a reason to remain. Now the world is full of wanderers who cross the land. They throw up their huge houses and turn the cottagers away so that they can surround themselves with parkland. It was never easy here: we dwelt in the midst of the unhomely from the start. I scarred the forest to make a clearing. First, as ever, comes the usurper. We can never have the old forest back. We have separated out its mixture and now it is all, with us, piles of this or that: heaps of charcoal or ash, fruits, grains, ores, leaves, debris, dross.

'Well, Mr Spellman, at last: Wormshill. This place is home to me.'

I looked up for the first time in many minutes and attempted to focus my eyes. A most peculiar building emerged from the kaleidoscope of dark shapes. It had no particular colour. The walls were long and very low, as if pressed into the ground by the weight of the enormous turfen roof. The windows were slits so small that the cottage appeared to have closed its eyes in sleep or death. Chickens pecked in the gravel around the door. There was a pile of logs nearby, and a chopping-block with a hatchet. These things and the scattered wood chippings brought to mind, inappropriately enough, my father's workshop in Canonbury. For a moment I saw him bent over his plane.

The door scraped open in answer to the charcoal-burner's knock. I found myself shaking hands with a woman in her early fifties. From foot to neck she was the robust and hearty farmer's wife of popular fancy – trim, cleanly and warm of welcome – but her face was gaunt, her hair hung thick and grey in unkempt tresses and her eyes were dark and wild.

'Have you brought back a dead soul with you, this of all nights?' she asked her husband irritably.

He replied with patience. 'No ghost. Only a lost stranger to be our guest.'

'He has a wound on his head.'

'He fell down the gorge.'

I was immediately – so speedy was the quickening of her compassion – hurried to a chair by the fire. The charcoal-burner's wife washed my temple and applied some sort of salve before carefully winding a bandage round my head. She then left me in peace under a warm rug to take fuller account of my surroundings.

At first it was the size of the cottage that astonished me, so out of proportion did it seem with its own exterior. The beams arched above my head like those of a modest church and from them hung hams and sides of bacon, strings of onions, bushes of rosemary and lavender and thyme. A roughly constructed set of stairs, set snugly against the rear wall, led up into a small loft which I assumed was used for storage.

Two vast dressers dominated the interior. One, placed near the stairs against the rear wall of the house and perhaps the larger of the two, carried an enormous array of china teacups, saucers, plates, serving dishes, cut glass fruit bowls, pewter trenchers, earthenware mugs, decanters, vases, flasks, preserving bottles with muslin coverings, herb and spice jars, tea caddies, kettles, teapots, coffee pots, tureens and skillets.

The second dresser was laden with an even greater variety of things. Yet these objects had, to my eye, little to do with the business of everyday life. One would have been forgiven for thinking that they were the collected treasures of an eclectic antiquarian, only they seemed in no way placed for the purposes of display. Here too was a range of bottles and smaller jars, phials of different shapes in stone and glass, ampoules and tiny boxes. There were paints, pens and a stock of paper, bones, mosses, ferns, flowers, strangely-shaped vegetables, sands, shells, materials, patterns.

Between the two dressers – the patriarch and matriarch respectively of the house – was a profusion of other things. Yet there was no sense of disorder or uncleanliness. The laundry chests seemed only that day to have been polished with walnut oil; the coffers and the caskets were free of dust; the barrels and canisters and baskets, the casks, the kegs, the tubs, the buckets: all had their place. On hooks from the chimney breast hung gleaming brass saucepans and leather pails for water. A cauldron simmered over the fire. Ewers and stoups, urns and pitchers stood in a neat row along the wall by the front door.

In the flickering light of the tallow candles, my eyes had strayed amongst these inanimate objects for some time before I became aware that there were also living things around me. As I placed my hand on the arm of the rocking-chair, I startled a small lizard which scurried onto the fender and paused before the fire, its head bobbing as though it was attempting to swallow too large a morsel of food. Inside the ingle-nook, two small animals were curled up together. I took them at first for household dogs but my assumption was almost immediately proved incorrect when one of the animals extended a delicate cloven hoof and raised its head to look at me with large dark eyes. It was a roe deer. Its uplifted head revealed another more cunning but no less beautiful skull: that of a sleeping fox whose ears pricked now and again when a branch crackled in the fire. Above these two creatures, looking down on them silently and with considerable wisdom, like some grey judge in Chancery, was a jackdaw.

The charcoal-burner sat with a newspaper at the table, reading to his wife in a low voice which did not reach me. I then noticed two further souls. One of them sat in the deepest recess of the ingle-nook: a rheumy-eyed old man who nodded to me in taciturn greeting as our eyes met and then began to cough heart-rendingly. His fingers continued to move nimbly, however, over the knitting he was engaged in and his needles flashed as he worked. Beside him in a basket were many balls of loosely spun wool. The other person was a young girl of perhaps twelve years, pale of face and silvery-blonde of hair. She sat in a corner at a small writing-table, holding a quill which, as I watched, she dipped into a pot of ink. A slightly shadowier version of herself sat writing within the frame of a large mirror which was propped against the wall.

The charcoal-burner's wife approached me and asked if I should like some soup now that I was settled. I accepted and watched her as she busied herself over the cauldron. The food had a fineness of flavour which had not touched my palate in years and I ate greedily. When I had finished, the charcoal-burner put away his newspaper and began to point out the curiosities and treasures of the cottage. We came to a halt next to a delicate flower stand on which stood, in a beautifully shaped and un-figured white pot, a plant which I could not identify.

'Pliny called it *lunaflora*,' said the charcoal-burner, noticing the direc-tion of my gaze, 'but it is not of the same species as our own moonflower. It is from the Orient: rarer, some say, than the unfading amaranth. It blooms in winter and the flowers, opening only at night, turn towards the dark.' As he had said, the petals had indeed begun to open and bask, oddly, in the shadows. They had a clear but waxy texture and were of the strangest colour: pure white with a hint of silver or of blue, a colour more like that of some mineral, some milky quartz, than that of a flower's flesh. 'It has been found sometimes in caverns far from the light,' the charcoal-burner continued, 'but perhaps the strangest thing about the lunaflora is that it does not belong to itself and has no root at all. The most beauteous of parasites, its wind-blown seeds find purchase in the forks and clefts of other fleshy plants and grow there, taking all their sustenance from the host plant which, remarkably, transforms itself into a root for the service of its guest, thereby renouncing its chance to propagate itself. Such,' concluded my interlocutor, 'are the sacrifices made even by mute vegetables for beauty.'

'It provides no other service for its host?' I asked, intrigued.

'None whatsoever.'

I was somewhat at a loss for words. 'Your wife,' I said at length, 'must gain great pleasure from it.'

He looked across to where she sat, painfully piecing together a column of newsprint with a frown and a moving finger. 'She is not my wife.'

'The – ah – the elderly gentleman?' I did not wish to seem over-inquisitive concerning their domestic arrangements.

'The old man? Ah, I see your implication. No, she is not married to him either. He was here before us and is no relative of ours. The cottage belongs to him. He was the youngest brother in his own family. The others died. The father died. It came to him by reversion: he never expected it. It was a very long time ago.'

'Your child,' I said, changing the subject and turning towards the girl who sat at her desk holding a brush such as is used by oriental scribes, 'your little girl seems very happy in her work.'

The charcoal-burner smiled ruefully and shook his head once more. 'Neither is this my child, sir. Nor indeed a child at all. She was exactly the same as she is now, except a little thinner, when we found her, like you, lonely and lost, twenty years ago. She has not aged since. We –' he nodded to the woman I had taken for his wife '– we think, sometimes, that she is older than ourselves.'

My glance towards the subject of our discourse was answered, to my discomfort, by a cool and level stare, an appraisal which seemed certainly beyond her apparent years. I looked away again, ashamed to appear curious. I had always been fascinated by human oddity. Perhaps this was because I was myself a kind of freak. But an old woman who looked like a child – ! In his wonder, Sophocles was to speak of the triumphs and masteries of men, of trapping and artful taming, but disease and deformity escaped his incantations, legions of madness and hosts of oddity.

Within the confines of the city walls, we still told our pathetic story and emptily celebrated our victory over the wild horses. All our history tried only to jump out of its own skin in order at last to see itself without the trickery of mirrors. The end of the journey, however – how quickly we forgot! – was to find, through wonder, that the other we sought was always within and that never, through any twist, on any corner, would our own image answer us or reach out to take our hand. Everything was strangeness; order was an incident in chaos.

The charcoal-burner tapped me on my shoulder. 'You seem lost in thought.'

'I am,' I replied, 'I must apologize.'

He brushed my words away as though they had not answered his meaning. 'Let us approach our aged child,' he proposed, 'and see what she is doing.'

The girl did not look up as we drew nearer but I was able to confirm at last that the charcoal-burner had spoken nothing less than the truth. Although from across the room this woman had the undeveloped physique, the snub nose, the largeness of eye, the pouting lips and rounded cheeks of a young girl, at a distance of three feet one could see that her hair was also streaked with silver, that she had lines around her eyes and mouth and that her neck was slack with age.

In front of her and to one side lay a faded and tattered manuscript written in an unfamiliar script which might have been Arabic or Hindoo. She was transcribing these characters on a fresh sheet of parchment. Her precision was remarkable: quite without hesitation. It was as if she was completely at home in the foreign script. The charcoal-burner spoke quietly in my ear. 'As you see, she copies with great accuracy. But she cannot read.' I turned to him in astonishment. 'No, no, I assure you she cannot. Nor can she speak – at least as you or I can. In all these last twenty years I have never heard her utter a single human sound. Yet she can hear more acutely than any of us.'

'That is truly remarkable, considering the sharpness of your own ears,' I said, trying to suppress a note of disbelief which had crept into my voice and remembering how the charcoal-burner had known of my presence in the clearing whilst I had not been aware that I had made a sound.

'It is remarkable, and I assure you that it is true. Not only is her hearing sharp, it is also subtle. She knows immediately the catch in your voice if you try to tell a lie.'

'The text that she copies,' I asked after a few moments, 'what is it? What is the purpose of it?'

'It is, I believe, a spiritual text in Devanagari, one of the older scripts. She has told me in her way that it is a discourse in metaphors on the journey of the spirit, its whirled repetitions. I do not know the answer to your second question, except to say that it is beautiful and that thus she allows something to survive. She always copies decaying documents.'

'And where does she find them?'

'She had them with her in a trunk when we found her.'

'Do you think she minds us talking in her presence like this?' I enquired below my breath. My answer came from the woman herself. Raising her head, she smiled beautifully and shook her head. Then, with great rapidity, she made a series of gestures which to me resembled a sketch in the air of letters or hieroglyphs, followed immediately by an action similar to that of a mother rocking a child in her arms. An obvious gesture of approbation concluded her display.

The charcoal-burner translated on my behalf. 'I had not known it before, but my suspicion was correct. She says that to copy something that is about to decay or die is as good as giving birth or lending nurture.'

'You seem to understand her sign language with ease,' I said.

He looked at me. 'Was it not evident to you what she meant?'

I said that I had understood the essence of her message but had only partially made out the phrases which he had translated for me.

'You see,' he said, 'that it is not so difficult to be wordless and yet to make sense. In a way, she has a larger vocabulary, a greater expressive range than myself. For us, a word is a transient thing, a breath. We forget it. But when we read stories to her, she remembers word for word. After hearing something only once she can repeat it back to us in her language without missing a single detail. Even if it were a story we had known all our lives, she knows it better than us.' The charcoal-burner considered a moment and then continued. 'The sign language, however, is only her day-to-day medium of communication. On special occasions, or for new things, she resorts to another language altogether.'

He guided me to the second of the dressers which I have already had occasion to describe. Never in one place, I think, had I seen so many things in such a variety of categories. The only comparison for it that seemed appropriate was that of the witch's store cupboard: a repository of ingredients for all kinds of spells and magics.

'This,' said my friend, 'is her lexicon, her dictionary, her word store. It is the most complex tool I have ever seen. I still do not fully understand how it works, how she uses it. But I know that it generates language – a language, at that, far more pertinent than any which we can speak in the tongues of daily life. All these natural and artificial things: these bones, twigs, stones, shells and plants; all these jewels, ornaments, perfumes and cosmetics – all these are her vocabulary. Instead of making noises with her tongue, she presents the thing by way of a detour through this box of tricks. All the things take on a complexity with her and it has taken me many years to get to know them. She is always inventing new things and new things in turn for them to resemble, so that after a while it is not in the things themselves but in the associations they evoke.'

The charcoal-burner scanned the dresser, searching for an example. 'Take the scent of apple, for instance, preserved in this little bottle. There are many things called up here. Roundness, perhaps: it is used for balls and baubles and also for the world. She sometimes uses it to represent greenness. Occasionally it is Paradise, sometimes faith. Or pride. Or a fall, depending on the context: all forms of sin and fakery and mischief. It is knowledge, too: the collision of opposites like good and evil.'

'So am I to understand,' I put in, somewhat confused, 'that to speak or comprehend the language of the dresser is to pose and solve a sort of riddle or charade?'

'Call it a riddle if you like, or an allegory, or a parable. A charade makes it sound trivial, which it is not, although it has a great deal of comedy in it. The only difference is that both of us know the answer to the riddles.'

He began to search again across the surface of the dresser and I noticed that his large hands moved carefully, delicately. 'Here is another example – a familiar one these days: charcoal. It can mean black, or burnt, or hidden, or "after" – after the fire. Often it is used to refer to my work, my daily life. Recently it has become a nickname for the old man over there.' I looked across to the ingle-nook, where the ancient gentleman coughed and spat into the fire. 'Yes, he smoulders still,' the charcoal-burner continued, 'like an ember of the rebellious son he once was. He tried to throw off his father's yoke, you know. But he succeeded only in immortalizing him with superstitions. He fears his father's return one day, one night, a paternal Alastor. He hates himself, of course, his entrapment in an inherited face, as if he were a reduced image of what went before. He hates age too: the depletion, the shrivelled skin, the inevitable slide into the past.'

The charcoal-burner smiled grimly and once again I felt uncomfortable. My friend was too intimate, too familiar with these strange things. We fell silent for a few minutes. At length I made an attempt to return my companion to the less awkward subject of the child's language. 'Why have you not taught her to write? Would that not have been easier? Then she could have been understood by all.'

'Easier? I don't know. We tried, but she refused, she did not want to know our letters. It would have been too cruel to take her own language from her and replace it with black and white. Some might say, in any case, that her language is the older and more honourable one, that it comes from a time when words were things still and talking was pointing.'

All the time the charcoal-burner had been talking, I had been leaning against a small mahogany chest of drawers. Confused by the matter-of-fact way in which these wonders were described, my hand had carelessly begun to trace the surface of the chest and at some point had come into contact with a glass vessel which I had not previously been aware of. Without realizing it, each sentence of the charcoal-burner's became marked in my mind by the stages in the small journey made by my fingers, lingering here over some flaw or imperfection before sweeping on across the smooth surface.

The charcoal-burner looked at me intently and said, again with that laconic manner of his: 'Your hand, I see, has found out another of those things you call wonders.' I looked around at the jar and at first saw inside it only loose-packed earth. 'It is the first resident. The Founder, you might say: the Guardian Spirit whose rest guarantees our own.' My eye began to piece shapes out of the earth. I saw a twist, as of some pale body: a coil, a segment. A head came into view and my baffled eyes focused. The creature was the colour of an earthworm but it was much larger. Its mouth and eyes were those of a snake but its body fell into sections like that of a millipede. Coiled in the bottom of the jar, it seemed to sleep peacefully.

I hardly noticed the low voice of my friend, so fascinated was I by this beast. 'It reminds me, Mr Spellman, of the serpent Nidhögg gnawing away at the Tree of Life.'

From her writing-table, the small scribe beckoned us closer. She made a series of eloquent gestures which were once more translated for my benefit. 'She wishes to tell you a story, Mr Spellman: you are very honoured. She says that you have some partial understanding of her language.'

The child smiled up into my eyes with her lined face. She could not have been more than four feet tall. With her translucent skin, she reminded me of some figure seen in a waxworks. It seemed, as she gestured, that I began to understand. She took my hand and led me to the dresser, to her narrative machinery, so that she could begin. The story was one that had often enchanted my idle moments in Thomas Carlyle's fine translation: *The Golden Pot*, by Hoffmann. Her telling of it, however, was beyond Hoffmann's German or Carlyle's English. The figures of speech were figures of speech and yet they were also something else again which partook more closely of what they tried to conjure. Anselmus's love for Serpentina was rendered so rapidly and with such vivacity that it had the immediacy of a play put on a stage and the pitiful pages of script withered and fell away like leaves.

That night, much later, we sat and waited for the ghosts. I looked into the fire and recalled the events of this day of all souls and I sipped from a glass of sweet wine. Sometimes we all smiled at each other and I felt even a little ashamed that we had agreed to play the game with such comic serious-ness. Although we were still and silent, the fire seemed to take sudden life from us and, catching a new log, sent all the objects and shadows in the room dancing round as if at the fair. At other times, and especially later, when the fire had sunk very low, we would look into the silvered mirror and know, all of us, that shapes lurked and moved in that beyond over there, behind the patterns of the mirror's rottenness. The shades had answered our call with a solemnity which seemed to mark their acknowledgment of the spaces that lay between us. I will not say who I saw: their faces were mere glimpses and I did not want to mislead myself. Perhaps we all saw different ghosts; I will never know, for none of us spoke. Yet the past appeared that night; its presences were with us as guests in the long low cottage.

'We will have no sleep tonight,' said the charcoal-burner towards dawn as we watched the last glimmers fade away into the mirror. 'I will take you back to the circus, Mr Spellman.'

We went outside and watched as he harnessed his mule. I thanked the woman and the old man and the child, and my voice was swallowed up in the forest.

During the long ride back we spoke only occasionally. The dim shapes of trees fell away behind us into the mist. At last, we arrived at the gates of the circus meadow. I got down from the trap and, looking back into the face of the charcoal-burner, offered him the opal ring. He would not take it from me.

I was only just in time, for the circus was leaving that morning. There were shouts of welcome; my friends gathered round and the air was thick with questions. In memory, I see myself turning to them, pointing to my bandaged head, describing my fall in gestures. Somewhere in the confusion of explanations, I missed the charcoal-burner to say a last goodbye and the trap had moved away without my noticing and disappeared.

'Where have you been?' asked Mimi.

'To Wormshill. I met a forester,' was all I could reply.

'A foreigner?' She misheard me in the commotion.

'He was that too.'

And then at last, after the walk across the meadow, I fell onto my palliasse. Undisturbed through the day by the jolting and tipping of the caravan, I dropped into a deep and strangely dreamless sleep.

22

The Flight of a Paperweight

WE HAD arrived at Canterbury. The cathedral loomed dimly from the dusk as, awakening, I peered out of the caravan window. A flock of rooks swooped and circled in the upper air. The old streets echoed to our coming. In the houses lamps were being lit and people were sitting down to an early meal. I could see their crockery and their silverware and their fires as if through the windows of a series of doll's houses.

Our arrival produced only a dim re-awakening of the enthusiasm shown in previous years. Some boys shouted and threw stones and ran away. An old man stopped to stare. A child in the arms of its mother called out with glee and wonder before the woman, with a pinched, impassive face, passed out of sight.

The next morning, a little restored by my long rest, I went out to wander along the banks of the Stour. The meadow, to the north of the town, was regularly provided for our use on the night of the last performance of the season and as winter quarters.

The circus still suffered from a kind of atrophy and the empty ones were becoming increasingly difficult to deal with. Those who were left with their faculties intact spent larger and larger amounts of time giving out reminders, orders and instructions.

As I walked, memories of the evening before last spread and danced again across my inner eye. That morning I was oddly sensitive to sound, and the noises made by harnesses hanging loose on grazing horses began to give me the impression that my life was being led inside a purse filled with jangling coins.

I passed a team of men hauling on ropes in order to erect one of the main poles of the big top. A mountain of canvas billowed in front of them and began to rear up like a grey leviathan in the gloomy morning. Then, as if with one accord, the men paused in their work and started giving out line.

'Pull!' I shouted, '*pull*!'

Blinking sheepishly, they obeyed. We all stood there as the canvas slapped against the pole, frozen into a tableau of mariners on a clipper, straining impossibly for speed in a dead calm.

A little further onwards, I came across our captain. Collapsed into an enormous deck-chair which had been specially constructed to withstand his weight, however, he bore a greater resemblance to a figurehead. In his fleshy hand he held an empty bottle of spirits. His impatience during the latter part of the season seemed suddenly to have turned into lethargy. Now, with a bleared eye, he stared off across the ocean of meadows without noticing the activity around him. That morning he had refused to sanction the purchase, for our winter employment, of the brightly-coloured paints we used to liven up the summer's worn surfaces and to provide the necessary sparkle for next year's act.

'D'ye think I'm made of money?' he had ejaculated to the nervously waiting machinist.

With his top hat grotesquely awry, Croop looked like a dispossessed monarch in a comic opera. All that was left of him was a dogged meanness and a dangerous hypertrophy. His skin shone like a balloon at bursting point. As I watched, Pesto emerged from the caravan and stood above Croop at the top of the steps. Descending, he thrust a new bottle of spirits into his master's absently receiving hands.

A voice sounded in my ear. 'He's lording it with his guv'nor isn't he? Haven't you noticed?' I turned and found myself looking into Wilf Patchkey's face. 'Haven't you noticed?' he repeated.

'Noticed what?'

He shrugged. 'I've heard them anyway, late at night, when I've been creeping.'

'Creeping?'

Wilf looked somewhat secretive. 'They argue,' he briefly said.

I pressed him to elaborate: 'Argue? What sort of arguments?'

'Terrible ones. Low-voiced ones in the small hours. Hissing ones and spitting ones, like cats. I can't hear it all, the things they say.' Once more he looked shifty. 'I creep because of the desire, Jacko, because of the itch in me, to work it off. That's when I hear things that the others don't. I see secrets without meaning to.' He glanced at me significantly.

'But what do they argue about?'

'Debts, mostly. You must have noticed what's going on round here. Ten years ago, when you came, we were flush. Now Croop eats and drinks it all. He's been fed up like a calf by that dwarf.'

'So the circus is in debt?' It did not surprise me.

Wilf took a little time to reply. 'Oh, I don't know. Probably. You can feel it, can't you? This place is big and gaudy on the outside, but it's all shrunk up in the middle. And Croop – the gambling – you know about that?'

I said that I had a vague idea of it.

'Croop's at it every night these days,' continued Wilf. 'Sometimes he wins, sometimes he loses. Mostly loses. He doesn't win very much at all, in fact – not to make up for his losses. The dwarf probably gives him a run now and then to keep him on the boil.'

My partner looked over his shoulder to make sure we were not overheard. 'When I'm creeping, I can hear Croop telling the dwarf that he's cheating. The dwarf denies it all, of course.'

A couple of days previously I had seen another side to Pesto, although even I could hardly believe that he was prepared to run such risks for his money. 'He can't be cheating – surely. Can he?'

'I don't know,' said Wilf, scratching his head. 'If he is he's doing it very well. Croop knows most of the tricks: he's no novice. But then Pesto learned his dice and his cards from Zanzare, who's a master.'

'From Zanzare?' I had never heard of any connection between the conjuror and the clown.

'They knocked around together for years,' said Wilf. 'Didn't you realize? They've been together at least since 'sixty, when they arrived in England. And probably before that in Italy, in Zanzare's "days of old".'

'Zanzare is a sentimental man.'

'The dwarf isn't, and nor am I.' Wilf pulled at my sleeve. 'Come on, Jacko, let's go and have a few drinks. I'm sick of this place. We won't be missed.'

I was reluctant at first but my companion insisted. Taking a last look at the figure of Mortimer Croop, now lying prone in his deck-chair, we sauntered away with affected nonchalance. Behind the circus joiner's shed we crawled through a hole in the hedge, crossed some fields and gained the road which led into town. As we went, I thought what a sad old tyrannical showman Croop was. There would soon come a time, however, when any one of us would have welcomed him back with a generous spread of arm.

It was midday and we could hear the cathedral bells beginning to chime. At the gate to the cathedral close, a verger in a black surplice crossed our path and said good day. Now and then men lurched from hotel doorways to stagger back to work.

Wilf and I called for strong beer in the snug of the King's Head. Over the first glass, I told Wilf my tale of the charcoal-burner and the wife who was not his wife and the child who was a woman and did not belong to him. To my tale of wonders his only comment was a curt: 'Odd place, odd people.' He became more animated, however, when I told him how I had watched Pesto in the cave. 'Hundreds of pounds, you say, Jacko? Are you sure?'

'Certain.'

'And he was chunnering to himself?'

'He was chattering like a magpie!'

'But how on earth did he get hold of it all?'

'I haven't any idea.' I put my hand in my pocket. 'But he left this behind by mistake.' I showed Wilf the opal ring. He put it musingly into the palm of his hand and it sparkled in a ray of sunlight which had somehow penetrated the stained windows and smoke-laden atmosphere of the King's Head. 'I cannot understand how he could possibly have got his hands on that.'

'Somebody,' said Wilf darkly, as he swigged at his beer, 'is up to no good. I would lay a bet that somebody wouldn't be very amused to discover that you had this ring.'

I got up to buy another drink. We finished that and then had another. Changing the subject, for again he said that he was sick of the circus, Wilf began to run on as he occasionally did when he had had too much beer. He was getting out of the circus, he said, cutting loose. He had a little money saved up with his parents in Nottingham and he was going to buy himself the leasehold on a greengrocer's shop.

'I'm thirty-three, Jacko, and it's time to perpetuate the name of Patchkey. I can feel it within me – that longing to multiply.' He rubbed his belly and stared gloomily at the table. 'That longing is a religious urge, Jacko: a sanctioned, a permitted, a holy thing. A wife big with child, that's the ticket. Tomatoes laid out all nice in boxes, and customers ringing the bell. Me behind the till, smiling at them all.'

I drained my glass and shivered involuntarily. I had no wish to stay in the circus and stagger around with a new partner: if Wilf left, I would follow. Despite my unease I had to acknowledge that he had only expressed my own stifled desire: I too wished to be gone. I suggested to Wilf that perhaps he could find me some work in the back room of his shop. He smiled and, with a brief, embarrassed glance over his shoulder, whispered into my ear the old lament:

'I want a girl, Jacko, to be my wife. A woman for children, with hips like handles to hold onto. And to hear her feet in the room above the shop and see the baby in its cradle, all pink and puky.'

Wilf was sentimental, but he meant it. He looked into his glass and a small tear formed at the corner of his eye. Then he sighed and finished his beer. We left the King's Head in some disarray and, arm in arm, with the perfect synchronization acquired through long practice in the horse suit, staggered the half-mile back to the circus meadow. Nobody had noticed our absence. Indeed, as we squeezed once more through the hole in the hedge behind the joiner's shed, the meadow seemed completely empty.

91

Turning the corner, however, we at once saw a large and voluble crowd surrounding Mortimer Croop's caravan. This sort of demonstration had never once occurred in all my years in the circus and with mounting curiosity we made haste to join it.

Everybody was there, waiting expectantly. The tents and caravans were empty and no work was in progress. The big top remained in much the same state as when Wilf and I had escaped some three hours previously. It was held to the ground by ropes, which stretched in every direction and were attached to harpoon-like stakes. Pushing to the front of the crowd, which formed a partial, milling circle around the door of Croop's caravan, Wilf and I found ourselves standing next to Mimi and Bessie. Their gazes were fixed on the open door and they did not respond to our questions.

The most peculiar mixture of noises emerged from the caravan: shrieks and curses, laughs and taunts, together with the sounds of heavy objects colliding and the splintering of glass or china. Suddenly, a glass paperweight was hurled through the door. Falling unbroken to the ground, it rolled slowly across the grass. All eyes followed it, as if attempting to assess its significance. The paperweight was hollow and inside, on a green field, a painted carousel with minutely modelled figures span round and round.

Shortly after the little roundabout had stopped moving, a series of crashes rocked the caravan. At the top of the steps, Mortimer Croop appeared. He had lost his wig in the tussle and was wearing only a vest which was torn in several places. In his flabby arms he carried the frantically struggling Pesto. As we all looked on in an awestruck silence, Pesto very deliberately turned his head towards Croop's chest and bit his master in the nipple. Croop roared with pain and hurled his burden to the ground. None of us stepped forward to assist the dwarf. The magnificent Mortimer was breathing so heavily that he looked as if he was about to expire. He seemed naked without his wig. Tears of anger, pain and frustration rolled down his cheeks. Pesto twitched uncontrollably at our feet but his eyes were on Croop and he seemed perfectly capable of continuing the struggle.

It was then that the strangest thing happened. Noticing his audience apparently for the first time, an indulgent smile began to spread across Croop's face and he seemed to bask in our attention. 'Ladies and gen –' he announced, struggling for breath. 'Ladies and gentle – ... ladies.' Spreading his arms in his usual oratorical fashion, he descended the steps with trembling legs and began to address us. 'Here stands before ... before ... lies before you ... the vile ... vilest ... worm.' It was all too much for him. He fell to his knees, his mouth open, swallowing lungful

92

upon lungful of air. He looked like a beached sea monster but the odd thing was that this was his finest performance.

'Magnetized the bloody table.' With these enigmatic words, Mortimer Croop fell, face downwards, onto the grass. Rising to his feet, Pesto cautiously began to circle the recumbent and heaving figure of his master. At length, confident that there would be no reprisals, Pesto drew closer and put his hand on Croop's shoulder. After a few seconds, a muffled sob was heard. Pesto helped the great Croop into a sitting position and held him steady. With his legs spread wide apart on the grass, his usually shiny black boots unbuckled and muddied, blood trickling from his torn nipple and the rouge running down his cheeks, Croop presented a sorry figure. His face creased and crumpled. The sobs came faster, and he burst into a flood of tears. 'Oh Pesto! Where is my Pesto?' Standing behind Croop, the dwarf patted his master reassuringly and looked at us with venom. A few members of the crowd began to drift away. 'My darling, my good companion, I didn't mean to insult or hurt you.' There was something repulsively fawning about Croop's manner now. He seemed aware that he had gone too far and now wanted to take back his words, to rescue a few tattered fragments from the scene. 'I should not have blamed you for my ruin. It was never your fault, dear Pesto.' For the first time, Croop seemed to become soberly aware of his audience. He reached an embarrassed hand to his denuded scalp and a few of the younger members of the audience, I regret to say, began to giggle.

'Ladies and gentlemen,' he began again with regained control. 'Friends all, I present to you Pesto: the noblest little man, the best-hearted clown to walk the face of the earth!' The predatory features of the dwarf twisted into an appreciative smile. He sketched a bow. It was all a pathetic farce: Croop was not sincere but nor, I think, did he intend any irony. He was too terrified for that.

'Begone, friends, please, I pray you. This was an insignificant incident, a difference of opinion which should have been earlier resolved as it usually is among – er – friends. My words, ladies and gentlemen, were misjudged, and I take them back, I swallow them.'

Croop's breathing came easily now but his features were still distorted and his eyes bulged. Mimi and Bessie moved away. Alf Hagsproat strode off to resume his duties. The tober began to assume the semblance of normality. I was the last, with Wilf, to leave the scene. As we walked away, I turned round to look behind me. Croop still sat on the grass and, as I watched, the dwarf approached him. Bending slightly, Pesto spat viciously and accurately into his master's upturned face. Croop only smiled and wiped the spittle away.

23

In the Air

Early the next day I received, by the hand of a small and grubby messenger boy, a letter which had been awaiting my arrival in Canterbury for some time. With great excitement, I sat down at a small table in the caravan and tore the envelope open. The letter was from Amelia and since I have it before me now, Mr Secretary – the paper is yellow and the ink faded – I shall read it in its entirety.

> My dear young Jack – But you will not be so young as you were and maybe you will not want me to call you by your first name, it has been so long. But Jack – let it be Jack – you are probably wondering how I know where you are. Well, I know Gerty Desmoulins and you will remember her. She is with me now in the Plough and Stars Inn in Blackfriars Lane, which is the place I own, and she is quite well and sends you her best wishes. She says to tell you that she is sorry she did not say goodbye when she left the circus.
>
> Yes, I am the landlady of the Plough and Stars. Over the door there is a sign of a rosy ploughboy on his lonely furrow with a bright star in the sky and he reminds me of you. I married a Mr Randidge but he passed on four years ago and there was some money from another source. So I bought something for my old age, Jack. I'm fifty now, stouter and shorter of breath. But I still have my red hair and no illness to speak of thank goodness. I hope this letter gets sent on. I am sure it will. Jack: come and see me soon. There's plenty of room and Gertrude says the circus is a miserable life these days. I wouldn't like the moving around, myself. A pub stays still. And I wouldn't have anything to do in a circus. I only ever had one trade but I can pull a glass of beer as good as the next. Jack, I am sorry I drove you away. I couldn't help it. You reminded me of someone perhaps I'll tell you one day. I hope

94

to be seeing you soon Jack but now I must be going to bed as it is past midnight. Yours with every best wish,

Amelia.

PS. Remember: the Plough and Stars Inn, Blackfriars Lane.

Amelia came into my mind so clearly that I might once again have been watching as she washed herself. I had never forgotten the disgust and repulsion she had shown towards me that day so long ago. From then onwards I had always felt marked out. It was a strange coincidence that, the day after Wilf had talked of leaving the circus, some sort of possibility had also opened up for me, if only of a place to stay, a shelter should all else fail.

I had borrowed a sheet of paper from Bessie's writing-case and was about to frame some sort of reply when the door of the caravan flew open to admit a dishevelled Mimi. She seized my hand and pulled me outside. I found myself running behind her across the meadow towards the newly-erected big top.

Once inside the ring, everything was oddly silent. The stands had not yet been put up and were stacked to one side. The grass was uncut and free of sawdust. The place was like a church. In the distance, to complete the resemblance, a knot of people had gathered and for some reason were looking up into the air. A ray of sunlight penetrated the canvas vault through an opening far above, and in its brightness hovered spinning motes of dust. My eyes followed the ray down from the roof and yet still further down, until the line of my gaze intersected that of the crowd. There, hanging by his neck from a length of rope attached to the high-wire, swung slowly the figure of Mortimer Croop. He was naked and I turned away. But Mimi led me closer.

Wilf had climbed up to the trapeze and was about to lower the body. Alf Hagsproat stood beneath to steady the dead form of our proprietor. The physical effects wrought on Croop by the manner of his death were typical, I believe, of such cases: the blackened tongue, the loosened sphincter. Directly below Croop a wreath of red roses lay on the ground. Six feet in the air, against the central pole of the tent, was nailed a neatly written notice in our ringmaster's hand. It read as follows:

> To the Employees of Mortimer Croop's Travelling Circus: My dear friends,
>
> I have to tell you that I am an utterly disgraced man. Of my own volition, therefore, and being in full possession of my faculties, I have decided, as you will be able to see, to take my own life. I took this step after lengthy, serious and profound

reflection, cogitation and cerebration. I was neither assisted nor encouraged; responsibility for this act is mine and mine alone. If you look beneath my feet, you will notice that I have taken the liberty of sending some flowers to my own funeral. On the desk in my caravan, the following items will be found:

Item 1: A letter to my sister in Eastbourne.
    " 2: My last will and testament.
    " 3: The name and address of a reputable lawyer.
    " 4:   "   "   "   "   " "   " doctor.
    " 5:   "   "   "   "   " "   " firm of
           undertakers.
    " 6: Some personal items: my fob-watch, cufflinks and tie-pin; a paperweight which had some sentimental value; my wig, boots and top hat.

It only remains for me to hope that we may meet, one day, in a better place and to entrust my soul to the universal ringmaster.

            The once Magnificent Mortimer Croop (Prop.)

By the time I had finished reading Croop's final message, his body lay outstretched on the grass. Somebody covered it with a blanket. We whispered amongst ourselves; nobody quite knew what to do. Having descended from aloft, Wilf Patchkey finally stepped forward. Shuffling his feet nervously, he began to speak:

'Well, I suppose that in our hearts some of us may have suspected that it would come to this. There's not going to be a show tonight, so what I say is that I will go into Canterbury – Jack Spellman here will help me – and fetch the doctor and the lawyer. We will see what is to be done and try to do it well. The rest of you might as well stay quiet in your quarters and prepare yourselves for an uncertain future.'

'There will be a circus tonight!' called out a loud voice from behind us. It was Pesto. As he stepped into the centre of the ring, the crowd parted deferentially in front of him.

'Mr Pesto, out of respect for the dead, surely –'

'Don't lecture me about respect for the dead!' interrupted Pesto. 'There *will* be a circus tonight!' he reaffirmed with all his passion.

He approached and knelt beside the body of his erstwhile master. Unwillingly, but under the intense and vicious gaze of his opponent, Wilf stepped back. Pesto licked his lips as he looked down on Croop. He spoke again: 'Is it not what dear Mortimer would have wanted?' The use of the familiar appellation made me wince. Pesto looked at each one of us in turn and then raised his shoulders by the merest fraction as if to indicate that he too was bemused by the enormity of what had occurred. 'I – was close to my master. None of you will ever know how close.' He scanned us once more, tested our resistance. 'I knew Mortimer Croop and I say that there will be a circus tonight because I can be absolutely sure that this would be what the performer in him would have wanted. For once we will all work hard. And for once it will be a good circus with nothing slipshod about it.'

Despite themselves, Pesto's audience murmured their assent. What else was there to do, what else was waiting? Only unemployment and perhaps vagabondage – what were we good for? For tinkers and street musicians or prostitutes and thieves.

The twitch at Pesto's mouth had appeared again, as it had that day at the gorge. 'To work, then!' he called out, beginning to bustle us out of the tent. 'I will execute my master's wishes. And at six o'clock we will meet together again in the smaller tent.'

There was still a degree of reluctance amongst us but we had lost ground and, like sheep, obeyed. Pesto ordered one of the stands to be brought over so that Croop could more easily be moved back to his caravan where he would be washed and prepared for burial. Alf obeyed and Pesto then lifted Croop on to its receiving surface. It was, I think, adequately impressed upon all of us that if Pesto had the strength to lift his master dead, he had probably had the strength to lift him alive.

I did not have any time to take this thought further. Work occupied me throughout the day to the exclusion of all contemplation. That afternoon some of the old energy of the circus seemed to have returned. We summoned up our last particles of strength and commitment. Some of us, I know, caught ourselves at moments in a mood approaching jollity. But in reality all this was the final trembling of a dying body, a dramatic access of full life before the last fall of the curtain.

Later that morning a doctor arrived and after him, the undertaker. In the early afternoon a besuited lawyer gingerly crossed the muddy meadow to knock on the door of Croop's caravan. All these comings and goings were directed by Pesto, who held court in the caravan where his master lay in tawdry state.

During the course of the day, one rumour after another started up. One of these was to the effect that Croop had first attempted his death from the hook in the roof of his caravan. It had proved too flimsy however and so, evidently firmly set on his course of action, he had walked across to the big top to try once more. A couple of people claimed to have seen his nude figure flitting across the meadow in the early hours.

At about six o'clock we foregathered in the smaller tent which Pesto had named for our meeting earlier in the day. By this time, most of us were partially dressed and made up for the last performance. Even now a few early members of the audience were drifting from booth to booth.

Pesto appeared after a few minutes and stood before us on a small raised platform. Behind him, a placard advertising 'The Magnificent Mortimer Croop's Travelling Circus' had been crudely altered so that it now read 'Luigi Pesto's Authentic and Original Travelling Circus'. Pesto was accompanied by Mr Gant, Croop's solicitor. He was a lean and elderly man with white hair and he evidently went in terror of the small typhoon at his side.

Pesto inaugurated the proceedings with a disparaging allusion to his erstwhile master's rhetorical flourishes. 'I will not lady and gentleman you. You do not need to be soothed and coddled with soft words. I expect you all know why we are here. Gant: proceed to the reading of the will, if you please.'

Mr Gant stepped forward and unrolled a sheet of parchment, the seal of which had already been broken. 'I am here to read the will of the late Mortimer Aloysius Croop, proprietor and manager of the Magnificent Mortimer Croop's Travelling Circus.'

'Yes, yes,' muttered Pesto.

Mr Gant coughed with dignity into a large white handkerchief before continuing. 'The will was signed and sealed in my presence on the fifth day of December in the year of Our Lord eighteen hundred and eighty-eight.'

'Tut!' Pesto chewed his nails irritably.

'This, then, being the last will and testament of Mor –'

Pesto suddenly exploded into a fury of impatience: 'Come on, Gant, you can leave the formalities aside and get down to the meat of the matter. Take it from the tenth paragraph like I told you. We have a performance to give in half an hour.'

'But there are some minor bequests,' Mr Gant spluttered, 'the fob-watch and the – er – wig and paperweight.'

'They will be attended to, I assure you. Please proceed at once to the main clauses.'

'Very well,' said Mr Gant in an injured tone. He began to read.

There is a tradition in the circus, as there is in some clans and monarchies, for the outgoing ruler to name his successor before his death. Without the shadow of any legal doubt, Pesto had been named sole inheritor. He owned everything now, from the properties and caravans to the costumes we wore and the food we ate.

As Gant talked on monotonously, turning his pages with clerkly flourishes, Pesto examined us all. After a time, a smile of triumph spread across his face. The audience did not so much listen to Gant's words as watch the changes that had come over Pesto. Twenty-odd hours previously, during his altercation with Croop, he had been prepared – to a point – to play his part, to be humble and quiet. Most of us, probably, had never heard him utter more than a dozen words in public. I was one of the few who knew how voluble he could be in private. Now, on two occasions, we had all seen the ease of his assumption of authority, his bluntly commanding tone and, more than this, his overweening delight in power. He positively wriggled with joy on the platform.

Mr Gant finished speaking and stood to one side. Bringing his heel down with a startling crack, Pesto himself began to speak:

'You have laughed at me and insulted me and abused me behind my back these many years. I endured it all because I loved the circus and my master. Unlike so many of you, I was willing to suffer and to obey. It is a pity that you did not learn to respect me for now my time is come and yours is over. I am advanced and you stay still. You have no power over me. Justice is done. Thanks to Croop, may God reward him, I am now the owner here. I will not fail him: I will outdo him. This circus will once more be as great as it was in the times of old, of which many of you will have heard Signor Zanzare speak.'

We all looked to Zanzare but he bowed his head and said nothing. I wanted to stand up and shout out that Zanzare's nostalgia was only the rambling of an old man, that it had nothing to do with Pesto or his viciousness. I wanted to stand up, but I could not. It was then that the heaviest blow fell.

'As I am speaking of Signor Zanzare, let me continue a little longer. I entertain an enormous respect for the purity and beauty of his daughter, Miss Aramind. I would like to inform you, since some of you may wish to congratulate me, that Signor Zanzare has generously acceded to my request and given me the hand of his daughter. Step forward, Aramind my dear!'

A hush fell over us all. Aramind joined Pesto on the rostrum. He took her hand and displayed her engagement ring to the audience. Her head was bowed but as Pesto pushed her back towards her seat, she threw one glance towards me and my eyes could not but respond.

Pesto seemed not to notice our look. At any rate, his face was exultant as he called out to the assembled crowd:

'We have a performance to give and I am the new ringmaster! To work!'

24

Horseplay

IT WAS undoubtedly the finest performance that we had ever given. Was this because we knew that it was to be not only the last of the season but the last of all? Or, more esoterically, was it because the essence of a thing tends to emerge most authentically at the moment of its extinction?

It happened, in any case, both because of Pesto and in spite of him. As I checked the seams of my horse-suit that evening I had to admit that the cruelty of his energy had always figured in the dynamism of the circus. Set against that energy, however, was our own disordered resistance, our amnesiac indifference to authority.

Whatever the causes of this supreme performance, one could not number amongst them the presence of a large and enthusiastic audience. The very opposite was true: the stalls filled slowly and many rows remained empty. They cheered enough, I suppose, as the evening progressed but I think that my memory has magnified the sounds of their applause. No: in the end, this was a performance that we gave to ourselves.

A prolonged trumpet fanfare burst upon the audience and cowed them into a partial but expectant hush. Two tall-stilts walkers entered the ring, their striped pantaloons flapping loosely around their extended legs. Twenty feet into the air, on their shoulders, stood Pesto. He had somehow acquired a perfectly fitting ringmaster's uniform. His top hat, his brass buttons and black boots gleamed in the torchlight. He carried in one hand a whip proportional to his size and, as his carriers reached the centre of the ring, he cracked it several times. There was complete silence.

'LAAA-DIES and GENNN-TLEMEN!' he cried. Wilf and I exchanged astonished glances, for Pesto no longer spoke with his old, grating voice. Instead, he was imitating to perfection the tones of Mortimer Croop. The pauses, the gestures with the hand, the very phrases: all belonged to the man whose body lay now, dressed for the funeral ceremony, in his caravan.

'Gentlemen and ladies! Allow me humbly and gratefully to welcome you all to this mighty canvas dome, this oasis of wonders in a desert of

100

prose, this palace of delight and of illusion. THIS! ladies and gentlemen –
is Luigi PESto's Au-THENTIC and His-TORIC TRAVEL-ling CIR-
cus!'

There was a burst of applause and a volley of fireworks was let off.
Earlier in the evening Pesto had refused to flatter us, his workers. But he
did not shrink from ingratiating himself with his audience; indeed he
beamed his pleasure from aloft.

'Gentlefolks all!' he continued in somewhat quieter tones, 'a word
about what you will see here tonight. The living core of this circus was
formed in the Piedmont thirty years ago and more, when I was smaller –
than I am now.' Some of the audience laughed at this point. 'Oh yes, ladies
and gentlemen, I may be only four foot dead in my stockinged feet but
tonight – as you can see -- I stand on the shoulders of GIANTS!'
Scattered applause greeted this witticism, and Pesto acknowledged it
graciously. 'Thirty years ago, more or less, as I say, all this began in that
most beautiful region of the most beautiful of countries.' He looked
around him at the assembled faces and raised a hand as if he wanted to
qualify what he had just said. 'But the traditions of this circus go back
much further than that: who, ladies and gentlemen, can say how far?
Further back than Joseph Grimaldi of famous name. Oh yes, certainly.
And further back than all the Grimaldi. Some say, ladies and gentlemen,
there are some who say that we were born in the time of the troubadours,
that we were wandering players who gathered together for safety on the
roads. But I say that we are older still than that, by far. Yes, we were there
during the Crusades, we juggled outside the strong white walls of Acre.
But we were there also in the darker times before. We sang to Charle-
magne in the forests and we were there in Byzantium and at the Sack of
Rome.'

Once again Pesto looked down into the faces of his hushed audience.
Then he smiled and spoke more quietly still: 'Were we, ladies and
gentlemen of our modern age, were we those strange hordes that came
from the east? Interlopers? Goths, Vandals? I do not think so, for we were
there even before them. Yes, before Christ, our cymbals sounded before
his birth. Who can say? It is a riddle written in sand long blown away. Let
us then, my friends, leap forward through the millennia to a mere thirty
years ago, when I was young.

'I joined the circus because I believed in wonder. I joined when my own
people still believed in magic, and spirits of wood and water and stone and
fire. Some of us still practised magic. I know this, ladies and gentlemen,
because my mother was a witch. Oh yes – ' Pesto smiled, raising his hand
again. Barely a murmur of dissent was heard. 'Yes, she gathered herbs and

mingled potions. But all her knowledge could not save her from the stray bullet which killed her, during a battle, in 1859.

'There are hardly any witches now and there are fewer stray bullets. It is a less dangerous age but a more complicated one. Things have changed so much for me. I am in another country, speaking another language. I am speaking in the tongue of an Empire which grows daily larger. The mills hum, and the mines clamour. Steel is forged, and money is made. Everywhere there is the chatter of business and change.

'But remember this, ladies and gentlemen, I have only this to say: if you believe in us and watch with innocent eyes you will see wonders before you tonight. Later, when you go home, you will know that for two long hours nothing has changed at all and that this could have happened anywhere, in any time.

'I talked to you fondly a few moments ago of the Italy of my youth, of the spirits of lakes and forests. I would like to present to you tonight, as the first course in a meal of marvels, a spirit of the sky. PUT your hands toGETHER for BESSIE LANGRISH!'

The audience applauded wildly. There was another fanfare of trumpets and, still carrying Pesto, the stiltsmen retreated from the ring. The air was free of words when Bessie descended on her trapeze.

I had never seen her soar so high as on that night. She span so fast and for so long that she seemed bound to miss her handhold, her meeting with the swinging bar. It is all too easy to say, I know, but Bessie appeared at moments to be on the point of escaping altogether the will and law of gravity, and the audience gasped with fear for her safety. Reaching the edge of her capabilities, for a few seconds she pushed herself well beyond what she had known.

Bessie had always started off the evening show; her flight stood for the overcoming of the ordinary and this, of course, was the myth that we existed to purvey. She was the incarnation, that night, of the stretched tightrope tension of the circus. Far above the earth, she was very close to disaster, but for the moment, the present moment alone, she was transcendently alive.

As the applause began to die I took a last look round the ring before burying my head in the body of the horse: it was the turn of Wilf and me. We had fixed the dimensions of the ring in our minds and were now guided by the inner compass of instinct. We knew the audience, their manners and their types, knew where to turn for a low laugh and where for the appreciation of the class.

The ring was like a gigantic inverted cake composed of many layers and varying richnesses. Or have it that the whole thing, that flimsily fixed cathedral, was a merry-go-round hurling us all into the oblivion of pure sensation. I do not believe, Mr Secretary, that I have previously had occasion to describe in detail the prancing performance of our pantomime horse. I am glad, then, to be able to tell you about our finest hour. We played all our pranks. Oh yes, there was not a single missed gesture nor a stumble that had not been calculated.

Making our entry, we strolled calmly and with great elegance towards a painted wooden lamppost which stood in the centre of the ring. Leaning against it, we looked casually this way and that along an imaginary street as if we were waiting for a lady companion: a pantomime mare. Wilf began to whistle a tune; I flicked my tail in time. A little competition began to go on between the whistle and the flick as to who should have, as it were, the last word. We quickly realized, however, that we were running the chance of making ourselves look ridiculous should our equine Juliet arrive for her tryst. We assumed an attitude of extreme urbanity. Wilf lifted his leg in order to admire his well manicured hooves. He turned his vain head this way and that to catch his beauty from all angles. Becoming aware for the first time of the audience, he tossed his mane coquettishly. 'Yes, I know,' he seemed to say, 'I am the nonpareil of stallionhood.'

Stallionhood? Certainly: the pantomime horse had always been male. It lacked of course, for decency's sake, the verifying organ but I could never think of ourselves as other than masculine, even though that masculinity was entirely theatrical.

Wilf began to examine his other hoof. It was at this point that the back leg of the pantomime horse began to behave awkwardly: it too wanted to be admired. Wilf's foot brushed it away with impatience but mine cautiously returned, craving the attention that was surely its due. Again it was rejected and once more it returned. Then our feet fell to fighting and all hope of a successful meeting of lovers was gone. The scrambling, the ducking and weaving, the twisting and turning, the staggering and stumbling had begun. It was a parody horse at war with itself and with each mistaken step it lost its precious dignity. As ever, the cruel laughter began. It was not consciously cruel, I suppose, but nevertheless it gloried in our debasement and our folly.

Fourteen boxes had been spaced equally around the perimeter of the ring. By now we had completely given up our dignity and were showing off disgracefully. With a neat leap we landed on the first box, staggered, and fell. As we gathered ourselves together, a clown emerged behind us from his hiding place in the box. The clown was angry that his rest had been disturbed and began to chase us. Hurriedly cantering away, we performed an out-of-time tap dance on the second box. Another clown emerged and joined the chase. We missed the third box entirely because we were too vainly preoccupied with the impression we were making on the audience.

Now, rubbing their eyes, three clowns were pursuing us. Then a fourth, and a fifth, and they were gaining on us rapidly. Now seven – and eight – and nine pursued us round the ring. On the tenth box I lifted Wilf into the air, twirled round and fell over. Clown five threw a pie at us but it hit clown eleven as he sleepily opened the lid of his box. We foolishly made too much of our cleverness and ran straight into another, thrown by clown twelve. On the thirteenth box I performed a handstand on Wilf's back and waved my legs in the air. On it went to the end. We were caught by the clowns and kicked in our rear and covered with cream pie and duly chastised. The fourteenth clown, whose costume sprouted papier mâché vegetables (Joey Grimaldi's old trick) jumped on our back and rode us to the edge of the ring. At the curtain, with a last gambol, we were gone and the first half of our performance was over. This was the spectacle, subject to a few minor alterations, which we had performed most afternoons and almost every night, eight months of the year, for the previous ten years. Wilf and I emerged from the horse suit and when I had wiped myself down I decided to watch the remainder of the performance from the backstage entrance to the ringside.

The old eyes of elephants smiled down on me with fathomless sadness. A camel brayed peevishly and the stench of its breath was in the air. They paraded round the ring in the torchlight: cart horses, buffalo, two shaggy yaks and a troupe of llamas – the great animals from five continents displayed for our audience's delectation.

Then the horses, fleet and unfree, careered out their paces. Their nostrils jetted vapour into the cold air, spume flecked their chests and their hocks were lathered. Still supported by the stiltsmen, Pesto called them in and ordered them off, put the trainers through their paces. He was in a narrow nirvana of delight and gestured wildly, grandiosely, galvanized by some force beyond his own control. He gyrated and cavorted like a puppet.

The lions knelt before their tamer. They rolled over and licked his face. They delicately took morsels of flesh from his extended hand. Finally the tigers and the lions, the bears and the malicious leopard sloped off to Pesto's directions, hating with every fibre the training they were unable to transgress.

Now it was Zanzare's turn. Tonight he made no mistakes. His daughter handed him the tools of his trade with downcast eyes. Zanzare seemed younger: his cheeks were rosy and suffused with life. Even his eyes glittered as of old. The objects emerged from their hidden places with many a sleight-of-hand with which I was delightedly familiar and, tonight, with the occasional twist that I had not noticed before. The rabbits, the doves, the snake, the apple, the coins from behind the ears of small boys, the lighted torch hidden beneath the coat, the feats of memory and calculation, the disappearing daughter, the reappearing daughter: all the old favourites were performed. She was pale, Aramind, and she looked at nobody.

There was an interval. Mimi began the second half of the show, riding bareback into the ring with consummate control. She was the highlight of the night. The arena seemed to contract or expand: I was never afterwards able to tell which as she cantered around it on her favourite chestnut mare. She stood on the beast's withers, extended one leg, performed a handstand, then seated herself backwards on the horse. Still it galloped, faster and faster, sending the sawdust flying. The counterpoint of its footfalls was easily audible in the hush. Mimi stood up again on the horse and caught an item of clothing thrown to her by a clown. She put it on, and then another garment and another, each one flung to her and deftly caught. I was mesmerized: this was a new feature of Mimi's act. At such a pace, she seemed deliberately to solicit disaster. Some catastrophe surely awaited her around the next bend. She was bulkier now and she seemed to stoop with age. When, suddenly, she showed her face, she had the wizened plastercast mask of an old woman. She was frail and incapable yet still she galloped on. By now both horse and rider were in the extremity of old age and slowly they came to a halt. Mimi descended feebly as the orchestra played the Dead March from *Saul*. Clowns brought her a coffin and placed her inside and closed the lid. Before she could be carried from the ring, however, Mimi sprang up again, having miraculously changed her costume. She had become a skeleton dancing to an accompaniment of bone music played on the xylophone. The clowns begged her not to terrify the little children and once more she suffered them to lay her in the coffin. Nevertheless, before they left the ring, Mimi was up once more in a final incarnation, leaping onto her horse in the white robes of a fugitive ghost.

Clowns with painted faces and outsize clothes scattered around the ring. Their story was 'Orpheus and Eurydice', an old piece of Grimaldi's. Harlequin as Orpheus followed Columbine's Eurydice – played by Aramind – down into the Underworld where Pantaloon, playing the part of Hades, opposed them with his magic. Harlequin got lost; disguise succeeded disguise. There were caves and Gothic ruins – all part of the latitude allowed the pantomime with regard to scenery – and a good fairy. Pierrot was the Chief of Ghosts, Pantaloon's right-hand man, spectral in his bismuth make-up.

Orpheus charmed the ghosts with his music; they gathered round him to listen. In our final appearance, Wilf and I played the spirit of Bucephalus. In this version of the myth no tragedy of decapitation awaited Orpheus. Eurydice was restored to him: Eurydice, who should have stayed for ever in the Underworld as sad Persephone's companion. That was the way things were in the circus. We twisted the myths into the shapes we wanted and at the end we were all transformed back into our proper clownish selves. The dark scene was over; everything was over. General merriment prevailed as we took our bows.

After the audience had left and as the stalls were being taken apart, Wilf and I still gazed into the sawdust ring. At last he pulled at one of the straps on my horse-suit and looked into my face with an expression of incomprehension.

'Why do they do it, Jacko? Why do they want so badly to be gulled? Shuffling to their seats in their grey overcoats and all to be fooled and waste their money.'

I risked a cruel irony. 'Why Wilf, to see wonders of course: to believe in magic again and spirits of wood and water.'

Wilf spat contemptuously on the ground. 'Ain't nothing to do with spirits, Jacko. It's more fleshy than that. And yet I don't and I never will know the reason why.'

As we walked away, I took up the voice of Dickens's Mr Sleary. 'People mutht be amuthed, thquire, thome of the time.'

25

The Turning of the Tide

WILF AND I set out across the meadow. Although it was late, small groups of circus workers were still taking down the booths and stalls. A crescent moon silvered the dark sky and here and there a lantern flickered and threw darker shadows across the ground. There was a great and silent sadness between us. It had been a fine performance but our situation was increasingly untenable. It was then that Wilf stopped and pointed across the meadow. 'What's that over there, Jacko, outside Zanzare's tent?'

'People,' I replied, 'there are people standing outside.' Considering the lateness of the hour and Zanzare's misanthrophy this was an unusual and even unheard-of occurrence. It was hardly likely that the magician was receiving visitors.

As we approached, the picture emerged more clearly. A couple of hands stood around in attitudes of idle but not unsympathetic curiosity. A light hung by the door and two of the elderly women who prepared the food were boiling water on the fire. As they moved around or sat stiffly on their stools, I could not help but be reminded of other eerie figures on a heath. I went up to one of the crones to ask what was happening. 'He will be gone with the turning of the tide,' was all that she replied.

Diffidently, I entered Zanzare's tent for the first time in years. To one side the conjuror lay outstretched upon his bed. Even now he appeared younger than at any time during the previous five years. But with a thrill of certainty I realized that this youthful flush was the symptom of serious illness.

Aramind sat at the bedhead wiping her father's forehead with a piece of cloth as she had once wiped mine in my delirium. At the foot of the bed, looking down on the failing prestidigitator, stood Pesto. He licked his lips and smiled at me with his carious teeth. Then his gaze flicked across the tent to Aramind. The air was sweet with the smell of sickness.

We stood in silence by the side of the bed for about an hour. Then Wilf beckoned me over and whispered into my ear:

'I'm going away now, Jacko. This is no place for me.'

I was surprised. 'What do you mean? I thought you knew Zanzare well.' I remembered how Wilf had persuaded him to tell my fortune and I mentioned this to my friend.

'Not particularly,' Wilf replied. 'I got Bessie and Aramind to butter him up.'

'Don't go,' I pleaded with him. 'You won't sleep wherever you are.'

'I won't,' he agreed, 'that's true. But I still don't want to hang around here.'

Wilf disappeared through the door of the tent and I felt very lonely. Pesto, Aramind and I did not speak to each other. Zanzare occasionally muttered to himself in his sleep. With each passing quarter hour, mercilessly marked by a single chime from the cathedral, his breath shortened and the hoarse rattle in his lungs grew louder.

At about three o'clock in the morning, Zanzare rallied a little. When his eyes opened, he was looking directly at me. He did not seem to be aware of the presence of anybody else.

'Spellman, Jack Spellman,' he whispered. There was no longer any recrimination in his voice. I bent my ear to his lips.

'I have been reading your book again, Spellman,' he murmured before pausing to clear his clogged throat. 'Many things emerged which I had not seen before. I had not realized it was such a tale.' He smiled feebly. 'They gave me leave, you see, the ghosts, because I am almost one of them – all but in name.'

Zanzare looked around the tent but I do not think that he saw anything. His fingers sought my hand. 'Certain things cannot be altered now, Spellman. The text is complete. It is not your fault. Perhaps it was my fault – I don't know. Many years ago, before the story started, it might have been different. The ring will do you no harm.'

I winced and almost glanced behind me at Pesto, afraid that he might have heard. But he stood motionlessly and without interest at the foot of the bed.

Zanzare pulled me closer. 'I see further now but it is not for me to tell you. Everything has its time.' His hand fell back upon the sheets and he was silent for a while. Soon, however, he gathered his faculties for a final effort:

'The fire draws closer – so close it scorches me. See – my cheeks!' They were indeed aglow, and his eyes like embers. 'Not one of noble birth but two. And other faces behind them. They wrote it before I could reach my hand to the page. It is all in bringing things to life, Spellman. But the others come to steal our little efforts and the precious web becomes a chain of useless ornaments . . .'

Zanzare fell into a restless sleep. His last words to me had come from so far away that I could barely reconstruct them.

I went outside to clear my head. The water was boiling on the fire in readiness for the washing of the corpse and the old women still kept their vigil. I thought that they had gathered here out of some desire to triumph over their own last ends. They were confabulating in their toothless voices, mumbling of days gone by. Death had made their past years live again and strengthened their hold on mortality. I listened without thinking. One of the women said that Zanzare had been ill for some time. The other added that he had refused to see a doctor. After a while, the first woman said that she thought the news of Croop's death had dealt the final blow. The second woman nodded and looked into the fire:

'The tide turns at five. Already at Southampton the water will be running out.'

I shivered. I could bear neither to go nor to remain yet somehow, pacing up and down, I stayed.

Towards the darkest hour of the night, Zanzare's crepitus became audible through the canvas. The old women looked at each other and the flame of life seemed to burn more brightly in their faces. Zanzare's panting came faster but shallower. Separated by several seconds, two sentences issued from his lips – the last he was to speak.

'My daughter, I have signed away your life!' This was spoken calmly, with an immense but distant grief. Then, with a hatred I would not have believed expressible:

'My son! That such evil could have come from me!'

Pesto gave out a long, low laugh. The old women arose, wrung out their cloths in the water and went into the tent. The exequies had begun.

26
Sawdust and Scalings

Z ANZARE AND CROOP were buried on the same day, in the same churchyard outside Canterbury. Our two patriarchs had gone within a day of each other and now only one ruled in their place. The little Norman church was full; everybody was there. Resting next to each other on trestles at the end of the dusty aisle were the two coffins. After the words had been spoken I helped to carry Zanzare's casket out into the pale light. The autumn had come and the morning was cold but the frost had melted from the grass at the graveside.

I stared numbly at a pick-axe and a shovel which leant against a tombstone. Then we lowered the coffins into the soil and sang a hymn. The vicar said something about travelling men being laid to rest at last. A bird sang from the depths of a nearby yew tree. Each of us threw some soil into the graves with a little silver trowel and, singly or in pairs, departed.

That day and for many days after, as the properties of the circus were taken down and stored away, I tried not to think too much. I only had the strength to watch. My eyes wandered about in the world of things, traversing surface and inspecting shape with no sense of curiosity or of emergent meaning. There were so many things in the world. One's gaze passed over them and sometimes they seemed marvellous, bursting with structure and sense. Now things were only a tedious queue. I stared across the meadow and they cropped up at random in the line of my vision: mute, inert.

For some reason I could not take this opportunity to leave the circus. I stayed on from day to day, living in an absent, hand-to-mouth sort of way. Although some of us remained to slow the seepage of the circus population, we were not a dedicated band of the faithful. Mimi and Bessie stayed for no better reason than that it mattered not where they were so long as they were together. Wilf stayed, I suspect, because of me. Alf? He stayed simply because he was too miserable to do anything else. He began to drink heavily in his caravan and did not speak to anybody.

Why did I stay? Perhaps out of an absurd chivalry, a desire to be there should Aramind need me.

110

Pesto was named sole legatee in Zanzare's will. This did not surprise us: even the phrasing of the document echoed that of Croop. No separate provision was made for Aramind on the assumption that she would soon be married. The banns were up for their wedding and the service was to be in late November, in the same church where Croop and Zanzare had been buried a few weeks previously.

When the ceremony was held and the vicar asked if any of us knew cause or just impediment why these two persons should not be joined together in Holy Matrimony, I was silent as before and did not stand and declare to the church: 'I do. They have the same father.' This was not from fear of Pesto, although as the vicar's words were spoken he glared vengefully at us all. It was partly because Zanzare had said that everything was written and could not be altered. There was another reason as well. Although I loved Aramind, I had come to hate the decade I had spent hoping for a sight of her. I had promised myself to follow my fate through to the end and to outlast it; I was going to stand and watch it pass and do its worst until it was quite, quite utterly spent and every detail had been unravelled and come to rest. As for the pain I felt, I was used to that. It was a given part of my condition. I am no anatomist of the movements of the spirit, however, so let us pass on.

We waited. We marked time through the days of late November and darkening December. Meat was a thing of the past with us and we ate little, keeping to ourselves and the glow of our lamps. The meadow came to resemble the encampment of a departed army; spars and bridles commemorated the vanished soldiers; dancing shoes and scraps of ribbon bore witness to their victims. Sparrows gathered to drink from the edges of half-frozen puddles. It was at this time, Mr Secretary – I see that you are alert to my eccentricities – that I developed a fondness for sparrows. They are pragmatic creatures, cocky and unsentimental. I fed them with breadcrumbs from the steps of Mimi and Bessie's caravan and they accepted my tributes without gratitude. 'So,' they seemed to say, 'he has decided to keep us through the winter; well then, it is his affair. We care not.'

The details concerning Pesto's inheritance from Zanzare gradually became known. We had been aware, of course, that Zanzare was a cultivated, an educated man. Nevertheless it surprised us to learn that he sprang from a family of minor aristocrats and that Pesto had in consequence come into possession of the extensive but impoverished estates in northern Italy.

After the wedding, Aramind was not to be seen. She kept to Croop's old caravan where Pesto had now taken up residence and where she too had moved on the night of her marriage. Perhaps she remained indoors for her

111

own reasons; perhaps – and this I thought more likely – the firm hand of another intervened to close the door on her contacts with the outer world.

We speculated that the couple would move out to the Italian estates, but Pesto, although he had never quite lost his accent, was no more naturally Mediterranean than I. He cared little for the land of his birth; his adopted habitat was this stricken England. When we visited the great towns of the north, he would seek out their more noisome parts as if with some feeling of affinity. He took a great deal of pleasure in poverty. There was nothing that amused him so much as a child with rickets, the way it staggered and toppled. There was nothing he relished more than the mansion abutting on the slum.

Pesto spent much of his time away during these weeks and I guessed that he was returning to the places spoken of in his litany, his secret stores of wealth and trash. When he returned each Friday evening his dogcart was more heavily laden than when he had left. He would unload a chair, a little cabinet: purchases he claimed to have made so that Aramind should feel at home. Yet at the same time he was gathering up his goods, calling in the debts, allowing the vortex to spill out a stream of wealth at his feet. On Monday mornings he was regularly seen on the steps of a bank in Canterbury, waiting impatiently for the doors to open.

Pesto said nothing of his little outings. It was rumoured that he had been to Hull and Manchester, to Rochester and Cambridge. We sat in our caravans and chafed our knuckles. Only the sparrows were doing well, fattening themselves on a few crumbs. They could live on nothing and I admired them for that, for not giving a damn about this world of things which weighs us down.

Pesto acquired a new costume: that of the businessman. Trimly besuited, he would stalk the circus meadows avoiding the icy puddles and from time to time looking about him and laughing as he smoked on his cigar.

One day I had been out to see what could be had for nothing. Returning, I had rounded the corner of the joiner's shed when I ran hard into Pesto, who was peering into a water-butt and giggling to himself. I dropped my load of scrumped apples. 'Now then Spellman, careful as you go!' he chortled as I bent to pick them up. 'More haste, less speed!'

I had muttered some reply and was about to go on my way when Pesto restrained me with his arm. 'Pleased to see you my lad. Delighted!' I overcame my distaste and responded with a forced politeness. It was then that he looked up quizzically but mockingly into my face. 'What do you think of meadows, then? Meadows. In a general way.'

'Too windy and too muddy,' I said, wondering what he was getting at.

'Oh really, Mr Jack. *Generally*. In a general way, I said. You're taking too narrow a view.' He looked at me pityingly before drawing my attention to our surroundings with a broad sweep of his hand. 'Don't you think the meadow is a marvellous place? Look at it, young Spellman! What a good place it is, isn't it?'

I remained silent but Pesto did not wait for my reply; I was merely the audience to his performance. 'Yes, the English meadow. So –' he hunted for the right word '– so *English*. And so much better than – Italy, for example. I take it as an example because Italy is there, as it were –' his voice dropped, as if he was talking to himself '– whereas the meadow is most definitely here.'

Shifting uncomfortably from one foot to the other, I must have attracted Pesto's attention since he turned to address me directly. 'You might be interested to know, Mr Spellman, that I have some land near Turin which is worth this meadow and the next and the one after and still a deal left over if Caravelli pays as I know Caravelli will.'

I nodded wisely and wondered why Pesto was telling me all this. My companion extinguished his cigar and raised his hat. 'Thank you, my lad. Most grateful. Endlessly grateful.' He tapped his forehead with his finger. 'What a head for business you have, young man. Extraordinary for your years. Exceptionally acute.' Lighting another cigar, he was gone in a trail of smoke.

After this exchange – I call it an exchange although in reality it was he who spoke my side of the dialogue as well as his own – Pesto sought out my company with increasing frequency. He knew that his presence repelled me and I imagine that to be in my company, therefore, must have given him great pleasure. He saddled me with the reputation of a business genius in order to give out select details of his financial manipulations and he also forced on me the character (entirely falsely, as you will appreciate by now, Mr Secretary) of a great lover of women so that he could dangle scraps of Aramind's pain under my nose.

'Spellman, you fast dealer, you,' he said one day, 'what would you think of iron scalings now, in a general way?'

The next week sawdust was on his mind. 'I see that you are laughing at me. Yes, sawdust! For stuffing dolls and puppets – very useful. What would you think of that, purely in general terms of course?'

On another occasion it was bone-meal. 'Quite, quite, I see your point entirely. My, you're as sharp as ever! But guano is altogether a different kettle of fish, don't you think?'

The first snow fell; it was a Friday night. I had gone to bed early and had just succeeded in gathering round me enough scraps of blanket to achieve a certain degree of warmth when I heard the familiar jingle of Pesto's dogcart. Mimi and Bessie had left to spend a few days with Bessie's aunt in Dover, so I lay alone in the caravan as I waited for the noise to pass. Instead of proceeding in the direction of Pesto's caravan, however, the rattling cart rapidly drew nearer to my own sleeping-quarters. A few seconds later my door was flung open and Pesto leapt onto the palliasse beside me in an insane frenzy of delight. He screamed with laughter and kicked his legs in the air. He embraced me and kissed me on both cheeks.

I pressed myself back against the wall of the caravan and enquired what purpose he might have in this late visit. This set him laughing until the tears rolled down his cheeks but he stopped suddenly and looked me in the eye. 'Of course, Mr Jack. Of course! You don't *know*!' Once more he fell victim to the humour he saw in the situation. It was some time before he recovered. 'I had thought – such are you the sharer in my humble plans – I had thought that you must know. But I forgot to tell you! Forgive me. Wait! I need the papers to show you and I must fetch a celebratory cigar.'

He was out again and through the door. A few moments later, he returned puffing upon a large Havana and carrying in his arms a sheaf of papers. 'Now then, young Spellman, prepare yourself for a shock, you wily old rascal you.'

He unrolled and spread before me a number of sheets covered with draughtsman's projections, measurements and figures. Then, with a proudly inflated chest, he handed me a blueprint perhaps four feet square. I saw before me an impression of one of the strangest buildings that I had ever seen.

'Isn't it lovely, Spellman? Ooh, it's beautiful. But don't tell her, you mustn't!' He seized me by the ear and pulled my face round until I was looking into his eyes. 'Mum's the word, Mr Jack. Silent as the grave!'

I asked, of course, to whom he was referring.

'Who else? My dear, my darling wife, my Aramind. Don't be obtuse, you rascal! She must not know until Christmas, Spellman. This is to be a surprise, a Christmas present, a wedding present.' He gestured towards the blueprint. 'It's to be a little modest house in which she can be the little modest woman she is. Spellman, my lad – really, your acuity fails you for once – this is – going – to – be OUR HOME!' Pesto rolled about with glee. He would have started kissing me again if I had not pretended to sneeze. 'Our wedding home! Here: in the MEADOW! And isn't it just the most beautiful, the most cottagey-looking place you've ever seen? Look at it, lad! Just look at it!'

The drawing in front of me represented, in plan and elevation, a building whose effect was half-way between that of a factory and a ship. There were echoes, too, in the gargoyles which punctuated its perspectives, of Canterbury Cathedral.

Pesto saw the movement of my eye. 'You like the gargoyles, you love

114

'em! I knew you would. So do I. I'm very fond of gargoyles, Mr Jack: they brighten the place up no end, and I never liked a grim, serious sort of building.'

Yet this was that building and Pesto did but dissimulate his true purpose. A grimmer and more serious building I could not have imagined. It had also something of a prison or an asylum in its design: there appeared to be no windows on the ground floor and all the higher ones were barred.

'Keep the plans hid here, Jack, will you? Keep 'em safe so me sweetie won't know.'

I found it hard to imagine how Pesto could seriously request me to keep secrets from Aramind as though I had only seen her yesterday or last week. He had kept a firmer hold on her than even Zanzare. I said that I would keep his plans safe and – felt like a collaborator.

'That's it, Jack. Hide 'em good and I'll know where they are!' With these words Pesto leapt from my bed, leaving his cigar stub smouldering in my pillow, and disappeared into the night. A flurry of snow swept through the caravan. He had not closed the door.

27

Seventy Pounds

I N THE week before Christmas workmen were called out to the meadow to begin work on the foundations of Pesto's mansion. Guide-ropes and marker lines soon criss-crossed the field, turning it into a sketch of Pesto's nuptial fantasy. There were odd nooks and jutting pillars, passageways which seemed to lead nowhere. The sound of pickaxes could be heard impaling the frozen ground.

On the third day – it was the twenty-first of December – the workmen uncovered some bones and old coins. Pesto swooped with delight, a chattering magpie. The coins, it transpired, were all but valueless. This was a disappointment to Pesto but he vowed nevertheless to have the skeleton, which had suffered somewhat during its long interment, re-articulated and varnished so that it could stand in his hallway to greet his guests.

I kept my peace but I found it stranger and stranger that Pesto could leave his blueprints with me in order to preserve his secret from Aramind when, every day, outside their caravan (which was to be built into and included within the structure) the actual work had already commenced. Throughout that week, however, the curtains of their caravan remained drawn and nobody but Pesto went in or out. It was almost beyond belief, yet I could find no other explanation for it: in order to spring his pleasant surprise, Pesto had compelled his wife to live in darkness.

In this last week of advent, Pesto travelled no more. He was busy overseeing the work on the foundations, hopping across the lines, into and out of trenches, holding animated conversations with the labourers. As before, he would occasionally explode unannounced into my caravan, bursting with excitement at his new project. On Christmas Eve, however, the subject of Pesto's discourse took a new and unexpected turn. This time he buttonholed me outside, where I was roasting potatoes in the fire.

'Ah, Spellman! Keeping the wolf at bay, I see!' He gestured at my meal with his foot. 'Clever lad, sound mind, extraordinary.'

'Thank you, Mr Pesto. Will you have some?'

His lip curled. 'Not now, thank you. No, not now.' He squatted beside me to light a cigar from a flaming branch and smoked quietly for a while before opening the conversation.

'Now here's a nut for you to crack. It baffles me but then I haven't got your mind. Australia, my lad! What do you think of Australia in a general sort of way?'

I replied that I thought it was warmer than here.

'Oh dear, you're being narrow-minded again. Why not take the broader view, Mr Jack?'

I tried again, still unsure where Pesto would come out. I said that many men had been transported to penal settlements in Australia.

His eyes glinted. 'What sort of men, Spellman? Honest types, were they?'

No. They were criminals: convicts.

'Ah, convicts! Brilliant, most astute. I knew you would get there. Yes, plenty of convicts in Australia, to be sure. Adulterers. And thieves, Spellman, thieves.'

I stiffened slightly and became more attentive. He knew, whilst pretending not to be aware of it, that I knew. I am certain of that.

'I take it, however, you old seducer of the yellow-boys – it's a mere speculation – that Australia is not the only place where convicts lurk?'

No, I said. Certainly not. Where there were people, there would be criminals; they were spread the whole world wide. Almost all the wise world, in fact, was little else in nature but parasites or sub-parasites. Pesto looked at me askance. It was a well-known fact, I added, with an unpleasant sensation of straying into deeper waters, that wealth bred crime.

'Ah, breeds crime does it? I see.' He scratched his head and gave me a chilling little smile: 'The converse, I suppose, is also true?'

I became preoccupied with turning my potatoes in the fire and so avoided the need to reply. When I glanced up again he was standing over me and still smoking.

'Crime, wealth, what does it matter? We are digressing, I think, from our topic. Australia.'

I said nothing.

'Swagmen and prospectors and – gold!' He spat out this last word with all his force. 'Gold, Jack Spellman. And other precious things – such as opals, my fine young knave, yes: opals!'

At that very moment, burning through the lining of my pocket, lay the girasol ring which I had found in the cave near Wormshill almost two months previously.

'Now then, Mr Jack, would you say – putting your business cap on – that opals were a good thing in their way? Are they sound, Jack? Are they solid? Tell me now, please do.'

I said that I thought that opals, like other precious stones, probably made a very good investment.

'Quite so, quite so lad. Very sensible, very true. You wouldn't say, then – how shall I put it? – that they were divisive? Don't give rise to greed, do they? Jealousies? Not likely to lead men into evil ways, are they? Because I have heard tell that in Australia, which is a savage place where one man's life is led against another's and this one rises at the cost of that one's fall, in Australia – but no, even in such a place! –' And he shook his head from side to side as if to throw off an unpleasant dream.

'In Australia? –' I prompted. It was too late to avoid the subject.

'– There are men who murder for opals.' Pesto looked down at me: 'Must be a folktale.'

An 'undoubtedly' was the only response that I could muster.

'That sort of thing could never happen in good old England, could it?' Pesto disappeared, leaving me with little appetite for my lunch.

A couple of hours later he returned. I saw him bobbing across the meadow at great speed and my heart sank. When he was within a few yards of me, he threw his cigar into the fire and breathlessly took up his theme once more:

'Absolutely fascinating and such an interesting coincidence: I thought I would come and tell you all about it at once, Spellman. I've just been talking in a friendly sort of way to Alf Hagsproat – poor man, he drinks too much, he's falling to pieces – on the very subject of opals. "Alf," says I, "what are they worth then?" And what d'ye think he said? It's the subject of a little homily, it really is: the fickleness of Mammon. "Twenty years ago," says Alf as he takes a swig from his bottle – he has the shakes these days, have you noticed? – "I made me a little ring of gold and opal in Australia. The gold was worth a fair bit then but not as much as now. In those days," he says – listen, Jack: here's the point, "the opal was next to valueless. It was a newish thing and there wasn't the demand for it." "Why did you put it in the ring then, Alf?" I asked. He hummed and hawed a bit before he admitted that it was his woman made him do it. She liked the colours, you see, they pleased her possessive little eye for prettiness. Alf didn't want to do it because a black man had told him that the red opal was bad luck. But his woman said it couldn't be bad luck as long as he loved her, so Alf went ahead and made the ring. The silly old fool got quite sentimental about it all. But guess what, Jack?' He seized me by the shoulder. 'For the same weight of stone now, you'd pay seventy pounds! Now ain't the public such a fickle thing to value that little piece of planet, that tiny jumble of nature's atomies at such a deal of cash?'

Pesto clapped me on the shoulder. 'What a lovely Christmas present that would make, Jack Spellman! Eh? Something to warm your heart in the long evenings.' He ruffled my hair in a tyranny of affection and told me that I was a donkey. Then, with his strange leaping gait, he was off across the meadow in the direction of his caravan where, in the fading light, the workmen were putting away their tools.

'I've got great plans for you,' he called back to me. 'Oh yes, you knave, great plans!'

That night the circus showed the first definite signs of its imminent collapse. Tossing and turning on my palliasse, I was visited by the most peculiar series of dreams. At one point, I remember, I was trapped inside a gigantic paperweight and at another I was fleeing from a nameless pursuer on the back of a nameless animal. Then the scene changed and suddenly I became unbearably hot. I dreamed for a while that I was in a bed in Hell with Pesto beside me and that Pesto was licking my face.

Awaking with a start, I found myself looking into the pale blue eyes of a tiger.

I froze.

In a strange slowing down of time, I saw a droplet of saliva trickle down one of its incisors and hang for an age before it fell, with a tiny *plop*, on my face. It is very odd to know the fear of violent death in one's own bed.

I looked at the tiger. The tiger looked back at me quite calmly but a little possessively. Its great weight was half on top of me and I could feel its coat against my skin. It was clear that the beast had escaped from its cage but why, in particular, it had sought out me I could not imagine. I recognized it as the largest male of the three owned by the circus; it must have been eight feet long and it was muscled like a wrestler. Yet still it did nothing but look at me as the slaver dropped from its jowls.

We must have remained together like this for an hour but such was the clarity of each instant that it seemed far longer. Each minute I thanked God for sparing me so far and prepared myself to face the next. After some time the tiger's head began to droop and sink. Its eyelids closed and it lay its head upon my chest. I could feel its deep slow purr.

If I was to die, I thought that I could claim with some justice to have been cheated. Hadn't Zanzare talked as though I would survive? Yet perhaps this was the fire in the night that he had mentioned; perhaps this was the conflagration which had warmed his dying cheeks. Or alternatively, maybe Zanzare had himself been cheated. Perhaps the ghosts had allowed him to leave their territory clutching a misleading parable, a snaring riddle. All the same, how could one then account for the remainder of his prophecy? Other faces, apparently, and other scenes were to have gathered on the path in front of me.

As you may imagine, Mr Secretary, I had plenty of time and the extremity of stillness in which to ponder these things. The hoarse rumble in the tiger's throat ceased and it fell into a deeper sleep. Sweat trickled from its fur and mingled with my own cold perspiration. I considered calling out to Mimi and Bessie in order that they, at least, could save themselves by climbing out of the window at the far end of the caravan. It was impossible, however, since the slightest sound might wake the beast whose weight was almost stifling me.

It was dawn. Some remarkable compensatory faculty must have enabled me to sleep and so escape for a couple of hours my terror. I awoke to discover that my nightmare, after all, was true: the tiger still slept soundly, its head upon my breast. I remembered that its name was Nico. Nico the tiger.

I heard a tiny noise at the door of the caravan and turned my head slowly and carefully, expecting to see a mouse. No, it was the door itself, which was open to the width of half an inch. Surely it had not been open before? Surely – on these frozen nights – one of us had closed it tightly before retiring? In that case, how had the tiger gained its entrance? My thoughts were again interrupted by the almost inaudible scraping noise and I saw that the door was now open at least three quarters of an inch. Over the next minute, the gap gradually widened. It was a small enough and slow enough movement, to be sure, yet compared with the enforced immobility of the past few hours it seemed as momentous as the toppling of some huge piece of masonry. The gap between the door and the jamb was now a full three inches. With enormous circumspection, a thin metal rod was being inserted into the gap. It took me a few seconds to recognize this object as the barrel of a rifle. My first thought was that somebody had decided to shoot me as well as set wild animals upon me. The barrel of the gun was extended still further into the caravan by some steady but as yet unseen hand.

Nico stirred in his sleep and the barrel hovered motionlessly at the door for a minute or so. At the same gradual pace as before, its owner's hand came into view, steadying the piece against the side of the door. A face could be seen behind the stock and an eye looked steadily along the sights. The face was partially obscured by a peaked cap and the eye was a cold grey; I was familiar with neither.

I had come to the end. Imprisoned by a tiger, I was to be shot down like a dog. I knew that Pesto had done this, that he had somehow found out about the opal ring and decided to take his revenge on Christmas morning, of all days in the calendar.

A last few outbursts of consciousness remained to me. I saw myself, very small and at a great distance, opening a box and taking out a painted horseman.

There was an intensely bright flash. I cannot recall hearing any sound, although of course there must have been a loud report in such a confined space. Everything went white, then black. I wondered if this was how death began. Did the mind continue to function for a while? How long would it be before consciousness failed? I felt moisture spreading over my chest and assumed that I had been shot in the heart. Even now (although, being dead, I could feel nothing) the ventricles were pumping blood into each other and the blood-tide was coursing back upon itself, cancelling out all circulation.

'It's all right, laddie, I got him! First shot!'

For some reason I was able to open my eyes. I found myself looking up into the smiling face of the man who had been holding the gun. This person stooped and, seizing with both his hands the scruff of the tiger's neck, dragged its disfigured carcase away from me.

'First time, eh? Straight through the head. Mind you, I had to finish him off with one shot or he'd probably have taken you with him. I expect a mortally wounded tiger gets a shade truculent.'

Amiably addressing me, the man stood in a widening pool of blood which steamed in the cold air. He turned his cap round in his hand. 'Sergeant Pail. Delighted to make your acquaintance, sir.'

He shook my hand briefly and began to reload his carbine. 'Better not waste any time, sir. Can't tell what might come through that door next.' He peered cautiously outside. 'Seems all right. We'd better get you out of here and over to the joiner's shed with everybody else.'

I managed at last to speak. 'What – what on earth is happening?'

Sergeant Pail pushed me out of the caravan without replying and began to walk me across the meadow at a brisk pace. Snow lay on the ground and the wind whistled fiercely. There was nobody about.

'You've had a practical joker, sir,' he said at last. 'Not very funny, especially on Christmas Day. Released all the animals late last night. Two young women came into the Station about three in the morning. In what we call a state of disarray, sir. Said you had a tiger lying on your chest.'

'That would be Mimi and Bessie,' I interrupted.

'That's right, I think those were their names. Naturally, we didn't believe them, not at first. Professional caution, sir. It was only when we found the lion-tamer that we began to take them seriously.'

'Found him? Where?'

'By a milestone on the Dover road. He was in a bit of a mess.'

'Dead?'

'I'm very sorry sir. Knew him well, did you?'

'No. I –'

'Everybody else is unhurt, as far as we have been able to ascertain.'

We had arrived at the joiner's shed. Sergeant Pail knocked three times on the door and was admitted by a uniformed police officer. As soon as I had stepped inside, Wilf, Alf and Bessie rushed forward to greet me. Pesto growled in a corner. Aramind sat, silent and composed, by his side. Pail approached the officer who appeared to be in charge and who was engaged in taking a statement from Mimi. 'I rescued the young man, Inspector Williams.'

'Good work, Sergeant. What about the tiger?'

'Got him, sir. First time. I think it must have been the big one.'

'The male? Excellent, excellent.' The Inspector called over a young policeman who was clutching some papers and a notebook. 'Right, Billet, you can cross off the oldest male tiger from Mr Pesto's list.'

Billet flicked through his papers. 'Bears . . . buffalo . . . lions . . . tigers. Yes sir, that would be Nico wouldn't it? Twelve years old, eighteen stone?'

'Well, now,' mused Pail who was standing nearby, 'I'm not sure I recall him telling me his age.' The young policeman flushed.

'Enough of that, Pail,' snapped Inspector Williams. 'Come on, Billet. Pull yourself together. Just strike out the senior male tiger. Now, what does that leave us with?'

'Well sir, there's the elephants,' said Billet, sucking at his pencil. 'And the llamas – we haven't found any of them yet.'

'Never mind the llamas. Let's deal with the carnivores first.'

Billet leafed through his papers. 'Certainly sir. We've shot two of the lions, another tiger and one of the wolves. That leaves four lions, three wolves and one more tiger. There's also the leopard, sir – they're very cunning, I believe. That's about it. Oh yes, and the two camels.'

'Herbivorous in any case,' remarked the Inspector.

'One of the camels went missing months ago,' growled Pesto from his corner.

'Very careless,' tutted Sergeant Pail. 'Where was that, may I ask, sir?'

'Norwich.'

'Report it to the proper authorities, did we?'

'No.'

We remained inside the sanctuary of the joiner's hut all that day as the police scoured the meadows and surrounding countryside. We exchanged our Christmas presents under armed guard. Despite Pesto's baleful glare, I received from Aramind (you may remember that I had occasion to mention them earlier on in the story of my life, Mr Secretary) Dickens's

Memoirs of Joseph Grimaldi and the *History of the Stage* by Thomas Dibdin. It could not be said that Aramind was particularly pleased with Pesto's blueprint, which he presented to her, wrapped and sealed, with an exaggerated bow. He slouched sulkily off to his corner, where he could occasionally be heard muttering to himself beneath his breath.

The afternoon was punctuated by the sound of shots. Every hour or so, Sergeant Pail would return to claim another trophy. Some of the circus animals, however, were to survive the police hunt. An elephant was cornered on Boxing Day in the Cathedral graveyard, having earlier drawn attention to itself on the High Street. The llamas joined a herd of sheep and were discovered in a meadow a mile or two from the circus. By the end of Christmas Day, what the Inspector had described as the 'carnivores' had all been killed, with the exception of the leopard which was found dead, twenty miles away, a few days later, and a single wolf which was never seen again. We returned to our quarters at about ten o'clock in the evening, having taken the precaution of loading some of the circus guns to keep by us in our caravans.

With the help of Mimi and Bessie, I managed to drag the tiger outside and mop the floor. My palliasse was so bloodstained as to be unusable and I was forced to lie on a spare blanket. I wrapped it about me, checked the rifle at my side and tried to sleep.

We were destined, however, to have a second disturbed night. At about three o'clock in the morning, we woke to the noise of hammering at the door. It was Wilf; he was in a state of panic.

'Fire! Croop's caravan is burning!'

We rushed headlong into the night. A hundred yards away, great flames rose thirty feet in the air. I was already too late: if anybody remained inside there was not the slightest possibility of their survival. The windows had burst in the heat and incandescent paint dripped onto the wheels. We attempted to put out the blaze as best we could, flinging buckets of snow through the door.

Sergeant Pail and Inspector Williams arrived again at dawn, the sergeant as equable as before. The burned wreckage of Croop's caravan was carefully examined at first light but, to general relief – at least with regard to Aramind – no corpses were found. Neither Pesto nor his wife had met their deaths here. Where, then, were they? The Inspector asked us all a few questions. Nobody had heard anything; nobody had seen anything. The first person to notice the accident, if such it was, had been Wilf, woken from his sleep by a series of sharp cracks as the objects inside the caravan began to explode.

'You heard no domestic disturbance, no arguing or anything like that?' the Inspector asked.

'Nothing.'

The Inspector was clearly irritated. Pail stood nearby and stroked his chin meditatively. 'Perhaps we should commence a search for the couple, sir,' he suggested. 'We could scatter in different directions.' He pointed towards the Broadstairs road and the meadows on the other side of the Stour.

I found Aramind. I had squeezed through the hole in the hedge behind the joiner's shed when I came upon her. She lay motionlessly on a bank of snow and her black dress stood out clearly. I ran over to her, knelt beside her, touched her on the shoulder. She did not move. In hopeless desperation I turned her over and saw that the left side of her face was badly burnt. It was then that her eyes flickered open and she looked at me:

'My face was so hot, father, that I put it in the snow.'

I turned and shouted for the others. As they came running across the meadows, she continued to speak in the same flat and distant voice. 'He said he wanted me to be the core of his hoard, father, the centre of his dead treasure which doesn't move any more, which is where all the dreams and dragons in the world are stored up. He said he'd bought me like a whore and paid a fair price. I was a thing: his concubine. He drew the curtains and made me dance without my clothes on.'

By this time the others had gathered round me. Aramind did not appear to notice them. She started to shiver. Pail put his coat on her shoulders and we led her back across the bridge and through the hole in the hedge to the circus meadow. Mimi, Bessie, Wilf and myself: we all tried to make Aramind tell us what had happened to her the previous night. Despite all our coaxings, however, she would not reply. She only repeated the things that she had already said over and over again and, unless disturbed, would sit gazing at nothing in a sort of trance.

Nothing was seen or heard of Pesto either that day, or the next, or the one after. The police forces of five counties were alerted and the ports were watched but he had simply disappeared. You, Mr Secretary, may – as I – have come to hate him, but since we have no means of punishing him and can hardly hope for the intervention of divine justice, this is a useless exercise. In any case, the blame did not lie with Pesto but with the energies that moved him. He was merely a puppet who wanted to make the world into his circus.

On the twenty-ninth of December, the fastidious figure of Mr Gant was again to be seen in the circus meadow. He carried with him a large and blackened box which had been discoverd by Sergeant Pail amongst the smoking remnants of Croop's caravan. Mr Gant's first act was to dismiss

124

the workmen. Over the previous few days they had loitered about the trenches disconsolately, afraid that, with their master gone, they would not be paid. Somewhat to their surprise Gant gave each one his wage packet. Later, he wandered about the meadow, knocking on caravan doors and asking us to gather in the joiner's shed.

'I expect you will have guessed what I am going to say,' he remarked in his cultivated voice after we had all assembled. He opened the box he had been carrying and took out a number of singed but still legible papers. 'What remains of the circus is to be put up for auction in the spring. This document –' he held it up for our inspection – 'which was signed by myself and witnessed by Mr Pesto on December the twelfth of this year, provides me with executive power should Mr Pesto, for any reason, be absent.'

Mr Gant replaced the document in the box and cleared his throat awkwardly. 'I am afraid to say that your employment with Luigi Pesto's Authentic and Historic Travelling Circus must cease forthwith. I must also ask you to vacate the meadow within the next forty-eight hours. I am empowered to give you all a week's wages.'

Mr Gant looked about him and his gentlemanly distress was evident to all of us; he did not find it easy to act the employer. He took a canvas bag from the box and started to count out our coins. As we began to line up to receive our pay Mr Gant glanced at us through dusty spectacles: 'I am very sorry to be the one to bring you this bad news.'

That afternoon I went to visit Aramind in her cell at the police station. Before I was allowed to see her, however, Sergeant Pail called me into his office. 'She's still not talking, Spellman.'

'Really? Nothing at all?'

'Absolutely nothing. You know, I'm sure I overheard her speaking to you just after you found her. She was muttering something when the rest of us came up, wasn't she?'

'I told you what she said. She thought I was her father.'

'Oh yes sir, of course, I remember now. Of course you told us.' Pail looked at me speculatively across his desk. 'You don't think you could play the same trick again now, do you Mr Spellman?'

'What trick?'

'Well – make her think you're her father.'

I frowned. 'What on earth for?'

'To get her to talk,' smiled Pail patiently. 'To find out what happened, whether this Mr Pesto was involved at all. It won't make any difference to Miss Aramind,' he reassured me, 'she's bound for the asylum whatever happens.'

'Who started the fire Aramind? Was it Pesto?'

She shook her head and clutched the blanket which covered her more tightly. Her burnt face had been dressed and bandaged.

I looked at Sergeant Pail who indicated that I should continue. 'Was it an accident, Aramind? Did you knock a candle over?'

' – '

I took a deep breath and asked the question that I did not want to ask. 'Was it you, my darling? Did you start the fire?'

Her voice was very low. 'Yes father, I started it. I set light to his bed.'

'Why did you do that, my dear?'

'He was asleep, sound asleep. I didn't think he would wake up. I sat in the chair and watched him.'

'But he did wake up, didn't he Aramind?'

She nodded, then bit her lip. 'Father?'

'Yes?'

'I let the animals out as well.'

'Did you, Aramind?'

'Yes. I wanted them to turn on their master.'

Sergeant Pail caught my eye. He had got his evidence. I embraced Aramind but she did not seem to notice me. The sergeant and I tiptoed away, leaving her gazing expressionlessly at the blue sky through the bars of her cell window.

The next day, on the thirtieth of December, the court in Canterbury sat to hear the case of Aramind. She was pronounced clinically insane by a doctor, who had also found her to be pregnant. In the absence of her husband and until further notice she was committed to an institution at Dover run by the Siriso Charitable Trust.

On New Year's Eve, Wilf, Alf, Mimi, Bessie and myself packed our belongings and prepared to leave the circus. We stood at the gate which led into the meadow and looked back on all the years of our past. At that moment the urchin who had brought me the message from Amelia on the morning of Croop's death ran up to me and pressed a letter into my hand. I thanked him and, without further thought, put the unopened envelope into my pocket.

At the railway station, the five of us purchased third-class seats on the London train. It was already dark when our journey began and we had no chance to watch Canterbury slip away from us into the evening; all that could be seen from the windows was an occasional spark shooting through the night. Inside the carriage, the five of us looked blankly from one to the other. Nobody spoke.

We arrived at Victoria Station at about eleven o'clock in the evening. Pushing through the milling crowds outside, Alf managed to secure a cab for us and we all got inside.

'The Plough and Stars Inn, Blackfriars Lane,' I said to the driver. He tipped his cap and motioned his exhausted nag forwards.

As a nearby clock tolled out the last moments of 1889, I rapped with my knuckles three times on the door of the Plough and Stars. It seemed that this noise marked, as much as anything else, the ending of my youth.

Knock, knock . . .

INTERIM

1

Visceral

I<small>T HAS</small> been a long time since we returned to ourselves, Mr Secretary. I am not, in fact, at the door of the Plough and Stars Inn in Blackfriars Lane. I am sitting beside a warm fire, thirty years later, in Bartholomew Square, face to face with you and sipping Madeira wine. We have delved deep into the entrails of the past and I have regurgitated it all for you as best I could. My voice, turned now into typescript, stands in a neat pile on my desk and half my work is done.

I do not know what use it has.

As a hard-bound book, I think, it would make a good replacement for a missing bed leg. At least then I could not be accused of disturbing anybody's sleep.

What faces me now is the little matter of trying to find some junction between the two halves of these walnut memoirs. The circus has been left behind and I am searching for a bridge to cross over into the city. But it is out of character for me to hope for such a clear path: my narrative usually has a more visceral quality. I find myself fascinated, endlessly, by loops and convolutions. When he detects this interest asserting itself, the Recorder sighs sadly and bends lower over his stenographer's pad. At such times he reminds me oddly of Wilf Patchkey.

I saw this look on his face only the other day. When, at length, I enquired whether anything was troubling him, I eventually extracted the doubt which had been lurking in his mind, hedged in as it was by a thousand evasions and an excess of discretion. The Pencil felt that an autobiography of one so unknown as I (you will find me in no biographical dictionaries, I lurk in no lists or registers) needed to enliven it, if not as its *raison d'être*, some account of my meetings with famous men and women.

I was happy to be able to reassure him that these celebrities were drawing nearer by the minute. He looked happy too; we were both happy and we smiled at each other like mental deficients. It was then that he said – the matter had been worrying him for some time – that the work, so far, lacked tension.

I stared at him. 'You mean something to be resolved? A mystery, something like that?'

The Pencil thought for a moment and then said that 'there wasn't a struggle'.

I put my glass down on the table very slowly. So I had not struggled against the black magic which gives some things a ghastly life and wraps our everyday lives? I tried to be patient. 'Wait and see,' I said. 'Wait and see.'

The Secretary may have to wait a little while yet: our progress has been much slower than I had hoped. We started in the middle of March and it is now the end of May. Both the Secretary and I have been ill, of course, and this has delayed us somewhat. The real reason, however, lies in the utterly unforeseen variety of things which has come to light. I feel a sense of urgency because of this; providing we manage to keep up this pace, however, all will be well.

I have now read the manuscript straight through for the first time. I began in trepidation, knowing that the narrated events would be different from those I remembered or those of which I had talked. I almost expected that the story would seem to belong to another. Indeed in a way it did, for I have to say that I was deeply shocked by my own obscenity and want to dissociate myself from it. I knew all along, of course, that I dealt in corruptions but surely none such as these! In future I must watch my tongue and take care not let it stray into libidinous regions, as it has already done so joylessly. I think, however, that I might adduce this lack of joy in my defence. I did not wish to arouse; in any case, writing has neither the necessary flesh nor the friction to attain this end. Tears are the only fluid it can produce.

Nor did I wish to offend either the Secretary or my readers. It is true that I have no respect for prudery, which generally disguises salaciousness. I can only say that such shock as may have been produced could only proceed from an animistic attitude taken towards the word, in which the mention of the phallus, for example, is superstitiously thought to conjure up the thing itself. Although magic is dead, there are some who still wish that the text had a body which climbed upon them in the night. Let me say then, to end the matter, that the erotic sprang without my knowledge like a tiger onto the path which wound widdershins behind me.

Another aspect of the case worries me far more. Naturally, my dictation takes place *in camera* and I can hardly blame the Secretary for taking down my words: it is his job. Yet it deeply disturbs me that I cannot remember having said these things. It seems that the dictator acquires a trance-like attitude of dissociation from the words he speaks, which sound upon the air as if divested of their usual ties. They seem unconnected to the acceptable solidities of things in the outer world.

On the other hand, I also feel that the Pencil has become a fine mimic of my words. His accuracy is such that, upon reading the typescript, I sensed on several occasions that my voice had been stolen from me and even that I had become a sort of doll which he ventriloquized. I comfort myself with the observation that it is never the ventriloquist who is applauded but the puppet which he breathes life into with his speech. Nevertheless, a few days ago these feelings grew so intense that the writing seemed to have something about it beyond parody. The Pencil's style worked too well and cast an inappropriate transparency over everything. It was as if, after all, the parable had turned out to be a concrete history. Perhaps I did not review the Secretary's engagement after the initial probationary period with sufficient seriousness. 'He's not perfect,' I merely thought, 'but he'll do.'

He will do: I am used to him now and shall retain him as my amanuensis until the end.

I would have liked to tell you here that the circus is over and long dead, since it feels that way to me. Did I mention? I went back to the meadows outside Canterbury a year or so ago. Some houses had been built on the land and the view over the Stour to the Cathedral was obscured. I found no remnants of my own past until, about to leave, I suddenly came across the unfinished foundations of Pesto's mansion. At first I had not recognized them because the outlines of the trenches had blurred and the spoil heaps were overgrown with grass. It looked like a village abandoned centuries ago.

No, Mr Secretary, the circus is not dead, although it no longer goes under the name of Mortimer Croop or Luigi Pesto. Its properties were purchased by another circus and now, in other tents, are worked by other hands. Bessie's trapeze supports a different human weight. The dumb-bells are lifted high into the air by a younger Alf. One might conclude, in fact, that all along it was the properties which used us and not we who played on them for our tricks. All the circus people I once knew had long disappeared. The things, however, with a business sense all of their own, had got themselves a new position with servants to keep them in the style to which they had become accustomed.

I stayed in the meadow, on that visit a few months since, until after darkness fell and I was swallowed up in the belly of the night.

To pass the time I began to throw pebbles into one of the choked trenches below. Occasionally they struck, with a small sound, a loose brick.

Tap, tap . . .

2

Pontifical

Tᴀᴘ, ᴛᴀᴘ.
Look, Mr Secretary, down there, the blind soldier with a stick.
There! At the corner of the square, in a khaki uniform with brass buttons
and gaping seams. He is carrying a placard. *'Hungry,'* it says.

Yes, the world has changed since I knocked, thirty years ago, on the
door of the Plough and Stars. The city has changed too, neither for the
better nor the worse: these are relative terms when what we need are
disjunctions. The streets certainly seem wider and less twisted, although
perhaps this is only me.

I said that the knock on the door seemed to signify the ending of my
youth. I would not like you to conclude, however, that I identify the city
with my maturity. Youth, maturity: for me they are words without
connotations. This is not the story of my ethical evolution.

True, Mr Secretary: things are changing. We are approaching the city,
but that does not mean that there is any progress. Not at all. To start again
in the city is just – to employ an inappropriate metaphor – to move into a
new field. Have it, if you like, that this city thirty years ago is a photograph
taken in negative where the circus lights turn into shadows, and *vice versa*.

That soldier down there has stopped moving. How thoughtless of me,
he needs some stuff to eat. Ring for Martha, Mr Secretary. We'll get her
to run across and give him some money. Then, like deities, we can watch
the effect of our investment.

You know what he feels like, the private down there, don't you Mr
Secretary? He feels like an alien, he feels like an exile in his own country.
Naturally he does and with more reason than those who whine that the
heart has been torn out and the language broken. Their precious language! The words they can so well afford! Others say that the war was an
illness from which we will recover. The first ones start complaining that
the borders are coming down and that there is no room left for vagueness
or indecision. The patriots answer that we must work harder for less
money, all for the sake of the nation's health. Whose nation, whose broken
country? Once, it seems – they all agree on this – there was a path which

135

now has dwindled and given out. Yes, yes: but it has always been like that. Optimism was only a stage in a society which was already rotten. The infantine linearities of progress seem to me to be a fantasy projected by those who have forgotten that they are living in transit and that nothing is a pattern for all time.

Some people are trying to hunt down a meaning. They can afford the space in which meaning is possible: the ample living rooms, the leather-surfaced writing-desks. Yes, Mr Pencil (I can see you watching me) just like this room, this pleasant bureau. 'What is the meaning of all this, of life?' they ask. Fools! They ought instead to consider the life of meaning: it is brief, was born but yesterday and will not necessarily be alive tomorrow. 'The light has gone out,' they all protest. There never was a light. 'Dead end,' they moan, unaware of the suicidal tendencies of all ends including their own. Snakes and ladders, say I. Even that has too much structure to represent the contingency we deform into history, that void we fish in for a sign.

Stuff and nonsense, Mr Secretary! Especially stuff. Senseless, inert materiality, mere weight and resistance and difficulty. We make stuff, use it, trade it, but it will not shape itself as we want; it generates conflicting energies. It is only a little later that we find we have given the stuff a dreamlife. We actually think it is alive! Alas! We are the puppets of waxworks. The images on the faces of coins play with us. Dead gold uses up our lives and gold only figures stuff – without the addition of nonsense.

The optimists and meliorists scatter along the street, knocking on all the doors with their progressive schemes. 'It is your birthright,' they pant, spreading in their beneficence a thin paste of happiness over misery. They perpetrate the injustices that anger them so. In their hearts they think that if you are nice to people then they will produce more stuff.

Everybody is looking for a new religion. People's eyes light up: 'Why?' they ask. Always 'why?' They want the clarity of answers, a lamp to lead them back to grandeur. Oh, the nostalgia spouted by those whose lives have been warm and safe! That grand path which brings a tear to their eyes was the golden age of stuff-storing. So much stuff was stored, in fact, that it began to seem worthwhile to bicker about it all and to pour millions of bodies and billions of stuff-symbols away, all in its defence. Stuff makes stuff to seize stuff: that is what happens when the transformations begin.

Unless we end the reign of these totems we will be performing the same dance over and over again to the same queasy barrel-organ music. We must look the images in the eyes and tell them that magic is dead and their mysteries are fictions. We will still be talking to ghosts, of course, but the life of meaning is strong and vigorous: it is hard to tell it that it never existed. Always, in some shadowy corner, the images regroup and multiply with uncanny fertility. We are just bodies, pale and nude. The automata we have made are already far beyond us and the likelihood is that our belief in them will never be overthrown.

I have become pontifical. People will think that I have a dogma to sell. The Pencil already does but he is not sure what it is. Let us leave all this and go down into the streets.

Book II
THE CITY

1

The Plough and Stars

KNOCK, KNOCK . . .

We stood in the icy street and waited for the door to open. The lamps had been lit; the only sound was that of the receding hansom cab. Snow had been shovelled against the walls of the Plough and Stars to clear a path and the pile was studded with a hundred lumps of coal.

'Look,' said Mimi, 'snowmen's eyes.'

Perhaps they had fused together to protect themselves from the city.

It was Amelia who opened the door.

'Jack!' she cried out after a moment's hesitation, 'Jack Spellman!' There was something in her voice beyond mere surprise, a note that I would not understand until much later. She held me in her arms and her fragrance was still familiar after all those years.

I had introduced everybody to each other when Gertrude Desmoulins emerged behind Amelia, as much the neat French gentlewoman as ever. There was another round of greetings and embraces.

Amelia beckoned us in with her hand. 'You are the first to cross my threshold in the new year,' she said. 'You will have good luck.'

In the hallway a low and confused babbling could be heard through the darkness. Amelia opened a door and light flooded into the passageway. At the same time the babble turned into a roar of cheerful voices.

In one corner of the public bar a drunken man with white hair and no teeth stood on a rickety chair and attempted to address the crowd who sat beneath. He swayed unsteadily this way and that. His audience, however, paid no attention to him. They were looking in the opposite direction, where a man and a woman were dancing on a table. Beer spilled from the glasses of the dancers and spattered onto the faces of those below. They did not object to their soaking, however, and merely wiped the droplets from their eyes like tears of mirth. Everybody was drunk. It was almost as if, in the pandemonium, the room itself had become inebriated and had started to spin round in a festive jig. Dogs ran about under the tables and lapped at puddles of beer. In yet another corner – this tap room seemed to be all corners, each one teeming with the details of human physiognomy –

two men were brawling. The surrounding crowd applauded each blow and a great cheer went up when one of the men finally collapsed on the floor with a bloody nose. Amelia moved through it all like a lifeboat through a heaving sea, carrying tankards of beer, trays of bottles and glasses. Gertrude assisted her but although she was evidently in good humour she had the somewhat arch look of a baroness caught in a brothel. It was a great bibulous babel. Within a few minutes, our party of refugees became separated and in different parts of the room we were being winked at, pinched, or bought drinks. People I had never met before kept coming up to me and shouting incomprehensible things in my ears. At length, however, the company began to thin out. There was many an exaggerated 'ssh!' as the customers went out into the quiet street and did their best to assume upright and sober postures.

When the doors closed we followed Amelia and Gertrude upstairs where, in the corridor, an uncanny line of figures met us with fixed gazes. Darwin, Joseph Grimaldi and Charles I: Gertrude's collection of wax-works had found a new home. Through the open door of her room I saw portions of bodies which had never attained the full status of human figures: wax arms and legs, noses of various shapes, a spare eyeball which glinted in the candle-light.

Amelia's room was at the end of the corridor. I was pleased to see her old piss-pot wink at me from beneath the gigantic bed. We sat on the floor and in turns, with many interruptions, told Gertrude and Amelia every-thing about the collapse of the Magnificent Mortimer Croop's Travelling Circus. For the second time I recounted how Pesto had hidden his stolen wealth and how I, by chance, had found the opal ring which I had given to Aramind. I took it out of my pocket and we all looked at it. Silent and apart from us, Alf began to cry. When Bessie crossed the room to comfort him, he held her tight and hid his head in her lap. 'It's all my fault,' he wailed. 'The black man told me that the red opal was bad luck, but I didn't believe him. I thought that love was stronger.' Bessie stroked Alf's hair to quieten him and after some time he fell asleep.

We thought hard that night and at length decided to join forces for the remainder of the winter. We pooled our money on the floor and I threw in the opal ring. Wilf tossed several gold coins onto the pile and we looked at him in astonishment. 'Found 'em under Croop's caravan when I was creeping,' he confessed with some pride. 'Didn't think Pesto would miss 'em.'

This led us all to wonder once again about Pesto. Perhaps what Aramind had said at the police station had been true and, surprised by her attempt on his life, he had fled the circus meadow without retrieving his loose cash. Nevertheless, with the money he had in the bank at Canterbury he was unlikely to starve and the sale of the circus would, in his absence, proceed under the direction of Mr Gant.

What of ourselves? We had enough money to keep us in food for perhaps two months. Amelia offered us three of her rooms free of charge provided that we were eventually able to find other accommodation. If this proved impossible, the hay loft across the courtyard was always at our disposal.

As we lay down to sleep that evening, we all felt, I remember, a provisional security. 'But in the spring,' we were thinking, 'what will happen to us in the spring?' Outside, along winding alleyways, in basement rooms and by the sludgy edges of the river, a million miseries waited for the light of day: one for each heart that beat in the night.

January was a frozen month. Our small pile of savings gradually diminished but none of us, as yet, made a move to find work. Like invalids we needed a period of convalescence and the healing process was slow in the gusting, unforgiving weather. Mimi, Bessie and Alf moved into cheap lodgings across the street from the Plough and Stars whilst Wilf and I spent our nights in the hay loft. Amelia fed us with scraps from her kitchen. Although we lived in poverty there was no longer, amongst us, the old intensity of unhappiness. We seemed to choose as a group to forget the past. There would, I suppose, have been many ways in which to talk of it but to begin would have been to never end. The circus dropped from our conversation, although each night, in my dreams, I was transported across the Downs to Dover and found myself outside the building on the clifftops, searching for the cell where Aramind lay her burnt face on a pillow belonging to the charitable hospice for the criminally insane. I thought of her powerlessness and of the way in which, despite Zanzare's better impulses and death-bed regrets, she had been treated as furniture to be disposed of in his will. Why had Zanzare done this callous thing? Had his hand too, like Croop's, been forced? Had Pesto somehow been able to direct the fall of the dice? In any case, it had come to this: that in a striped grey dress and with a shaven head, a woman lay on her bed and looked off into the distance with grey and vacant eyes. Nurses and doctors moved briskly along the white wards and well-lit corridors. Nobody came for Aramind; nobody answered for her. Her dance had long stopped and there were no more turns on the path ahead by which she might escape her pursuers. There was, however, perhaps one freedom left to her: the freedom not to be a precious jewel, the freedom to scar and vacate herself so that nothing of value was left.

It was the middle of February. Our money had dwindled to a few shillings and we would soon be forced to sell the opal ring. I happened one day to be searching through the pockets of my coat when I came across a crumpled envelope. It was the letter which, six weeks ago, I had stuffed unopened into my pocket in the disordered rush of our departure from the circus.

2

A Tiny Spot of Blood

'DEAR MR SPELLMAN,' the letter began. It was dated the fifteenth of December, 1889:

We have not met but I am familiar with you and there is a possibility that you may have heard of me.

I was returning from a trip abroad in early November accompanied by a friend of mine and my eleven-year-old niece, Elizabeth Tramont. We had docked in Dover early that morning and I was for continuing our journey to London.

My niece, however, noticed the advertisements which publicized your last performance of the season and demanded to be taken to see Luigi Pesto's Authentic and Historic Travelling Circus.

I was in no mood – I rarely am – to refuse her wishes. We put up for the night at Canterbury and attended your evening show.

My ward was enchanted and I feel no shame in admitting that I was too. Elizabeth particularly enjoyed the antics of the pantomime horse, although she protested that the clowns were too cruel to you. After the show, my friend took the trouble to find out the names of that splendid costume's occupants and I stored away your name and that of Mr Patchkey in my memory.

Elizabeth Tramont is to be twelve years old on the twenty-eighth of February next year. I asked her yesterday if she had any particular requests for her birthday party and suggested that she and her friends might like to see a juggler or a conjuror. The mention of the conjuror must have stirred her memory – I remember your Zanzare – for she immediately indicated her desire to celebrate the occasion in the company of a pantomime horse.

Mr Spellman, I am not familiar with the arrangements made

by the companies of travelling circuses for the winter period. I suspect, however, that these are in general impecunious months. Would you and your partner, therefore, care to attend our celebration and mount some small performance for an audience of about a dozen twelve-year-olds?

I take the opportunity of requesting your services so long in advance in case you might make other commitments. I would be pleased to see you at my home address at any time that may be convenient.

Yours sincerely,
Lady Magenta Tramont

I could not believe my good fortune in having paid work presented to me on a plate but I was horrified at the possibility that I might be already too late owing to my long delay in opening the letter.

I rushed across the road to borrow paper and a pen from Gertrude and, in her uncanny museum of a bedroom, surrounded by dismembered effigies, scribbled an ungrammatical reply, my prose style broken perhaps by the anatomical disjunctions around me. I apologized for my delay in answering Lady Magenta's letter, hoped it was not yet too late to make some sort of arrangement and suggested the following afternoon as a suitable time for an appointment. I spent my few remaining coins to have the letter delivered by hand and, a few hours later, received a reply agreeing to the following day's meeting.

When Wilf returned that evening I asked to borrow his best suit, for I did not have one of my own. Although he agreed I could see that his curiosity had been aroused. I showed him Lady Magenta's letter and he at once became inordinately excited. After some minutes I managed to discover that he was already familiar with the name Magenta Tramont.

Wilf was an avid reader of the society columns in any newspapers or magazines that he could acquire. He had carried around with him, on his circus travels, a large number of these out-of-date publications. From time to time he cut out the articles that interested him and pasted them into a large album which he now showed to me. After some hurried leafing back and forth, he pointed out Lady Magenta's profile in a lithograph from one of the illustrated magazines of ten years ago. It had been commissioned to coincide with her twenty-first birthday.

Wilf was certain that Lady Magenta was the daughter of a gentlemen photographer and geologist who had died in the 1870s. She had, he thought, become at one point a minor celebrity for her charitable work with orphaned children. Wilf also seemed to remember that she had been one of the founder members of an organization devoted to the care of such waifs. He could not remember what this charity was called but it had somehow reminded him of the strange names which astronomers give to stars; it had sounded foreign.

We pored once more over the grubby, ancient and fly-spotted illustration. Even through the years' accumulations the beauty of the face had remained fresh. For some reason Lady Magenta had been depicted as Persephone with a cut pomegranate in front of her and a withered bunch of field flowers, her last earthly possession, in her hands.

Next morning I washed myself, shaved, brushed my hair and, having put on Wilf's dark suit, started out across London on foot. The wind carried grit in its icy embrace; all London seemed to be struggling for scraps to feed a withered life. As I neared my destination the buildings became grander and more opulent. The snow had been carefully shovelled from the pavements; brass numerals gleamed on every door. Pollarded plane trees stood around the edges of the square which Lady Magenta had named in her letter and, behind them, great four-storied houses a century old eyed me disapprovingly. I knocked twice on the door of number fourteen and was admitted by a shy but not unfriendly maid who showed me to a beautifully furnished room upstairs, offered me a seat and asked me to wait whilst she informed her mistress of my arrival. The mere maid, with her starched apron and her tightly gathered hair, seemed to me the quintessence of privilege. I felt like a piece of litter blown, in an unguarded moment, through the temporarily opened door.

Lady Magenta came into the room. It was immediately clear that, although she was now ten years older than in the engraving, this picture had done her scant justice. She moved with a grace that seemed like Aramind's dance contained within a single stride and there was the same indescribable melancholy about her. It was not the ennui of the idle classes, however: she greeted me straightforwardly and as an equal. There was not the faintest trace of haughtiness in her manner. I felt immediately at my ease and reiterated my apologies for the temporary loss of her letter. She said that she was sad to hear of the demise of the circus. 'Do you have any plans for the future?' she asked.

'None at all,' I replied. This had accounted for the eager haste in which I had dashed off my note. I hoped that it had made sense. I described the room in which it had been written and suggested to Lady Magenta – as I have already suggested to the reader – that its dismemberments had smuggled themselves into my orthography.

'I am surprised such things disturb you,' she said. 'I have always thought of dismemberment as a somewhat happy state.'

My look of incomprehension must have prompted her to amplify her observation.

'It attracts me – the thought of being free of the body's usual order. My right hand, for example, could write its letters in London whilst my left traces the inscription on a stone at Pompeii. My eyes see clouds passing across Mont Blanc, my ears listen to the final aria of an opera in a concert hall in Paris, my tongue tastes eastern sweetmeats whilst my nose inhales the scent of the Spice Islands. And all the time my legs have been walking the shoreline near Sorrento.' Lady Magenta looked at me and began to apologize. 'I'm sorry, Mr Spellman, it was a rather far-fetched conceit.'

'And your hair,' I said impulsively, 'your beautiful hair on a model of Persephone at Madame Tussaud's on the Marylebone Road!'

Such a strange knot of memories gathers here, Mr Secretary! My mention of Persephone has quite disconcerted me and broken my stride. I had not recalled that comment in thirty years. This therapy of dictation must calm me and allow the lost details to re-emerge like shy forest animals after the hunter has passed. Yes, they are timid, these creatures, these various Persephones. Yet how they complicate things as they twist the phantasmic umbilicus which stretches behind me into the dark.

Wait a moment; hold steady and wait. Surely, amongst the shifting shapes and shadows, surely some fine suture can be seen, a threadlike parting on the seemingly so seamless screen. We have only to wait patiently and the split will widen. Then, like Bilharz's Egyptian flatworm, we can select the most minuscule point of entry into that host we shall henceforth consume with pious greed.

Lady Magenta passed off my presumptuous remark with good humour and took no offence. She did not allude to the connection between my reference to her and the society portrait in the illustrated magazine. Perhaps she had simply forgotten: the lithograph had, after all, appeared many years previously. What details, even of my own existence, could I myself claim to remember after such a lapse? For everything is forgotten and lost in that night.

My interlocutor turned to the subject of our meeting. Elizabeth Tramont's birthday was only a week hence, since today was the twenty-first of February. Lady Magenta was worried that in so short a time I would be unable to make the necessary preparations. I reassured her by saying that my ten years in the circus had, if nothing else, taught me the art of improvization.

She understood; she was sympathetic; she passed a hand across her hair, which glowed darkly in the dim light; she was elsewhere. Then she coughed convulsively and perhaps for half a minute into a handkerchief: a dry, hollow cough the like of which I had never heard before. I suppose that I was solicitous for her health, but she brushed aside my questions: it was only winter, a London winter, the filth of a London winter. As she slipped it back into her sleeve, I noticed on her handkerchief the tiniest spot of crimson or, darker than that, of carmine. It was the only colour in the long, dusky room, the only distinct sign.

She asked me what arrangements needed to be made. I was nervous, being unused to playing the part of the actor-manager. I wondered whether, besides Wilf and myself, there might be some part for Mimi, Bessie and Alf. Lady Magenta assented: certainly this would be a good idea; it was up to me to communicate with my colleagues. Did I need any particular equipment? I thought a little before replying in the negative, having decided then and there to revisit the winter quarters of the circus at Canterbury in order to retrieve whatever properties might be necessary. Mr Gant had said that the circus was to be auctioned off in the spring and I doubted whether, as yet, anything would have been removed.

'Would you like to look over the room I have in mind, Mr Spellman?' asked Lady Magenta. 'It is, I think, the most suitable venue in the house.'

We left by another door than the one through which I had been shown in. By walking the length of a long passageway at the rear of the house we reached a second, smaller staircase which led to the scullery and the kitchens. In this latter room the maid was polishing certain pieces of brass and silverware, amongst them one in particular of a most unusual design. It was, I think, some pasha's hookah enamelled in vermilion, with extensive filigree work representing scrolls and strange plants. We crossed the kitchen and the shy domestic watched us from the corner of her eye. Lady Magenta threw open a door and invited me to precede her. I found myself in a vaulted conservatory which rose almost to the full height of the house. Around the walls, under the great panes of glass, dark and mossy tanks were set into the floor and I could hear the slow drip of water. A breeched and booted figure who I took for a gardener stood at a distance attending to some orchids which sprouted from a terracotta pot.

It was then, as I looked about me, that I began to notice orchids everywhere. Great masses of these strangely shaped flowers basked aloft in the warmth and humidity. Others bloomed in pots which stood on pedestals of marble or porphyry. Every shade of red and blue was represented here: carmine, vermilion, scarlet, indigo, cobalt, mauve, crimson, maroon, mazarine, violet and purple. One looked in vain for white and yellow. It was almost necessary to search for green, so scantly, it appeared, was this colour valued. Between the urns of flowers stood classical statues. In one corner, a vine stretched its questing tendrils towards a bunch of stone grapes which depended from the hand of a marble Dionysus.

'This,' said Lady Magenta whilst I remained, speechless, at her side, is what my father used to call the Red Room.'

'I have never,' I said at last, 'trod on such a stage.'

Lady Magenta did not seem to hear me. 'My father,' she continued, 'was a great collector of orchids. They were the only plants, I think, that he truly loved. He fed them and bred them and, occasionally, put them to death.'

I hesitated. 'There is something – how can I put it? – unnatural about them.'

'Oh, yes,' she agreed. 'They are entirely the products of cultivation.'

'But don't you find them – grotesque? Monstrous?' The flowers had an animalism which one did not normally associate with vegetable life. Although dressed in the lurid colours of a vibrant life, however (it was as if blood, not sap circulated through their veins) these plants were more vulnerable than even the most fragile blooms of our temperate woodlands. I looked about me and remarked that a frost would be fatal here.

My companion pointed to some ducts of about the thickness of a man's leg which ran round the walls of the hot-house. 'The pipes heat the air,' she said. 'It takes as much coal to heat this room as it does to heat the rest of the house. The pipes ensure that the temperature remains constant to within a degree or two's margin. Orchids are so fussy, so delicate. I continue to care for them,' she added, 'because of my father. He died many years ago but I know that he would have wanted it.'

By this time, walking slowly, we had reached the far end of the conservatory. Before speaking, Lady Magenta tightened the catch on a window. 'Tell me, Mr Spellman,' she said at last, 'do you think you could do anything with this room?'

'Absolutely anything,' I laughed. 'Words are completely beyond me. This is the circus in miniature: it has all the qualities I could ask for.' I pointed to the other end of the building. 'Look, your ladyship, look: we can seat the children over there. And the door behind us is a perfect stage entrance. Does it lead back into the scullery? It does? Excellent.'

Everything was decided; everything was perfect. All that remained, over the next week, was a considerable amount of hard work.

In the scullery the maid had finished polishing the hookah and started on the cutlery. We returned to the reception room; it was four o'clock. Lady Magenta took a small silver key from her pocket and unlocked a mahogany escritoire which stood against one wall. She withdrew a velvet bag from one of the drawers and handed it to me, saying that she was prepared to provide further funding if the need arose but she thought that for the present this would suffice. It certainly would. I looked inside the bag and saw at a glance more than double the amount I had been prepared to ask for. This would keep my friends and me for another two months. I told Lady Magenta that her generosity was excessive but she would have none of it. I had one final worry. Would her niece not find a circus without clowns somewhat dull?

'She hates clowns,' was my answer.

It sounds a little grandiose, I know, but the next decade began that morning. Here, Mr Secretary, is where my narrative closes one of its circles, for the room in which my voice sounds now is the one in which I first met Lady Magenta. Yes: it happened in Bartholomew Square. Outside, at the back of the house, is the conservatory which was once so full of orchids. Perhaps I will show it to you one day, when our work is over and the manuscript is bound. We will go out through that door and along the passage which stretches the width of the house. We will descend the second and smaller staircase and pass through the kitchen. The shy maid has gone but Martha will be sleeping in front of the fire. I will force open a door and invite you to precede me.

Outside: a bleak, chill light. The heating ducts have fallen from their supports onto the ground; the tanks are dry; broken glass scatters the floor. Over there lies the remains of a stage, riddled with rot and spattered with bird shit. Here, a broken terracotta pot. There, an ageing Dionysus who looks down, without grief, on the sarcophagus which stands in the centre of the room. The grapes have dropped from his hand, the frosts have cracked the statue and the tomb. And over here, Mr Secretary, brushed into a corner maybe twenty years ago, the single, parched flower of an orchid whose colours have long since faded.

3

An Unfortunate Accident

THE NEXT day, Wilf and Alf caught an early train to Canterbury, delighted that our period of inactivity had come to an end. Before leaving the circus at the end of the previous year, they had locked most of the properties into the joiner's shed and so they expected to find everything intact upon arrival.

For my own reasons I did not accompany them. To have returned to the circus would have brought back too many memories of Aramind. At that time I did not want to see the jumbled meadow ever again.

On the evening of the twenty-third of February I was sitting in Amelia's bedroom in the Plough and Stars when I heard the rumble of a cart in the lane. Alf and Wilf had hired a waggon which was filled with tools, coloured balls, lengths of canvas, musical instruments, ropes, wires and everything else which furnishes the materials of our trade. The pantomime horse had been flung over the rattling goods to protect them from the rain. Fortunately it had deteriorated little during it spell in the joiner's shed. There was only a slight smell of mildew to add to its other aromas.

'The "For Sale" signs are up,' said Alf as he took out his dumb-bells.

Wilf beckoned me to one side. He told me that in a corner of the shed, hidden beneath the horse suit, he had discovered the skeleton which Pesto's workmen had unearthed whilst digging the foundation of his madhouse. 'There were two guineas in the eye sockets, Jacko. I'm sure we never left it like that.'

I was sure too. We speculated that Pesto had planted a mocking clue for us but we decided not to tell our companions.

That afternoon, in the hallway at Bartholomew Square, Lady Magenta gave us two keys. One enabled us to enter by the rear gateway; the other fitted the lock of the hothouse door. My friends were as delighted as I had been with our new stage. On that first day, we would occasionally stop in our hammering and sawing to admire once again the peculiar appropriateness of our surroundings. We put up a stage with a curtain and a winding device; we stretched a tightrope ten feet above the ground.

Lady Magenta was little seen during the days that followed. On the day preceding Elizabeth Tramont's birthday party, however, she came to inspect the progress of our work. Although he had briefly met her on his first day at Bartholomew Square, Wilf stood before Lady Magenta in undisguised awe. His mouth fell open and his eyes drank in her presence. His dog-eared illustration had stepped from the page, but he was far too shy to speak.

Whilst her niece played amongst the stage props and chattered excitedly to Alf, I mentioned to Lady Magenta that, in harmony with our surroundings, we had thought of performing a pantomime set in the jungle. It would be easy, with a little dye, to convert the pantomime horse into a tiger. Mimi had already made a papier mâché head for the beast. Lady Magenta put a finger to her lips and glanced in Elizabeth's direction. 'No,' she said, 'no, I think not. Elizabeth's father – my brother – was killed last year, you see, in India, by a tiger. The poor child still has nightmares.'

'Ah, I see.' I felt clumsy. 'Of course not. A tiger would be very inappropriate.'

The evening of the birthday party arrived and everything was ready. Between us we had patched together a little script and learnt our speeches. Our new story was a version of the Piramus and Thisbe playlet from *A Midsummer Night's Dream*. We had taken out the lion and expanded the part of the ass, played, of course, by the pantomime horse. For the wall which divides the two lovers we had substituted a curtain. Bessie, on her tightrope, was to play the part of Diana on Olympus. As we assumed our make-up and costumes and peered through the coin-sized aperture in the stage curtain at the gathering children we were all, I think, more nervous than on previous performances. The lights were dimmed and we played our part.

Afterwards, Lady Magenta brought Elizabeth over so that she could thank us in person. Clutching her aunt's hand, the little girl dropped a curtsey which humbled us all. It had not been a particularly fine performance: we had lacked the cruel spark of the clowns. Lady Magenta asked us to join her in the drawing-room. We climbed the stairs with trepidation, hearing a cultivated conversational hum ahead of us. Passing through the opened double doors, we came into a great, well-lit space where groups of besuited gentlemen talked to ladies in silk dresses. On tables stood vases of dried flowers which had been dyed purple; two chandeliers threw their faceted glitter onto the clinking glasses.

This was my first experience (although Joseph Grimaldi, for one, had preceded me) of the odd privilege granted in certain circumstances to the performer. For sometimes and in certain places those that follow my profession are granted access to riches and can cross for a few minutes, for an evening, the thresholds of class. We are given a limited licence to mingle with titled reticences and noble cultivations. We were all unused to this. For some reason I was tacitly elected our collective voice. I answered questions; I tried to be polite; I felt most uncomfortable. Lady Magenta did not notice my awkwardness but others, I am sure, did their polished best to accentuate it.

A lean, pale gentleman approached and introduced himself to Bessie. Amongst the murmur of voices I did not catch his name. It was then that Wilf tugged at my sleeve and pointed wordlessly across the room. There, in a dark frame on the wall, was the portrait of Lady Magenta whose reproduction in a yellowed cutting had so fascinated Wilf and myself a week ago. The lean gentleman smiled down on Bessie and began to toy with a lock of her hair. His face was a ghastly white and he looked as if he had only just recovered from a long illness. I noticed that Mimi could barely restrain her irritation and judged that it was time to make our exit.

Having said farewell to Lady Magenta at the drawing-room door, I turned towards the stairs and met with a most unfortunate accident. I was carrying the horse-suit over my arm when I suddenly felt it brush against something. In my instinctive recoil I somehow succeeded in knocking a large wooden object from a pedestal which, stupidly, I had not previously noticed. There was an immediate hush. Lady Magenta was already protesting that I should not worry and need not apologize when the saturnine gentleman who had approached Bessie stooped to the floor and picked up the object I had dislodged.

'The lens, at least, has not been broken,' he commented. 'It should be possible to repair the casing.' He indicated the extent of the damage with an elongated finger. 'See, it needs only a little veneer work. Any experienced cabinet-maker could repair it.' His tone was balanced and measured; he pronounced his 'r's in an unusual way; he was completely the master of the situation.

I was suddenly seized by the strangest impulse and felt as if it was only now and not an hour ago that I had stepped onto a stage. Moving forward and taking the damaged object in my hands I said that I myself could mend it. I had been my father's apprentice and had not forgotten his trade.

The pale gentleman raised an eyebrow and looked at me disapprovingly. 'A carpenter and a clown? Well, well: you are indeed a jack of all trades.'

Lady Magenta intervened: 'There's no need to be gruff, Sir Rodney.' She looked across at me and smiled: 'I am afraid, Mr Spellman, that this joyless man claimed to be bored by your circus.'

'You do me a grave injustice, Lady Magenta!' Sir Rodney demurred. 'I was enchanted with Luigi Pesto's circus. The performance itself, it is true, was unbearable. But I enjoyed strolling around and peeping into the tents: the sight of honest poverty is always amusing.'

Lady Magenta put out her hand to say goodbye. 'Thank you for your offer, Mr Spellman. You shall mend our camera: you shall go away and mend it.'

4

The Secret Life of Colours

THERE IS no clear beginning to dye and so, as usual, I must mix up false starts and web my way without a clue.

I would like to introduce you to Mr W.H.Perkin – Sir William as he became. You may have heard of him, Mr Secretary: his death in 1907 was much obituarized. He was an idiosyncratic man, a pioneer: the briefest death notice would have told you that. Before your time? You surprise me. Surely? Not even as a boy? No?

Well, I will tell you.

Mr Perkin's discipline was chemistry but I think that a drop of the old alchemists' blood ran in his veins, the faintest tinge of the charlatan, the confidence trickster. At any rate Lady Magenta's father, Lord Tramont, had confidence in Perkin: he lent the charming youth the sum of two thousand pounds for purposes of research into deriving colours from coal or, to put it more precisely, coal tar.

Do not imagine for a moment that Tramont was duped: Perkin was not Giuseppe Grimaldi. His new dance may have started off as the Sorcerer's Apprentice but it soon turned into the Goose that Laid the Golden (or in this case Indigo) Egg. Perkin was able to repay his noble friend many times over. Tramont extended the loan in 1856, shortly after the fall of Sevastopol and his return to England. He had not fought in the war, having gone out to the Crimea solely in order to take photographs.

I imagine that Mr Perkin took the money with a young man's ingratitude. He purchased his ingredients and settled down to his mixing and stirring. He was only eighteen years old at the time. Either Tramont was remarkably perceptive, which I doubt, or Perkin communicated an authority and inspired a confidence beyond his years. Tramont was twice his age but believed wholeheartedly in his charismatic protégé. The youth had a fixed look in his eyes: he was so disenchanted with the things of the world that one could be certain he would conjure up something new or sink into a hopeless obscurity. That was the way that Tramont put it anyway, according to Lady Magenta, who had these drawing-room tales from a talkative governess.

At the age of fifteen, Perkin had enrolled as a student at the Royal College of Chemistry. His father, a builder, had wanted his son to apprentice himself to an architect. Since his own father had been a bricklayer, this seemed a natural refinement of the paternal line. But Perkin *fils* saw things differently. Although ambitious, he was more interested in the sophistication of matter than of his genealogy.

Tramont shared Perkin's fascination. His lordship was essentially a dilettante; a keen amateur geologist and palaeontologist, he had a couple of articles to his name in the learned journals. In 1849, in sand layers at Hunstanton, he had discovered the fossilized remains of an extinct species of mollusc of the genus *Murex*. His residence, number 14, Bartholomew Square, was filled with specimens of ore-bearing rocks from mines and quarries all over the world.

They talked, I imagine, Perkin and Tramont – the one a novice and the other an amateur – of matter: its peculiar varieties and its odd qualities, the extracts that it yielded. Tramont, charmed, wrote out a cheque for a considerable sum of money to a man he barely knew. His lordship had been married less than a year. There were some who warned him that his happiness was making him over-generous.

Despite his natural arrogance, it must have been a worrying time for the young Perkin. After all, his first major scientific project had been an unmitigated disaster. In the previous year, he had failed utterly to synthesize quinine. This was not surprising: the goal was ridiculously ambitious and had already eluded scientists more brilliant than he. Perkin had therefore turned his attention from attacking the income of the South American peasant growers of cinchona, the bark of which shrub yields quinine, to undermining the livelihoods of the Indian exporters of natural indigo cakes.

I am in a position to tell you, Mr Secretary, that Perkin has now succeeded. Twenty years ago, the value of indigo imports outstripped the value of artificially produced indigo by a factor of four. Last week I noticed in the newspaper that the synthetic variety has now almost completely displaced the natural and swallowed the market.

Perkin, with his fund of confidence, toiling in his laboratory day after regular day, remained calm. He tested the effect of treating aniline sulphate with bichromate of potash. The precipitate, aniline black, was susceptible to separation. This, then, was ! w aniline blue, otherwise known as mauve, first saw the light in the year 1856. To be fair, mauve had already been derived from a variety of lichen by Dr Stenhouse in 1848 but Perkin's product was the real thing: an entirely derived, purely artificial aniline dye. Perkin took his results in their liquid form to an immediately excited Lord Tramont, who saw himself already as an aristocratic patron, a Medici of industry with a Leonardo of dye in his employ.

To the great annoyance of the housekeeper, Perkin called for a white linen sheet and poured the contents of his flask onto it. He allowed the beautifully coloured stain to spread and be taken up by the fibres of the cloth. When all the liquid had been absorbed, Perkin held the sheet up to the light. Lord Tramont was as silent with wonder as if he had just been shown a fresco. The housekeeper, standing to one side, sniffed contemptuously.

Two weeks after this incident Lady Tramont gave birth to her first child. The baby girl was duly baptized Mauve and, despite the house-keeper's violent protests, the stained sheet did office as the baptismal gown. The following year, again with Tramont's help, Perkin set up his dye works at Greenford Green near Harrow. The name was inappropriate since green would never issue from this factory. Perkin registered his company and set up a sign at the factory gates: 'Imperial Dyes Ltd.'

In 1858, Lady Tramont produced a son. Perkin and his lordship, again entrusted with the problem of nomination, pondered long and hard. The lad was eventually christened Ronald Indigo Orlando and their choice was politely applauded. Ronald porphyrogenite, one might risk, for the dyes were just beginning to bring in an income. Ronald born in the purple to inherit aniline, usurper of indigo. Ronald born with the Viceroyalty out of the death of the East India Company.

A few months later, on New Year's Eve, Lord Tramont gathered together his family and servants. Champagne was poured and, as the clock began to chime, Mr Perkin, who had naturally been invited to the celebration, raised his glass and proposed a toast.

'To dye!' he cried.

'To dye!' they all responded. Even the dour housekeeper was seen to sip from her shining glass.

What would the new year bring?

It was the best of years and the worst of years; the year of wisdom and of foolishness; the year of a clear, bitter drug and a deep, sweet dye; the year of a searing light and the year of a smothering darkness.

In a canoe half a world away from London, the botanist Richard Spruce struggled against the current of the Rio Pastaza, that mighty tributary of the still mightier Amazon. He bore with him a letter from Her Majesty's Secretary of State for India which had been procured for him by Sir William Hooker at Kew Gardens. The letter instructed him to secretly gather and to remove from their natural habitat the fertile seeds of the plant known to science as *Cascarilla roja*.

Spruce was a keen cryptogamist but a reluctant criminal. Many a time he was tempted to stop and examine in more detail the luxuriant mosses which were the love of his life. Nevertheless, suffering from bloody catarrhs and guided by headhunting Jiraro tribesmen, he ascended the Rio Puyu and pushed onwards into the Rio Bamba. Threatened by revolution in nearby Ecuador, he had little time to perform his task, which was made doubly difficult by ravenous ants and caterpillars.

It was then that a second man arrived on the scene. Clean-shaven and dressed, apparently, for nothing more strenuous than a game of tennis, Clements Markham (later President of the Royal Geographical Society) carried with him two dozen Wardian cases. These were to provide a more secure environment for Spruce's nibbled seeds. Within two months, Spruce was travelling downstream on a balsa wood raft with a hundred thousand germs of *Cascarilla roja* in his possession. Reaching Manaus, he was to hear with great sadness of the death of Baron Alexander von Humboldt, the father of Amazonian exploration: Humboldt, much beloved of Charles Darwin, who had taken the *Voyages* with him on the *Beagle*. It was perhaps fortunate for Richard Spruce that Mr Perkin had turned his attention from quinine to coal tar. For *Cascarilla roja* is more commonly known as cinchona and yields the most powerful natural tonic and febrifuge known to man.

As the miraculous seeds began their voyage across the Atlantic, Lord Tramont and Mr Perkin began to reap the rewards of their three years' collaboration. In June 1859, however, before the twenty-one-year-old Perkin conjured up another dye, two battles were fought in Italy. The first of these occurred near a small town called Magenta, which lies approximately mid-way between Novara and Milan. It was a remorseless and rather bloody struggle. Supported by the French, the Sardinian forces eventually defeated those of Austria. Outside the walls of Magenta there stands to this day a commemorative ossuary which contains the picked bones of nine thousand men and, to my knowledge, at least one woman: Luigi Pesto's mother, Zanzare's mistress, the witch struck down by a stray bullet as she gathered herbs on the battlefield. It was Magenta that determined Zanzare and Pesto to leave Italy. The ambitious Piedmontese, they realized, spurred on by Cavour and Orsini, were for the moment more concerned with *panem* than *circenses*.

And so, in the year when things went two by two, Perkin commemorated a battle with an artificial flower and named his new blue-red dye Magenta. So also did Lord Tramont baptize his wife's third child. It was a good name. Like the best names of all, its origins would be lost in obscurity. It was a better name than Solferino, for instance, which was the site of the second battle in the War of Italian Unification. Solferino too gave birth to a colour, and also to an organization. For it was here that Henri Dunant was marked for ever by the carnage of war. It was here that he decided to found the Red Cross.

Whilst Dunant travelled across Europe in his attempt to succour the sick and the dying, Charles Darwin talked more clinically of the survival of the fittest. It might be said – perhaps we stretch the point – that his *Origin of Species* painted a picture of nature red in tooth and claw. On the hills and in the plains, from the wide seas to the distant islands and from the beginning onwards to the end of time, surplus populations struggled for survival and brothers died that their brother's sons might live.

A death which made for life; a paralysis which burst the seeds of change. Blue against red: in Karl Marx's *Critique of Political Economy* the forces of money and the forces of labour were locked together in the logic of history. All this as John Brown led his rebellion of negro slaves against the white men who held the arsenal at Harper's Ferry and began a civil war.

It was the year of empire and of revolution. It was the year that a flying trapeze swung between them for the first time, now this way, now that, ticking the double beat of history. It was also the year that Blondin crossed the abyss at Niagara on a tightrope, the year that de Lesseps began to drive the cleft of Suez between Africa and the near east, the year that John Brown was hanged by his neck.

Between these doubles, in the midst of these battles, a colour and a drug, a forgery and a theft. Two liquids, two movements: life-bitter quinine from the Amazon to the Indus; death-sweet aniline replacing the Indus with the Thames. Can we make a triangle? Find some third term? Not at all. Later, however, there is a second theft: of rubber.

The following New Year's Eve Mr Perkin and Lord Tramont could have toasted their success in Erasmus Bond's Aerated Quinine Tonic Water, which had been patented but a few months since. What the glasses held on that particular occasion is not, however, recorded.

Time went on and money accumulated. Perkin erected new sheds on the land belonging to Imperial Dyes at Greenford Green. He bought giant ceramic vats to mix his colours in. The value of the company's shares doubled, and then doubled again.

The year 1869 looked like being another *annus mirabilis*. Another dye was well on its way and Lady Tramont was big with child: the partnership was again working its magic. The successful synthesis of Alizarin, however, produced only a ten-day companionship with the child of the same name. The little girl died of cyanosis; Lady Tramont sickened and a month later also passed away.

Lord Tramont was inconsolable. He travelled the world but he could not leave his grief behind. Towards the end of this period, during one of his increasingly brief returns to Bartholomew Square, he decorated much of the house in Perkin's sombre colours. Magenta's governess speculated that his lordship was preparing for a longer stay. She was the only member of the household who seemed able to soften his features into a smile and the housekeeper, whose manner had if anything hardened with age, shook her head knowingly at every opportunity. Nothing came of it: a couple of months later, Lord Tramont died suddenly at the early age of fifty-four. It was 1874; Magenta Tramont was fifteen; I, Mr Secretary, was ten.

Mauve was confined to an institution shortly after her father's death and committed suicide in 1880. Ronald Indigo was mauled to death by a tiger whilst travelling in the upper reaches of the Indus Valley. Magenta thus entered into the hereditary title and full possession of her father's mansion in Bartholomew Square, together with a considerable legacy. She was a rich woman but she felt as if she were rowing in an open boat on Acheron, river of woe. The Amazonian orchids, the red room, the statues collected during her father's travels in Italy, Greece and North Africa, the paintings, the collection of photographs, the cameras and photographic equipment, the geological specimens, the eclectic library: all belonged to her. She wandered the house for weeks, thinking of her father and of all the deaths that had enriched her.

The housekeeper died. In a drawer in her bedroom, Lady Magenta discovered Mauve's baptismal gown folded neatly away. The dye that Perkin had spilled enthusiastically from his flask, one afternoon thirty-three years ago, was faded now and looked like an old blood-stain.

Black and red and blue: her father and Mr Perkin had omitted white and yellow. Every shade and hue of black and red and blue but no tints of grey and green, no ochres, oranges or earths. Only with great generosity and a leap of the spirit could we allow that aniline, through coal tar and coal, retains at a fossilized distance, over a crevasse of aeons, some link with vegetal green.

William Perkin remained a close friend of Magenta's through all these catastrophes and became to some extent an honorary father. Sir Rodney Rouncewell, an erstwhile colleague of Lord Tramont's, was a more avuncular but no less attentive figure.

Perkin's career grew in distinction. During the early 1870s, whilst his aristocratic patron mourned his wife and found no tranquillity, Perkin – aided now by two assistants – began a series of investigations into anthrapurpurin. In 1879 he received a medal from the Royal Society to reward his work. His love of music was well known and he collected instruments from all the countries of the world. In his spare time he attended concerts with his friends or invited them to recitals of chamber music at his house in Harrow. Lady Magenta accounted his violin playing better than that of any amateur she had ever heard: it was like a rendering to the ear of his soft, sad colours.

Perkin became President of the Chemical Society in 1883 and was knighted in 1906 on the fiftieth anniversary of his production of mauve. He died at his home near the dyeworks on 14 July 1907. At the end of June he had returned from Rome a desperately sick man, having contracted hepatitis by drinking polluted water.

Yes, Magenta was the first beginning to spring up in my path. The camera was the second: it lassoed the decade ahead even as I held it in my hands and watched Lady Magenta smile as she spoke: 'You shall mend our camera, Mr Spellman: you shall go away and mend it.'

Or was it rather Persephone, hung upon a wall, discovered in an album, who sprang all this upon me?

Magenta is not a natural colour, Mr Secretary: it blooms like the winter flowers in Giuseppe Grimaldi's garden. There is something sinister about it, as if dye evokes death. I confess myself consumed by figured comparisons. Did you realize that likeness begins, at least etymologically, in death? Each likeness threatens us with the discovery that appearance is a mere image: a corpse, a phantasm.

The deployment of colour is generally called painting. The effect of painting is to multiply the number of likenesses in the world. Any such multiplication immediately starts up uncanny resonances and echoes. It is important to understand this uncanniness now, for at some point in the future the world will be populated solely by images.

What happens when an artist, exhausted after his labours, stands back to look at a finished painting? In a corner, his model drowses on a sofa. He makes a move across the room to wake her, to pay her, to fasten the buttons on her dress. Then, in front of his canvas, he pauses. His appraising eye moves from the picture to the woman and back again.

Doubleness has entered the scene. The picture's flesh is his model's flesh, its hair is her hair, its shape resembles the shape on the sofa. There is, however, also a difference here. In life, the model drowses and the painter can hear her soft respiration. In his picture, on the other hand, she looks at him with an eye still bright, alert, full of desire. The painting, which has begun in the deployment of mere stuff, has ended by promoting a spectral illusion which has the force of another life.

This originally base and still to some extent imaginary life is dead, but in every studio the images continue to multiply with a fertility in comparison with which our fleshly lusts are feeble. Paints, pens, brushes, canvas and paper. Colours written in water: we trace out the lines and tones until stuff gives, magically and equivocally, like shadows dancing on cerements, the appearance of life.

If dye evokes death, it also calls up a die. To use colour is to throw dice which always turn up deuces. Worried by these things, Socrates sought about for an original criminal. He found his counter-Prometheus in Thoth, the god who played draughts with the moon in order to win extra days for the birth of Osiris. It was Thoth who invented dice and who allowed myths to be born by giving us writing so that we should not forget. When did it all go wrong? Was our original sin mimetic, mnemonic or simply ludic?

It is hard to stop once you have begun. To begin is to enter the unstable realm of likenesses, where every colour is prone to mixing and every rhetoric solicits your investment. The charade will never end because, although secondary, many likenesses survive their originals. The portrait outlasts its sitter with a tenacity which characterizes only the most malevolent of fleshly parasites.

I have come to a point where I am subject to the strange fear that paint alone is solid. Life, ideas: they pass. When I put out my hand I find nothing but stuff surrounding me: pieces of parchment or papyrus, flesh or grass which we disfigure with tattoos like cannibals. Colour is a drug which makes us dream that there is something there. I have become frightened that when I go out into the world, I will meet, everywhere, only a death which survives me. There is nothing real in this city, only million upon million shaded simulacra. Every object is labelled in this vast museum, but the labels refer to nothing.

The world has become a veil to me. It is a costume, a painted face with no flesh beneath. There is no possibility of nakedness. Colours are free, like scarves and ribbons. Is there anything there? I feel as if I am table-rapping. Can we have things in black and white? Can we clear away these misty figures and see hard forms underneath, lit up by the white light of truth? Unfortunately, optics tells us that white, too, is suspect. It is a compound of all the other colours, the most impure light of all. All paints run, stains spread, cosmetics blur, dyes bleed into each other. Unfixable, ungovernable liquids, there is nothing to contain them. How can you master the play of reflection, refraction, distortion and interruption? Particles of pigment shift endlessly, lifelessly, in their liquid medium. Nothing is pure. Everything is adulterated. Order is an incident of chaos.

In this circus of sham and feint and cover, there is, perhaps, another reason why paint and dye are suspect: they have such odd sources. Can anything incontrovertibly good arise from nature's more extravagant oddities? The cochineal insect, for instance, has given us carmine, crimson and purple lake. An insect, Mr Pencil! And a lichen produces natural mauve! Indigo and saffron lurk in strange fleshy plants. The molluscs *Purpura* and *Murex* yield dye and in the armoured world of the crustacean there is also a pageant of colour. It plays a central role, too, in the lives of soft cephalopods: squids secrete black ink, cuttle-fish squirt sepia. Flowers, roots and ores; alien versions of earth and underearth, world and underworld.

This is where Persephone comes in again. She made all this multiplication possible, although she is hardly its perpetrator. Blame Hades, blame Demeter, or Zeus, or Ascalaphus: it is more their fault than hers. But it is she who has been persecuted as the one who destroys the light, who sinks into a frozen silence with her blue-grey eyes, her eyes of Persian blue.

Persephone stands quietly in the middle of our myth, stands with a quietness that is like the purple stain of twilight, like a shadow cast on snow, like porphyry wine-dark as the sea. And in a moment, Hades in his chariot, all black hornblende and damask feldspar, will burst through the volcano from Phlegethon, river of fire.

'Not far from Henna's walls,' as Ovid tells us (inadvertently adding yet another pigment) 'there is a deep lake, called Pergus.' Beside the lake, on a sunlit afternoon, Persephone was gathering scarlet poppies.

What a sign is scarlet! As the reader knows, it is a colour which has marked my life, a flagrant intensity which stands proud of the flesh to proclaim its lurid story. I believe that is is related – may the etymologists curse me as they will – to that other significant mark the welt, the weal, the cicatrice, the *scar*.

I forget who writes that Persephone was gathering scarlet poppies on that sunlit afternoon: the colour, even the species is uncertain. Ovid, who calls her Proserpine, casts his vote for violets or 'shining lilies' and in the Kore version of the myth, they are mysteriously transformed into narcissi. Let's say poppies though; yes, poppies picked in sunlight. Their scent makes her drowsy and she lies down on a bank to rest. It is then, near the pool, that the ground buckles and gapes. The chariot of Hades bursts into the day. Its master is inflamed with passion; his horses rear and prance. One of them is white, with dark eyes. A noble creature, it obeys every command. But the second is a crooked, lumbering beast, brutal and as stubborn as a mule. Hades, whom the pious call Pluto, rich owner of all ores, seizes the startled Persephone. He cracks his reins, which are 'dyed a dark and sombre hue.' The horses give out an unearthly whinny and the chariot moves forward. Persephone struggles frantically but the strong arm of Hades is around her waist. They descend into the underworld mid-way between Cyane and Arethusa. Before they disappear through the portal which opens into the dark, Persephone rends her garment in her distress. The flowers she has gathered fall from its loosened folds and lie withering in the sinking sun.

Cyane, a nymph who inhabits the dark blue pool near the opening which leads to Tartarus, Cyane with her green-blue eyes, is so upset by the incident that, on the violet evening of the rape, she is washed away by her own tears. Ovid says that at last, 'instead of living blood, water flowed through her softened veins and nothing remained for anyone to grasp.'

Demeter is distraught. She would move heaven and earth in her mother's agony. I see her as a painted figure on some Athenian vase, her hair in disarray, her eyes wide with grief, a hand, perhaps, stretched out in supplication. She searches fruitlessly through the ancient world and in gratitude to Triptolemus teaches him the arts of agriculture. Finally, in despair, she visits Zeus, the father of the gods and also (in the shape of a stallion) of Persephone herself. He is angered by his younger brother's violence but refuses to intervene on Demeter's behalf. The goddess descends from Olympus and in her wrath she breaks the ploughshares of men and spreads plague amongst farmers and oxen alike. Zeus is forced to negotiate.

Pomegranate-pink caused the disaster which led to dye: the seeds of the pomegranate, which are living crystals. According to Ovid it is Ascalaphus, a friend of Hercules, who sees Persephone eat the seven fateful seeds and tells his tale. In revenge, Demeter turns him into a screech-owl, a 'harbinger of woe for mortals'. For a certain portion of the year Persephone remains in the underworld with Hades who has a helmet of darkness and a staff to drive the wailing ghosts. She sits on the banks of Cocytus and listens to their dissonant cries; a world of absences is born.

That is the end of most versions of the story. In a few, Persephone later conceives a chaste passion for Adonis, brought to her as a baby in a coffer by Aphrodite. In the dim halls of her master she sings blue-grey lullabies to the child, in whom she finds a type of herself or, further back, of Orpheus, or, more distant still, of Tammuz, the lover of Ishtar who was persecuted by Allatu, Queen of the Infernal Regions. Behind Tammuz, at the source of all the stories, is Osiris, whose death is commemorated when seeds are sown in a coffin filled with sacred earth and watered with Nile water.

At the beginning the stories are blurred. Osiris contains both red Persephone and black Hades, as well as a multitude of other sprouting possibilities. Perhaps it was the very potency of Osiris which led his brother Seth to tear him into fourteen pieces in a fit of fratricidal jealousy. It is related that thirteen parts of the anagrammed corpse were recovered by Isis and Nepthys, the devoted sisters of the god. One part only could not be found, since it had been eaten by the oxyrhynchid crabs which inhabit the Nilotic mud: the phallus. Embalmed and resurrected in a ritual which the Egyptians would henceforth devotedly repeat, Osiris paradoxically becomes the castrated lord of life who reigns in the underworld. Having, like Demeter, taught his subjects agriculture and the arts of making bread and wine and beer, having abolished cannibalism, he is himself murdered and eaten repeatedly by his double-dyed worshippers.

A partial ending to the stories, the beginning of some sort of history: we pay for our summer with winter, not that it was anything to do with us. The gods teach us the knowledge necessary to survive their curse of infertility. Storing, ploughing, sowing, growing: we delay and plan ahead, we put things off until the omens are auspicious. When it is cold we have clothes to cover us which we dye in bright colours to remind us of dead nature, or sombre indigo to mourn its loss, dark aniline, blue as the upper reaches of the Nile, deathly as the weeds worn by ullulating crones. We hide together in cities, inventing all kinds of games to pass the time and rituals to repeat, turn and turn about, year in, year out, all in the hope of conjuring a sunlit afternoon, a good harvest.

We need the magic. When the seed sprouts in spring, we convince ourselves that the god we have made has brought new life to the fields. Underneath we know that life always comes from death, that death is first, followed by oblivion. Nevertheless, on the surface, we continue to forget Lethe in our rituals. We dress ourselves, paint ourselves and drug ourselves to resurrect the dead, to dye into life.

Thus ends a whole raddled tapestry of stories. I know that you have been watching me uneasily for the past couple of days: forgive my rhetoric, Mr Pencil. I seem to have strayed from my path but I glory in my vagrancy because colour is such an emblem for me.

Gold, purple, indigo, black, mauve, magenta, solferino, alizarin, crimson, perse, damask, scarlet, violet, cyan, pink: these tropes are a way of life for me, an addiction. I step forward as the curtain closes behind me; proudly I take my bow as the blanket of silent applause begins. I claim this purple prose and these enamelled flora.

5

Veneers

LET US go back, Mr Secretary, to that strange device on which I had set eyes for the first time at Elizabeth Tramont's birthday party: the camera which I had offered to mend.

In the hay-loft at Blackfriars Lane that evening, I took the camera out of its leather case. Although of no great weight, it was nearly three feet in length and a foot both in width and depth. A polished glass lens which could be covered and uncovered by the use of a rotating opaque disc had been encased in brass and set into one end. It was possible to adjust the length of the camera in order to focus it, and this adjustment could be measured with the assistance of a calibrated brass scale. There was a narrow rectangular opening in one side which presumably allowed the insertion of the sensitized plate. A mounting, again of brass, was fixed to the base and I speculated that this permitted the camera to be positioned on a tripod. Although I wanted to satisfy my curiosity as to what form of machinery was concealed within the instrument, I did not dare to open it for fear of causing further damage. It was to be some months yet before these penetralia became familiar to me as merely a dark and empty space.

I examined the injuries which the camera had sustained and was immediately reassured to find that the workmanship which had gone into its casing was known to me of old. As a boy I had produced pieces of marquetry with an exactitude and degree of complexity at least equal to this. The veneers were all of wood and laid on oak of the highest quality. On further examination, however, I began to foresee difficulties and became a little worried. The veneers were made by hand and I had never seen their like, those since the middle of the century having been produced exclusively by mechanical saw. In addition to this, the ornamented surface of the camera was made up of two different sorts of wood and, although I recognized one as yew, I had not previously encountered the other. This second veneer was hard, fine-grained and of a purplish colour. I thought that it was probably some tropical hardwood since, had it not been for the colour, one would have taken it for mahogany.

The next day I possessed myself of the requisite tools: a pot of glue, a knife of the sharpest, a small saw and a vice which I converted into a marqueter's press with the addition of some wooden blocks covered in zinc plate. I searched in vain, however, for the veneers I required. Yew I found and even in veneer form, but never of the correct thickness, and none of the tradesmen with whom I spoke had ever seen so much as a splinter of the other, stranger wood. One of them suggested that I should dye a piece of mahogany to the correct shade, but for the moment I resisted the temptation. Instead, I wrote to Lady Magenta to explain my position and to ask whether she had any knowledge of the origins of the camera, since it bore no maker's plate or other mark. She could not answer my question. The camera was no longer used, having long been superseded by more sophisticated apparatus. It had belonged to her father and had been constructed according to his specifications in the 1840s. She was certain, from what both he and, later, the housekeeper had said, that he had taken it with him on his expedition to the Crimea. Beyond this, Lady Magenta had no information, except to say that Lord Tramont had been accompanied on his journey to the war by a Polish aristocrat whose name and address she appended.

The baroness mentioned in Lady Magenta's letter lived in Hampstead. Having nothing better to do, I set out at once to visit her. And this was how I made the acquaintance of one of the strangest women in London.

The gate was rotten and stiff on its hinges. Dark laurels hung over the pathway leading to the door and rain dripped onto the broken tiles. Beneath the portico, the paint on the door was cracked like chapped skin. I rang the clanking bell and, after some time, a maid answered my call.

'Dzień dobry,' she said.

And all at once, after all these years, my mother's tongue sprang to my lips and I replied in kind: 'Dzień dobry. Baronowa Hrocka jest w domu?'

The maid gave a knowing smile which made me feel uncomfortable. 'Proszę wejść,' she said as she beckoned me in.

I was led into a large room at the back of the house. It was early afternoon but the curtains were tightly drawn and a fire burned in the grate. The air was laden with some perfume which I could not name. At the prompting of the maid, I moved forward towards the hearth.

In the depths of two armchairs placed on either side of the fire reclined a pair of somnolent gentlemen. Between them, lying on a rug made out of the skin of an animal which I could not identify, and evidently luxuriating in the warmth, was a woman whom I assumed to be the Baroness Hrocka. She looked perhaps fifty years of age, although I found out later that she was nearer sixty. Unlike her two companions she was naked.

Taken aback, I hesitated. The baroness did not appear to have noticed my entrance and I wondered whether to take advantage of this and quietly retreat. At this moment, however, the baroness, who appeared to have been absorbed in the contemplation of the flames, turned her head towards me. Her languid eyes brightened. Then – I have to confess that it was the most confounding gesture she could possibly have made in the situation – she glanced quickly at each of the two gentlemen, both of whom appeared to be in some sort of trance, and looking again towards me without as yet a single word having been spoken, she gave me a single, palpable wink. Thinking that the gesture was meant for the maid, I glanced round. But the young woman who had admitted me had disappeared. I saw the handle of the door turn slightly, as if she was waiting just outside.

The baroness laughed like a distant bell, amused, it seemed, by my awkwardness. Then, also in Polish, she asked me my business. Since she betrayed not the slightest trace of self-consciousness I could only state, at some length, the purpose of my visit. I spoke haltingly and the baroness smiled at my errors. Yes, she had certainly been in the Crimea with Lord Tramont – a delightful, virile man. But no, alas, although she could recall the camera in question, she knew nothing of its manufacture. At this point she shifted into perfectly pronounced but oddly constructed English. 'I remember well the unusual purplish colour of the wood. I remember also Tramont delicately picking his way through fields of carnage like a ballet dancer who had put on too much weight.' The baroness looked into the fire for a moment before continuing. 'Tramont's camera, I recall, was suitable only for the capturing of corpses since, with the length of exposure required and all the chemical hocus-pocus, the image of any living model would inevitably blur.' She smoothed the rug with her hand and sighed. 'I am sorry that I cannot enlighten you concerning the variety of wood with which it was constructed.'

One of the gentlemen started from his sleep. 'Eh? Wood? What?'

The baroness pretended to be put out. 'Well, Mr Bellowes, I declare! I spend an afternoon with you recounting the most, absolutely the most libidinous stories and you sink softly into a doze. And then at the mere mention of wood you spring to life! You dendrologist you! But I wonder,' went on the baroness as I waited, 'I wonder, Sidney, whether perhaps you can be of some use to our visitor.'

'Eh? Visitor? What?' Mr Bellowes turned his head this way and that in vague distress. He was very short-sighted and so, stepping forward with an extended hand, I introduced myself. 'Spellman, eh?' said Mr Bellowes as he attempted to blink the sleep from his eyes.

'Mr Bellowes is a botanist, you know,' said the baroness. 'Kew Gardens and all that. He's just putting the finishing touches to the tenth volume of his *Survey of the Trees and Flowering Plants of Amazonia.* Aren't you, Sidney?'

Mr Bellowes nodded and his tiny eyes gleamed through the thickness of his spectacles. 'Is there something I can do for you, young man?'

I repeated my enquiry and mentioned Lady Magenta.

'Ah, the good lady of Bartholomew Square,' said Mr Bellowes appreciatively. 'A fine woman. I knew her father: collected orchids for him on the Putumayo.'

'Stole them, you mean!' said the baroness in a teasing voice.

'Quite, quite, my dear lady.' Mr Bellowes looked a little hurt. 'Now then, Mr – er – Spellman: do you have a specimen of the wood in question?'

Fortunately I had had the foresight to provide myself with a sample of the veneer. I handed this to a now alert Mr Bellowes, who began to examine it carefully with a magnifying glass which he had taken from an inner pocket of his jacket.

'Yes, Mr Spellman,' he said at last, 'a nice specimen from a fine, healthy tree. It's name is descriptive: this is a piece of purpleheart wood, a native of tropical South America.'

'You clever old thing!' exclaimed the baroness with admiration.

Mr Bellowes gave her a sly smile: 'Purpleheart is another theft, of course, dear lady. Like Spruce's cinchona and Wickham's rubber.'

He offered to send me some sections both of yew and purpleheart, which he would cut to the thicknesses I required.

'Poor forest!' he murmured after I had thanked him. 'How violent were the sons which Humboldt fathered upon it!'

Without clothing herself, the baroness took me to the front door. As I stepped out under the portico she put a hand on my arm to detain me. I turned towards her. Some rain-water fell on to my cheek from a broken gutter and she reached out a hand to brush it away. 'Perhaps you will call again, Mr Spellman,' she said. Her hand moved along my arm, feeling the flesh beneath my overcoat. 'It is so dreadfully lonely on this damp hill. I wish you would, Mr Spellman.'

In order to secure my liberty, I said that I would be pleased to return one day, perhaps, but there was something acquisitive in the baroness's eye and I did not trust her. I felt like a horse having its hocks examined, or a stick of furniture in the corner of a curiosity shop. Before I knew it she would be poking about in my cupboards, looking for woodworm.

Mr Bellowes sent his samples round to Blackfriars Lane a couple of days later and I was able to set to work. I cut, fitted and glued into place the new veneers. Then I smoothed and polished them until the damaged area blended in with the old surface. It was not perfect, I knew: I was out of practice at this trade. Nevertheless, at the end of the week I felt with some pride that it would take an experienced eye to detect the point at which the old ended and the new began.

I went, therefore, at an hour previously appointed, to return the camera to Lady Magenta at Bartholomew Square. Sitting with her ladyship, the best, the most intimate of friends – almost the picture of a maiden aunt – was the Baroness Hrocka, who seemed delighted – absolutely delighted – to renew my acquaintance. She was gregarious, she was garrulous, she was gossipy. Within half an hour, a selection of the most famous personages then in London were paraded before myself and Lady Magenta and morally, so to speak, undressed. The baroness showed no false respect for authority; indeed, she delighted in its idiosyncrasies and peccadilloes.

At length the baroness departed, leaving us with the tale of Lord Eldred's recent rupture. She was going to hawk her wares of dropped breeches and pensioned maidservants elsewhere.

'I have never met anybody quite like her,' I said when she had closed the door.

Lady Magenta laughed loudly and began to cough. 'There is nobody like her,' she said through her tears, 'nobody at all.'

And so another tumbler turned and fell into place within the mechanism of futurity. Over the next ten years, as we grew closer, Lady Magenta was to show me the poverty of London and its wealth. The baroness, on the other hand, became my tutor in delight. She took me to museums and galleries, to the opera, the gambling house and the brothel.

When I left, Lady Magenta rose to take my hand. She thanked me for the work of restoration that I had done on her father's camera. For some hours afterwards, I could feel the cool pressure of her palm in mine.

6

Southwark Bridge

'OF COURSE, she's not a real baroness: ten to one she's a fake. They always are, especially the Polish ones.' As the speaker of these words turned to me with his vapid features, I looked across the garden to distant trees beneath which the pale shapes of evening mist were gathering.

Gossip operated as a sort of currency in these circles. My interlocutor, the Member of Parliament, as I recall, for South Kensington, was merely repeating what had been told him – 'in the strictest confidence' – by Lord So-and-So, at Such-and-Such's dinner the previous week.

The Member of Parliament for South Kensington collapsed into an armchair by the window and beckoned me towards him. His breath smelt of spirits. 'I have it on the highest authority – the highest, Mr Spellman – that this Hrocka woman serviced an entire troop of the Polish cavalry in a town with an odd name – all consonants – which is the very devil to pronounce. She had the captain twice, first and last, I do assure you.'

I cannot recollect the reason for my being at Bartholomew Square on this occasion. Certainly, after the episode of the broken and mended camera, Lady Magenta and I had no contact for several months. I returned to my garret in Blackfriars Lane across the courtyard from the Plough and Stars.

It was during this period that the friends of the previous decade began, one by one, to drop away from me. Mimi and Bessie, true to my fantasy, bought themselves a small sweetshop in Chalk Farm. Early in the summer, Wilf and I found a scarcely articulate note from Alf Hagsproat. We gathered that he had gone abroad, perhaps with the ultimate intention of returning to Australia. He left the opal ring with me, saying that so long as it was in my possession he thought that no ill-luck would come of it. He hoped that someday he would leave the beast behind him. In late August Wilf returned to Nottinghamshire. I felt as though someone had removed a part of my own body. Only myself, Amelia and Gertrude Desmoulins were left.

Lady Magenta wrote a few times to ask me to help with various repairs and odd jobs at Bartholomew Square. In the autumn I began to run the occasional errand for her, picking up some box of goods from a bright shop to take to her door.

First a carpenter and then a London messenger! I began to have a sense that history was repeating itself. I almost began to expect a second version of the circus. In any case, on one of my visits to Bartholomew Square, invited upstairs, I found myself with the Member of Parliament for South Kensington.

I moved on, across space but perhaps across time too. For some reason, Mr Secretary, I find it impossible to situate my recollections of these months in any chronological order. I telescope them together here for convenience and representative value.

In another corner of the reception room a bishop and a cardinal were debating the case of Parnell. Both, from differing points of view, shared essentially the same opinions. In the middle of the room, two gentlemen were engaged in a loud and earnest discussion.

'William, you simply cannot imagine the agony your appalling attitude is causing me. I cannot comprehend why you choose to take that line. It is astonishing to me, astonishing!'

'It seems perfectly straightforward to me.'

'Not at all! It is so patently obvious that Lady Emma's buttered scones are far, far inferior to Lady Magenta's. These are manna spread liberally with ambrosia' – he gobbled one as he spoke and blackcurrant jam rolled down his chin – 'Lady Emma's are as hard as her impregnable heart.'

'If you insist on arriving three hours late for her Tuesday soirées, what in Heaven's name do you expect, Gussy?'

'I expect, William, something edible. Since I never get it, I line my stomach as a precaution at a chop-house in Euston.'

Lamps were being lit and soft-footed waiters moved around the room collecting empty cups and plates. The conversations continued. I drank in these urbane phrases more greedily than the tea; I feasted upon cultivated fragments more keenly than on buttered scones.

'They simply fly into one's sights, my dear man. It is most obliging of them, for I cannot call myself a shot. But it's an amateur sportsman's utopia: they whirr across the moor to drop obediently at one's feet.'

'And his wife's a pretty woman, I hear.'

'True: ah yes, very true.'

Somebody tapped me on my shoulder and turning, I found myself face to face with a young, effete gentleman. His blond hair curled around his collar and an extravagance of brightly coloured handkerchief protruded from his breast pocket.

'I believe I saw you in *The Lions of Mysore,*' he said.

'I beg your pardon?'

'Barnum's thing – with the animals. *The Lions of Mysore:* a little jungle piece, wasn't it? I enjoyed it ever so much. I say,' he giggled, 'how awfully embarrassing! You are the circus chappie, aren't you? I was sure that Lady Magenta said it was you.'

'I never belonged to Mr Barnum's circus –'

'– Alas!' sighed the pretty man.

'Yes sir, alas. It would have been a great position for me. The circus to which I belonged was a much smaller affair.'

'No, no: you misunderstand me. I mean alas for Barnum's death.'

I stared at him. 'Barnum – dead?'

'Indeed sir, two days since.' He put out his hand. 'My name is Rupert Dinmont. Pleased to make your acquaintance.'

We talked, I remember, for some time and shared many anecdotes of the circus, a form of entertainment he prized above all others. Mr Dinmont was a charming, witty and infinitely trivial man. He had inherited his father's silk importing business and told me that his breast pocket was as good as a shop window to him. But he had the grace not to appear to notice my poverty, my threadbare clothes.

These people controlled the nation and owned large parts of it. They ran the Empire and defended the English faith. They legislated and carefully restricted the availability of ideas. For the most part they were venal, self-serving rogues who were unable even to make themselves a cup of tea without an army of paid slaves (to think, Mr Secretary, that I have become one of these men! – that I have my Martha to bring me – look – the coffee, the evening paper). Circling around, Lady Magenta's guests brushed against each other, preened themselves and then moved on, as lonely as cats in the midst of these sociable forms. When they left at last, I found Lady Magenta half-hidden behind a curtain, gazing listlessly out of the window. I tentatively put my hand on her shoulder. She remained motionless and her blue-grey eyes seemed to be focused on a point beyond the night.

'Let us walk,' she said.

And so we walked aimlessly into the darkness of that city so vast that it seemed to have lost its edge. We left Bartholomew Square at about two o'clock in the morning and the streets were quiet. The late crowds from the theatre had long since disappeared. A steaming horse stood under a lamp; the dozing cabby, hoping for custom, looked up at us and sank his chin back onto his chest as we passed. Lady Magenta knew this city better than anyone I have ever met, far, far better than I. She seemed to have a map before her eyes as we progressed and she never faltered once, not even in the narrowest of alleys. Although I had taken her arm it was she who led me. Time and again I was surprised as we came suddenly upon a square that I was familiar with only from a different direction. On several occasions, my companion cut in half the distance that I would have expected to traverse between two landmarks on my accustomed routes. We threaded the city as though it were a sampler and Lady Magenta the fine, slim needle.

We talked of many things; perhaps it was London that spoke through us, its sentinels. I recounted the story of my time in the circus, how it was over now and I did not know what to do.

'I have two lives,' I remember saying, 'the past and the future. This very moment is a sort of limbo between one working day and the next. Only two lives, Lady Magenta: the circus and the city.'

Lady Magenta spoke of her childhood, her parents and their death, the years in Europe with her governess. 'All the stages of my life seem so separate,' she said, 'like differently coloured fragments, like a broken plate.' We walked on a little way before she continued. 'And even now my life seems all jumbled up, day after day of bits and pieces, never settling to anything.'

'What bits and pieces?' I asked, surprised. To me, her life seemed full of finish and integrity.

She thought a little. 'There's my life with Elizabeth, that's one piece: easing the burden for Ronald's poor wife. And then there's what you saw tonight.'

'Tonight?'

'Yes: "appearances," that's what I call it. "Keeping up appearances," you know.'

'Oh,' I said, 'I see.'

'Do you?' she asked sharply, 'I'm not sure that you do. It's only through appearances that I am able to live the most important fragment of my life. But it's all so exhausting, so frustrating.'

I glanced across at her and saw, by a street lamp on some empty thoroughfare, that the lines around her eyes which I had taken for the traceries of a life led in ease were also marks of care.

'I raise money, Mr Spellman, you see, to help orphans. I curry favour with the powerful. I attempt to force a way through their blindness, to make them respond to interests other than their own. I can never, in this, seem to be serious or I would be taken for a bore and they would not pay, they would no longer come.'

Fragments. Little sibylline leaves cast into the vast and ignorant machinery of society, appearances. Lady Magenta's words turned and twisted, lost themselves. The orphans and Siriso . . .

'Siriso?' I enquired.

'It doesn't matter,' she sighed, 'perhaps another time.'

There were other bits of this particle life: the Baroness Hrocka, Dr Garth-Thompson, bohemians, radicals, aesthetes. They were more free than the rest, but also more desperate.

We had stopped halfway across Southwark Bridge and leaned over the parapet, following the current of the river. Down it went, slowly down, carrying in its grip a crate or a dead dog. Beyond St Paul's and the distant Tower it flowed, past wharves and the great hulls of ships, at last to filter through the docks and pass out beyond the mudflats, out to sea.

I felt very close to my companion and yet very far away. Although I could have touched her with my arm, it felt as if I was watching her through the wrong end of a telescope. I gazed along the landing stages on the south side of the river, where the buildings seemed thrown upon each other like half-collapsed houses of cards.

'This city: it's a heap of jackstraws,' I said. 'If, by an unlucky chance, you picked the wrong one, then the whole lot would come tumbling down.'

'Lon-don Bridge is fall-ing down,' sang Lady Magenta to herself, 'falling down, fall-ing down . . .

'Will things change, Mr Spellman?' she asked suddenly after a silence which had lasted some time. 'Can things change in this city?'

She put the question with such urgency that I was taken aback. It was as if she thought I had the answer. 'Surely things change all the time,' I said. 'Streets are built, buildings fall down. Powerful people die and others rise to the top of the pile. Goods change hands.'

I looked about me: 'What is most striking is this ceaseless movement, ebbing and flowing like the river.'

Lady Magenta made a small, impatient gesture: 'And like the river, all according to one law. You think of it as a picture, different under different lights, immensely alive, teeming with faces and things. Yet underneath it all, there's only the dead hand of one law, stationary and fixed for ever.'

I rattled some loose change in my pocket and leaned on the balustrade. 'I don't know: perhaps you're right. I'm more familiar with the circus than the city. If the city was the same as the circus, maybe there would be less of that one law. You could choose, if you wanted, to believe in the magic, to believe in change. Then, perhaps, all the objects in the world would come alive and return your gaze. It would be like a gigantic kaleidoscope. But . . .'

'But you don't believe in that?'

I looked hard at the current beneath me for a long time. 'No. I do not believe in that.' How could I? It was dead. In the middle of the bridge, in the middle of the night, I could say out loud my doubts. There were no barriers between us any longer, only the immensities of distance which separate each from each.

'What are you thinking?' she asked.

'I am thinking that even the best juggler in the world sometimes makes slips.'

We walked on. The late September dawn began to flush our vast, vague Babylon. Yet the black perspectives and blank walls of warehouses still loomed up; hooks and cables still swung from abandoned gantries. Piles of empty boxes stood around us and our footsteps echoed in the stillness.

Then, slowly, emergent life. The signs above the doors of shops became legible. Sleeping on the pavement, an old man moaned his way to wakefulness. In the markets, people were huddling around braziers and blowing on their fingers. Others heaved crates of meat and baskets of vegetables onto their shoulders. Slowly the light grew, yet still we lingered.

The crowd – composed of a million routes and pathways like a giant web – came out upon its business. At points we came up against its hardness and its roughness but to be amongst the crowd was most of all to be surrounded by the softness of a living body which advanced and receded like a wave rattling the pebbles of the shore, a great wash of oppressed life. The shouts of buying and selling began. We had emerged from limbo. A newspaper vendor outside Victoria Station shouted the headlines into the passing crowd, but its noise drowned his voice. From across the street, we saw only the jerkiness of his movements and the steam of his breath.

In Kensington, a rag-and-bone man drove his cart down the middle of the road and shouted into the doorways: 'A fair price for printed matter! Your books and magazines, your old newspapers please!

'Old bedsteads, old iron, old mattresses, old sheets!

'Cutlery, broken crockery, rusty metal!

'Your rags, your bones, your ashes please!'

I accompanied Lady Magenta to Bartholomew Square and then returned, exhausted, to Blackfriars Lane. The noise was louder now. The city was a huge orchestra forever tuning up, all random percussiveness and jarring sound. I rubbed my eyes in the sunlight. Dust particles seemed to be caught under my lids and I tried to blink the motes away. For a few moments I saw everything through my tears. I felt as though I had lost my edges and become a part of another, slowly breathing organism. Or that I was full of holes like a sieve, or that the city around me was composed, not of solid bodies, but of interstices. The masonry was pitted with voids and the buildings were cubes of sugar or even Swiss cheeses.

177

It seemed that morning that I had gained new edges, harder, brighter ones. I was a coin tossed high into the air, spinning now heads, now tails. I was just a bit of cash, of loose jack: a penny rolling drunkenly this way and that, a coin amongst coins.

A few hundred yards to go, but still the threat, amongst the pressing, milling crowd, of a thousand scratches and marks. It was a fencing match or a ballet. I danced along, absurdly in control of my tired body, absurdly in love. I parried every thrust and at each point tried to forget the teeming images that thrust their way inside and threatened to displace the image of a single face.

There would soon come a time when I would be forced to confront these crowding details, forced to sort out the chaos for myself. Now, so many years later, the whole story, my life, emerges like a bloody child through a rent in the protective fabric. The Secretary, like an undertaker, lays it coldly, reverently to one side.

An Evening in Pompeii

S IR STAFFORD Singleton, QC, eminent jurist, noted bibliophile: a pillar of his profession. It was the Baroness Hrocka who introduced me to him in one of the filthiest gaming houses in London. She knew him of old but their friendship had seen the lapse of several years.

Yes, dear man, she had been away – for her sins – in Rome, Vienna and Warsaw. Stafford hoped that her sins had been pleasurable. Yes, dear boy, certainly. And prolific. She fixed him with her eye and a furtive smile passed between them. But she had been back for months and – memory quickly fades. Unless it is renewed, dear baroness. Undoubtedly; and what had he been doing with himself? – things more interesting, apparently, than paying visits to her. Stafford was contrite. Well, he had been in London, of course, during the sessions. He had changed his chambers, published a couple of books – oh, trivialities of no interest at all, really: none. Mere esoterica. Yes, he loved beyond anything to pore over old manuscripts, the charts and narratives of the age of exploration. He had risen, yes, socially, professionally. Had he risen for his sins or in spite of them? Another smile passed between them. Stafford hesitated. Perhaps his pleasures were sins but he did not care; let it be left as society chose to leave it: that he had lacked, when young, the moral guidance of his parents. But his pleasures, yes, dear baroness, had been intense – if both infrequent and insecure.

The roulette wheel span; Stafford had lost. He was losing a considerable sum but he maintained complete equanimity, chatting away negligently as the pile of counters dwindled before him.

'And what,' the baroness asked archly after a particularly ruinous *coup*, 'is the man's name, dearest Stafford?'

He laughed uproariously and exclaimed that she was the most inquisitive of women. She agreed and reiterated her question, telling him that he was avoiding the subject.

Stafford could only oblige. 'His name is Andrew, and he is a Ganymede. Has a brain too: they tell me he's a fine surgeon. Such delightful down on his face, not stubble. And so strong!'

'Dear me, Stafford,' said the baroness sadly, 'you never learn. At first they're catamites, but in the end you tell them they're bloodsuckers and kick them from your bed. I suppose you are going to tell me that Andrew is different.'

Stafford gave her a rueful glance. He staked all of his remaining counters on black. The croupier called red; he had lost. Looking completely unconcerned, he rose from the table. 'That is the limit for me. Shall we to pastures new, baroness? How young you look tonight!' He took her by the arm and returned to the subject of their conversation. 'Nevertheless, Andrew *is* different, despite your cynicism. I know that I have said the same thing before, but I have never meant it as I mean it now.'

The baroness inclined her head and reserved, for the present, her judgement. 'Unlucky at dice, lucky in love: I suppose that's the way of it.'

As Stafford helped her into her coat, the baroness suggested that we go on to Pastorelli's. Whilst we waited for a cab outside, I was aware that Stafford was discreetly scrutinizing me in the lamplight. I knew that he took me for the baroness's lover and that the baroness was aware of this. Nevertheless, she did not try to correct him; perhaps his mistake amused her. Instead, she took every opportunity to put her hand on my arm or to smile up into my face.

Signora Pastorelli was in those days the proprietress of one of the most exclusive brothels in London. It was much-praised in some circles for its immense luxury and the exotic taste with which it had been furnished. The place specialized in the purveyance of women of Mediterranean origin and the private chambers were named after famous artists and writers. The whores took upon themselves the names of fictional characters. On various occasions I was introduced to Madame Arnoux, Mademoiselle de Maupin and the Princess Casamassima. These ladies were, however, little seen on the ground floor, which was furnished in the Classical style. Both Stafford and the baroness were well-known here and we were immediately provided with a table to one side of a small fountain which was adorned with frolicking marble nymphs. As I gazed wide-eyed from the strutting peacocks to the frescoed ceiling, the baroness talked in a low voice with Stafford, who had already ordered a bottle of champagne.

The place was laid out in the likeness of the baths at Pompeii and a distant mural represented Vesuvius glowing by night. Stars sprinkled the ceiling and, amongst the soft lights, the tables receded into the shadows, where exhausted or expectant men engaged in private conversation. Steam emerged from an archway, which led to the *tepidarium*, or warm baths.

Stafford relaxed his reserve as he became accustomed to my presence;

he had long been on intimate terms with the baroness. Their wit was pricked by each other's presence and I merely listened to them, asking only, for politeness's sake, the occasional question.

Some time had passed before Stafford mentioned that he always took, on his excursions into pleasure, the precaution of disguising himself. He must have been practised in his art for even I, with my experienced eye for cosmetics, would never have noticed. When I mentioned my admiration, he thanked me for the compliment and continued: 'Such, Mr Spellman – alas but be thankful – are the subterfuges one learns from associating with the criminal classes.'

He began to point out the features of his assumed costume. His extravagant suit was not his normal, more sober one and his reddish wig belied his silvered hair. He had no scar, as now, across his cheek. When he went out on his forays, he affected a limp and assumed a false name; he carried misleading papers which did not belong to him. Nothing connected him with his home – he was married, with three children – or his profession.

The baroness differed from Stafford. She had no use, she said, for disguises. The stories that were told about her already! Her presence in a mere brothel could serve only to quieten and disappoint rumour. Yes, such stories were told! Such fantastic extravagances! Yet many of them – she grinned lewdly – were tarnished and poor compared to the things she had done.

At last Stafford tossed off his glass of champagne and got up. 'Well, baroness: I am lonely tonight. These long nights, the past week, with my musty papers! Perhaps Signora Pastorelli will find me some company.'

The baroness raised her eyebrows and began to formulate a question; he answered it before she spoke. 'Oh – I forgot to tell you: Dr Garth-Thompson is away in Scotland. Any port in a storm.' Stafford departed for the upper storeys.

On the way home I had a confused sense that, two millennia later, the Roman senate still resorted, for its pleasure, to the baths, where polite attendants took away their purple robes of office and they could be naked again.

Are these the personages of repute that you desired so much, Mr Pencil? The famous men who influence little, lower lives? I should not wish to disappoint you.

8

The Mirror of Memory

ELEVEN O'CLOCK of a June evening. Bartholomew Square is deserted and the open windows let the darkness in. A few stray insects which have survived the city hover around the lamp or wriggle, with singed wings, on the table.

Ah, and here is Martha with her convivial tray! Think of the amount of liquid with which she has fuelled our evening sessions! Put the tray over there, Martha: next to the Secretary. He will pour the coffee.

Not coffee? Iced tea? I see: bearing in mind as it seemed suitable. Bearing in mind the hot weather, the parched streets, the dust. Well, I would know nothing of all that. How should I? – confined, a voluntary invalid, to the upper rooms. I have noticed that there is less darkness than there was three months ago.

Nearly thirty years in three short months! Yes: there is less darkness. What's that you say? Midsummer's Night? Such things were significant to me once.

I have know Martha more than twenty years, Mr Secretary, and yet I feel that I do not know her at all. I purchase her labour, you see, and therefore friendship is outside the script. I admit that I am uneasy about our relation. We speak to each other so infrequently that I am reminded sometimes of my own father and mother.

In twenty years Martha has only said one thing without my prompting. It was back in February, a week or two before I met the Ghost. Perhaps it could even be said that Martha's words were the cause of our meeting and that without her there would have been no scratch of the stenographer's pencil in the night.

Yes, Martha. I had never thought of her before as the sower of the seed. What she said was so completely mistaken that I have produced these pages only to show how wrong she was – as well as to persuade myself that I, after all, was in the right. I concede that it is a larger task than I had anticipated; even now I am not at all certain of success. What was it she said – the germ? Hand me the first page of my memoirs, would you? Let me remind myself.

Yes . . . here it is.

She hands my medicine to me. As I pour it from the bottle a droplet falls onto the rug and glistens like a ruby. I am chattering indiscriminately, attempting somehow to make the air vibrate. I can hardly breathe; I am panting; my throat is sore. Every word I utter is absorbed by the blanket, the curtains, the wallpaper. But Martha was impressed, even if I was not. It was then, as she pulled the rug up under my chin, that she said how interesting I was. I did not believe her, of course: she was merely trying to make me feel better. But she insisted; she said that I had many stories, that my life was like a fairy-tale. 'It only seems exotic in contrast to a life of soups and cakes,' I said.

If you look more closely, Mr Secretary, you will find that it is Martha's life and not mine which makes a better subject for a story. Real strangeness is to be found, not in Africa, but in a London kitchen. A pause for thought; a sip of this iced tea.

How is it you ask?

Cold; thin. I prefer coffee and its brittle, palpitating wakefulness. Yes: I am perfectly well . . . am I? It is so hard to tell when one never moves about. The borderline between health and disease tends to disappear in these upper rooms. I think that I must be a little unwell. There are more pains, at least, than there used to be. Stabbing . . . twistings. I think that it will be a short session tonight.

Josiah Wedgwood and John Flaxman poured slurry into wax moulds to produce their famous Jasper Ware. Josiah's son, Thomas, was interested in a different form of reproduction, less palpable impressions. In June of 1802 his paper, *An Account of a method of copying paintings upon glass and of making profiles by the agency of light upon nitrate of silver*, was published in the *Journal* of the Royal Institution.

The shift between father and son is most instructive. Both were interested in the production of likeness but the one lived by firm moulds and solid china whereas the other, the latter, was all ephemeral traces, light beams caught by the action of a chemical. The tradesman's son was a magician whose ghosts emerged on paper by a sort of automatic writing. The magician was nearing the end of his brief life when his paper was published. Had he lived, perhaps he would have been able to find solutions to the problems involved in his new method. As it was, Humphry Davy defined these difficulties on his friend's behalf:

'Nothing but a method of preventing the unshaded parts of the delineations from being coloured by exposure to the day is wanting to render this process as useful as it is elegant.'

The colouring referred to by Davy was a violet thing which, do what the

investigators would, inevitably spread over the exposed paper and submerged the original image.

Lady Magenta and I stood in her studio in Bethnal Green. Outside, grey
snow covered the window ledges. A few cries floated up from the street far
below. The light was beginning to fail and, above the hiss of the gaslamp,
Lady Magenta had been talking for some time of her interest in photography. I handled the plates; I looked at the earliest cameras. We tried to
reproduce those first, tentative discoveries. Bags of chemicals stood
around the walls of the attic. Outside, clouds raced across a dark-blue sky.

Photography is a technique with an uncertain paternity. Thomas Wedgwood was not the first to investigate the peculiar properties of silver
compounds. We cannot name him as the founding father. In 1777, K.W.
Scheele had studied the darkening effect of sunlight on silver chloride
and noted that violet blackened the substance more effectively than any
other form of light.

Wedgwood, Davy, Scheele: these were the progenitive gods. François
Chaussier was a lesser deity. In 1799, he discovered hyposulphite of soda
but he could never have dreamt of its uses as a photographic fixative.
Seebek too was a demigod. He was the first to experiment scientifically
with producing natural colours by photographic action. At Jena, in 1810,
he projected the complete spectrum onto silver chloride paper.

There was one further Prometheus who knew the patriarchs and
prophets yet to come: Nicéphore de Niepce. He called the process which
he developed between 1814 and 1827 *héliographie*. In his studio, he would
drop oil of lavender into a wine glass which contained powdered asphal-
tum. This mixture would be heated gently and then used to varnish a
polished and prepared plate. After exposure, Nicéphore placed the
metallic plate into a tray containing a petroleum solvent and the parts
which had not been exposed to light rays dissolved away. Although his
pictures were extremely faint, Nicéphore had found a way to stabilize the
photographic image. But he did not know of Chaussier's work and so it
was left to his successors to introduce a fixative in the true sense.

Late into the night the lamps burned on in Lady Magenta's studio. I sat
rigidly in a chair, my chin supported and steadied by a metal contraption
which, beneath my jacket, Lady Magenta had strapped around my chest.
The slightest movement of my head would have blurred the photograph.
As it was, my eyes were destined to appear as milky and glazed as those of
a blind man: I had blinked and inadvertently shifted the direction of my
gaze during the exposure.

It was after dawn when Lady Magenta lifted with delicate forceps a small piece of paper from the immersion tray. This was the first photographic image of which I could say that I knew the processes by which it had been produced, the chemicals employed to make such a strange record emerge. That photograph, taken on the twenty-first of December, 1892, lies now in my lap and I, a man of fifty-four, look down into the past at that man of twenty-eight who was me, the dead image of me as I was so long ago. Lady Magenta stood in the centre of the atelier, holding the photograph in front of her and smiling, strangely smiling.

The *agon*: Nicéphore de Niepce against matter and light. To continue the struggle, he left behind two images of himself: his son, Isidore de Niepce, and his nephew, Niepce de St Victor. So began the reign of the patriarchs: the men who were to fight tooth and nail for copyrights and patents. Ironically, it was Nicéphore's more distant relative, Niepce de St Victor, who maintained the less predatory relationship with his predecessor. Niepce invented the albumen process on glass. He treated a prepared plate with a mixture of five fresh eggs, a hundred grains of potassium iodide, twenty grains of potassium bromide and ten grains of common salt. He dried, exposed and developed the image as before, discovering that albumen succeeded in holding the iodide *in situ* as no previous process had done. Until the advent of the collodion process in 1850, however, both the albumen and starch prefigurations of film quickly deteriorated.

Over the next eighteen months I devoted myself, with Lady Magenta's encouragement, to learning the rudiments of photography. I spent long nights in the attic at Bethnal Green, sometimes alone and sometimes with my friend. I read all the journals and the manuals. I familiarized myself with the uses and characteristics of a world of strange ingredients. At first my practical efforts were disappointing but the quality of my work gradually improved and by the summer of 1894 I think I had become a useful assistant.

What of Isidore de Niepce, the silver son who saw the evening of the age of gold? Unlike his cousin Niepce, Isidore was able to keep in close contact with his father. He bent his ear attentively to Nicéphore's ramblings during the illness which, beginning in 1828, ended only with his death in 1833. The old man became an invalid; he needed disciples to be his hands. But his mind was as clear as his idea of the perfect photograph. Lying in his bed, he carried out lengthy investigations in his head. His thoughts crystallized into a single substance: iodine.

'Fight violet with violet!' he muttered to himself in his bedroom. An anxious maid, taking the words as a sure sign of the onset of her master's final delirium, informed the housekeeper, who called immediately for the son. Isidore arrived to find his father more alert than he had been for weeks.

'Make violet receive violet!' the old man shouted ecstatically and fell back upon his pillows with a contented smile: 'Let violet rape violet.'

Nicéphore punned, with an old man's lack of concern for comprehensibility, on the homophony of the French *violer*, to rape, and the colour *violet*. Behind this pun lay another which played on the relationship between violet light, so effective in blackening silver chloride, and the element iodine, whose name derives from the Greek *ion*, violet and *iodes*, violet-like.

Eventually Nicéphore was persuaded to explain his riddles. Isidore happened to pass on the information to an acquaintance who had of late been much in his company, a man of forty called Louis Daguerre. Together, they rifled Nicéphore's cellar and eventually discovered, in a sealed jar, some black crystals which emitted a distinctively-coloured vapour. Iodine! As dark and sweet as the aniline dyes which Mr Perkin was yet to invent.

After Nicéphore's death in 1833, Daguerre and Isidore devoted themselves to pursuing the dead prophet's clew. Both of them would have been incensed by any suggestion that the victors in this contest with matter and light would be those who tinkered with previous discoveries or adapted prior inventions. Monsieur Daguerre in particular would have been driven to fury by the accusation that it was to be thieves, in this struggle, who left their names behind. Louis Jacques Mandé Daguerre was a subtle man who knew his moment and his chance. He seized both firmly and was rewarded with immortality.

One day, the maid rushed into the laboratory in a state of great distress. She had been arranging flowers in the room where Nicéphore had died and claimed to have heard a word, twice repeated. Turning, she found nobody behind her. A strange sensation had come over her and she must have fainted.

'And what was the word?' asked Daguerre testily.

' "*Voleurs*," ' the maid replied. 'Twice, in *his* voice: "*voleurs*".'

Neither man, of course, needed to ask who 'he' was. Isidore went rather pale. But Daguerre was not superstitious; at least, if he was, he was able to control his fear and reassure his younger comrade. For the next six years, patiently and painstakingly, the two men perfected the new technique.

They took a silvered copper plate and cleaned it with finely powdered pumice and olive oil, then with dilute nitric acid. They polished the plate with the softest buff until it was brilliant. Daguerre, in particular, was a meticulous workman and knew that the slightest trace of foreign matter, the merest of particles, would be fatal to the production of a picture of the highest quality. Isidore on the other hand, with his youthful impatience, could be somewhat careless and his partner would often scold him for wasting expensive materials.

Once the plate had been polished, Isidore would scatter tiny fragments of crystallized iodine over the surface of a saucer, which he then covered with gauze. Daguerre placed the prepared plate face downwards over the saucer and together they waited for the iodine vapour to form a surface of silver iodide on the plate. Gradually it began to change colour. By trial and error they discovered that maximum photographic sensitivity had been achieved when the plate had become golden in colour. Withdrawing this transmuted plate, they placed it in the dark slide of the camera. The duration of the exposure was at first a matter of guesswork but Daguerre and Isidore soon learned to allow seven or even eight hours for a landscape subject in normal light.

One summer's evening, they were in the laboratory with an exposed plate which they had just carried in from the garden. The weather was warm, and they were in their shirt-sleeves. Suddenly Daguerre noticed that they were both due to attend a dinner party in half an hour. Isidore had been negligent with his time-keeping and Daguerre hurried away to dress with a few sharp words. The unfortunate Isidore put the undeveloped plate into the dark cupboard before following his friend.

Resuming their labours the next morning, they were astonished to discover that the plate had partially developed itself overnight. Since the cupboard was packed with dozens of improperly stored chemicals (a state of affairs for which Daguerre was not slow to blame his colleague) a lengthy process of elimination was necessary to ascertain that mercury had been the agent responsible.

Isidore, with a trace of his father's love of punning, remarked that there could have been no more suitable element. Mercury – the god of thieves – had supported his own. Daguerre was not amused. Had he been a superstitious man, which he was not, he might have thanked his stars for bringing him into contact with Isidore. Instead, however, he regarded his gift-horse with ill-concealed contempt. The young man, doubtless, was not particularly intelligent. It was he, nevertheless, who stumbled on most of their innovations.

Daguerre and Isidore ordered new stocks of mercury and began to refine the process they had discovered so fortuitously. They placed exposed plates over cups of mercury heated to varying temperatures. Daguerre was soon able to establish that the optimum temperature was 75° Celsius, at which point the mercuric vapour condensed on the portions of the plate where light had acted on the silver iodide in exact proportion to the extent of the action of the light.

Having perfected two new techniques, they began in a leisurely fashion to prepare their results for publication.

The daguerreotype: Lady Magenta and I produced many images by this method. Each morning we would climb onto the roof of the studio, position our camera and insert the sensitized plate. Throughout the day, as we busied ourselves with other things, the horizons of Stepney and Whitechapel or the gloomy dome of St Paul's would materialize in our box like trapped ghosts.

We were zealous in the recovery of every detail of photography's brief but rich history. We revived and re-staged each method and process, wondering always whether, amongst all the obsolete techniques, there lurked anything which could be of use to us. I remember that we became particularly fascinated by the cameo effect to be found in numerous daguerreotypes. This was created by the primitive methods used to sensitize and develop the plate, which allowed iodine and mercury vapour to spread unevenly: more concentrated in the centre of the plate, thinner towards the edges. We also experimented with using bromine instead of iodine and replacing hyposulphite of soda with potassium cyanide, as Martin and Marc Antoine Augustin Gaudin had done in 1853.

These were dangerous chemicals with dangerous vapours and our work was frequently interrupted by violent fits of coughing and even, occasionally, vomiting. Lady Magenta seemed more sensitive to the chemicals than I, perhaps because of her more prolonged exposure to them. Sometimes, even in the depths of winter, we were forced to throw open the windows and allow fresh, icy air to enter the room. Shivering, doubled up with pain, the tears streaming down our faces, we must have looked like two patients in a sanatorium for incurables.

Louis Daguerre published his work on 6 February 1839 and was furious to discover that he had been beaten by a short head to the winning-post and beaten, at that, by an Englishman. William Henry Fox Talbot had published an account of his own process on 25 January 1839.

Fox Talbot's name would also echo down the generations but his authorship was as questionable as Daguerre's and depended in a similar way on one whose name, once mentioned, sets off not the slightest reverberation of memory: the Reverend J.B. Reade.

188

I find it strange, Mr Secretary, that photography (a technique which of all others most closely resembles the operations of memory and which promoted ease of identification to an extent never before seen) should, at its very beginning, have been so marked by violent displacements, erased or missing persons and an almost drunken forgetfulness. Nicéphore and the ghostly Reverend Reade wander around Hades whilst we drink from Lethe as fast as we can, desperately pinching each other to convince ourselves of our own substantiality.

Fox Talbot: the fox, at least, is appropriate. A vulpine eclectic, he reminds me a little of Autolycus. Littered, like Daguerre and the jesting Isidore, under the sign of Mercury (a type of Thoth) he is also a snapper-up of unconsidered trifles, whose traffic is photosensitive sheets.

In Fox Talbot's case, the trifle was the gallic acid which the Reverend Reade had used to develop his photographic images in the dark. Gallic acid! As clear and bitter as Richard Spruce's stolen quinine. The liquid is derived from gall nuts, the spherical excrescences on oak trees resulting from the ravages of a fungus, a bacterium or various species of insect. With such a strange origin one must also be reminded of the peculiar sources of the dyes which I have already had occasion to mention. It comes, therefore, as no surprise to learn that gallic acid is used in the manufacture of ink. Owing to its powerfully astringent qualities, it is also used in the treatment of the disease purpura.

Lady Magenta and I purchased large quantities of gallic acid to use in Fox Talbot's calotype process. We carefully selected paper for its consistency of grain and, as in Wedgwood's original process, soaked it in a salt solution before brushing it with a solution of silver nitrate in water. After the paper had dried before a low fire, we dipped it into a further solution of potassium iodide in water for a period of two to three minutes, after which time silver iodide had formed on the surface. The paper was still barely sensitive to light and it was at this point that we brushed gallo-nitrate of silver over its surface. We prepared this solution by dissolving one hundred grains of silver nitrate in two ounces of water to which we then added one sixth of its own volume of acetic acid and, immediately prior to application, an equal volume of a saturated solution of gallic acid in water. The paper thus moistened was now ready for exposure. It developed itself in darkness and was then washed and dried.

There were five other techniques with which Lady Magenta and I familiarized ourselves during this period: the Collodion Process, developed in 1850 by Frederick Scott Archer and P.W. Fry; the Moist Collodion Process of 1856, patented – in the year of mauve – by Sir

William Crookes and J. Spiller; the use of dry plates, made workable in 1854 by Marc Gaudin and G. R. Muirhead; the Collodion Emulsion Process of 1864, registered by W.B. Bolton and B.J. Sayce and, dating from 1871, the Gelatin Emulsion Process.

These developments, together with the advent of rapid plates with C. Bennett's work of 1878 and the supersession of pyrogallic acid by hydroquinone in 1880, brought photography to the point where it was possible to take and develop photographs easily and quickly. Because it was no longer necessary to prepare plates in the field, the camera became an increasingly mobile eye. With the Eastman roll-film camera of 1888, which Lady Magenta and I also used, my brief history of photography is at an end.

We had passed through the fire. Lady Magenta and I now knew in detail most of the available photographic methods. The studio in Bethnal Green contained an arsenal of chemicals in various states. There were sacks and boxes of silver chloride, lead oxide, pumice, crystal iodine, gold, salt, potassium cyanide, starch, gelatin, tripoli powders, ferrous sulphate and zinc nitrate; jars and flasks of ammonia, oil of lavender, olive oil, liquid iodine, gallic acid, bromine, hyposulphite of soda solution, spirits of wine, acetic acid, black varnish, nitric acid, distilled water and carbolic acid (the last of which was essential to prevent the decomposition during hot weather of the broken eggs with which we made our strange omelettes). There were racks of glasses, pipettes, mixing vessels and immersion trays, cupboards full of silver, glass and japanned plates, paper and waxed paper, row upon row of eggs. And there were chamois leathers, silk handkerchiefs, light filters, screens and shades, china crucibles and pestles, great rolls of crape to block out the light. The place seemed like a mixture of an undertaker's parlour, a public house and an explosives factory. Our hands were chapped and raw, blackened by silver iodide; together we held them up to the dawn light, as pleased as oarsmen with the marks of our labours.

It was a remarkable decade. In those years the photograph had a magical quality which now belongs only – and even this will fade – to the moving film, the history of which to some extent recapitulates in its suspicions and mysteries, its accusations and authentications, that of the still image. In 1889, for example, Louis Augustin Aimé Le Prince, who patented the first single lens film camera a year before Friese-Greene, died in unusual circumstances on the Dijon to Paris train. Adolphe, his son, was bequeathed the patents and made an attempt to establish Louis as the true father of cinematography; he had still not succeeded when he too was found dead in a wood on Long Island.

The city took up and used this magic. It saw in photography a process which enabled information to be recorded, accumulated and retrieved. The police took likenesses of murderers and victims alike. They photographed the corpse of Louis le Prince in Paris. The police photographer was regularly to be seen in Whitechapel during 1888. The scene of a crime would be examined miles away and the face of a suspect, should one be found, could be blazoned to the world. Mimetic or mnemonic, the photograph reflected our original sins in its silvered remembrance.

Photographs were reproduced: there were photographs of paintings and photographs of photographs. The likenesses were multiplying in the offices of police stations, in family scrap-books standing on mantelpieces, behind the tawdry windows of journeymen photographers. Faces left signs behind them; a mere visit could leave a trace which lasted for years, record an embarrassment never to be expunged. For the first time doctors were able to make a precise record of the typical progress of a disease. Photographers became the pimps of women who prostituted themselves without fleshly contact, who made themselves available to the eye but not the hand. People collected whole boxes of these appearances. Frozen personal transiences accumulated amongst the memorabilia in second-hand shops. Memory, sparking its pictures of long ago, was a vast library of snapshots. Our eyes, which we had trusted for so long, were shown to have misunderstood the movements made by a horse when it galloped.

I have before me, Mr Secretary, two volumes of photographs. The first shows the streets and monuments of Paris as they appeared in the late 1840s, before the Baron de Haussman began his boulevards. I stroll around looking up and down the alley-ways, noting the time told by a stopped clock, the angle of the morning light. The second volume contains photographs taken during the aftermath of the uprising in 1871. Corpses pose for the spectator. A line of coffins contains cramped, creased bodies of communards killed by MacMahon in May. I see figures standing in doorways wearing clothes long mouldered. And then I look out of the window into the London dark.

It must be almost dawn. The Pencil has not had the short night he expected. He looks tired, drawn.

Me? I have never felt stronger.

I can still remember in all its details the first time I stepped up to the camera in my own right. It was 21 September 1893. I remember the date because it was my birthday: I was twenty-nine years old. I covered myself with the dark hood and, applying my eye to the viewfinder, saw a minute and inverted image of Lady Magenta. She was dressed as Persephone and she held a flower in her hand, a poppy or a violet. On a table beside her lay half a rose-red pomegranate which soon – alas – was only to appear in black and white. I bent down, spreading and settling the cape over my shoulders and head. Suddenly, except that now I could see a little more, I felt just as I had done inside the pantomime horse.

The years, then and now, disappear in a magnesium flash.

9

Porphyry and Prophylactics

BY THE middle of 1895 both Lady Magenta and I felt ready to test our photographic expertise in the world outside the studio. We left London on the Bath Road, having equipped a carriage with the tools of our trade. Riding in a second conveyance, we were able to use the first as a travelling dark room. Each day we spent hours in its cramped belly. Our subjects were roadside wanderers: peripatetic agricultural labourers with grimy shirts and tanned, wrinkled faces; men with pipes who wore frayed trousers and grinned over gateposts. We photographed a troupe of travelling performers on their way to give a performance in Salisbury. We captured the image of a quack doctor selling his remedies in a market-place and of a bargee asleep on a tow-path with his horse grazing beside him.

These wayfarers had tales to tell which our methods could not record and it was often difficult to stop the mouth of a vagabond whilst he posed for his picture. On and on the tramps and pedlars, the tinkers and gipsies talked; on and on without ever reaching an end.

A week after our return, we spread the photographs before us. One picture in particular arrested our attention. A dusty road rose into the distance, where it met a grey, storm-laden sky; to the right, a caravan stood in a bleak field. In front of it was a group of travelling performers. Some were looking into the lens of the camera and some were not; some were posing for their portraits and some were lounging around in the remnants of the previous night's make-up. In the immediate foreground was a crate on which two dwarfs were playing chess.

It was then that we had an idea.

Later in the summer of 1895, Lady Magenta and I journeyed by train up and down the country seeking out the stopping places of as many travelling circuses as I knew or we had been able to discover from advertisements and publicity notices. We collected hundreds of images of scenes which had once been familiar to me.

But the circus had changed in the five years since I had left my profession and the steam engine was now its beating heart. Whirring wheels and belts powered displays and moving structures more extrava-gant than any I had seen before. On enormous merry-go-rounds, children screamed as they flew through the air. Amongst the growling, smoking machines it seemed more than ever that the circus was a factory, a mill thrown up overnight by a nomadic work-force. We had great difficulty in persuading the overseers of these steam roundabouts to disengage the motors and stop their contraptions from moving so that we could take our photographs. Otherwise, we would have recorded only an indecipherable blur superintended by an oily mechanic with a rag in his hand.

Lady Magenta had more enthusiasm for her subject than I, but I wondered at the time whether it excited her only because she thought it was free of the city. It was different to her; it brought back no memories. She turned a blind eye to the machines and saw only the myths.

With meticulous care, we amassed a gallery of types. Owners in the pride of possession stood with their legs splayed. Their hands rested on ornamental walking sticks and blades of grass were reflected in their polished boots. Bareback riders were so energetic and so hard to keep still, even for a moment, that we had little luck with them: a nodding plume, a single, focussed leg which extended from the blurred surge of a galloping horse. A lion tamer darned his socks on the steps of a caravan. Bent over their tin plates, a line of despondent clowns sat at a long table. The lens of our camera lingered lovingly on the giant, the fat lady and the thin man; on the Siamese twins, the midget and the three-legged boy.

Lady Magenta was delighted with our work. But she noticed that something still troubled me and asked what it was.

'I can't put my finger on it,' I replied. 'The circus – the tents and roundabouts – it's a good enough backdrop, I suppose. But it all looks so smug, so quaint. It's as if – I don't know – all the people *belong* here.'

'But Jack!' exclaimed Lady Magenta, selecting a photograph at random and pushing it towards me. 'Look at these people: the circus is their home, their work, their life. They *do* belong. That is what we are recording.'

I held the picture in my hand. It showed a mechanic enveloped in a cloud of steam.

'Nobody belongs,' I said. 'On the streets, people are alert and frigh-tened. In the city nobody is immune.'

Lady Magenta looked at me almost pleadingly and I saw the sense of mission in her eyes. 'It is our privilege,' she said, 'to be able to make ideals visible. We should show all the paths that lead out of the city.'

'I don't see that at all,' I replied with an irritation which I could not pin down. 'That's just what the circus tried to do.'

'Well? What's wrong with that?'

'It's whistling in the dark, pretending we're not afraid.'

Lady Magenta sighed and looked at her stained fingers. 'Perhaps you're right,' she said. The next day, she left for Dover on a visit of a week's duration and I had nothing to do.

A couple of days later I took a walk over Hampstead Heath and decided to call on the baroness before returning to the Plough and Stars. As I opened the drawing-room door and stepped across the threshold I found that for the second time I had intruded upon an intimate scene and once again it seemed that I was the only embarrassed party.

On this occasion the room could be seen in daylight, although it was a brightness so filtered that I felt as if I had entered a vast aquarium. The laurels beyond the French windows had been allowed to grow freely and their leaves pressed against the window like the hands of drowning sailors immersed in a great green wave. The baroness knelt on a *chaise longue*, naked to the waist. She smiled at me and made no attempt to cover herself. Standing behind the baroness with his hands on her shoulders was a man in early middle age. As I greeted my friend, his pale pink hands began to twist the upper portion of the baroness's body into a series of remarkable and presumably therapeutic postures. I thought it strange, I remember, that a powerful man should have such a deficiency of hair. His eyelashes and brows were almost invisible and his ginger moustache was as downy as his sandy side-whiskers.

The baroness introduced her companion as Dr Garth-Thompson. It did not take me long to remember that on our first meeting several years previously, Sir Stafford Singleton had mentioned this man in the fondest terms.

'Andrew,' said the baroness in a slightly strangled voice, 'has a flourishing practice in Chelsea.'

The doctor nodded diffidently in my direction and then forced the baroness's head between her knees. A clicking, as of the readjustment of traumatized vertebrae, could be heard.

'So have you come to take our photograph, Mr Spellman?' asked the baroness when her treatment was finished and she had replaced her upper garments. 'I should love to be in a medical textbook – or a peep-show.' She leered at the doctor, who turned away to hide a smile.

The maid served tea. On the pretext of helping Dr Garth-Thompson to a biscuit, the baroness began a whispered colloquy with her guest. She seemed to be suggesting something which at first aroused the physician's doubts. At length, however, he acceded. The baroness asked me to stay: there was an arrangement in view which she thought I might enjoy. I gladly accepted the invitation.

The conversation drifted onto the topic of social health and occupational diseases. I happened to mention that I had spent my youth as the back end of a pantomime horse. Garth-Thompson's shyness disappeared and he expatiated for some time on the longevity of the circus performer – barring, of course, the usual accidents:

'It really is quite remarkable: there has been a study of two of the phenomena. The circus seems to be a far healthier place than the city, with all its problems of poverty and overcrowding.'

For the next hour or so, the young physician mapped out before us a topography of disease as it existed at that hour in the capital. We went from scarlet fever to diphtheria and cholera, from typhus and polio to tuberculosis. Finally, the doctor discussed the spread of syphilis.

We were interrupted by the arrival of Mr Rupert Dinmont, the ineffectual but good-natured silk merchant I had met once before at Bartholomew Square. On this occasion, he was provocatively attired in a checked green suit with a purple necktie.

The baroness began to regale him with her inexhaustible fund of gossip. Rupert listened with rapt attention whilst she went over the details of a fist-fight between two Members of Parliament which had recently interrupted the performance, at Covent Garden, of one of Verdi's operas.

'A woman, was it over a woman?' inquired Rupert excitedly.

'Mr Dinmont!' cried the baroness reproachfully, 'you think in clichés! According to questions reported in Hansard, the "disagreement" concerned the "treatment of Mahdist insurgents in Egypt".'

'Rubbish!' exclaimed Rupert. 'It was a woman!'

The baroness smiled. 'Mr Poynter, the Member of Parliament for South Kensington, who happened to be one of the parties involved in the "dispute", would, I think, deny your accusation.'

Rupert sank back in his seat. 'The vulgarity of it! At the opera, of all places!'

'You like the opera then, Mr Dinmont?' asked Dr Garth-Thompson.

'I adore it,' said Rupert, gazing into the air. 'It is the only reason I stay in London.'

'But surely – your business?'

'Pah!' replied the young man, toying with his necktie. 'Business! I despise it!'

A short while later, we were joined by Mr Sidney Bellowes, who lumbered short-sightedly around the room to shake our hands. I had seen him on several occasions over the previous few years and I always enjoyed his scholarly presence. Speak to him of the morning's paper and his eyes glazed over; mention the forests of Brazil and he radiated enthusiasm. Mr Bellowes was accompanied by a gentleman whom I had not encountered since our first meeting. On that occasion he had been sound asleep in his chair; now, although a little older, he looked intensely alert. He introduced himself to me as Mr Lionel Zabel. I discovered later that he was an American millionaire. He had made a fortune in zinc before turning his attention to rubber, in which he had doubled his assets in two years. Then he tried copper, made another mint and began to feel bored.

Over the next few minutes, I began to realize that Mr Zabel, Mr Bellowes and Mr Dinmont were all involved in the mysterious plan which the baroness had mentioned.

At length Mr Zabel looked at his watch and announced that his barouche was waiting at the door. As the company gathered itself together, the baroness took the American to one side and asked him whether he should mind my attending the evening's entertainment. I was a friend of hers, a sort of pupil.

'We are all your pupils, baroness,' he said as he looked at me across the room. I saw the steely eyes of a born money-maker. 'I should be delighted. Mr Spellman is most welcome.'

The six of us surged through the evening streets in the luxurious carriage. I talked further with Dr Garth-Thompson, who sat next to me. Had he any plan or suggestion to lift the burden of misery from London? He had many suggestions, certainly, but whether he was by nature a cynical man or, as he maintained, merely long used to disappointment, he held out little hope of any improvement sponsored by authority. Authority, he said, was not unhappy with the present situation, because Authority knew that a rising birth rate meant a rising pool of labour and thus its cheaper cost. Improvements could only be expected if the death rate began to exceed the birth rate, for this would be reflected in rising labour costs. For that situation to come about, however, public health would have to deteriorate to such an extent that, compared to it, this modern London would seem a paradise of salubrity. The doctor sank into a preoccupied silence whilst Mr Dinmont entertained us with his affable trivialities.

We travelled westwards through the autumn evening along the banks of the Thames. London died away, a distant hubbub, and a succession of mansions which bordered the river came into view. Mr Zabel pointed out one or two of these edifices, mentioned the names of their owners and drew our attention to their more interesting features. But in the end, he drawled, he preferred his own little cottage.

The little cottage was approached by way of a gatehouse and a half-mile avenue of oak trees. It was called Fairfields.

The baroness later gave me other examples of Mr Zabel's penchant for understatement. He had a 'house' in New York which took up a whole block and a 'mansion' upstream from Manaus which was reputedly the size of a Renaissance palace. He had filled it with quattrocento furniture and classical statuary and would bring his friends to visit in a Venetian gondola which breasted its passage up the Rio Negro amongst electric eels and crocodiles. Surrounded by primeval swamps, European tenors and sopranos sang duets on the piazza in the warm nights and courtesans were thrown into the fountains.

Sir Stafford Singleton arrived at Fairfields by a separate conveyance shortly after we had sat down to dinner. The usual insouciance of his manner was notably absent. Making a circuit of the table in order to reach his own place, he ignored Mr Zabel's welcoming gesture and put his hand on Andrew Garth-Thompson's shoulder. The doctor, over his soup, could not have noticed that his friend's face twisted momentarily with pain. But Sir Stafford quickly mastered his distress.

The conversation turned for a while on a second century Athenian vase which Mr Zabel had recently acquired, and which stood now in pride of place on the table. It had once been painted but now only the lines remained. The rim and base were decorated with heads of corn, and around the sides were depictions of the Eleusinian Mysteries. One of the illustrations was turned towards me and I was able to examine it in detail. It showed the goddess Demeter in the first agony of her loss, wild-eyed, her dishevelled hair streaming behind her.

'My dearest Andrew –' Sir Stafford had broken the silence and I dragged my eyes away from the distraught figure on the vase. 'Andrew, Andrew: are you entirely and absolutely sure that you want to go through with this absurd wager? Baroness, I have to say that I blame you entirely.' He looked across at her but, fork in hand, she merely raised her eyebrows and shrugged. 'You have set my poor dear boy on, baroness.'

There was an awkward silence for a moment and then Sir Stafford turned again to his friend. 'Andrew, the mark of the mature man, surely, is discretion. It is not too late to draw back: nobody could blame you.'

The doctor moodily tore a bread roll asunder. Stafford had to lean across the table to secure his attention. 'Andrew, are you determined on your course of action?'

Dr Garth-Thompson put the butter knife down with a small *clink* and, looking directly at his older friend, replied firmly. 'Sir Stafford: I have never been more determined than I am now. I am afraid to say that your entreaties only harden my resolve.'

'So be it,' said Sir Stafford, looking gloomily down at his untouched soup. The play of conversation resumed slowly, but without his participation.

Determined to appear unmoved by Sir Stafford's distress, Dr Garth-

Thompson began to draw Mr Zabel out on the subject of political economy. Did it have any ascertainable prognostic value?

Mr Zabel wiped his mouth with a damask napkin before replying. 'Well, Doctor, I'm not sure that I can answer your question. I can't see into the future, you know. I'm not a magician.'

'No, I quite see that. But aren't you more like a physician? Can't you speculate on the likely progress of the disease?'

'Ah, I understand your distinction, doctor. Yes: I suppose I can make informed guesses.'

'Then what do you think's going to happen?' interrupted Mr Dinmont. 'In what way?'

'Oh, you know: politically and all that sort of thing.'

Mr Zabel smiled gravely. 'Quite frankly, Mr Dinmont, I see only a great conflagration. The economic pressure to expand markets will surely lead to territorial disputes. Look at Egypt: it's happening already. These skirmishes, I think, will eventually but inevitably escalate into a major political, and then military, confrontation between the European powers.'

'What about America, Mr Zabel, what will she do?'

'America will pursue her policy of isolation as long as she can.'

'And England?'

'Oh – England,' said Mr Zabel softly, 'smothered and stifled old England! She will continue in complacency and passivity until forced to act. Once roused, I think that the lion may well show all its old strength. But it will be the end of her as a great nation.'

Later Mr Zabel guided us across the lawns to the chapel at Fairfields. We took our seats in a spacious gallery above the aisle. It was as if we were at the opera. Twenty feet below us, standing at the centre of the stage, was a gigantic block of porphyry perhaps ten feet square and four deep. Besides the opera and the church, there was something here, too, of the surgical theatre, for stretched out on the cold stone was the naked and motionless figure of a corpulent woman in late middle age. She looked like the subject of a lesson in anatomy. Her hair was lank and the insides of her thighs were covered with bruises. This lent her a mottled appearance which, Mr Dinmont observed, went well with the porphyry. The baroness began to giggle but the lesson in anatomy did not share her amusement: she looked directly upwards at the ornamental ceiling and there was not the flicker of an expression on her face.

I sat in a corner. On my right, the baroness and Mr Dinmont whispered with Lionel Zabel. Beyond them, Sir Stafford chewed his nails and looked both exasperated and ignored. In the far corner, Mr Bellowes made up our party: Dr Garth-Thompson had made his excuses and left us immediately after dinner.

Mr Zabel and Mr Dinmont were still pursuing the analogy – and the incongruence – between the pitiful body of the lesson in anatomy and the noble stone on which she lay when, with a sharp intake of breath, the baroness suddenly leant forward over the gallery railing.

Naked beneath us, Dr Garth-Thompson had entered the chapel. As he approached the porphyry altar I noticed that he had equipped his already erect penis with a prophylactic made of greased gut.

The doctor was evidently something of an athlete but nevertheless I was completely unprepared for what followed. He fucked that impoverished and bedraggled woman for a period of over two hours, a time during which my companions passed in and out of the gallery as if between the scenes of a play. He fucked her doggedly, tenaciously and with an inconceivable violence. He fucked her until her weighty body – it was like a murder – bounced off the stone with his force. Throughout this operation, the lesson in anatomy stared over his shoulder at the ornamental ceiling, on which golden cupids twined. In the end, her body juddered and she emitted a strangled shriek. Garth-Thompson's audience showed their appreciation by cheering and clapping and, as the lesson in anatomy moved spasmodically on the stone, the doctor bowed towards us and left the chapel.

Sick at heart, I stumbled down a flight of steps and escaped into the garden. I wandered for some time over rose beds and between moonlit avenues of yew before being approached by one of Mr Zabel's waiters, who offered me a glass of wine. I detained this person and tried to make conversation, feeling desperate for –

For what? I don't know. In any case, my accent – something in my tone – was no longer right. Whatever I said, the waiter shied away from me: he refused my intimacy, he gave me only respectful deference.

10
Hurdy-gurdy

'DON'T YOU think she was paid well enough? Don't you think she probably earned more money last night than she had ever seen before?'

The speaker was the baroness. Sitting in the carriage which had called that morning to take us away from Fairfields, I could not reply. Perhaps she was right. In sombre mood, I looked through the window at the meadows and the mellow mansions. 'It seems to me that money alone could never make up for such an outrage.'

'Don't be dull and sentimental, Jack, or I shall ask you to get out and walk. It was a bargain: she wanted it, she was paid, she came.'

'She was pounded into porphyry.'

The baroness became impatient with me. 'It doesn't make any difference! What difference could it possibly make for such a woman?'

I tried to be clear. 'Andrew Garth-Thompson behaved brutally.'

'Oh come, come, Jack.' The baroness was getting more irritated by the minute. 'Didn't you see?'

'See – ?'

'Evidently not. There were bruises on her thighs before, you know.' And she looked at me meaningfully.

'That's got nothing to do with it,' I said. 'The point is that Dr Garth-Thompson was utterly merciless.'

'The point is,' returned the baroness, 'that all women suffer that; all men do that.'

I was incredulous: '*All* of them?'

The baroness gave me a level stare. 'Don't you know?'

'I –' For a moment I gave up, completely baffled. 'And you,' I said at last, 'do you suffer that?'

'Suffer it?' she laughed. 'I enjoy it!'

'But people aren't waxworks to do with as we will.'

The baroness laughed again. 'On the contrary: the older I get, the more people seem to me to resemble nothing so much as waxworks.'

'And you *enjoyed – that*?'

My friend looked out of the window. 'It passed the time didn't it?'

Later, as we entered the London streets, the baroness spoke of her latest lover, an Italian hurdy-gurdy man with curly black hair and so many ear-rings he looked like a pirate. Two days previously, he had been dragged unceremoniously off the Hampstead pavement with barely enough time to tether his dancing monkey to its pole. Having temporarily satisfied the baroness's lusts, he had been paid off and forcibly ejected from the house by the serving-boy, Tom. Once in the street, the organ-grinder had untied his monkey and beaten it for trying to hide the money it had collected. He had then spent several hours walking up and down the avenue and reciting at the top of his voice all that had occurred between himself and the baroness.

The baroness had ignored the furore and remained in bed, smiling to herself and sipping her tea. She was immune to blackmail; what difference in the end, true or false, did one more story make? In any case, the organ-grinder's accent was virtually incomprehensible.

11

Offensive Images

W HEN I next saw Lady Magenta, in October, we returned almost at once to the subject of our previous conversation. She had clearly been thinking in the interval for she had taken up my unformulated thoughts with a force and eloquence I could never have matched.

'*Gealla*,' she said suddenly, 'was the Norse word for a sore on a horse.'

'Ah – *gealla*.'

'*Galli*,' she added a moment later, 'meant a fault.'

I had not lit the lamps and her face was dim in the long atelier. 'I'm not quite sure I follow you.'

'Don't you see?' she asked excitedly: 'Fox Talbot's gallic acid has found us our subjects! The satirists were gadflies, so let us too make gall our ink.'

She began to pace up and down the attic and her shadow flickered on the sloping ceiling as she continued. 'The circus is buttoned up in its own performance. But the city is etched with wounds: it is these engravings which we must photograph.'

I worried that even if we were able to freeze for a moment the collapsing wharves and warehouses as they left their imprints on the soft bodies of their subjects, these photographs – like the city – would still be only a semblance of presence. In each case something – a soul, a voice – would always escape us.

Nevertheless, in late December 1895, we spread out our new photographs on a trestle table and began to review them. An unemployed stevedore leant back against a bollard and turned his head to watch his silhouetted comrades unloading a barge on the other side of the river. His wooden leg stuck out awkwardly on the cobblestones.

A woman of perhaps twenty-five, her face eaten away by phosphorus from the match factory, sat on a kerbstone with a placard which read: 'HUNGRY – 4 CHILDREN.'

A ray of light illuminated the stained clothes of a woman who nursed a baby. Until you saw the mother's face, you might have thought that, frozen in the blink of the mechanical eye, there would have been no way of knowing that the child had died.

A one-eyed man; a woman with no fingers; a pock-marked child. Chemical factories, paper mills and dyeworks. Boats and trains, stations and wharves.

What we could not capture was the dynamic which had produced this freakshow, the incomprehensible tongue of steam hammers, the rationale of squealing winches. The camera does not question the sufficiency of mute things. In its eye the peeling signs, the warehouses and rubbish heaps needed no afterword and had no case to answer; they were so many shapes.

Despite these reservations, Lady Magenta and I made an appointment to see the Member of Parliament for South Kensington at one of his surgeries. Hoping to use it as a sort of petition, we took our portfolio with us.

The Member of Parliament for South Kensington was not upset by the content of our photographs: he barely looked at them. He was outraged by the fact that they had even been shown to him:

'I will not have this obscene charade, this catalogue of depravities in my house for a single instant longer than is necessary to show you the door! These images are offensive to civilized people, Lady Magenta. I am surprised and deeply shocked that you have taken it upon yourself to poison the atmosphere of my drawing-room.' The Member of Parliament for South Kensington looked me up and down as if to suggest that I was the agent responsible for Lady Magenta's action and puffed in self-righteous indignation. 'I am astonished at your gall and frankly, well – it *galls* me.'

Lady Magenta stepped forward to take back the portfolio. 'I had thought these pictures illustrated the need for intervention,' she said calmly.

'They illustrate, madam, the dung heap and the midden! They are improper and as such I . . . I . . . ' Scarcely articulate in his fury, he made a gesture with his hand as if to sweep our photographs out of his way.

Lady Magenta rose to go and as she did so was attacked by one of her fits of coughing. Once again I noticed that there was blood on her handkerchief.

When we reached the door, the Member of Parliament for South Kensington had become calmer. 'In any case, madam,' he said as we passed out of the room, 'those people are not my constituents.'

Returning to Bethnal Green, Lady Magenta and I sat up until dawn to discuss this incident. The Member of Parliament for South Kensington had responded as if our photographs were an incitement to revolution or an act in itself revolutionary. We knew that he was no radical and yet we had not expected such a display of blindness.

We could only conclude, in the grim early light, that our photographs had failed. It was not the camera's fault but our perception of its possibilities. So excited by photography had we become that we had begun to attribute magical powers to it. As if the mere image had ever changed a stubborn heart!

Wearily we reassessed the scattered pictures. 'In any case,' said Lady Magenta after a while, 'misery is only incidentally pictorial. Its essence lies in the accumulations of history. It needs a narrative, a duration of impossibilities, some sense of weight and density.'

We had produced mere floating eye-blinks of suffering, little jabs that the viewer could brush away like gnats. It was not the camera's fault but nor, in the end, we decided, was it ours. It was not even the fault of the Member of Parliament for South Kensington. The fault lay in whatever it was that made us shut our eyes. It seemed that nothing reached us any more; we had all been inoculated.

It occurs to me now, Mr Secretary, that our pictures were worse than this, that they were something like thefts. There was a vacant space here in which tormented flesh became the desired and purloined object.

Out of the past, a mother looks down at her dead child whilst on her doorstep, two people from another world commit an offence which is recorded in the moment of its execution. It would be the perfect crime, had not the photograph left a single trace behind: itself.

I think now that the mind is a rapist and that each mental act is a violation, an incursion into alien territory. Thought thinks itself by ruptures, exposures, dissections. The camera's poking eye turns everything into a woman which it masters for its pleasure.

I am not entirely serious, Mr Secretary. If you think that I am, you are reading me for a window and not a door, trying to see through me, to turn me into a ghost.

NEW YEAR'S DAY, 1896. I walked between two beautiful women, either one of whom could have been my mother in the matter of age. Their arms were passed through mine and they were giggling like schoolgirls. We were still a little unsteady on our feet: the celebrations at the Plough and Stars had been more than usually unruly and it had been after dawn when we had finally retired to bed. Lurching now along the Embankment, we were laughing uproariously at the people who crossed the street to avoid us. The day was quiet and bright, with a diaphanously blue sky across which scudded the smallest white clouds. Ice crisped the edges of the Thames. Geese, unsteady and bemused, stood on the ice. A packing crate was frozen into the ice. Cleopatra's Needle was sharp and pale against the tangled black trees. I thought what a change of climate it must have been for the monument when, in 1878, as a tribute, Mehemet Ali had sent it from Heliopolis to our own City of Fog.

New Year's Day. The newspaper talked of the achievements of the past year. Marconi had transmitted the first message by wireless. Röntgen had discovered X-rays. Invisible pulses of energy existed beyond the red and violet ends of our own spectrum; rays and waves bounced around the world beneath the atmosphere. We were beginning to conduct our business by means of the intangible.

Later, wrapped in blankets, I lay on my bed in the hay-loft and watched, through the skylight, the passing clouds. On my bedside table were two letters which had arrived shortly before Christmas. The first was from Mimi and Bessie. I had not seen them for a couple years now. They said that they were well and still lived above the sweetshop in Chalk Farm. Just as I had imagined, they were slowly and ruefully ageing; just as I had imagined, they were still intensely and passionately in love. Somehow I felt that for them I was still the pale youth of 1880 or even, perhaps, one of their own young customers, penny in pocket, nose pressed against the glass of the shop window.

Mimi and Bessie had news of Aramind. She was still confined in the asylum at Dover: Luigi Pesto had not appeared to claim her and had eventually been given up for lost. They had visited Aramind a couple of months previously, in the autumn, and they said that their hearts had sunk when they saw the vast, gloomy building on the cliff top. Inside, the aproned nurses had scrubbed faces and bony hands. All kinds of howling came from locked doors. Aramind sat quietly in her room; she had seemed to recognize them but they were not sure. A nurse had told them that her child had been stillborn.

My second letter was from Wilf. He rambled on illegibly and enthusiastically about his greengrocer's shop in Nottingham before springing his surprise: he was married! Six months married to a coal-miner's daughter! 'And she was used to the filth, Jacko, just like I said. So I was glad I could carry on same as before. And she didn't mind about the – about the smallness, you know, Jacko. Said she liked a small one if it was springy. Oh, and it's got some sap in it these days!'

Wilf's wife was called Laura; she was very pregnant; they were obviously fascinated with each other. In the evenings, Wilf wrote up his accounts in a special book and at the weekends, if she felt well enough, Laura would check it for him. 'Profit and loss, Jacko, plus and minus: two columns, two halves – it's just the same as it used to be.'

It was all rather heart-warming and made me feel very lonely. I huddled in my blankets and stared at the darkening sky. I squashed a bed-bug – one of the million motes in this smoke-chamber of a city – and fell into a dream. I was my own toy soldier, fighting the tiger, aware that I, an automaton, had come to life only for a moment and that soon my mechanism would run down. Then I was sitting at the table in Regis Street and Zanare was dead, or somebody was dead, and my father's legacy was to be taken away from me and buried where I would never find it.

The next day, I received a telegram from Lady Magenta asking me to meet her at the studio in Bethnal Green.

In the long, narrow room she rose from an armchair and faced me determinedly, as if we had an unpleasant task ahead of us.

'You and I, Mr Spellman, are going to pay a visit to Sir Rodney Rouncewell.'

She picked up our portfolio and, taking me by the arm, dragged me down the interminable, echoing flights of stairs where children peeped from doorways and brooms leaned against the wall. Lady Magenta refused to utter another word until we were rattling and swaying in an Underground carriage on the way to our destination.

'It's time for Rouncewell to pay his debt.'

'Debt –?' I fished for further information.

'He must prove that he means what he says and that his wallet is where his heart is.'

'But where should his heart be?'

'In the right place, of course. He could help us: he is powerful and he is rich. Sir Rodney could pull strings.'

'For the photographs?'

'For the children: the hungry, the orphans.'

'You are going to ask him for money?'

'I'm always asking the old wolf for money, every year. And he always gives it – but then he has a great deal to spare.'

Lady Magenta put her hand on my arm and raised her voice above the noise of the train once more: 'You have already met Sir Rodney, haven't you, Jack?'

Yes, of course I had met him. It had been six years previously, during the party at which I had damaged Lord Tramont's camera. I still remembered the way he had smiled at Bessie and toyed with her hair.

For the remainder of the journey I wondered at Lady Magenta's continuing enthusiasm for our photographic endeavours. There was an inexplicable joy in her manner. I for one had lost my illusions the moment we had entered the house of the Member of Parliament for South Kensington and nothing, now, could have been more calculated to depress me than a revival of this interest.

We found Sir Rodney sitting in a darkened room, his ravaged features thrown into relief by the firelight. His skin was as pale as if, immediately prior to our visit, he had applied Harlequin's bismuth make-up. His hair had receded from his temples but still curled thickly over the collar of his smoking-jacket. It was dyed to the unnatural blackness of a crow's wing.

It was hard to engage him in conversation; he knew that we had come for something other than politeness's sake and refused to be drawn by our pleasantries. To me, his manner was curt and contemptuous; to Lady Magenta he was absurdly flattering. His manner seemed to say: 'I am lying, of course, my dear lady. But for you and your beauty I have agreed to play for a while the attentive fool.'

At length Lady Magenta sat on the arm of Sir Rodney's chair and proposed that he should examine our photographs. She lit a gas lamp to cast a pool of light over his shoulder.

'My dear Lady Magenta,' murmured Sir Rodney, 'surely you must realize that to withdraw, even for a minute, my lingering gaze from your charms – illuminated so marvellously as they now are – will be to suffer a tragic agony that even the pen of a Sophocles could not record.'

The reader will have noticed a peculiarity in the typographic rendition of Sir Rodney's 'r's. He consistently affected the rolling French pronunciation of these, in the court fashion of a hundred years ago, and they are so characteristic of that bored but unnerving voice as it comes back to me from across the chasm of years that I have no option but to ask the secretary to represent them by a supplementary mark.

Lady Magenta shouted with laughter and threw back her head to show her full throat and the white points of her teeth. While she was thus for a moment unconscious of his gaze. I noticed that Sir Rodney salaciously devoured every detail of her physical form as far as it was revealed by her clothing. She looked down at him and I noticed that her eyes were very bright. 'You old wolf, you flatterer. Well – if you can bear to take your eyes off me for a moment – look at these photographs.'

Together they turned the pages of the portfolio. Lady Magenta occasionally directed Sir Rodney's attention to a particular image with her hand, or, with a finger, alerted him to a detail. I strolled around the room, looking at the smoke-blackened paintings on the wall in their smothered chiaroscuro. I was particularly drawn to a landscape in oils depicting a mythologically sylvan scene. Time and smoke had turned it into a poisoned industrial panorama. That swain did not tend sheep: he worked a power loom, and his companion, a nymph, was surely a dye-mill girl. They reclined, not on a pregnant Arcadian bank, but on a slag-heap where the paint had bubbled as if with the application of acid.

Sir Rodney and Lady Magenta finished leafing through the portfolio and Sir Rodney, placing it on his lap, positioned his hands over it as if it were a piano that he was about to play. His pale, delicate fingers were extended eloquently; his beautifully manicured nails touched the kidskin binding of the album and I half-expected them to cut into it, so sharp did they seem.

'A remarkable series of images, Lady Magenta: I congratulate you.'

'Do you find them – powerful?'

The pale gentleman thought for a moment. 'Certainly they arouse powerful emotions, feelings perhaps as intense and as obscure as those engendered by erotica.'

She was puzzled. 'You find them – erotic?'

'In a certain sense, yes. One receives from them the same vicarious sense of – what? – exposure. They do great honour to the voyeur. They assert his security, his imaginative majesty.'

Lady Magenta was baffled but fascinated. She did not seem to realize that this meant the end of all our hopes. 'Am I to understand, then, that you think of these pictures as pornography?'

Sir Rodney made a vague gesture with his hand. 'They feed a most specific craving. They seem to record a certain perverse interest – which I share, I do assure you – in the varieties of human misery and deformity.'

He paused for a moment before turning to the picture of the match girl which I have already described. 'Your – ah – assistant and you, Lady Magenta, have done particularly well here, I think. This waif has a singular beauty which is rendered only the more extravagantly fascinating by her decayed jaw. The definition of the image is so sharp, it captures so well the tormented flesh. And here,' – he indicated something with his little finger, 'this delightful smudge across her cheek. Dirt, madam, or a bruise? Charming, charming.'

I looked across at Lady Magenta but her eyes were fixed on Sir Rodney as he continued to speak. 'The dispossessed are so – I struggle for the right word – *picturesque*. I would expect to find such litter in the streets of Naples but I am most gratified to discover it so close to my own doorstep. Something about the English climate, its rigours, the moisture and the cold, gives these wretches an added charm.'

Sir Rodney seemed complacently unaware that he had shocked Lady Magenta and me beyond measure. I could not but feel that the sheer aestheticized lust with which he now again flicked through the portfolio was a response more deeply obscene and more profoundly immoral than that of the Member of Parliament for South Kensington. I realized with astonishment that even the Baroness Hrocka, with her limitless capacity for the erotic, would have been incapable of this. Lady Magenta left the arm of Sir Rodney's chair and stood in front of him, smoothing her skirt. Then she turned her head towards the fire and her whole posture became slack, resigned. Her arms hung loosely by her sides; once again, she seemed to offer herself to Sir Rodney's gaze. For a while they remained like this: she, mastered, averted her face; he, negligent, was completely at his ease. I decided to act on Lady Magenta's behalf. It did not matter that I no longer had the least confidence in our pictures.

'Sir Rodney, can you not do something about this?'

He affected incomprehension but he knew very well what I meant. 'Do, Monsieur Jacques? – may I call you Jacques? – I do so hate the plebeian Jack. Do? They are very fine photographs: it seems plain to me that neither of you need my assistance.'

I pursued my point. 'Can you not do something about them? Something to help?'

For a moment a smile of understanding passed across his face but a second later he continued to protest his ignorance. 'I, Jacques? Do? Help? A mere individual, an ailing bachelor?'

He glanced across to Lady Magenta in her abandoned pose. The room seemed darker than ever. I waited for Sir Rodney to continue. 'And, by helping, would I not erase your subject-matter – poverty, misery, ugliness, deformity?'

'Yes.'

'And would I not therefore make such photographs impossible?'

'Yes, Sir Rodney, yes.'

He shrugged his shoulders. 'But I rather like them: it is not my intention to interfere with the work of artists like you. I think there should be more of these things' – he indicated the portfolio in his lap – 'not less.'

Lady Magenta hesitantly placed her knee on the arm of Sir Rodney's chair and her hand on his shoulder. He touched the material of her dress and stroked her thigh as though she were a cat. 'Sir Rodney,' she said in a strangled voice, 'could you not, as before, give money to Siriso?'

Siriso? Where had I heard that name before?

'Money! so there's the rub!' Sir Rodney laughed until the tears ran down his face. 'You made me think that you wanted criticism, appreciation! If it is mere money – ! I will have a cheque sent to you tomorrow, and you can fill out the amount for yourself.'

Once again he put his hand on Lady Magenta's leg: 'How could your ladyship ever doubt my fidelity to the Siriso Charitable Trust?'

13

A Literary Figure

I COULD not sleep after our session last night, Mr Secretary. My mind returned to the pages which have accumulated on my desk and I became convinced that somewhere I had left something out. It was as if I had been sweeping out, not my own chapters, but the rooms of a large and abandoned house. What was I looking for? Perhaps a small article which I had left on a table downstairs: a scarf, a paperweight. Or maybe a pile of dust which I had forgotten to clear away. I wandered through the house but found nothing. And oh! the increasing sense of emptiness: forty-two vacated rooms!

Ill?

You have asked me that before. Why do you keep asking me that? No, Mr Stenographer, it was not illness that kept me awake last night. I will tell you what it was: it was happiness, relief, release. I had worried that I was disappointing you but something you said made me realize that the confession I had planned was unnecessary.

A revelation? Are you hoping for that? No, Mr Pencil, it is not that. I know that these are gloomy days and the grand path is – how shall I put it? – somewhat pot-holed. That makes it only the easier: if you want to forget the nightmare of stuff then there are plenty of attractive schemes in the streets. Prophets are waiting round every corner.

Last night you said that you continually had the sensation of having read all that I dictate somewhere before; you felt as if you had strayed into a museum of half-remembered fragments, broken snatches and partial passages from old books. You called it *déjà lu*. Nothing could have flattered me more; I was ecstatic. You, too, knew that others had preceded me and that I had concealed myself behind them – or rather, perhaps, that they, like an ambush, were hidden behind me. I am only a secretary, Mr Secretary: everything I say has been said before. Last night, however, my ecstasy gradually turned into a sort of horror: what had all this writing, these forty-two chapters, been about?

Grave-robbing, soul-stealing, spirit-possession.

Whose soul, whose grave? Was it those others I had submerged in my lines, or was I, after all, only the ventriloquist's dummy? Since the gamekeeper has confessed himself a poacher, should I therefore now play the legal jack and track down my list of missing persons? The sources: even now I feel them scatter through the text like nervous animals who have sensed something hostile in the air of the forest.

Let me be more specific and brush some of the moss away from the face of this interred statue the figure of the writer. He is a Thoth, of course, who gambles on behalf of others. He is also a Mercury with a conscience, a Hermes tormented by his own dishonesty. There is always plenty of opportunity for guilt since the materials of the statue's trade are stolen: a shaving here, a veneer there; occasionally the odd plank. In order to continue the game at all, the figure must acquire the mask of a trespasser with nothing but contempt and envy for the property of others. He is out to fleece us. In his darker moments, however, the figure knows that he is played by his own game. To continue to imitate is to lose one's self, to have one's picture confounded with the original.

Worse still, it is to lay oneself open to burglary. The figure senses that others want to invade his power and dignity, to topple him from his cardboard throne. He takes steps to protect his property and to safeguard the legitimacy of his children. The old subversive, knowing that he is a black marketeer, sets himself up as an honest tradesman; the creator, realizing he is only a copyist, protects himself with copyrights. Thieves obey the same laws as men of property: both know that in the market you must sell dearer than you bought.

The words that the figure speaks will not be unaffected by this new awareness. At first, he believed in a world where words were things. The song of Orpheus, he thought, could bring Eurydice back from the ghostlands. His incantations could make her pallid face flush once more with life and his words were not bound by the laws of likeness, they were not copies of copies or ghosts of ghosts. No: they originated solely in themselves. Because he was young the figure wanted his readers to see the things he described as clearly as if they were really there. He wanted them to feel his effects like the symptoms of a disease or an impassioned love. He felt no guilt for prescribing opiates. Indeed, as he made his twists and turns and played his tricks, he had a gambler's sense of potency.

One of these figures, once, talked about the two halves of the panto-mime, but he had no sense of their junction. He rejected the 'serious' legends depicted in the first half of the show and plumped, in his still guiltless magic, for the comic trickery of Harlequin. The world of Hades is a story which is told; only after the ghost has been appeased, only in the horseplay is there any life. Gradually a shadow steals across the face of the figure. At a certain point he realizes that horseplay is the oldest ghost story of all. Suddenly he feels that his tricks no longer belong to him. Everything is artifice; transplanted flowers.

Like a tyrant, the figure attempts to reassert his authority over his stolen subjects. But in his heart he feels a great loss and a sense of dismemberment. From now on, his words will be set against themselves. There is still the old dream of a romance between words and flesh but now there is also a new consciousness: that words belong to words, back and back with no end.

At about this time, after the prescriptions and frenzied commands, the figure will begin to issue edicts and manifestos. Legislation is introduced concerning the figure's figures, his past analogies. From now on, for example, it is no longer right to compare the theatre with the world: this is a false comparison. The figure becomes as pedantic as a priest; refusing to see likenesses, he is always trying to penetrate differences and contrasts. The figure becomes as eccentric as a millionaire; he inserts borrowed and untranslatable nonsense into his writings because he thinks that only these inscrutabilities offer certain proof of their authenticity. He spends a lot of time signing adoption papers for his orphans and quarrelling about the parentage of ideas.

It is not all gloom, however. Sitting at his desk on a sunny evening, the figure still derives a furtive pleasure from his ornaments and embellishments. He calls them into columns and makes them march up and down his room. After that, he feels much better and is able to eat a large meal. He tells his guests that it is his sauces and secret recipes which make his food taste unlike any other. Old ladies nod wisely over their pearls. After dinner, the figure still feels some of the old warmth as he tells the tale of a thief who escaped because he was illiterate. Because he knows that people are watching, it amuses him to pretend to stumble in his narration.

The audience starts whispering that he has lost his way. Not at all. Only when he makes these errors is the old fox completely in control.

And who is this figure?

I should not want to give you the impression, Mr Secretary, that the nominal capture of a single ghost can solve our problems and so I shall withhold his name. Consider it consigned to a blank page or a missing chapter.

I trust that I will cast no revelatory light if I tell you that I too, dear reader, am a ghost. Tell me you can see my face, and I will know that you are lying or lost. Tell me that I am not haunting you, I who am also possessed, and I will know that you are not reading.

Siriso: I had heard this name before the visit to Sir Rodney. Lady Magenta had mentioned it, years previously, on Southwark Bridge. I seemed to remember, too, that I had heard the word long before this and even on another, more distant occasion. The word had been with me all my life, but I did not know why.

Our visit to Sir Rodney's house early in 1896, precipitated a new stage in the relations between himself and Lady Magenta. Their meetings became more frequent and throughout the spring of that year he regularly attended her soirées, where he was a distinguished although somewhat reserved figure. He took a particular delight in the barbed comment and the concealed insult. The Member of Parliament for South Kensington (who had quickly chosen to forget Lady Magenta's lapse from social form) would, in particular, had he understood these sallies, have suffered badly. He did not, however, and the evenings were in general pleasant enough affairs. Sir Rodney's presence even relieved the boredom of the ossified pleasantries and flabby politesse usually produced on such occasions.

Lady Magenta treated the pale gentleman as an uncle and delighted in teasing him, knowing that the wolf would deign to eat only from her hand. She would toy with his watch-chain and he merely smiled indulgently. She seemed younger than at any time since I had known her.

The exchanges between Sir Rodney and the Baroness Hrocka were a delight which I would not have missed for the world. They had known each other of old, had been lovers thirty years ago and more. But, perhaps finding in the other a mirror image of their own heartlessness, they had cursed each other for cynics and parted. Both the baroness's quaint English and Sir Rodney's whitened face brought back echoes of the previous century. The baroness always seemed younger than she was; Sir Rodney, on the other hand, appeared considerably older than his fifty-odd years. She had the aged bloom of artifice; he the rude health of sickness – the sickness of his own ancestry. He was like a gentleman disembowelled in polite company. By an act of will, he seemed to restrain

215

the articulation of some agony which racked him to the ends of his cultivated fingertips. It was the most astonishing act of self-possession and affectation that I had ever seen.

One evening in the middle of February, I was standing in the middle of the drawing-room at Bartholomew Square when Sir Rodney, passing by in the direction of the waiter, violently jostled me as though he had been unaware of my presence. I was affronted and spoke without thinking:

'I am alive, Sir Rodney. I am not a thing, or a picture in air: I live in flesh and blood.'

He smiled courteously and began to speak softly into my ear. 'Being little more than a paid slave, I am surprised that you take so generous a view of yourself.' He moved off to re-charge his glass, seeming, in spite of his insult, strangely pleased with me.

I was both astonished and perturbed that Lady Magenta seemed to find Sir Rodney's rottenness so compellingly attractive. For he was a deeply rotten man: not rotten *to* the core, as we speak colloquially of criminals and governments, but essentially and absolutely rotten *from* the core. The reek of it always surrounded him although he was never anything but impeccably dressed and, to the normal nose, perhaps even pleasantly aromatic.

I asked Lady Magenta that night whether Sir Rodney had anything in particular against me. She seemed worried as she replied. 'No, no, Jack. He was annoyed by something that happened yesterday, that's all.'

'Something to do with me?'

She picked up an empty glass from the table and stood uncertainly before me, turning it in her hands. 'There was a meeting between Sir Rodney and another man. He said something that Sir Rodney did not like, that's all.'

I learned over these months – mostly from the baroness – a number of things about Sir Rodney which were not generally known. He had been tried, in England, on three separate charges of murder. All, admittedly, had been in his youth and on each occasion he had been honourably acquitted. These judicial absolutions, however, as the baroness specu-lated, were not unassociated with the fact that he was able to provide himself, each time, with the services of the barrister Humphrey Singleton, Sir Stafford's paternal uncle, who was well known at the time as the most ingenious defence counsel then in practice. Nor were these results, in the baroness's opinion, unconnected with the astonishing wealth Sir Rodney had inherited from his father, Sir Thomas Rouncewell. For the Roun-cewells had been one of the richest families in England. At the tables, Sir Rodney could with little discomfort have seen Mr Zabel's wagers as far as Mr Zabel was prepared to go. Except that Sir Rodney would have won, for he had the luck of the Devil. He also took the precaution of betting only in gambling houses where he was on intimate terms with the owner. Mr Zabel had a great many dollars in his New York bank. Sir Rodney's gold, in contrast, was in land. The Rouncewells had not mixed well with industry but in property they were without equal: Sir Rodney owned halves of English counties, streets and small towns.

Despite his close brushes with the English judiciary, however, he was, in strictly legal terms, unimpeachable – utterly: as pure and clean as a freshly printed banknote. He doubled his rents – and what if people were forced onto the streets? They had exploited his generosity for too long.

The first half of 1896 passed quickly, as the years now increasingly did for me. Lady Magenta was frequently away from London, speaking at rallies or raising money for her orphans. She said that she had decided to take a more direct role. During March I went to see her address an assembly of Trade Unionists in Birmingham. Dr Garth-Thompson was also on the platform and later passionately condemned the insanitary conditions in which the poor were forced to live. I could not help feeling there was a marked disparity between his public pity and the pounding he had given the hired woman at Fairfields. I too, during this period, rattled the imploring can on many a windy corner.

During the six years of my residence at Blackfriars Lane, I had lived from hand to mouth. My longest period of employment during this time was of some ten months on a Thames dredger which worked the docks and the reaches of the river below Tower Bridge. At various other times, I was a butcher's boy, a fruit vendor and, once again, a London messenger-man. I was a grave-digger in Highgate, a doorman at Brown's Hotel and, reverting in some sort to the circus, a lion-feeder at London Zoo. I spent a couple of weeks as the model for a new design of artificial leg. J.W. Stride, Manufacturer of Prostheses (a rather grand title for a carpenter who couldn't sell his banisters) informed me that I was fortunate enough to possess the perfectly average appendage. In the periods between these diverse avocations I was able to support myself by doing odd jobs both at Bartholomew Square and in the Plough and Stars. I had no savings, no security, and not the slightest means of support should I fall ill.

I could not know, however, as I sat in the hay loft late in May contemplating a beautifully printed invitation which lay on my desk, that this small piece of pasteboard would provide me with a competence for life. Sir Rodney Rouncewell invited me to a celebration of the summer solstice to be held at his family seat in Axbridge, to the west of the Mendip Hills in northern Somersetshire. The card was bordered by a frieze of phallically over-endowed Cretan boys and confirmed Sir Rodney's oft-repeated claim to be a 'red-blooded pagan'. I wondered with some anxiety

217

what form his extravagant tastes might take on this occasion. Some Bacchanalian orgy? Naked dancing by moonlight? Had it not been for Lady Magenta's persuasiveness over the next couple of weeks I would have returned a polite refusal.

I went down to Somerset on the day before the solstice in the company of Sir Stafford Singleton and Dr Garth-Thompson, who met me at Paddington, where they insisted on purchasing a first class ticket on my behalf. I recall that I was embarrassed, having insufficient funds for this luxury. On the platform, waiting for the arrival of the train, they laughingly waved my objections aside and even seemed slightly offended that I could question so trivial a favour.

I underwent a strange interrogation in that carriage, the purport of which I only understood much later. Had I any attachments in England, any relatives? Sir Stafford asked the first question and I answered that my parents were long dead, mentioning Amelia as my closest approximation to next of kin. They were interested, they were intrigued: at what age had I lost my parents? How old was I now?

Dr Garth-Thompson then suggested to Sir Stafford that a general medical examination might be in order. I was somewhat anxious, as the doctor seemed prepared to commence his investigations on the spot in the public carriage and had even risen to draw the curtains. Fortunately Sir Stafford waved aside his friend's idea:

'No, no Andrew: don't be ridiculous. Can't you see that Mr Spellman is in perfect health?'

The doctor reluctantly agreed and gazed moodily out of the window. Their friendship was beginning to take a pettishly argumentative turn.

The questions continued. Did I know any languages? Had I any experience in business? Would I describe myself as responsible? Was I used to travel and a certain amount of hardship? Had I any private wealth? My answer to this latter question appeared to cause some difficulty. I told them that I had nothing. I said that my father's poor legacy had been swallowed up in debts. I did not mention the opal ring, my only asset, which I carried everywhere with me.

Sir Stafford and Dr Garth-Thompson started to whisper to each other and I caught, here and there, snatches of their conversation: ' . . . Even if he had a little . . . not insuperable . . . could persuade them . . . Feste . . . Rouncewell will be difficult.'

It proved impossible to return to casual conversation and the three of us fell silent, watching the countryside pass by out of the window of the train.

We took a trap from the station and arrived at Rouncewell Hall as the light was failing. It was an impressive building, comprising an Elizabethan core with many later additions, although even from outside it was apparent that it had fallen into disrepair. A fire had entirely gutted one wing of the house and through the blackened archways of the windows one could see the sky between charred beams.

The next morning I was up early and had my breakfast alone. I was taking a stroll on the daisy-strewn lawn when I was met by Sir Rodney who wished to secure my company for a visit to Cheddar Gorge, which lay three or four miles to the east; Lady Magenta would join us for the expedition. Somewhat surprised by Sir Rodney's pleasant manner, I accepted. We agreed to meet outside the stables in an hour's time.

I had wandered from my companions in the bright day and now stood before a wall of stone which, layer upon layer above me, made up one of the larger projections of the famous landmark. There seemed no plan in the variously hued and textured strata; the rough red lay unsifted beneath the finer orange shale. Hard, soft; smooth, coarse: the rock face was like a great disjointed novel written on shuffled cards.

I was surprised when I felt a hand upon my shoulder and, turning, encountered Sir Rodney's saturnine visage. His ghastly pallor was absurdly at odds with the scene around us and, as his cracked, rouged lips parted and I felt his rank breath upon my cheek, he did not even seem to be a creature of the day.

'You have been named, Monsieur Jacques.'

'Sir Rodney?'

'Somebody has named you for Siriso. "Put you up," as they say.'

'Siriso?'

'Sir Stafford and Dr Garth-Thompson have generously seconded the proposal.'

I was baffled and tried again: 'Siriso, Sir Rodney?' But I received as little satisfaction as before. Sir Rodney's answer, when it came, was a series of further questions to which I could only assent.

'Do you love Lady Magenta, Monsieur Jacques? Do you like the baroness? Do you have faith in the work for orphans? Are you not an orphan yourself? Do you need money? Should you not wish to travel somewhere far from England?'

Yes, Sir Rodney, oh yes, yes.

'You shall go then to Alexandria as an emissary for Siriso. Tonight you will put your name on the list: yours, Monsieur Jacques, will be the last. You will sign and we will pay you generously for your work, for your labours on our behalf. I have to say, Monsieur Jacques, that I did not approve of your admittance, but you have persuasive friends and – well, in short – I acceded.'

Sir Rodney's manner changed and he now laid a patronizing hand upon my sleeve. 'This will be a considerable advancement for you, Master Jacques. I doubt that you are worthy of it but – for Lady Magenta's sake – I hope that you will try to be.'

Sir Rodney left me and, utterly bewildered, I watched his gaunt frame and his long legs as he descended the slope to the carriage, at the window of which Lady Magenta was watching me with a solemn look upon her face.

That evening we sat around a table in the great hall. Small rivulets of water spread across the cracked marble floor and the leaking roof issued a series of staccato drips into metal buckets. Distant thunder could be heard over the Mendip Hills. Despite the rain it was warm and the French windows stood open. Sir Rodney sat at the head of the table, flanked by Lady Magenta and the Baroness Hrocka. Along one side were Mr Bellowes, Mr Zabel and Mr Dinmont; along the other, Sir Stafford, Dr Garth-Thompson and myself. All of these people, excepting only me, were members of Siriso and today, far from being a celebration of the solstice, was the annual general meeting. In spite of the occasion, our conversation was at first informal. Mr Bellowes had almost completed the twelfth volume of his *Survey of the Trees and Flowering Plants of Amazonia*, although he had recently been devastated by the news that many of his finest specimens had succumbed to a fungal infection on the voyage from Belém.

'The forest is punishing me for the sins of my fathers!' he joked unhappily.

The recent disaster had made him more concerned than ever at the prospect of another trip to Brazil in order to research the thirteenth volume of his work, which was to be devoted to orchids (a subject continually in his thoughts, he said, since his labours for Lord Tramont on the Rio Putumayo in the 1860s). Dangers these days, however, came not so much from disease – thanks to Richard Spruce he had his quinine from the plantations in India – but from the rubber baron's rifle. Sir Rodney agreed that the difficulties to be met with in tropical regions might discourage the most ardent traveller but he maintained that still greater dangers were to be found in the Arctic. Thirty years ago, of course, Rae had established beyond all doubt that the survivors of Franklin's expedition on the *Erebus* and the *Terror* had resorted to cannibalism. His own experience was poor in comparison but he had once been buried for some days in a Spitsbergen crevasse where, with great regret, he ate his favourite dog in order to survive until a rescue party could reach him.

The proceedings were formally opened at eleven o'clock in the evening by Sir Stafford Singleton, who read out to the assembled company two apologies for absence. One was from W.H. Perkin but I did not recognize the name of the other, an Italian who was at that time away in Egypt.

Questions were asked and suggestions were made. I have to say that it was all a strange language to me. I looked out of the windows and across the terrace to where distant lightning played on the hilltops.

A clock struck the hour of midnight. My name was mentioned; my turn had come. All eyes were upon me. Lady Magenta handed me a sheet of parchment on which I read the names of the eight people present and of the two who had registered their absence from the meeting. Three other names had been obliterated with a single stroke of blue ink: Stephanides, Ronald Indigo Orlando Tramont and, simply, 'Tramont', Lady Magenta's father.

Somebody offered me a pen and, in the first minutes of the second half of the year, I added in red ink my name, the fourteenth and last, to the register. I did not know what I had done.

I still do not.

16

A Gift

AFTER THE ceremony at Axbridge in which I was inducted into Siriso, Sir Rodney remained in the country whilst the rest of us returned to London. I found the solemnity of this occasion – the blood-red ink on the roster, the whispered voices – enigmatic but faintly ridiculous. I almost felt as if I had been asked to open a vein and sign my way into a mystic fraternity. Despite my doubts, I had already committed myself, and after all, I could hardly complain about my share – the fourteenth – in Siriso. I was informed that, since three of the fourteen members had already died, the annuity would be divided only eleven ways. With a single stroke of the pen I had become a moderately rich man.

My passage to Alexandria was booked for two months hence and, in the over-heated London of July, I found myself with time on my hands. I discussed my prospects with Amelia, who was delighted on my behalf. When I offered to tell her about Siriso, she put a finger to her lips and begged me not to go on. The world of business, she said, made her head spin.

I wrote to Wilf Patchkey and to Mimi. A week later, I received a brief note which bore a Nottingham postmark. Wilf was the proud father of a four-month-old baby boy, shortly to be christened Jack. It had been a difficult birth but, day by day, Laura was regaining her strength. Wilf was relieved that the child's genitalia, if not his surname, appeared to have been inherited through the female line, 'so it looks like he won't have problems in that direction, which is all for the best as far as I can see.'

A few days after this, Mimi wrote to wish me well. She suggested that I try to find time to see Aramind before my departure: 'You never know what the sight of a familiar face will do.'

In early August I took the pantomime horse out of the cupboard in the hay loft at Blackfriars Lane and brushed it down. Later that day I took it over to Bethnal Green, where Lady Magenta intended to use it in her studio.

After that, I had very few preparations to make: I could have left on the morrow. London sweltered in a sun that seemed like an augury of Egypt.

To pass the time I called frequently on Lady Magenta at Bartholomew Square, where I usually also met the baroness and Mr Bellowes, the former having remained in the capital out of perversity and the latter from the demands of scholarly research. The three of them willingly provided enlightenment concerning the nature of my task and the extent of my duties to Siriso.

The organisation had been founded in the April of 1871 by Lord Tramont, Sir Rodney Rouncewell and Mr W.H. Perkin. It originally had two aims: first, to examine the possibilities of setting up a trading company and, secondly, to promote various forms of charitable assistance to the poor. His conscience perhaps pricked by the growing impoverishment of oriental indigo manufacturers, Mr Perkin took charge of the latter operation, whilst Lord Tramont undertook to organize the former. I discovered that Tramont's visits to Italy, Greece and North Africa had partly been made with the intention of establishing commercial contacts; through strenuous activity he had tried to overcome the grief caused by his wife's death. When Lord Tramont died, Sir Rodney took over the directorship of the Siriso Trading Company. In 1880, the overworked Mr Perkin resigned control of Siriso's charitable activities in favour of Lady Magenta. Perhaps his conscience had been allayed by the flourishing cinchona crop in India on land once devoted to indigo. By the year 1896, the Siriso Charitable Foundation was running two homes in London for foundlings, an asylum in Dover and several other institutions scattered around the country. In 1882, Ronald Indigo Orlando Tramont had travelled to India on behalf of the Siriso Trading Company. His death in 1889 had created the need for a successor to fill the ranks but, since the Siriso branch in that country was already well-established, it was decided that any new agent should not be inducted into Siriso. Dr Garth-Thompson had joined the club as its twelfth member in 1893; two years later Signor Feste was elected to the thirteenth chair. Since the maximum membership of Siriso had been set in the club's charter at fourteen, I was the last.

'But what *is* Siriso?' I asked at length, bemused by all these details.

Mr Bellowes coughed discreetly; the baroness and Lady Magenta allowed him to answer my question. 'Well young man, it is all that we have said.'

'But there's something else about it which I don't understand, something which makes it all cohere.'

'Well,' said Mr Bellowes, 'you're absolutely right. Siriso, you see, is a tontine.'

'A tontine?' I had never heard the word before.

'I detect your bewilderment,' said the baroness. 'Sidney: tell Mr Spellman what a tontine is.'

'Well, well, yes, mmm,' stammered Mr Bellowes, 'let me marshal my thoughts.' Behind his spectacles, his small eyes darted about the room for a few moments before he began. 'A tontine, young man, is a somewhat obsolete legal arrangement, more common in the last century and named after its originator, one Lorenzo Tonti. It works in practice as follows: a previously specified number of subscribers agree to establish a sum of capital which is invested and yields an annuity. The annuity is divided equally amongst the members of the tontine and, should a subscriber die, the shares increase until the last survivor gets all.'

'But I have nothing,' I objected. 'How was it that I was admitted to an equal share of the annuity?'

The baroness winked at me. 'You, Mr Spellman, were excused. We made a sacrifice for you. Perhaps you will have to make one in return.'

I thought for a moment and then spoke. 'I am very grateful for your generosity but, although I am poor, it is not entirely true that I have nothing.' And I felt in my pocket for Alf Hagsproat's ring before walking across the room to Lady Magenta, who was seated in a chair by the window. She looked at me enquiringly and I noticed that her face was very pale. Then I looked at the ring which lay in my palm and was once more to move along its strange circuit; its colour was as fierce as that of arterial blood.

'I hereby donate this ring to Siriso,' I said, holding the ring out to Lady Magenta. To my surprise, instead of taking it, she offered me her finger.

I should have been horrified had I known then what this ring was yet to do but, accompanied by the baroness's applause and the polite exclamations of Mr Bellowes, I slipped the ring, in a sort of trance, onto my friend's finger.

That night I dreamt of the circus for the first time in years. I thought that I was still inside the horse suit, struggling to get out. Somewhere close beside me, although they were unaware of my presence, I could hear the murmuring voices of all the people I knew.

The next day, I returned to Bartholomew Square, where I found the same company as the night before. It was as if they had remained in their chairs overnight.

'What,' I asked, during a lull in the conversation which followed the serving of tea, 'do the other members of Siriso do?'

Lady Magenta took it upon herself to reply. 'Until his recent death, Mr Stephanides was the agent of the Siriso Trading Company in Alexandria. My father recruited him during a visit to Egypt in 1873. It was Mr

Stephanides who dealt with our Mediterranean and African trade. Mr Bellowes –' she gestured to our friend, who smiled shyly from his armchair '– and Mr Zabel between them conduct our business in the Americas. Signor Feste, whom I have not yet had the pleasure of meeting – he was inducted a year ago, at Sir Rodney's instigation – is our business adviser. Sir Stafford is our lawyer, Dr Garth-Thompson our general practitioner.'

'But,' I began again in some frustration, still feeling that none of the pieces had fallen into place, 'what is our trade? What sort of goods does Siriso deal in?'

Mr Bellowes smiled, leaned forward in his chair and began to reply. He spoke for a long time, showing an enormous appetite for detail and a capacious memory. I have forgotten much of what he said but the bare bones remain.

The Siriso Trading Company dealt entirely in the exotic and luxurious, the rare and strange. It dabbled not in staples, but anything that was incidental or supplementary to life it readily supplied. Furs from Siberia, silks from India and Javanese batiks. Purpleheart wood from South America, toon wood from the Celebes, sandalwood and Cedar of Lebanon. Spices and strange delicacies, cosmetics and perfumes, drugs, poisons and pigments. Musical instruments which nobody knew how to play, old manuscripts and eerie relics, the tools of vanished trades, fragments of mosaic, icons and louring idols.

A question sprang to my lips so suddenly that I almost thought another had spoken and not I: 'Where does Sir Rodney own property?'

'Why, Mr Spellman, you surprise me with your curiosity and the sudden way you have of turning the subject!' The baroness leant against the fireplace and lit a cigarette. 'I have to say that I hardly know. Lady Magenta tells me that he owns a great deal of land in Bethnal Green, since she rents her studio from him; I believe that he also has some properties in the Blackfriars area. But as far as the capital goes, I am fairly certain that Canonbury is the core of Sir Rodney's landed wealth, the mucky jewel in his besmirched crown.'

The baroness tossed her cigarette, as though it was the subject of our conversation, into the grate. There was some peculiar vibration in the air like the rhythmic noise of a distant train. It was as if I was looking up at the trembling objects in the room from below, as if I had opened a trapdoor and was trying to get out. Putting a hand to my eyes, I asked a final question: 'Why is it called Siriso?'

The room was filled with the laughter of my friends. 'Siriso?' said Mr Bellowes, 'Siriso? Does it matter, Mr Spellman? What's in a name?'

Rouncewell . . . Siriso.

All at once it was upon me. For a second, before the links dissolved, my whole life seemed to come together in a hoop and I, a man of thirty-two, was one with the eleven-year-old child. Creditors dressed in black hovered around me as I sat at my father's table trying to read the piece of paper they had put in front of me. The words would not come out; the black print and the white paper merged into a single shimmering grey.

I knew at last that it was Siriso and Sir Rodney to whom, twenty years ago, my father had been indebted. It was Sir Rodney who had deprived me of my patrimony.

17

Voices from the Madhouse

I HAD one more week in England to wonder why it had taken me so long to piece these things together. Perhaps the only reason was that in my heart I had always known them. Siriso had taken the little I once had and what is more, to be near Lady Magenta, I had collaborated in my own dispossession. With camera and collecting tin I had spent years of my life in active support of Siriso.

I remembered Lady Magenta standing at dawn on Southwark Bridge; she looked down into the water and her eyes lingered on the floating detritus: a crate, a dead dog. Her sadness, of course, was for the orphans. But was it also for something beyond them? Was it linked, in some as yet occulted way, with my own? I had no answers then, had merely thrown up, like a juggler, reassuring phrases. I had still fewer now and it seemed to me that in the intervening years I had lost all my confidence. That once, that one time on a bridge: I had been happy then.

Dover: the morning of 4 September 1896.

I had just returned from the harbour-master's office, where I had left my trunk. Possessed only of a small hand bag, I sat sipping my tea in the breakfast room of the hotel. I was to embark that evening on the *Nepthys*. Our captain was Edward Shore and we would sail with the tide at dawn the next day. Today was for Aramind alone.

I walked uphill through the summer rain and left the town behind me. I asked a labourer for directions to the asylum. He silently pointed up the road ahead; I thanked him and walked on. A starved horse leant its head over a gate. I crossed a brook. I arrived at what I assumed to be the asylum about noon. It was a large building on the edge of the cliff, approached on the land side by an avenue bordered with hedges of yew. Its mock battlements and its dark tower stood out against the clearing sky. As I drew nearer, bars became visible at the upper windows of the building. There were no windows on the ground floor. Gargoyles stared down at me from the eaves.

I opened the heavy doors and crossed the red-tiled hall, where I stated the object of my visit to a sullen porter who dribbled over his lunch. Nurses hurried past, dressed, as Mimi and Bessie had written, in starched white aprons. They held ewers and metal trays in their chapped hands. Having had little luck with the porter, I eventually succeeded in stopping one of these figures, who immediately led me to the office of the principal of the institution, a Dr Chawl.

Dr Chawl sat behind a desk at the far end of an immensely long room. The rain must have cleared since he was illuminated by a brilliant pool of sunlight which fell through the window behind him, glowed from his bald head, glinted from the metal rims of his spectacles and glanced from the papers piled in front of him. Looking up, he greeted me politely and offered me a chair. Beneath an archway which apparently led into another room, two men were holding a whispered conversation. One held a hammer and the other a drill; they seemed to be engaged in fixing some piece of apparatus to the wall.

I again stated the purpose of my visit. As I spoke, Dr Chawl tinkered with a machine which stood on a table beside his desk. When I had finished speaking, he removed some kind of cylinder from this contraption and held it up to the light. The whiteness of his coat made him look almost transparent.

'So you must be Jack Spellman,' he said laconically.

Since I had not mentioned my name I must have shown some surprise. One of the workmen began to hammer a peg into the wall and, as Dr Chawl continued, it was difficult to hear his words.

'Yes, I know your name, you see. She mentions you when she talks to herself. Aramind: isn't that her name?' I nodded. 'But she never utters a syllable when others are present, Mr Spellman. I am afraid that my colleagues and I were forced to resort to a little innocent spying in order to make sure that she was physically and intellectually capable of speech.'

He passed the cylinder across the desk and I looked at it curiously. 'That wax disc, Mr Spellman, contains a few scraps of her ramblings.' His words seemed cold and I flinched involuntarily. Dr Chawl raised a forefinger and, in the brilliant light, took on a resemblance to a saint in an old painting. 'Yes, Mr Spellman: ramblings. For they are ramblings. I use the word descriptively and not pejoratively.'

I examined the cylinder as though it could speak to me. At one end, it was neatly labelled and dated: 'Siriso. Case 1400. Jan. 1890- Recorded 22 June 1896. Chawl.'

'*Siriso?*' I exclaimed.

'Yes indeed: this asylum is supported by the good offices of the Siriso Charitable Foundation. Did you not see the notice at the gate?'

I had not.

'In any case, Mr Spellman, would you like to listen to it?'

'I beg your pardon?'

Dr Chawl smiled at my confusion: 'That, Mr Spellman, is a phonograph recording. With the photograph we could see the past. Now we can also hear it. But I am afraid,' he continued, making vaguely deprecatory gestures with his hand, 'that it may well distress you. You must understand, Mr Spellman, that Aramind is not the woman she once was. It would be fair, I think, to describe her as an empty husk.' He regretfully fitted the cylinder into the machine and set it in motion.

There was a pause and then, as it crackled to life, I heard again the soft muttering of Aramind. It was an older voice – perhaps an emptier voice – but it was still, most definitely, recognizable as Aramind:

' . . . rain falling heavily on the terrace, rain falling through the broken roof, drops of rain falling into metal buckets, rivulets of rain twisting across the marble floors, clouds of rain massing overhead, lightning in the distance, over hills, but coming closer . . . signing his name . . . writing his name in blood . . . unknowing . . . '

The recording came to an end in a hiss of indecipherable noise. I sat dumbfounded. At length, misinterpreting my manner and my silence, Dr Chawl spoke:

'It has, of course, a certain poetry. I have noticed that this often characterizes the ravings of the clinically insane.'

Dr Chawl seemed a long way away from me. I could see his thin lips quite clearly as they began to move again:

'No core, you see, Mr Spellman. No sense of a self. These fantastic fragments are the only things left.'

He took the cylinder out of the phonograph and, opening the door of a cupboard, put it carefully away amongst hundreds of other cylinders which were ranked, shelf upon shelf, from floor to ceiling. Then he leant against his desk and folded his arms. 'I have to say, Mr Spellman, that in some ways she was more articulate in the first six months or so of her stay here. That was before the stillbirth, of course. After that, she relapsed into almost complete silence. I need not tell you that such words as remain have no link with reality.' He looked down at me sympathetically. 'I'm very sorry, Mr Spellman: it's a sad case.'

The workmen had paused in their hammering and were now listening unashamedly to our conversation. I suggested to Dr Chawl that perhaps I might now see Aramind. 'Oh dear,' he said reluctantly, 'we don't really approve of visitors. Bad for discipline, you see: upsets them.'

Nevertheless, he pressed a button on his desk and I heard the distant sound of a bell. The nurse who had guided me to his office appeared again; Dr Chawl directed her to conduct me to Aramind's cell and, putting out his hand, wished me good day. By the time I reached the door, he was already hard at work again, in the sunlight, amongst his papers. The workmen had resumed their hammering.

Another door, and another; a whole series of doors along a narrow, ill-lit corridor: doors at first swung open by the nurse who preceded me and whose steps rang out loudly in the confined space; then doors unlocked and locked again behind us. With each obstacle passed, the noise grew louder: the noise of madness, inarticulate, aconsonantal, a growing hubbub of shrieks and laughs. At length we reached the door of Aramind's cell: number 140. The nurse employed a final key and, standing back, indicated that I should go in. As I passed in front of her, she rattled her great ring of keys impatiently.

Aramind's back was turned towards me. Her once dark hair was now grey. It had been cut close to her scalp. There was a bed in the cell and through the open shutters I could hear waves pounding the base of the cliff far below us. As I stepped quietly towards her, I noticed that Aramind's shoulders were shaking with an effort which at first I took for suppressed grief. When I stood beside her, I realized that she was drawing with a fierceness I had never seen. She held a piece of charcoal in her wasted hand and was scoring the piece of paper before her repeatedly.

The stick of charcoal suddenly snapped and the point drove into the page, scattering particles of dust across her lines. Without moving, she gazed through the window into the sky. After a while, she looked up at me. I knelt beside her and grasped her grubby hand. To look into her face was to see a cloud slowly clearing. Her features, indistinct before, began gradually to shape themselves into the semblance of an expression. I saw the scars on her face and then I saw two small points of light in her dark pupils, two points that watched and recognized and knew.

I did not speak at first and nor did she. The only sound in the room was that of the nurse telling off her keys on their metal ring.

'Aramind,' I said gently, 'Aramind.'

The nurse sighed and began to scrape her shoe along the floor.

I tried again: 'Aramind, can you hear me?'

My old friend did not reply but a slow smile played faintly across her lips. I squeezed her hand and tried, impossibly, to send across the barriers of our flesh some pulse of life, but I could not find within me whatever it was that Aramind needed. Her silence rendered me mutely impotent.

I had risen to leave and the nurse was inserting a key into the door when, behind me, Aramind whispered in a voice which seemed to have forced its way into the air from behind some colossal impediment:

'Jack.'

In an instant I was at her feet. She seemed to struggle with herself for perhaps half a minute.

'The ring!'

'What ring, Aramind? The opal ring? What about the ring?'

My words only served to silence her.

The doors opened and closed in reverse order and when we reached the hall the nurse left me. I could see the great entrance way and, to its right, the smaller door which opened into the porter's cubicle. I wanted to leave the building as quickly as possible but, glancing into this room as I passed, I was astonished to discover the dark and lean figure of Sir Rodney, who was sitting with easy nonchalance on the porter's desk. This latter gentleman, having evidently finished his lunch (a few crumbs still adhered to his lips and chin) was gazing up at Sir Rodney with undisguised awe.

'Ah, Spellman: at last!' said Sir Rodney, turning round and noticing me. He leapt lightly from the table and crossed the room to shake my hand, showing no trace of surprise at our meeting.

As politely as I could, I asked him what he was doing here.

'In Dover, young man, or at this place?'

'Both.'

'Remarkable: there seems to be some sort of suppressed accusation in your eye, Monsieur Jacques. I see that I am on trial. So be it. Well, I am visiting this asylum in my capacity as one of the ten – I do beg your pardon, eleven – living shareholders in Siriso.'

'But Sir Rodney: I gathered that your interests lay in the Trading Company and not the Charitable Foundation.'

He looked at me out of the corner of his eye. 'I have wide-ranging interests. They extended even to you this morning, Monsieur Jacques. I ascertained from your breakfast waiter that you would not be embarking until this evening and theorized – quite correctly, as it transpired – that you were intending to pay a visit to Aramind.'

'How did you know of her?'

Sir Rodney ignored my question. 'My little theory was supported when I saw you leave the hotel, corroborated by a charming if inarticulate agricultural labourer I met upon the road and finally confirmed beyond doubt by me estimable friend here –' He indicated the porter, who scraped a little bow and smiled shyly up at us with blackened teeth.

'I see: you followed me.'

Sir Rodney made a placatory gesture. 'Monsieur Jacques, how could you? I did not "follow" – I indulged my interest in detection.'

'Yes – you have wide-ranging interests. But how did you know about Aramind? I didn't mention her to the waiter.'

'Of course not,' smiled Sir Rodney, 'you are discreet: Siriso relies on that. But Siriso, you see – in a friendly way – undertook an assessment of your life.'

'When? Now?'

He put his head back to laugh. 'No, long ago. Years ago.'

'You checked up on me! You pried into my life.'

'Oh, come now, Monsieur Jacques: we merely ascertained that you were worthy of our trust!' As if to cut short the discussion, Sir Rodney took me by the arm and walked me to the door, where he handed me a small envelope. 'Instructions, Monsieur Jacques. Something for you to read on your long voyage – you are fond of reading, aren't you? It contains details, suggestions, advice on accommodation – all that sort of thing.'

I thanked him and he opened the groaning door. As I began to walk away, he produced his parting shot:

'By the way, Monsieur Jacques: we have a mutual friend.'

'Who can that be, Sir Rodney?'

'Amelia, the landlady of the Plough and Stars. I have respected and admired her for more than thirty years.'

I stopped walking and Sir Rodney drew near to me. He was intimate and confidential; he bent closer to my ear. 'She has the most remarkable flaming red fanny-thatch that I have ever seen. Are you familiar with the beast, Monsieur Jacques? Quite wondrous. It shows, I think, a passion that exceeds the call of duty.' He clapped me on the shoulder in farewell: 'May the wake widen behind you, young man, and the sweet breezes follow! How I envy you your youth! How new it must seem to you!'

Half-way down the hill I turned and looked back. Reduced by distance, Sir Rodney gazed impassively down on me. I walked on. At the bottom of the slope, the nurse who had led me to Aramind's cell stealthily emerged from behind a laurel bush and ran up to me. She glanced around her as though she was frightened of being seen.

'Here: take these,' she said, thrusting another envelope into my hands. 'Her drawings – they destroy them!'

You may have realized, Mr Secretary, that I have them still. There, on the wall: sketches of the circus and strangely prophetic pictures of my life to come. They tell my story, perhaps, as well as I.

5 September 1896: dawn.

Petulant sea-birds beat their wings above the quarter-deck and the sun rose to my right amongst bruise-coloured clouds.

Suddenly the ship seemed to strain forward. The note of the engine changed as the screw engaged the current. I watched the wake begin to widen behind me until its V, like a pair of arms thrown open, stretched from shore to furthest visible shore. I thought of Lady Magenta who, at our parting, had coughed (not cried) with emotion and who, instead of a tear, had shed a bright red droplet of arterial blood into her handkerchief.

The land disappeared on my right, although to the west I could still see the pale cliffs as far as Dungeness. The sea-birds in our wake fell back and vanished. Other passengers, wrapped up against the cold breeze, leaned on the railings and gazed into the water.

It was like death: a gradual, solemn decline. We were quiet and we rubbed our tired eyes. It was also like birth.

18

A Hydraulic History

THE HARBOUR-MASTER, Mehmet Ali, sat in his office above the quay. In front of him was a small cup of black coffee and a bowl of sugared almonds into which he dipped from time to time with pursed lips and delicate fingers. He wiped his hands on a napkin, pushed some papers to one side and looked at me without interest.

'You wish to enquire about Mr Stephanides?'

I took my identification documents from my pocket. 'That's right. Mr Stephanides: the agent in Alexandria for the Siriso Trading Company. He died, I believe, some months ago.'

Mehmet Ali leaned back in his cane chair and placed a cigarette in a malachite holder. Lighting it, he smoked luxuriously for some time before replying.

'Mr Stephanides died in March –' He paused and, a few moments later, added listlessly: 'It was the twenty-fourth day of March when he died.' He picked up a newspaper and idly scanned its front page as if our colloquy had reached its natural conclusion.

'What did he die of?' I asked.

Mehmet Ali shrugged almost imperceptibly. 'The sickness.'

The sickness. There were so many ways to die in Egypt, Mehmet Ali seemed to say, that it was scarcely worth the effort to give a name to one more of the diverse manifestations of the same. I tried a different tack. 'I am staying at the Pension de l'Est.'

Mehmet Ali assented without looking up from his paper. 'Of course.'

'Mr Stephanides's rooms are directly below mine.'

'Yes – I believe that he lived there.'

I felt a little encouraged. 'You knew him, then?'

' – '

'Knew of him?'

Mehmet Ali was frigid. 'Evidently.'

I decided to be more direct. 'Mr Mehmet: my name is Spellman. I am the new agent for the Siriso Trading Company.' A flicker of curiosity passed across my interlocutor's face and I followed up my small advantage: 'I am told that the harbour company owns the Pension de l'Est.'

'Certainly. That is true.'

'I was told by the concierge – the *boab* – to present my credentials to you. I wish to obtain the keys to Mr Stephanides's rooms and – '

He interrupted me. 'Why?'

'I believe there will be papers there which I need.'

'I see. What sort of papers?'

It was my turn to be evasive. 'Details. Company matters.'

His eyes glittered. 'Can you not be more precise?'

'I am afraid not; I merely wish to obtain any papers or documents relating to the Siriso Trading Company. I was told that, two days before he died, Mr Stephanides paid his rent for the next six months and that consequently the room has not been occupied since his funeral. As Mr Stephanides had no relatives –'

'You seem to have had quite a conversation with the *boab*.'

'Yes: he has been very helpful. Since Mr Stephanides had no relatives,' I continued, 'it is reasonable to assume that his possessions – including any papers – will still be in his room. And,' I concluded, 'as Mr Stephanides's rent lapses today, I am afraid that his effects might be disposed of before I am able to establish my right to examine them.'

'I see.' Mehmet Ali put his fingers to his lips and considered the situation. 'Can you demonstrate that you are entitled to take possession of the company records which you mentioned?'

'Of course.' I pushed my papers of identification across the table towards him. He ignored them and, walking over to the salt-stained window, gazed down on the quay.

He remained in this position for a couple of minutes, after which I became impatient. 'Mr Mehmet: could I ask you once again for the key to Mr Stephanides's rooms?'

He raised his eyebrows and returned to his desk. As he finished his coffee he casually began to examine my papers. The noise of typing could be heard from another room. At length he sighed, unlocked a drawer in his desk and presented me with three keys tied together and a pale smile, a mere widening of the lips:

'These are the keys to Mr Stephanides's rooms in the Pension de l'Est.'

I was leaving the office when a thought suddenly struck me. 'Mr Mehmet: can you tell me how many shipments there have been for the Siriso Trading Company in the past year?'

The question sprang from mere curiosity and a desire to find out as much as I could about the activities of Siriso in Alexandria, but Mehmet Ali responded to it with something approaching alacrity. He called a clerk and together they searched through a filing cabinet at the far end of the office. After a minute he returned with a file through which he leafed officiously.

'There has been only one shipment in the past year,' he announced at last. 'It left port on the twenty-fifth of March.'

'I see. The day after Stephanides died.'

'Indeed.'

When I returned to the Pension de l'Est, Mistral – the *boab* – was waiting behind his desk. He rose to greet me and smiled, showing teeth filled with gold.

'I knew you would get them,' he said as he led me up to Stephanides's rooms.

High above the staircase, light filtered through a stained glass window and fell onto the walls of the landing below my own. I took out the small bunch of keys; opening the door, we stepped inside. Mistral crossed the room and threw open the shutters:

'This was his study, Mr Spellman.'

A fine layer of dust covered everything. Although I knew that the room had been empty for months and that its occupant was dead I still felt like an intruder. To cover my awkwardness, I asked the first question which came into my mind. 'Mistral. That's an unusual name. Why are you called Mistral?'

He thought for a while as though marshalling his English. 'I am from Algérie. They gave to me that name in Marseilles, in the docks.'

As he spoke, I began to notice a strange, spicy smell in the room and I sniffed the air curiously. Mistral was almost apologetic as he explained. 'Mr Stephanides: he like too much hot food. Chilli, ginger: he sweat. Pickles, chutneys. Stephanides eat more chutney than rice, meat. And salt – Mareotis salt. He cover his food with salt like – like –' He searched for the unfamiliar word and at length found it in French. 'Like *la neige.*'

'Snow?' I asked, absurdly. Even my French could rise to this.

'*Oui*, Monsieur Spellman: snow. His meals were like the Alps.'

I moved around the room; there was not much there. The chairs were covered with dust-sheets and the carpets had been rolled into one corner. A gigantic cedar beam which presumably supported my own accommodation spanned the ceiling. Fixed half-way along it was a large metal hook, perhaps for some lamp or chandelier which had been removed. Directly beneath the hook stood a small table with an arrangement of dried flowers in a vase.

There were three or four other rooms in the apartment, each of them equally empty. In one of them, I was amused to find on a shelf – as if in demonstration of Mistral's comments concerning Stephanides's dietary habits – a jar of anchovy paste and a pot of plum chutney. I returned to the study and noticed a large bureau standing against one wall. It was locked. Selecting the smallest key from my bunch, I attempted to open it. The key did not fit. I tried a slightly larger one and was successful. Inside the writing-desk was a stick of sealing-wax, a scarab signet, an ashtray containing several cigar stubs and a mahogany box which opened to the smallest of my keys. Inside the box, in a large envelope marked 'Siriso', were the records and ledgers I had been searching for. The seal on the envelope was broken.

'Can I take these?' I asked Mistral.

He spread his hands, palms upward. 'Why not? They are yours now.'

Suddenly I noticed a small drawer at the back of the bureau. It was unlocked and inside was a thick letter addressed to me. 'When did this arrive? You didn't tell me.'

Mistral looked a little sheepish. 'Three days ago, from Marseilles. Mr Mehmet himself brought it here yesterday, before you arrived.'

'He didn't mention that.'

'But it is true, Mr Spellman,' protested Mistral. 'Perhaps Mr Mehmet thought it was not necessary because you would find the letter with the keys.' Hurriedly, he closed the shutters. In the dim room, as we moved towards the door, I saw him looking at me out of the corner of his eye.

'What is it?' I asked.

'You look a little bit like Stephanides.'

I laughed. 'Thank you! Full of pickle and salt?'

'No. You are less fat and less old. But a bit the same.'

We left the room and, after locking the door, I gave the keys to Mistral. 'You do not need them?' he asked.

'No. I have got what I was looking for.'

'Very good: I can prepare for new occupant.'

I carried the company records and the letter back to my room on the top floor. Hearing the noise of cafés floating up, I went to the window and looked down into the narrow street, which rose steeply on my right. Washing had been hung out to dry on lines stretched between balconies. The sky was bright but milky. To the left I could look out over the port, where steamers were unloading. Workers ran to and fro between bales of cotton and chests of sugar or coffee. Maize, millet, wheat and rice were piled in sacks on the quay or, strapped onto pallets, hung from cranes and winches. As the ships turned slowly in the water by the harbour wall, I could hear the grinding of their engines. Other boats were being towed out to sea by tugs.

Slowly, at the desk, I began to read through Stephanides's records. His employment contract had been signed in 1873, with Lord Tramont as witness. Stephanides had kept all his salary receipts and pinned them together in their correct order. I turned to the ledger. It seemed that he had organized and superintended the first shipment for Siriso in 1873. Oddly, however, there were no records to show that Stephanides had performed any other service for Siriso during the next fifteen years. In 1888 there was another shipment which had been addressed to Ronald Indigo Orlando Tramont. After that there was a further lapse of eight years until Stephanides's posthumous shipment of March 1896. I turned to the bills of lading, the insurance certificates and the customs forms.

The first cargo, which had left Alexandria twenty-three years ago, seemed to have been composed of a variety of minerals and ores. Stephanides had written an inventory in his cramped handwriting:

Jamaican bauxite:	20lbs. Paid.
Sicilian anthracite:	15lbs. Paid.
Haematite (Tabora):	22lbs. Paid.
Graphite:	15 rods. Paid.
Galena, sphalerite, cinnabar:	12lbs. each. All paid.
Kaolin:	7lbs.6oz. Paid.
Kieselguhr:	3lbs.12 ½oz. Paid
Assorted fossils:	2 cases. Paid.

At the bottom of the page was a draft of a formal but not obsequious letter to Lord Tramont hoping that he would find everything in order and of the quality he required.

Fifteen years later, the second cargo comprised animals presumably destined for zoos and circuses in England. Three tigers in good health on embarkation. Six lions, ditto. Three wolves, ditto. One further wolf suffering from croup. One leopard in good health. One female elephant, ditto. Two camels, one ditto, the other with a cataract in the left eye and a tendency to bite. Everything seemed to be in order. The ship was the *Corsair*, registered at Marseilles, captain one Adolphus Franck.

The third shipment, which had pre-dated my arrival by six months and post-dated Stephanides's death by a single day, had an entirely different tenor. The inventory to this cargo was written in a more enthusiastic spirit and, from Mistral's information, I suspected that I knew why. The steamer *Messina* had left Alexandria on 25 March 1896 laden with exotic food and drink.

Sugared pineapples and mulberries, bael fruit, plums and cherries: –
12 tins of each.
Dried raisins, currants and figs: – 1 sack of each.
Cinnamon, green and dry ginger, pepper, cloves, nutmeg, mace: 1 bag
of each.
Sugared almonds: 15 boxes. Good quality, very good.
Betel nuts: 1 small sack. Quite nice.
Anchovy paste: ~~20~~ 19 pots
Plum chutney: ~~30~~ 29 pots.
Mareotis salt: 23lbs. Some of it is coarsely ground but most is fine to
the fingers and good.
Black olives in brine : 3 generously sized bottles
12 cans isinglass.
7 cans salted botargo.
5 cans bêche-de-mer.
5 cans chow-chow.
5 cans bardy.
12 cases Erasmus Bond's Aerated Quinine Tonic Water.
Arak – finest – three cases.
Vermouth: 6 cases, and very dry.
Mareotic wine, white, eight cases of it, which is enough to bring on a
paradisian torpor.

Strangest of all, however, was the last item on Stephanides's list: twenty-
five boxes of Abernethy biscuits. I could not understand what these
peculiarly British delicacies had been doing in Alexandria. Was Siriso in
the business of sending coals to Newcastle?

I went out onto the balcony again to clear my head. It was evening and
the quayside was quieter. Whilst I had been working, a gun-boat bearing
the English flag had arrived and now lay at anchor in the bay.

I returned to my desk and opened the letter addressed to me. Inside, I
found another letter and a curt note from Sir Rodney. It was even briefer
than the letter I had opened on the boat, which had simply directed me to
take rooms at the Pension de l'Est and to contact the harbour-master,
Mehmet Ali, concerning Constantin Stephanides. Sir Rodney's covering
note was dated the day after my departure and introduced me to the writer
of the enclosed letter, Signor Giovanni Feste. Signor Feste was the
thirteenth member of Siriso and the only one with whom I was unfamiliar.
It was he who had taken over temporary control of Siriso's Egyptian
interests immediately following Stephanides's death. Sir Rodney had
recalled him to London in July and the tone of his letter left me in no
doubt that Feste's services were more highly valued than my own. Signor

Feste, he wrote, was an excellent and most respected businessman. He had been elected to Siriso on account of a financial acumen that amounted almost to prescience. Signor Feste would be dealing with my affairs from London and would send his instructions directly to me in future.

Signor Feste's letter, which I opened at once, was more informative and for the first time gave me a clear idea of what I had committed myself to on the night of the summer solstice three months previously. He supplied me with details concerning the next two shipments from Alexandria – the fourth and fifth, respectively, of the Siriso Trading Company.

The first cargo was to be collected in Piraeus at the beginning of October; it would consist of textiles. The second, of 'assorted artefacts of value', would be acquired at Jebel Dukhan on the Red Sea coast. I should prepare myself, if necessary, to bargain for the goods. In each case I would arrange transportation to Alexandria, where I would check and examine the shipments. As far as possible, I was to identify individual items and label them suitably. Signor Feste was emphatic on this last point. He quoted a section of the Trademark Law of 1887, which demanded a label or certificate of origin on all imported goods. I was expected to supervise the packing and stowing of the cargo and to complete any necessary paperwork before dispatching it to London.

Signor Feste supplied two useful addresses. The first was that of the Colonial Club in Alexandria. He advised me to join this institution expeditiously and remarked that its well-stocked reference library might prove valuable for my research.

The second address was that of a Mr Feaver, the manager of the Occidental Bank, whose headquarters were to be found in the Rue de Londres. Signor Feste knew Mr Feaver as a charming and efficient man and a responsible member of the Alexandrian business community who, in his spare time and without additional payment, fulfilled the post of head coroner for the central districts of the city. Mr Feaver had been informed of my arrival and would be waiting for me to make an appointment to meet him. He had been acquainted with the financial situation of the company and would be making provisions for me to draw on the Siriso Trading Company account for any reasonable amount.

Signor Feste added that Mr Feaver would be able to arrange my passage to Piraeus and the trip to Jebel Dukhan. He also had with him in his office a set of keys to the Siriso warehouse near the docks. My correspondent ended his letter with some interesting information. He had been sent out to Egypt by Siriso in late February. Sir Rodney had charged him with the task of investigating certain inconsistencies in Stephanides's accounts and finding an explanation for the growing irregularity of his communications. Despite Feste's efforts during the early part of the year, however, there was little doubt that the March shipment had been deliberately interfered with: some items had arrived in reduced quantities and some not at all. More seriously, the amount claimed by Stephanides as reimbursement for his expenses was vastly greater than the sum of his purchases. No positive proof – before or after his death – had been found of Stephanides's guilt and it would therefore be improper to cast his honesty into doubt. Even so, his papers had been confiscated by the harbour authorities early in March and, as a precaution, he had been placed under virtual house arrest. Whatever the reason for the discrepancies, Signor Feste was sure that any problems would now have been removed and that there was no reason why my task should be exposed to difficulty.

'The currency – perhaps you do not know, Mr Spellman – fluctuates like the waters of the Nile. We bankers make our dams and dykes to conserve and funnel the flow of money but our economic theories are childish and inept. We have none of the ancestral experience of the *fellahin* out there in the delta, their age-old hands on the rope of the *shaduf*. Taking water from a channel that is full, putting it into one that is dry: restoring the balance.'

Mr Feaver was speaking. The manager of the Occidental Bank sat in his office high above the Rue de Londres and its groaning trams, pleased, as he put it, to have the opportunity of conversing with a fellow countryman. His pleasure was not evident in his voice, however, which was flat and monotonous, nor in his face, the features of which were set like those on an emblem or a coin.

Mr Feaver had indicated early on in our conversation that he thought he would prefer doing business with me rather than with Stephanides, a man whom he had personally disliked. 'Bit of a rogue, I thought, although far be it from me to cast aspersions.' He mentioned in warm terms, however, my immediate predecessor Signor Feste: 'A merry and most energetic man.'

'Yes, the balance is so critical here,' he continued, 'so fragile. Problems: always there are problems and disasters. Things change so quickly to violence.'

One of his assistants brought in tea on a silver tray. 'Believe you me, Mr Spellman: Gordon will be avenged! And in the Transvaal, the Jameson Raiders will be avenged! Do you take milk?'

I did. Mr Feaver handed me my cup and put a slice of lemon into his own. He praised its antiseptic properties. He had a delicate stomach. 'Of course,' he said, 'the situation has been relatively stable since 1875.'

I made an enquiry about the significance of the date, thinking at first that he spoke of his dyspepsia.

'1875? That, my dear fellow, was when Disraeli bought up the Egyptian government's shares in the Suez Canal Company. That, old man, was when we got our foot firmly in the door.' He sipped his tea and roared suddenly with vulgar laughter. I was surprised: he had seemed too grey a man to be coarse.

'Egypt is a factory, a workforce,' he continued. 'The government controls the Nile, of course – as far as such control is possible – but it makes nothing from Suez. Think of it, Mr Spellman: the wealth of the greatest of empires slipping through their hands with the grace of P&O.' He laughed again at his thought. 'And with the Assuan Dam project, there is the distinct likelihood that even the Nile, father of the gods, will be opened up for European investors.'

A deferential official placed before Mr Feaver a number of papers for him to sign. He waved this man away and, leaning forward, emphasized his words by rhythmically pushing a characterless forefinger into the surface of his desk.

'In my opinion the Egyptians have no reason to start causing problems. Yes, the currency rises and falls, expands and contracts like the waters of the Nile, like Belzoni's irrigation schemes, like Ctesibius's water clocks. It always has done. A hydraulic history, Mr Spellman – it's quite a theme, don't you think?'

Yes, it was most interesting. But –

'But by and large Sir Edgar Vincent did his work well. For the rest, we give this country eight million pounds a year. We buy a third of their exports.'

'Sir Edgar Vincent?' I was on unfamiliar ground.

Mr Feaver sighed reproachfully and began to elaborate. 'The architect of the single gold standard in Egypt, old fellow! A great man, one of our finest! In 1885 he made the unit of currency an English one: called it the pound Egyptian.'

He gestured at me with his teacup: 'I met him once, you know.' Smiling proudly, he began what was evidently one of his favourite stories.

'Yes, Sir Edgar Vincent: a courteous man – very. Tremendously aristocratic. Presence, demeanour, knew when he came into the room – that sort of thing. It was at the Club, I remember – the Colonial, of course. Are you a member, by the way? I'll write you a letter. They know me there, you see. Word of a friend, et cetera. Yes, anyway: Vincent. There was a group of us and we were all talking about Gordon's death. Khartoum had been captured and at the time things looked pretty bleak, I must say. But was old Vincent down-hearted? Not a bit of it! I remember his words clearly. "Trade first, battles second," he said, "that is the philosopher's stone which enables us to understand history."'

'What did he mean by that, Mr Feaver?'

He smiled down at me like a schoolmaster with a difficult pupil. 'He meant, of course, that battles are incidents of a history determined by trade.'

'He meant that trade causes wars?'

Mr Feaver became a little irritated. 'History tells us, Mr Spellman, History teaches us – the current of history is such that –'

'Yes, Mr Feaver. Such that –?'

He glared at me. 'What is the history of Egypt in the last one hundred years, Mr Spellman?'

I did not know. It did not matter, however, because he had already begun to tell me. 'The history of Egypt in the last one hundred years, Mr Spellman, is the history of the struggle of the European nations to secure the revenue that spills from the fecund laps of the Nile and, secondly, to preserve trade routes to the east. You will understand, Mr Spellman, that this latter task is the more important. Ultimately, Egypt is merely a staging post on the route to our colonies.'

Mr Feaver was in fine form: he relished his words and flourished phrases. I poured myself another cup of tea whilst he continued. 'Aboukir, 1798: that was the first time we knocked on old Pharaoh's door. We beat Napoleon there before he was beaten anywhere else, you know Mr Spellman. It was only his second major campaign; he was fresh from Campo Formio, having looted the art of Italy for the Louvre.

'Napoleon's army left but the French stayed on as traders. They kept Mohammed Ali in power; he went down into Nubia and founded Khartoum.

'The French thought they were onto a good thing when Thiers proclaimed the age of gold. "*Enrichissez-vous!*" he said, and they conquered Algeria. "Let us be rich!" everybody cried, and in 1859 they sent out Ferdinand de Lesseps to try another hydraulic project.

'We should be grateful to the French, Mr Spellman, for now we enrich ourselves at their expense. We run the Suez Canal Company and have our returns – all this without investment!' Mr Feaver laughed loudly once again.

'Price-fixing, Mr Spellman: that's the trick. We should also be grateful to Mohammed Ali, who wanted money for his wars so badly that he set the price of grain at a ridiculously low level. That was when British merchants began to arrive in floods. Also Syrians, Jews, Greeks and Armenians, all of whom saw easy profits in Egypt. Out there in the delta, unfortunately, the *fellahin* starved. Nevertheless, a great deal of money was made and, taken all round, that's always a good thing.

'I must say that the locals find ingenious ways to generate capital. Take old Asychis, for instance. There's a statue of him in the museum – my favourite. Realizing that the circulation of money was too slow, he decreed that a man could offer his father's dead body as security on a loan! Should the loan not be repaid, the money-lender obtained rights over the sepulchral chamber. Unfortunately, this is something that the coroner-banker of today would have to discourage. The Ancients, I often think, had a freer hand.'

I looked at my watch.

'One moment,' spluttered Mr Feaver, 'let me detain you just one moment, Mr Spellman. I see that you are pushed for time but please allow me to make my point.

'When, in 1881, we put down old Arabi Pasha, we managed to safeguard for the time being the revenue of Egypt's European creditors. Arabi, of course, had been muttering about Egyptian independence and so he had to go.

'There have been some skirmishes since, of course. The Italians, thank God, had the wind taken out of their sails by Adowa. And what else? Well, the dervishes are no longer a problem since we allowed them to die of thirst in the desert. In England, where as you know they don't really comprehend the extent of the problem, it was rather an unpopular measure. But we couldn't have them getting to Wadi Halfa and stirring up all sorts of nuisance.

'I would say, Mr Spellman, that the French are now our only rivals. They no longer threaten us militarily and they have been conclusively beaten in the economic sphere. Instead they're politicking with the Mahdists. Stanley has already had to rush across Africa to rescue Eduard Schnitzer – Emin Pasha, don't you know? That was another unpopular measure, and indeed it does seem excessive to sacrifice, for the sake of one man, 560 Zanzibari porters. As I said, Mr Spellman, things turn quickly to violence here. Have you seen the gun-boat in the bay? The *Orpheus*. That gives me confidence that we'll have Mohammed Ahmed before long. Oh yes, Mr Spellman: just you wait.'

I rose to go. 'I see. Your point is not that trade causes wars. You mean that wars are an extension of trade.'

Mr Feaver beamed as he showed me to the door. 'Precisely, young man! Precisely! Although I think that I had rather say in company that battles result from an "unfortunate collision of interests".'

That evening I dined at the Colonial Club, having presented a letter of introduction from Mr Feaver and paid my dues. I sat at a table looking out over the harbour, where the English gun-boat still lay at anchor in the fading light. I listened to a conversation at the next table:

'I feel so proud when I see the *Orpheus* in the bay, bristling with guns.'

'Absolutely,' a woman's voice replied, '*so* reassuring.'

I watched a lighter draw near to the distant vessel. A naval dignitary in a cockaded hat was being whistled aboard. Through the open windows of the club, several seconds after the stiff white figures saluted each other, the thin, steely sound reached me across the water.

Later, in the dim lobby of the Pension de l'Est, Mistral was sleeping at his desk. I leant across him and took my key from its hook: room 14.

Standing on the balcony looking down into the street, a number of questions occurred to me. Receiving letters, sending documents: what was I doing here? Was I to be merely a dead hand that held a pen for a corporation and signed indentures, contracts, bills of lading, certificates of origin, checklists and inventories? Or worse: not even a hand, was I simply a pen sputtering ink onto official paper, issuing the abbreviated language of trade?

I sat beneath a sun-shade on the southern shore of Mareotis. It was the middle of November and the Nile was leaving us. *Nili*, the season of flood, would last into the New Year but even now the waters were shrinking. Day by day, the land of the delta became more solid, the beach lengthened, the rushes revived and began to sprout. The *fellahin* were colonizing the fields again, flinging seed in wide arcs: cotton, wheat, flax. I watched them at a distance from beneath my parasol. I thought how indifferent the Siriso Trading Company would be to their crops.

I too had been broadcasting. A few days earlier, on the dockside, I had waved a mental farewell to my first fat cargo bound for the Port of London and the dainty hands of Mr Rupert Dinmont. A month previously, I had negotiated a price for each item of this shipment. It was in Eleusis, on the road between Piraeus and Corinth. Here on the Rharian Plain, my Baedeker told me, it was said that Demeter had sowed the first seeds of corn. In memory of this, the Field of Orgas was still planted with sacred trees. Festivals and celebrations had been held here, the name of the place perhaps hinting at their nature.

These rites, said the Baedeker, these first seeds, were reproductions of still earlier sowings, travesties of obeisances made to older gods: Egyptian gods. Herodotus, for instance, had given an elliptical account of the Mysteries at Saïs, held on the site of 'the burial-place of him whom I account it not pious to name'. In the 'sacred enclosure', he wrote, there stand 'great obelisks of stone, and near them is a lake adorned with an edging of stone . . . On this lake they perform by night the show of his sufferings.' 'Although I know,' says Herodotus of the significance of these ceremonies, 'I shall leave unspoke all.'

At Eleusis, in the room above his shop, I was introduced to the cloth merchant by his daughter. He was an old man, and he smoked foul tobacco in a pipe. The wind rattled against the window panes as he spread his yarns before me. Occasionally his grand-children would peep through the door and he would shake his pipe at them, call out to his daughter to take them away. Then he would smile at me and shrug as he pointed out the quality of a particular fabric. I began to jot down some prices. The cloth merchant's wife brought us coffee on a tray.

It was when I was away from England, by the way, Mr Secretary, that I first developed my taste for strong coffee. Now, of course, it is my main pleasure. Desire? Thank you, but no: I prefer coffee.

In the room above the shop, whilst the wind whistled around us, I bought all kinds of yarn in hanks and skeins. We agreed a price for the bundles of trimmings and braids: *passementerie* and orris, soutache and petersham. I took away with me great rolls of fabric, all the products of that spinning Harlequin, the worm that hides itself from the light: sarsenet, marocain, organza, poult-de-soie, samite, pongee, ninon and black bombazine, the cloth of mourning. There was organdie and damask, nainsook and cloth of gold. I bought splendid batiks, whose patterns were formed of dye which had penetrated the wax covering of the cloth. I purchased carpets and rugs from Syria, Persia, Tibet and China: a Bengali satrangi, an Indian numdah. From Piraeus back once more across the wine-dark sea I took lengths of silk from the looms in Cairo and Damietta. There were many other fabrics and cloths, but perhaps most incongruously – it was as odd as the Abernethy biscuits – I was sold three Axminster carpets.

I had been no expert in textiles but I became proficient through necessity. Once more in Alexandria, I rifled for the first time the library of the Colonial Club. Each morning I walked from the Pension de l'Est through the docks before settling into the opulent armchairs of the building on the Corniche.

I did my best with the ten volumes of the *Description de L'Egypte*, the survey of the 175 engineers and scholars amongst Bonaparte's expeditionary force. Clara Bell's 1887 translation of Eber's *Egypt, Descriptive, Historical and Picturesque*, however, was more succinct and accessible. Guided by some clues thrown up in my Baedeker, I also perused Macaulay's 1890 translation of the *History* of Herodotus, whose second book, *Euterpe*, contains an account of Egypt, as well as a meditation on the origin of languages.

The delta, writes Herodotus, is a supplementary land won by its people from the great river. It is also a place of curious inversions. The women trade whilst the men weave, and weaving involves pushing the wool downwards and not upwards. Men, it seems, carry objects on their heads whilst the women of the ancient world shoulder their burdens. Whereas men crouch to urinate, women stand up. Unlike the Greeks, Egyptian men are circumcised. Most peculiarly of all, to write or reckon in the delta is to carry the hand from the right to the left. Herodotus finds his homeland mirrored in Egypt, which possesses 'wonders more in number than any other land'.

Other books were more to my purpose during these days. In the reference section of the Colonial Club library I found Digory Reddle's comprehensive three-volume work, *Textiles of the Middle East*. With Lancelot Sturdiman's *Craft of the Weaver*, Bishop Trimmle's *Religious Vestments of the World*, Mrs Dorothea Burnham's *Oriental Rugs and Carpets* and Walter Bodkin's *Silk-Making and Silk-Weavers: From Orient to Occident*, I had all that I needed for my research.

I moved from shelf to shelf and along great lines of dark spines and creaking bindings. I wrote copious notes at desks whose blotters were marked with the spidered traceries of that day's dealings and, at last, I began to find my labels. Ten days later, in the warehouse, I was able to pack away most of the shipment in properly marked crates. Two unidentified cloths, however, remained to perplex me. I remembered that I had bought them almost as an afterthought and out of pure curiosity. Although the elderly cloth merchant had not set a high price on these goods, he had handled them more reverently than the rest of his stock; clearly, they possessed some sort of value to him. The cloths were made of a common and coarse material; they were stained as if with age. That they were cerements was relatively easy to determine, but this distinction did not necessarily mean that Siriso would have any interest in them.

It was only when the old man unrolled one of the cloths and held it up to the window that I saw upon it the image of a woman laid out in death. The points of nose, chin, hips and knees stood out palely against the shadows of the eye sockets, stomach and softer stretches of flesh. The other cloth held a similar image, except that it was slightly larger and represented a man.

After many hours leafing through my books, Reddle gave me, at least, a name for these things: sudaria. I cross-checked in Bishop Trimmle's *Religious Vestments* and found a more detailed treatment of the subject.

'The question of sudaria is a delicate one for a man in my position,' he writes at the beginning of his fourteenth chapter, 'but I shall endeavour to avoid the Scylla of an uncritical belief in the miraculous, whilst keeping at the same time clear from the Charybdis of cynical rejection. My position is that these strange shrouds should not be accepted as supernatural impressions or records of the passage of a spirit without scrupulous historical authentification. In many cases, I am afraid, the evidence is too slight and, for the time being, we can only say that we do not know if these things are forgeries or genuine marvels.'

Trimmle went on to describe various ways in which realistic images of bodies could be produced on cloth. Any application of paint, of course, was relatively easy to detect since particles of pigment would adhere to the fibres of the particular fabric used. Other methods were more difficult to discredit. The simplest of these was to place a wet cloth over a relief mould of a human figure and then allow it to bleach naturally in strong sunlight. An opposite effect could be achieved, said Trimmle, if a cloth soaked in an unstable dye was placed over a similar mould. In this case, the application of a bleaching agent allowed the raised areas to remain dark, whilst the hollows in which the bleach collected became paler in colour.

It became evident, even bearing in mind that my sudaria appeared to be neither bleached nor dyed, that their authenticity was in considerable doubt. I decided to dispatch them to London with a note to this effect. Leaving the Colonial Club that night, I walked down the Corniche and back to the Pension de l'Est. Trimmle's fourteenth chapter was still on my mind and, turning it over, I realized that I could think of two more ways to produce such images in addition to those my author had mentioned. Perhaps the process of death was itself responsible. George III, for example, suffered from purple sweats. Such stained perspiration might dye a cloth permanently, although it would be a difficult business for the investigator to prevent the deliriously tossing patient from smudging his image. Or alternatively, some unguent used in the burial preparations might contain a photosensitive substance such as the silver iodide used by photographers. In these cases it might be said that the embalmers would unconsciously take the photograph of a ghost. Surfacing from my thoughts, I looked along the crowded streets and heard around me the ceaseless murmur of many tongues.

Tomorrow, after my shipment left on the *Torino*, tomorrow I would go out to the delta.

In January of 1897 I made my second trip for Siriso. Once again, Mr Feaver organized my passage and issued me with the money I required. I took a train to Ismailia, a town north of the Great Bitter Lake. From there, I proceeded by river boat and then along the Red Sea coast by tramp steamer. I was deposited at a small village on the coast, where I was able to hire guides and mules to travel westwards in the direction of Jebel Dukhan, the location of the porphyry quarries worked by the Romans and by others before them.

The day after my arrival I stood at the edge of the desert and was met, from nowhere, by the Berber tribesmen. I remember simply that I turned round and they were there, standing silently before me. A camel coughed. One of the men lit a cigarette. They unloaded their artefacts and we entered the lingua franca of commercial negotiation.

I bought necklaces and loose beads of coral and turquoise from Sinai, translucent oyster shell ear-rings and amber brooches, some of which contained the trapped forms of extinct species of insect. One trader sold me a number of carved meerschaum opium pipes and also ornate narghiles and hookahs. There were ceramic amphorae, sacks of Roman, Greek and Egyptian potsherds; drinking vessels in majolica, jasper and jade. I paid out money for glittering champlevé plates and caskets made of brass or tortoiseshell buhl. A man with a long beard and a syphilitic lip unpacked crates containing busts and figures of Roman origin. I saw the gods in *nero antico*, *giallo antico*, verd-antique and breccia verde, the last of which had been quarried at Jebel Hammada to the south. I bought a porphyry vase depicting the legend of Persephone and knew that Mr Zabel, for whom the shipment was destined, would appreciate this companion-piece to his Demeter: mother and daughter would stand together on his mantelpiece. Last amongst my purchases was a series of ithyphallic statues of Egyptian origin. They were fashioned from both wood and clay; some held in the hollows of their bellies a waxy vegetable substance.

I was mystified by these figures and it was during my investigations into their origin and history that I first came across the fastidious and corpulent Mr Nopheles, shipping magnate, of Smyrna. I was sitting after my meal at a table in the Colonial Club with one of the figurines propped up in front of me – I remember the details because of the uneasy expression on the face of the waiter who served me – when a pink, fleshy hand entered the field of my vision and, hesitating as if to seek my approval, picked up the Bacchic figure with meticulous fingertips.

'Statuettes of Osiris such as this have been found at the necropolis in Thebes. Some had faces of green wax. Some, like this one here, had bellies full of grain mingled with wax.'

I put down the sugar tongs without looking round. The voice continued: 'In other places representations of the same god compounded of slime have been found between the legs of mummies. Larger automata or puppets were apparently brought out at his festival. They had one moving part – the virile one, of course, vastly exaggerated – and women operated it by means of strings. In the chambers of Osiris at Philae, near Assuan, the dead god is likewise represented with an erection. Piously, Herodotus will not say why the phallus is thus engorged.'

A few heads at nearby tables had turned to look at us. But the stranger continued his discourse. 'It is certain that the phallus is the most ancient of signs. Sesôstris, a king of the twelfth dynasty who was esteemed next in rank only to Osiris, subdued the whole of Asia and Europe as far as Thrace. As a reminder of his deeds, he left behind him a number of *stelae*, or pillars, in the countries he had conquered. Those races who had valiantly resisted his onslaughts were honoured with the sign of the secret parts of a man carved into the *stela*. An inglorious race, however, received the female pudendum.'

Nearby diners were beginning to murmur their protests. I rose to my feet and the stranger returned the figurine to me. He introduced himself with a bow and a click of his heels. As I shook his hand, I felt as though I had put my own into a nest of new-born mice.

This was my first taste of Mr Nopheles's enormous knowledge. It was he who was to be my index to the library of the Colonial Club, as well as its most useful encyclopaedia. He had read much and travelled widely – had only, in fact, returned to Alexandria in October having spent eighteen months aboard. He wrote his letters in the morning and spent the afternoons reading in the library. The best time to talk to him was in the evening when he drank coffee, smoked, and played chess in the lounge. He always won.

Over the next months I came to know him well. Sometimes, after a long day's work, he would take my arm and walk me down the Corniche until our ways parted. His gleaming cranium was full of the obscure and the abstruse but he was not a solemn man. Indeed, he had a childish love of mixed metaphors and conflated idioms. His puns were appalling but they often contained the most unforeseen associations.

'Strange that "mummies" are always – ah – daddies,' he said one evening at the Club as he moved his knight forwards across the chess-board, affecting bewilderment at the illogicality of my tongue. I am sure he knew that the word derived ultimately from the Persian *mum*: wax.

Returning to the game, I saw that once again my king was mated.

19

The Merchant of the Exotic

THE AMNIOTIC yellow light of an Egyptian dawn would surely be the most remarkable quality of this place, were it not for the Egyptian dusk: violet shading off into dim reaches of pearly, almost irridescent mauve. Or night – what of the night, stranger still? A hollow blue darkness in which sounds carry to tremendous distances.

And water: it was an agriculturalist's Venice in which a thousand dykes and channels distributed the vital fluid. In this hydraulic place it was hardly surprising that, centuries before Harvey, a colleague of Herophilus hypothesized the circulation of the blood.

The unripe maize undulated like a liquid. Green water flowed along the ditches which divided green scraps of land into shapes beyond geometry: a *feddan* here edged with poppies, iris and asphodel; one there, by the cypress grove where the buffalo turns the *sakia*; still another beyond the dyke, beyond the line of poplars. Down there, near the water's edge: a Pharaoh's rat stealing eggs from a nest.

I should have liked to pass over these details, Mr Secretary. I have no wish to riddle you, no desire for the exotic paragraph ripe with the fruit of strange tongues. Even as I dictate, I long for London: a cooler form of mortification.

Alexandria was disease-ridden and fly-blown and flea-bitten. A ten-year-old child touched my hand. Did the gentleman want company? I had thought she wanted guiding across the street.

The dead were buried quickly here, before the sun could swell their bellies. Two mornings a week, in the coroner's office, Mr Feaver signed death certificate after death certificate. Funeral cortèges queued at the cemetery gates, mingling with each other and gathering up passersby. It was not unusual, I was told, to attend the burial service of somebody one had never met.

The sun! I, one of the unfortunate living, ran into holes to hide from it: holes where fans whirred and glasses clinked. The art of conversation was still practised here in its original form: that of striking deals.

Chthonic city full of gibbering mouths.

It was not very different from other cities. Indeed, having erased, shattered, buried and dismembered its past, it was an exemplary city. Rootlessness everywhere, and yet it was here that Eratosthenes (perhaps, say the scholars: the details have been lost) calculated the circumference of the earth to within fifty miles and mapped out a place for us in the sky. Ruins and forgotten fragments, and yet it was here that Herophilus (perhaps, say the scholars: the details have been lost) performed the first human dissections and speculated that the seat of the intellect was in the brain and not as Aristotle thought, in the heart.

Cleopatra's palace on the Silsileh – gone. Sostratus's lighthouse, where candles burned for a thousand years – gone. The great labyrinth of Lacharês, which impressed Herodotus more than the pyramids – that, too, is gone. And the library. Of course, the library: burned down by Eratostratus in AD 391.

Over the following months I began to feel like some peculiar combination of a detective and a librarian. To follow Signor Feste's written instructions, which arrived regularly and were delivered by a smiling Mistral to my rooms on the top floor of the Pension de l'Est was certainly to be cast as a hunter who tracked things back to their source in books.

I wandered in a jungle of things, an efflorescence of exotica and all forms of rarity. I ploughed the encyclopaedias and sowed labels. I followed things through to the end.

There was in all this, however, a faint but disturbing awareness of being something other than a tracer of enigmas. This intangible impression left me sometimes for weeks together only to return with renewed force. I can only describe it as a feeling of being myself tracked and read, sifted for signs of origin. The feeling increased in intensity shortly before the departure of my third shipment to London in the April of 1897. In March, I had taken ship to Jounié, a port north of Sidon on the Syrian coast. From there I proceeded by mule and crossed the River Adonis. It was Easter and the little valley was carpeted with scarlet anenomes. Strange to tell, the river too ran red as if with dye leached from their falling petals. Having climbed the steep slope on the other side of the river, I reached my destination: Jbail, called Byblus by the Phoenicians. It is one of the oldest of cities and is said to have been founded by Cronos or a still more senior god, his predecessor.

Leaving the market-place, my guide led me through a crumbling archway into a large courtyard bathed in the spring sun. An old man sat on a bench in the shade. He greeted me as if he knew me, extending a hand stained green by the plants he nurtured. He had a red rose in his buttonhole. The old man took us through a doorway behind his bench and I found myself in another courtyard as large as the first. Once again I took out my wallet.

Here, in pots under glass, were martagon and poinsettia, heliotrope, betony and orchis, all in flower. Roses stood next to the Chinese paulownia. Rubber seedlings nestled against cinchona shrubs. I was sold in sealed packets the seeds and bulbs of many more plants. Then I was shown saplings of deodar and manuka; jacaranda, sapele and sabicu; primavera, rewa-rewa, jarrah and sissoo; quebracho, iroko, pipal, banyan and bo-tree. The old man laid before me planks of mahogany and ebony, great beams of the darkly-shadowed cypress, tree of mourning. There were shorter lengths of sandalwood which had been wrapped in oil-cloth to preserve their fragrance and flat trays containing purpleheart and tigerwood veneers.

Jbail is an isolated town and the cargo I procured posed great difficulties of transportation. I hired twelve carters and muleteers, whose loads leaned dangerously as we wound our way back down the valley. The ship that I chartered at Jounié was forced to take on board great tanks of fresh water in order to supply my delicate blooms during the return trip to Alexandria.

Installed once again in the Pension de l'Est, I would rise early and walk down to the Siriso warehouse on the quay. The gusting khamsin whipped sacks along the streets. I paused before the door and looked up. 'The Siriso Trading Company,' it said: black letters on a white ground. Letting myself in, I would water my thousand flowers before hurrying on to the Colonial Club.

I worked now in a different section of the library. Gladbushe's *Tropical Hardwoods* stood open in front of me; nearby, on a chair, was Augustus Browne's *Flowering Plants of Asia* and Fender's *Short Botany of Greece and Asia Minor*. My Bible during this time, however, was the monumental but as yet incomplete thirteen-volume *Survey of the Trees and Flowering Plants of Amazonia*, compiled by Mr Sidney Bellowes. This was entirely appropriate as, on the first of May, after many last-minute difficulties, a living cargo addressed to my old friend sailed from Alexandria bound for the Port of London and, eventually, Kew Gardens. Almost immediately, or at any rate within a week, the feeling of having to look behind me, the sensation of hot breath on my neck disappeared.

One evening, over dinner, I explained to Mr Nopheles the purpose and nature, as far as I saw it, of my appointment in Egypt. I began to discuss my responses to the profusion of things which were passing through my hands. I was, I suppose, naïve enough to hope that by sounding calm I would become so. At first, I said, I had been dizzied and staggered by the

253

task before me. The thought of spending whole days and even nights of research in a library had oppressed and dispirited me. Only very recently, I went on, whilst Mr Nopheles browsed placidly through his dinner, had all the significant details which at first disturbed me begun to disappear. The things, it seemed, were meaningless goods, mere problems: a certain series of unknown facts, a certain quota of space in the hold of a ship.

Mr Nopheles wiped his forehead with a handkerchief. 'Yes, Mr Spellman: I can quite see that as a natural response. One can easily grow resistant to difference and variety when they become the rule. Such things are stimulants, I suppose, and so quickly lose their effect.' I nodded in agreement. 'Perhaps,' he suggested after a while, 'you have been in Egypt too long: the delightful veil of the exotic appears to have fallen from your eyes. When was it, by the way, that you arrived?'

'September.'

'September of – ah – 1895?'

'No, no: last September. 1896.'

'So recently? You surprise me.' He looked at me attentively.

I was honest and indiscreet enough to voice my worries. 'A week ago, things were quite different.'

'Really? In what way? Please tell me.' He ordered coffee from a passing waiter.

'Well – I could not escape from the growing sensation that each item I labelled had some occulted meaning. I did not know its significance and I would never discover it but nevertheless, the thing was somehow full of sense. It was as if somebody somewhere knew and knew also that I didn't know –'

'Go on: you intrigue me.'

'I thought that it was as if I had been sent here to discover the *theme* of each cargo. The paperwork, the negotiations, the buying – all these are put in my way to distract me.'

'I see, I see.' Mr Nopheles had become quite excited. 'It's as if each cargo contains a – a what is it? – a crypt, no – a *code*.'

I almost banged the table: 'That's it! That's precisely the feeling I have. They are there to watch me and assess my performance.'

'"They"?'

'Oh – I don't know who.'

'You had better find out very soon or people might begin to doubt your sanity! Do you mean your employers?'

'I don't know. Whoever made up the code.'

'The problem with codes,' said Mr Nopheles after a pause for thought, 'is that the cryptographer needs to know which portions of a given message are encoded. It is only when you have already identified something as a code that you can set to work, can brush the moss away from the headstone and at last, in the middle of the forest, behold the trees.'

'But, then –' I felt uneasy '– in order to identify a code mustn't you know already how to break it?'

Mr Nopheles smiled beatifically. 'You have hit the head on the nail most neatly.' He was evidently pleased with his paradox but he must have noticed my anxiety since he tried to cheer me up. 'Never mind, Mr Spellman. It is only the ghosts that have worried you.'

'Ghosts?'

'The spring flowers that you brought back from Byblus.'

'I'm not sure I –'

'Oh, I'm sorry,' he interrupted, 'didn't you know? I thought from your reference to the stained water of the River Adonis earlier this evening that you were aware of the myth.'

I was not, but I begged him to tell me.

'The Phoenicians,' he began, taking a sip of his brandy, 'associated spring with the death of their god. The new flowers – anenomes, violets – rise from his slain body. They are, as it were, the ghosts of last year's harvest.'

'And the river?' I enquired, intrigued.

'Ah, the river. Well, it is not dye – as you thought, Mr Spellman. The water becomes red when the spring floods bring iron-rich earth down from the mountains to the east of Byblus. Once upon a time, it was the blood of the murdered god.'

Mr Nopheles drummed his soft pink fingers on the table and looked pensive. 'I wonder how many rivers have flowed miraculously wrong?' he murmured. 'During the reign of Nephercherês, the waters of the Nile were said to have been blended with honey for eleven days.'

I tried to bring him back to the subject under discussion. 'Who was the god killed by?'

He shrugged. 'By his followers, by his sons, by himself – there are different versions. The Athenians commemorated the occasion at their Festival of Flowers in March. Even today, many people say that poppies are the ghosts of warriors slain in battle.' He patted my hand. 'Hence, I suppose, the odd effect created by that name of which you are so fond: that Magenta who is both a battle and a dye.'

Mr Nopheles talked on, criss-crossing the separate fields of his knowledge and bringing distant things close together. No connection was too tenuous to generate a trace of meaning; every pun made sense and puns were everywhere. I was hardly listening. The words of Mr Nopheles had already set off too many associations and I was lost in remembrance.

' . . . and Nana, a virgin who became pregnant with Attis when she placed within her bosom a pomegranate which had sprung from where the severed genitals of Agdestis fell . . . further south it was the blossom of the almond tree . . . his death by a pine tree marked by violets springing from his blood . . . the Ptolemaic inscriptions at Denderah of which Plutarch writes . . . and anemones, of course, in the case of Adonis at Easter, a bloody spoor along the valley . . . or the rose which flushes with life . . . much beloved of the Egyptians and linked again to wounds and swoons . . . What did Keats say? "Drowsed with the fume of poppies" . . . and Marvell's massacred pastures . . . Always red in the green, an injury somewhere . . . Purple too, worn for both births and funerals . . . '

I saw the gleaming blade of Mr Nopheles's fruit-knife and suddenly started. He looked at me solicitously, but seemed unaware that I had not been following. With surgical skill he began to peel a peach.

'It was the most remarkable thing, Mr Spellman. The sheaves were piled in a corner of the field. It was evening and the *fellahin* were cleaning their scythes. He walked past me in the gathering dusk. I never saw his face but will always remember his words: "The old man is dead." Think of it! His words were older than his faith; he did not speak them, they spoke through him.'

The Colonial Club had closed for the night. At the bottom of the Corniche, before we parted, I happened to mention to my companion that at the beginning of June I would be travelling to the Oasis of Siwa to negotiate the purchase of another shipment.

'In that case,' said Mr Nopheles, turning his pale face towards me in the darkness, 'you must find time to visit the Temple of Jupiter Ammon, or, more correctly, Amûn – the Egyptian title of Zeus. Manetho thought the name meant "that which is concealed", which reminds me of the other god that Herodotus is too pious to name.'

I promised to visit the temple and Mr Nopheles said good night. 'Another great castrator with his sickle!' he called out as he walked away.

As usual before my departure, I visited the bland Mr Feaver who sat changelessly in his office three floors above the Rue de Londres. I had to collect my *khazna*, or treasury, which is made up of one thousand *kis* – each *kis* being five Egyptian pounds.

When I entered the office, I found Mr Feaver in discussion with Mehmet Ali. They both stopped talking at the same moment and looked at me curiously. Then Mr Feaver's face, as it occasionally did, took on a look of crude jollity.

'Look here, Mr Spellman, look!' He beckoned me over and indicated the papers on his desk. 'I am pleased and indeed delighted to inform you that the Occidental Bank in which you stand, manager Mr Lewis John

Feaver, has obtained in the face of great competition the right to deal with the account of the Assuan Dam Construction Company. Overseas investment will be hoarded here and, I fondly feel, the great stone edifice will block the valley almost at my behest.' He turned to Mehmet Ali. 'Ironic isn't it, my friend, that even as the Nile reaches its lowest ebb, an influx of foreign currency already gushes into our coffers?'

Despite his jovial manner, Mr Feaver seemed strangely relieved when I stated the object of my visit. He quickly issued me with the drafts and the paper money. After I had signed some papers and paid the standard charge for the transaction, he seemed positively glad to bid me goodbye. Mehmet Ali, in the background, cordially elongated his thin lips.

I returned three weeks later on the train from Cairo with a goods wagon full of musical instruments. As at Jebel Dukhan on my second journey for Siriso, the tribesmen had again emerged from the level sands of the Desert of Tripoli without my having observed their approach. They had unrolled their mats on the ground and silently laid out their goods. Squatting on their haunches, they had patiently begun to twist their waxed moustaches. For my part, I had only questions as I inspected and purchased the offerings. How had the Berber been informed of this meeting? Why did they so rarely haggle? Was I consistently giving too generous a price? Most mystifying of all, why was it that on this occasion the only things for sale were musical instruments?

I worried my way by mule and train back to Alexandria. My fears were somewhat allayed by a complimentary and approving letter from Giovanni Feste which awaited me in my pigeon-hole at the Pension de l'Est. Initially, however, as I tore open the envelope, I was greeted with sad news: Mr Bellowes and Mr Zabel were dead. They had been travelling together from Leeds to Manchester when their train had collided with another in one of the Pennine tunnels. Sitting in the front carriage, both had been killed instantly.

Adding up the dates, I realized that Mr Bellowes would not have seen his cargo of flora, although I thought it probable that, before he died, Mr Zabel at least had received his precious artefacts. For some reason, I was a little comforted by the idea that, on the mantel at Fairfields, daughter was at last reunited with mother.

With a business-like callousness that surprised me, Signor Feste enclosed a cheque for my share in the dividends of the Siriso tontine over the trading year June 1896 – June 1897. He pointed out that the amount was larger than I might have foreseen since, owing to the deaths of Mr Bellowes and Mr Zabel, the sum was to be divided only nine times and not the anticipated eleven.

The fourteenth and final volume of the *Survey of the Trees and Flowering*

Plants of Amazonia would never see the light now, and opera singers would no longer be heard in the swamp.

Feste ended his letter with a comment on the celebrations mounted in England for Queen Victoria's diamond jubilee: 'Scaffolds are thrown up along the streets, cheap gimcrack carpentry. The capital is defaced and the middle classes scramble to buy ringside seats.'

One evening, after a particularly ruinous game of chess on my part, I took Mr Nopheles down to the warehouse to show him some of the musical instruments I had purchased on behalf of W.H. Perkin at the Oasis of Siwa and which were to be shipped to London in a few days. Mr Nopheles was wearing a flowing cravat. Amongst the boxes and crates, he looked like a theatrical impresario reviewing a promising cast. He was particularly fascinated by the array of drums and cymbals which I had piled in one corner. He tapped a timbrel, sending its flat note around the warehouse, and began to make elliptic comments about the rituals surrounding the worship of Attis.

'By a superbly synaesthetic gesture food would be eaten from drums and liquid quaffed from cymbals. A sort of cultural glissando, is it not, Mr Spellman? A sound which consecrates the wine.'

Then Mr Nopheles began to weave the myths and, told back to back, they took on an isomorphic glitter.

Attis had castrated himself beneath a pine tree and bled to death: 'Violets sprang from the spot, as you will remember, Mr Spellman.'

There were ceremonies which, on the day of blood, had culminated in the frenzy of the Galli when novices left their severed phalluses on the altar. Later, these were buried in chambers sacred to Cybele. Marsyas the flute-player: a type, said Mr Nopheles, of Attis. Having outplayed Apollo in a musical contest, he had been tied to a tree, flayed and then dismembered by his vengeful opponent. Orpheus too; Mr Nopheles mentioned something about the limbs of a poet.

Returning to the Pension de l'Est that evening I heard quick footsteps behind me. Rapidly looking behind me in anticipation of some attack or confrontation I found that the street was empty. Mistral was absent from his usual post at the desk in the lobby. As I had done before, I took my keys from the hook and began to climb the stairs. Behind the door of Stephanides's old room, my attention was caught by the distinct sounds of a woman panting. Whether the sobs were those of grief or ecstasy, I could not tell.

12 August 1897. I had reached Cairo, where I was now recuperating at the Hôtel Les Deux Continents in preparation for my journey to the Selima

oasis, the most distant expedition to date. I was to travel south by riverboat to Farshut, where I would hire guides and camels to take me from Kharga to the Dakhla oasis, then southwards through the desert to Selima which, eighty miles west-south-west of Wadi Halfa in Anglo-Egyptian Sudan, was seven hundred miles from Alexandria.

In Cairo the flood celebrations were reaching their height. The Nile had risen twenty feet in a month, and now the circus had arrived to feed off the festival which surged in the streets. Funambulists practised their arts in crowded squares and, sitting cross-legged in front of reed baskets, snake charmers solicited their toothless reptiles with nasal chants. At the Khalíj, a canal which debouched from the Nile south of Cairo and was the artery of the fields on the west bank, an earth dam had been built. A cone of earth sown with maize had been raised midway along its lip.

I stood amongst a crowd of spectators and watched young men diving for money. A cicerone approached and started to tell me that, centuries ago, for the pleasure of the Nile and to ensure his fertilization of the cornlands, a virgin had been cast into the water during these celebrations. The dam was cut; people shouted and jostled for a view of the great green wave as it gushed along the watercourse and, gurgling into the transverse dykes, washed clods of water away with its force.

The Nile: the river described, in Wiedemann's fine translation of the inscription on the rocks at Jebel Silsileh as 'the living and beautiful stream, the father of all the gods'.

I looked across from the city to the plains and then I looked down at the guide who had seized the lapels of my jacket and was demanding baksheesh for his words. I paid him: I always paid: it was my job to pay.

A month later, back in Alexandria, I had turned antiquarian and archivist. Beneath the fans in the Colonial Club library I pored over the texts, pictures and maps which I had brought back from the margin of the great desert.

A copy on vellum of the Poetic Edda, a number of Masoretic commentaries, various Puranic poems and the Peshito, or Syriac version of the Christian testaments were all laid in specially constructed boxes and sealed with wax. I handled richly scripted versions of the Mishnah and the Gemara. I was swallowed by the bibliographical section of the library and wandered through books exclusively devoted to books. On several occasions, as my work continued into the evening, I reminded myself of the ancient child in the charcoal-burner's cottage who copied with such accuracy the contorted scripts she wished, for some reason, to preserve.

In the Siriso warehouse there were piles of mezuzoth in their original cases and phylacteries containing other Hebrew texts. There were Japanese woodcuts on mulberry bark and hieroglyphics on papyrus. Here, the

Upanishads and the Vedas. There, a late-seventeenth-century Moravian pharmacopoeia and a series of alchemical codices.

And here, an early translation of Benvenuto Cellini's *Autobiography* which included a description of his Monte Cavallo illness when, after several days of fever, he vomited from his stomach 'an hairy worm about a quarter of a cubit in length,' the hairs of which were, he wrote, 'long, and the worm was very ugly, being speckled of divers colours, blue, black, and red'.

There were writings in all alphabets, scripts and languages: Cyrillic, hieratic, Devanagari, Pali, Sanskrit, Aramaic, Greek, Latin and Arabic. But not all of them were sacred. I purchased a number of European curiosa: albums with photographs of naked Sicilian boys which I labelled, dated, and placed in protective binders. To my great surprise I discovered that a merchant whose face I could not remember had sold me a copy of my own and Lady Magenta's work. Since my departure from England she must have had a small edition of our photographs of the circus and the city printed privately. It was my first published work, Mr Secretary: the frontispiece showed me riding a horse on a carousel. I could not imagine how it had found its way out to Egypt.

I locked the door of the warehouse and returned to my room at the Pension de l'Est where, having lighted my lamp, I placed in a padded casket a first edition of Charles Marie de la Condamine's *Journal du voyage fait par ordre du roi à l'équateur*. There followed Bougainville's *Voyage autour du Monde*, Forster's *Voyage around the World on H.M.Sloop 'Resolution'*, Darwin's *Voyage of the Beagle* and Richard Spruce's *Hepaticae Amazonicae et Andinae*.

It was at this point that I began to become distracted. I had opened the windows to allow a cool breeze to circulate before moving on to my next text: the magnificent 23-volume *Voyage de Humboldt et Bonpland*.

As a young man desperate for the exotic, Humboldt had suffered a double setback. In 1797 Napoleon's army, looting Italy for the greater glory of France, had prevented him from instigating a complete geographical and geological survey of the volcanoes of Italy. Perhaps in his heart of hearts Humboldt had hoped to find the crevice in the earth through which Hades once guided the struggling Persephone. In the following year – never one to harbour a grudge in his pursuit of knowledge – he was unable to join Napoleon's scholars in Egypt. This time the impediment was a navy rather than an army, its nationality British rather than French.

Frustrated, Humboldt walked from the Alps to Madrid, took ship on the *Pizarro* and spent the next five years in the basin of the River Amazon. With the assistance only of the amiable Bonpland, he set out to classify and collect the most prolific part of the planet. A conquistador for the empire of knowledge, he accumulated 60,000 plant specimens during his travels – many of which remain unlabelled and unknown to science.

A moth collided with my lamp and startled me from my reverie. I packed away Humboldt, picked up my next book and once again made the fatal mistake of turning the flyleaf, where an illustration of a rubber plant stared me in the face. When Clements Markham and Joseph Hooker (son of William, the armchair pirate of cinchona) came upon this book in 1874 they considered that the time was ripe for another theft from South America. Henry Wickham, the unfortunate author of *Rough Notes of a Journey through the Wilderness*, was summarily dispatched to gather and remove rubber seedlings on behalf of Her Britannic Majesty. Like Spruce, Wickham performed his task as well as he could. Late in the summer of 1876 the S.S. *Amazonas* reached London with a cargo of seven thousand seedlings which were expeditiously transferred to the dark hold of the *Duke of Devonshire*, bound for Colombo.

Desperately tired, sunlight was streaming through the window of my room as I turned to the maps. Unrolling them on the desk, I gazed on patriarchal heads with puffed cheeks blowing from the four points of the compass. Anthropophagi roamed the southern tips of all the continents and whales spouted in the oceans.

At the beginning of October I emerged from my cocoon of notes and labels. My chests, safely sealed at last, had been hoisted aboard the *Patagonia*, and one morning, in the company of the *Orpheus*, the cargo bound for the dry and cultivated hands of Sir Stafford Singleton slipped over the horizon and was lost to view.

Soft, pattering steps behind me in the street. Turning – again nothing.

Despite the assurances contained in Signor Feste's letter of July, I continued to feel uneasy. The trip to Selima had unnerved me once more. I was spending large sums of money: surely too large for a mere agent of a trading company. I could not understand, although I realized that my purchases possessed undoubted value, how Siriso could survive if it traded on these things alone. My trips were unselective lunges and the objects so procured could arouse the interest of only the most rarefied specialist.

It was as though, in Egypt, I was staggering about in a darkened room filled with furniture. I was repeatedly knocking things over but whether they were priceless antiquities or mere lumber I had no idea. I became certain that I was no detective; I was the scapegoat.

Once again I confided my fears to Mr Nopheles over a game of chess. The leather armchairs and the ottomans, the quiet service and the gently circulated air: all this made a strange stage on which to voice my doubts.

After a while I trailed off into silence and, feeling somewhat absurd, attempted to concentrate on the game before me. With an air of quiet confidence, Mr Nopheles plucked his black knight from Kt3 and softly planted it on Q4. This was the overture to a sequence of moves which would result, I was sure, in my defeat. I moved my king's pawn forward to threaten the knight.

'Perhaps,' said Mr Nopheles reflectively, 'you would do better to stop thinking of Siriso – your endeavours, all your enquiries – as in some way significant. They seduce you, Mr Spellman, the things; they lead you on too much. You are too close to them, too familiar with them. Perhaps the secret of the code is that there is no secret at all.' He took my pawn. Recapturing, I was able to maintain the threat on his knight. Mr Nopheles looked down at the board and his brow creased. 'I have always wondered,' he said, 'why the piece called a knight is represented by a riderless horse. There is no knight on its back.'

'Perhaps he has been thrown off,' I suggested.

'Hmm –'

'I can never come to terms with the knight,' I added after a few moments: 'It springs its crooked surprises from nowhere.'

'Ah yes, the embarrassing fork.' Mr Nopheles moved his queen from the back row and set it down on B5. I was startled: he had chosen not to move his *en prise* knight. Mr Nopheles was amused. 'You see, Mr Spellman: you anticipated bafflement from the knight, but danger came with the queen.'

He was right. It was impossible for me to exchange queens because Mr Nopheles's knight would remain to win the exchange and my king was poorly defended. The only option now was evasion. After another two or three moves and an exchange of rooks, I offered Mr Nopheles my hand in resignation. 'I'm afraid I'm not much of an opponent,' I apologized.

On the Corniche my companion returned to the subject of our conversation: 'Siriso is only a trading company, Mr Spellman. It means nothing: it merely imports. Secrets – the things not named – they are often so obvious as hardly to need a name.'

Tap, tap . . . tap, tap . . .

The laboratory, the zoo, the larder, the mill, the herbarium, the concert hall, the library – and now the taxidermist's workshop.

In November 1897 I travelled to Zagazig in the very heartland of the delta. The Egyptians once called it Bubastus; in *Ezekiel* it is Pi-beseth. According to Africanus, a great chasm had opened in the earth here during the thirty-eight-year reign of Boêthos, a king of the second dynasty.

Through Damanhur and Tanta I crossed the lap, the great stomach of Egypt, its moist loins endlessly renewed, endlessly craving renewal from sowing to sowing and harvest to harvest, from the *fellah* to his son and his son's son.

The Royal Society had sent a group of geologists to this spot over a decade before. They had analysed the composition of the grey Nilotic earth with its glittering flecks of mica and, hiring local labour, erected a derrick and drilled down into the sand beds in an attempt to discover their depth as well as to map the fault line discovered by Napoleon's engineers in 1798. Having penetrated four hundred yielding feet without striking any solid floor, they had given up the task, dismantled their equipment and returned, disappointed, to England. The fault line, it seemed – a deep cleft in a seamless surface – stretched out to sea in the direction of Crete.

In a workshop adjoining the Zagazig slaughterhouse I met the subtle furrier and the stained tanner. The integuments of all dead things seemed to have been collected here. Hides were drying in the sun and leather from a score of animals was stretched out on frames of varying sizes. I was shown kolinsky furs and minks. I handled the skins of bear, rabbit, wolf, mongoose, leopard, snake and crocodile. The plumassier, a delicate man with gold-rimmed spectacles, arrived with boas flung over his shoulders and single feathers pinned on boards which he carried in a trunk.

I hired a cart to take my purchases back to the railway station and, in the abattoir yard, my notebook filled with figures and the wagon with furs. At one point I handed out a *kis* for a small box I did not bother to inspect. Heavier goods rapidly followed: the skins of two tigers, one Bengali and one Siberian, each with glass eyes the size of paperweights; a complete horse skin, beaver pelts, rhinoceros horns and walrus tusks, the stuffed and mounted heads of wildebeest, eland and pronghorn.

Two days later, in the Siriso warehouse, I stood contemplating the great pile of skins in front of me. Together, they were like the corpse of a compendious animal. Legs belonging to different species trailed in every direction. Reptilian, avian, mammalian: I hardly knew where to begin.

Through the salt-stained windows I noticed two English gun-boats in the bay where there used to be one.

I set to work, placing like with like and distributing the pelts around the four corners of the warehouse. When I had half-finished my task, I came again upon the little box whose contents I had forgotten to ascertain. It lay among the folds of the Siberian tiger skin. Inside the box was a ball of screwed up papers approximately the size of a human fist. I peeled away the first layer of paper and found that it was a certificate of authenticity signed by the plumassier at Zagazig whose name – Crute – I had happened to remember. Each succeeding layer of the paper ball proved to be an ever-earlier receipt or testimonial. Unwrapping the last layer of paper, I finally held in my hand a blackened walnut shell whose hemispheres had been sealed with wax. Splitting this miniature casket and looking inside, I found a hollow and carious horse's tooth nestling amongst fibres of flax and cotton.

Was this some sort of a joke? A *kis* for a chip of rotten enamel? I turned to the innermost paper wrapping.

Ten minutes later I was panting up the slope of the Corniche with the box in my hand. I burst noisily into the dining room of the Colonial Club. As I had hoped I found Mr Nopheles at his lunch.

'Bucephalus's tooth!' I exclaimed, waving the contents of the walnut box over his soup.

He was imperturbable: 'How fascinating. A relic of our founder has come home to roost. May I see?'

I placed the shell in front of him and passed across the papers.

'These are the certificates of origin,' I said. 'Letters from owner to owner back and back through the ages.'

'I see.' Mr Nopheles passed a hand across his smoothly shaven cheek.

After a few minutes, however, he had disappointing news. 'I am afraid, Mr Spellman, that these authentications – these documents – are fakes.'

'Can you be sure?' For some unaccountable reason, I had set great store on the veracity of the paperwork which had accompanied the tooth and to find it challenged was somehow, once again, to have everything cast into doubt.

'Absolutely certain.' Mr Nopheles shuffled the papers in front of him and sighed. 'The Greek, I am afraid, is wrong; the Latin is wrong; the paper is wrong. See: look carefully. Can't you tell that all these things have been written by the same hand?' There was undoubtedly a resemblance between all the scripts.

'Everything is wrong, Mr Spellman. So wrong, in fact, that one is tempted to smell a mouse. This is not just a bad forgery, it is a parody of a bad forgery. Eighteenth century, I should think. Possibly German, judging from the quality of the paper.'

Mr Nopheles evinced great interest in the shipment in progress and I offered to show it to him. We agreed to meet outside the Siriso warehouse that evening. Even as I was unlocking the door he had begun to mutter about the pigs which were once sacrificed to Dionysus. There was a window in the roof of the warehouse and I dragged the skin of an ox into its light.

'One of the old authors records the way in which these beasts were tested for purity,' said my companion. 'The cleanest of all were marked with a sign written on papyrus, which was then attached to the creature's horn and sealed in with clay.' He gazed upwards through the skylight and watched the evening clouds pass by. 'They would cut the throat and sever the head,' he continued. 'The ox would then be flayed whilst the worshippers uttered imprecations upon the sacrificial animal. "It is not we who kill you," they would shout, "retribution should not fall on us." Next they would remove the entrails, the fat, the legs, the end of the loin, the shoulders and the neck. This done, the body of the animal would be filled with consecrated loaves and honey, raisins and figs, frankincense, myrrh and every other kind of spice. Finally, they would pour oil over their sacrifice and offer it up.'

In February 1898 I received another letter from Giovanni Feste. It post-dated the arrival of the Baroness Hrocka's cargo of skins. Signor Feste had been particularly amused by the case of Bucephalus's tooth. He had recently made the acquaintance of a Dutch bibliophile who had become disillusioned with hoarding original manuscripts and first editions. Instead, he had redirected his collector's avarice into antique forgeries. Feste remarked with a mischievous pride that the bibliophile, one Pieter Van Wyck, had been prepared to pay a higher price for the fake than could reasonably have been expected for the real thing. Mr Van Wyck had also offered a generous sum for the forged sudaria which I had sent out in my first shipment a year previously.

Once more, with an oddly abrupt swing, Signor Feste informed me that he had sad news to relate. The Baroness Hrocka had died shortly after Christmas, apparently of heart failure whilst in the arms of one of her lovers, a diplomat who was, coincidentally, the Comptroller-General of Egypt. Feste hardly needed to add that the baroness had died as she would have wished and as she had lived: in the midst of a scandalous liaison which would live on in the gossip of London society.

Signor Feste's letter ended on an official note. The monies from London which were regularly paid into the Siriso account had apparently been miscalculated. In an unusual lapse of attention, Feste had recorded the remittance to cover my payment of maritime insurance as £155. 6s. 6d rather than the correct figures: £15. 6s. 6d. The account had consequently been over-funded to the tune of one hundred and forty pounds and Feste asked me to return this sum as soon as possible. I immediately complied with his request and, returning from the club that evening, slipped a banker's order into the overseas letter-box at the Post Office.

Tap, tap . . . tap, tap . . .

It was almost harvest time in the delta. South of Cairo, the *fellahin* would already be sharpening their sickles in preparation.

It is a peculiarity born of Egypt's latitude and the rhythm of the Nile that there the European seasons are turned topsy-turvy. Thus, towards the end of the northern Mediterranean autumn, sowing begins in Egypt. Throughout the temperate springs of Greece and Italy they are harvesting in the delta. In the north, the dead time lasts from December to the beginning of March, when Egypt is in glut. When Egyptian belts are tightened in June, July and August, however, the Italians and Greeks are making hay. Only in September, when the Nile reaches its peak, does the North African renewal occur, six months later – or earlier – than across the cradled ocean.

I travelled in March, therefore, from a country which was already beginning to murder and mourn this year's harvest across a border written in the sea to Cyprus, whose guilt flushed with the ghostly flowers of spring.

I disembarked at Paphos, the town which stole its name from the older place nearby now called Kuklia. Old Paphos is nearly abandoned now but, centuries ago, devotees of Aphrodite smelling of myrrh and dressed in indigo robes would, like the goddess they worshipped, mourn the death of Adonis. After praying at the shrine, they would walk in slow procession to the cliffs and there throw into the sea a puppet representing the body of the slaughtered god.

Returning to Alexandria about ten days later, I began to swing like a crazy pendulum between the Siriso warehouse and the library of the Colonial Club. Occasionally, towards dawn, I managed to snatch a couple of hours' sleep on an ottoman in the lounge whilst the waiter who had kept me supplied with coffee throughout the night collapsed, exhausted, in a nearby armchair.

After a week of frantic activity, I received a letter from a concerned Mr Feaver. He had somehow heard that I had hardly been seen at the Pension de l'Est and feared that I was 'overdoing things'. Could he perhaps help me to find an assistant who would shoulder some of my burdens? Had I heard, by the way, of the recent action of the Comptroller-General?

At first I thought that Mr Feaver was going to regale me with details of this gentleman's affair with the Baroness Hrocka, but he had something entirely different in his mind. It appeared that the Comptroller-General, notified and informed, no doubt, by his network of spies, had for reasons best known to himself ordered the establishment of a commission which was to be charged with the task of investigating the affairs of the Assuan Dam Construction Company. Absurd as it was when there were so many flagrant corruptions and abuses which, each year, went uninvestigated, the commission was to begin its sessions in November. Had I, by the way, been called as a witness? I barely had time to scribble a reply in the negative: I was not, as far as I knew, to be called as a witness; I knew nothing either of the commission or of the Assuan project; I needed no assistant.

The cargo was due to sail in the third week of April and was addressed to Dr Andrew Garth-Thompson at his private surgery in Chelsea. It was made up of an enormous range of pharmaceuticals. There were tonics and stimulants: cinchona, of course, and clear quinine in a stoppered bottle; Jamaica sarsaparilla; digitalis; cubeb, the Javanese berry used in medicated cigarettes; valerian; the bark and root of the quassia tree from Surinam, which yields a bitter tonic and insecticide; strophanthin, whose white crystals in solution stimulate the heart but become poisonous when taken in excess; tutsan, the St John's wort which was thought to heal wounds. Oils for use as unguents or in embrocations: oil of chaulmoogra from the East Indies, which is used against leprosy; oil of cloves and of eucalyptus, of juniper and peppermint and rosemary; poon oil; oil of savin and citronella and gaultheria. The astringents: arnica from mountain tobacco, used to treat bruising; kino from West Africa for tanning; South American rhatany; tormentil. Emetics: stavesacre seeds; ipecacuanha, which is mixed with opium in Dover's Powder; the purple berries of the American pokeweed. Cathartics: yellow and bitter podophyllin, resin of the May-apple; scammony gum from Western Asia; East Indian turpeth; colocynth extracted from a species of gourd; croton oil; oil of aloes. There was santonica too, derived from wormwood of the genus *Artemisia* and santonin, its extract, used as an anthelmintic against parasitic worms in the gut; viper's bugloss and male fern; stag's horn and pomegranate root; hyssop, heliotrope and calamint; purslane, manna-ash, sea-absinth and rue. Narcotics: henbane; hyoscine; white-flowered enchanter's night-shade, genus *Circaea*; hyoscyamine; all the disorientating legacies of the maguey plant: peyote, mescal liquor and buttons; Australian pituri; mandragora; Polynesian kava; dagga hemp from Southern Africa; opium. Aphrodisiacs: Chinese oyster essence; levigated oyster shells and rhinoceros horn; ginseng; dissolved pearls; the dried Spanish fly called cantharides. Specifics, diuretics, sudorifics, febrifuges, diaphoretics, aromatics, sera, irritants and counter-irritants, salves, balsams, antidotes, the fumigatory, pungent and mortifying drugs, panaceas. Poisons: curare resin; calabar beans; nux vomica and its bitter derivative, strychnine; the toxic berries of the black nightshade which is also called morel and belladonna; the mephitic purple fruit of the Madagascan tanghin tree, the kernels of which are used in religious ordeals. A world of other strange medicaments: horehound, theriac and a potion against grief; agar-agar, moxa, camphor and menthol; quebracho bark and asafoetida; stramonium; jaborandi and dittany; colchicum and kelp and taraxacum; vera-trine, tragacanth, manchineel sap and pellitory of Spain.

A small but deadly phial contained upas sap with which the Javanese tip their arrows in order to be certain of their prey. Finally there was the aromatic resin copaiba, the balsam of which is used in perfumery as well as in the treatment of certain venereal diseases and which can, like cinchona when taken in excess, cause the condition known as purpura – the tendency to bleed.

There were times during this month when I thought I would go mad. All the peculiar emanations and discharges of which the nature of five continents was capable passed before my baffled gaze. I had many opportunities to recall the fourth book of the *Odyssey*, where Homer ponders the essence of the origin of Helen's anodyne. 'Egypt,' he writes, is 'the land where the bountiful meadow produces/Drugs more than all lands else, many good being mixed, many evil.'

Some of these pharmaceuticals had labels and some had not; in neither case could any unity be imposed on sheer variety. This crimson liquid might be a deadly poison or an aphrodisiac. That resin, treated in a certain way – heated to a specific temperature, crushed or mixed with salt water – might calm the panicked chest of an asthmatic or release nematodes from the bowels of children.

There was no rule: everything was queer and counter. Each derivative deviated. Purified or mixed: the effects multiplied and once again proliferated. A poppy had a dozen uses; even poisons can save lives.

With a dim awareness that I had dispatched my finest cargo to date, I returned, after an interval that was like a spell in the underworld, to the Pension de l'Est, where I slept for three days.

In my dreams I seemed to worm my way back into the past. Years blanketed me and once again I stood with Lady Magenta on Southwark Bridge. We were watching the ships churning their way upriver from overseas. I saw a dead dog lying in a crate which floated downstream and received the passing impression of some ceremony, a fragment of ritual long since decayed into religion. At the edge of the river, the men who piled crates were diminished by distance and the profusion of warehouses and cranes.

The pictures shifted, contracted and vanished. Other pictures came to take their place. It was then that I had my dream of cinchona, whose history was part of my own. I saw the Countess of Chinchón in her mantilla and after the birth of her child they could not stop her sweating. Night after night, shivering in the heat of the Peruvian seaboard. And then

I saw the Jesuits distributing cinchona through Europe. I saw Oliver Cromwell die without it because it was the drug of idolaters. Then I saw Robert Talbor give Charles II quinine with his wine, and the king recovered and was strong. I saw the grubby Linnaeus working at his taxonomy and the slip of his pen as he misspelt the name of a plant he had never seen. And then all the categories collapsed because they were only rafts on a great river. How can we map currents in the stream? How shall we plot the purple droplets as they fall from the body of George III?

When I awoke I caught a cab to the Colonial Club where, in the refectory, I ate my first square meal in weeks. Later, over a chess board on which he was working at an end-game problem, Mr Nopheles watched me curiously.

In June I had sufficiently recovered to travel to Memphis and negotiate the purchase of what fortunately proved to be a less demanding shipment – the eleventh to leave Alexandria and the eighth under my supervision.

Memphis had been built on the ruins of an older city: Abydos. Here, a temple dedicated to Osiris had once stood over the place where Isis had concealed her brother's severed head. It was the holiest spot in all Egypt.

The Rouncewell shipment led me to a strange mixture of a place which contained equal quantities of the smithy, the armoury, the arsenal and the military museum. The red glow of a forge was reflected from the breastplates of a hundred suits of armour. I thought at first that the goods I bought here might incriminate me as a gun-runner. These were uneasy days and, back in Alexandria, three or four English gun-boats now floated in the bay. My fears, as usual, were absurd: the weapons which I placed in the coffin-like pine caskets were exotic, out of date and useless for any practical purposes.

I carefully nailed down the lids on sjamboks and kourbashes, parangs and snickersnees, yataghans, poniards, pangas and tulwars, nullas, kukris, falchions, jezails, a kris and a small Toledo. The smith – or was he the custodian? – then displayed a variety of tools which I examined carefully before purchasing: pitchforks, nose-rings and implements for removing stones from the hooves of horses; a small crucible and a pair of scales for the determination of the specific gravities of geological specimens; cutlery and crockery (there was a complete set of Wedgwood's Jasper Ware); needles, thimbles and weaver's shuttles; hammers, masonry chisels, gimlets and saws; a vasculum, several Wardian cases and an ivory-handled pair of secateurs; plectra, tuning-forks and metronomes; brushes, etching tools and pens with exchangeable nibs; a skinning-knife, a fleam, a bistoury and many types of snare and trap; phials, syringes, clysters, pestles and mortars.

There were tools here to make tools and I had no choice but to buy. The only procedure recognized by Siriso seemed to be that of inclusive accumulation: vices, anvils and bellows. Trays of soft cosmetic brushes made of squirrel hair and sable were set out. Pipettes, droppers and wads of blotting-paper; dice cups, dispensers for packs of cards, cribbage boards in ivory and ebony.

At last the smith took me confidentially aside, and with a wink, opened a case containing prophylactics in gut and bladder, as well as a range of rubber and wax dildos.

In July I was ordered by Signor Feste to take a holiday. My services would not be required until October and I was entitled to spend the intervening time as I wished. Feste advised me not to return to London and instead recommended Athens or Rome. The Piedmont, he had heard, was good walking country. He thanked me for the receipt of my cheque for a hundred and forty pounds. I was in no mood, however, for travel. I chose instead to sleep late. Towards midday I would get a shave in the Quarter. Then, in the afternoons, I would retire to the reading room of the Colonial Club where I had borrowed a newly-arrived copy of the first edition of Stoker's *Dracula*, over which I was lingering pleasurably.

In August I received a further letter from Giovanni Feste. Once again, with an insistence I found slightly peculiar, he encouraged me to leave Alexandria for a while. He informed me that Dr Garth-Thompson's cargo had arrived; apparently he was delighted with it. Mr Dinmont, unfortunately, had died of pneumonia (caused, in all probability, by having been caught in a shower of rain at a fête in Hertfordshire). I was once again disturbed by the bluntness with which Signor Feste remarked that the dividends of the Siriso tontine would now be split only seven ways since, as I would recall, the baroness had also died during the previous trading year.

Returning to my reading, I found myself travelling in the company of Professor Van Helsing through the trackless woods surrounding Dracula's castle, where we followed the evil back to its source in the imaginative maelstrom of the Carpathians. Standing on a border between the west and the east, I gripped the book more tightly as blood flowed along tubes stretched from body to body. Around me, merchants and businessmen talked softly and out there, in the delta, the algae-stained water diminished in the fierce heat of the afternoon.

One evening in early September, Mistral knocked on the door of my room. Entering, he presented me with a letter on the tarnished silver salver he kept exclusively for this purpose. Mr Feaver would be pleased to meet me in his office at the Occidental Bank to discuss what he called 'the situation'. The next morning I accordingly presented myself.

'I told you so!' he gloated. These were the first words he uttered after I had taken a chair. I guessed at once that I was in for another lecture on the British Spirit and Our Destiny in the World.

'Two years ago, Mr Spellman, I told you to mark my words. What did I say? "Watch the French, watch the Mahdists: they'll get their come-uppance."' He sat back in his chair and lit a cigar. 'How sweet is revenge! Kitchener for Gordon, Omdurman for Khartoum. British honour is satisfied, Mr Spellman; justice has been done. And Fashoda has pulled the French up in their tracks.'

Mehmet Ali was shown in. Mr Feaver welcomed him noisily, offered him a chair and ordered tea to be served; a clerk scuttled away to do his bidding. Mehmet Ali sat gracefully by the window. He watched me as he stroked his moustache.

Mr Feaver blustered on. 'No more Frenchmen snapping at our heels, eh? Marchand and his pathetic plans to encircle us. We've seen them off, haven't we, Monsieur Mehmet?'

Mehmet Ali inclined his head enigmatically.

'And Delcassé is weak, isn't he? *Faible*, Monsieur Mehmet, *faible*.' Mr Feaver glowed with patriotism and a sense of historic mission. He began to praise Lord Cromer's Cape-to-Cairo plan:

'Straight up the Nile, Mr Spellman: what about that? Mop up the Sudan, then southwards. And Cecil Rhodes leading the South Africa Company up into Uganda, Kenya and northwards. We have absolute security of tenure in Egypt now and can give the loyal Egyptians their Assuan Dam as a reward.'

Mehmet Ali shifted imperceptibly in his seat but remained silent. Mr Feaver burst into his vulgar laugh: 'Before you know it, we'll own the Nile as well as Suez! And then, Mr Spellman, we can truly say that we have fastened our teeth into the Egyptian neck!'

I shrugged.

'A few more battles, Mr Spellman, and the world will be open for business. Just a few more battles . . . '

I finished my tea and indicated that I had business to attend to. Mr Feaver showed me to the door, where he restrained me for a moment. He spoke more rapidly than usual. 'Yes, Mr Spellman: our Comptroller-General has glorious and laudable ambitions. But he is too suspicious, don't you think? I cannot understand the purpose of this Assuan commission. Can you?'

Once again I emphasized that I knew nothing of the matter and was not qualified to comment.

'Oh, come now! Surely you have discussed the case with Krzystof?'

'Krzystof, Mr Feaver?'

'Mr Pustynia: the director of the Eastern Trading Society. He is involved, as you know. It is generally believed, in fact, that it was he who made the suggestion to the Comptroller-General.'

I shook Mr Feaver's hand in farewell. 'I am sorry to repeat that I know nothing, either of the Assuan project, or of the commission, or of the Eastern Trading Society. I have never met this Mr Pustynia.'

'Surely – at the Club? He is easily recognizable. One eyelid droops and he tends to dribble.'

'No, Mr Feaver: he is not familiar to me.' I started off down the corridor but I sensed that the eyes of the manager of the Occidental Bank followed me all the way to the stairs.

Smyrna in October: stevedores laboured in the drizzle, feet slipping on the oily surface of the wharf as their hands fastened on the wet ropes. Or, with their collars turned up against the Anatolian rain, they sat disconsolately on empty drums of olive oil.

Later, I lay on my bunk with the completed forms on my chest, feeling rather than hearing the engine as the ship nosed its way amongst the scattered husks of the Sporades.

On the morning of November the third, after I had signed the requisite documents in Mehmet Ali's office, a rare and priceless cargo sailed from Alexandria on the merchantman *Ariel*. Amongst the paperwork on board was a letter from me to the destined recipient of the twelfth shipment, Lady Magenta. It was only a brief message, written in two parts on different days. At first I had tried to be cheerful about my surroundings. I remembered how she had once joked about dismemberment and how fine it would be for one's legs to walk the Mediterranean shore. I lunged now from description to description, trying in this way to capture some of the things that I had seen. For a while it had seemed to work but the next day, in a gloomier mood, I had acknowledged my disorientation and, in spite of myself, become entangled in the minutiae of trading laws and insurance agreements. These things would at best bore and at worst baffle her. They bored me and nor, certainly, could I understand them. Once, even a continental place-name had conjured up a vision of delight, but now, Sorrento was just another town. Nevertheless, I sent the letter. Why bother to destroy it?

What had I done over the last month? The details faded even as I recalled them. I had put the right figures in the right columns and added up my expenses correctly. Yet I had known, as I wrapped the stoppered bottles in lengths of wadding and packed them together in the wooden crates, that another total was lacking. Everything was labelled: once again I had ransacked the Colonial Club library. The waiters had learned to side-step me as I rushed past them with some new scrap of information. They looked on me, I think, with weary patience and good-natured contempt as an English eccentric with the money to fund his idiosyncratic *bêtises*.

Yes, everything was labelled, although to name was not to understand.

Perfumes: algabia and tolu, the Colombian balsam; myrrh, frangipani and olibanum; storax resin, Malayan ylang-ylang and orris-root; opopanax and stacte; attar oil from the damask rose; oil of mahaleb from the kernels of cherries; oil of bergamot and of neroli; sandalwood oil; vanilla and verbena oils; the dried leaves of the aromatic shrub santolina; ladanum, frankincense and Balm of Gilead. Bottled waters of delicate hue (I raised them to the light before packing them away): water of hyacinth, of rose and of orange blossom; lilac and jasmine water. The cosmetics and chrisms: steatite; rouge, which is derived from safflower; pearl powder, mascara and costly spikenard. Resins and gums and varnishes: japan; tung oil; insect lac and animé; megilp, terebinth and the child of terebinth, rosin; sandarac, dammar resin and colophony; gum benzoin and mastic. And all the pigments: madder root, which gives natural alizarin; bastard saffron; woad, henna, mummy and gamboge; orpiment, blue zaffre and the little worm, vermilion; verdigris and indigo and indigo's stepson isatin in phials of reddish-yellow crystals. Dearest of all: the stains, inks and dyes which spill and smudge, each one a genie in a bottle. Ancient *encaustum* (which, in abbreviated form, survives in our own 'ink') could be seen through the clear glass of a bottle. The purple fluid was extracted from certain shellfish and emperors once signed their names in it. Brazil wood from Tanazar in Rangoon and Mexican cochineal, which is produced by pounding the bodies of a certain female insect which lives on a cactus plant. Red alkanet comes from a root; purple or violet cudbear from lichen. Saffron's safranin; poppy-coloured ponceau and dyer's bugloss, the stain which also acts against worms. Crushed kermes insects and the red dye derived from their bodies: the word crimson is derived from their name. Insects whose homes were once taken for berries. Kermes oak and dyer's oak: wounds and gall nuts.

Dyes from wounds.

Scarlet.

Things, Mr Secretary.

Stuff.

Once upon a time, many chapters ago, you began to like the things. Just a little. Isn't that so? At first, like the bunch of flowers conjured from Harlequin's chequered sleeve, they set the scene vividly before your eyes. And then, like the objects flung high into the air by jugglers, they blurred into a hoop and you were not quite so sure anymore.

Was that a movement over there? Was there more life in things than you had allowed for, or in your heart of hearts desired? Wait! Did that silhouette stir? That puppet impertinently wink at you? Out of the corner of your eye, didn't you see that plaster mask flush a little with a shy life?

There? There! You must believe me!

I am sorry to disappoint you, Mr Pencil, but no such thing happened. There was no one behind the mask, nobody to work the dummy. Only faith or stupidity could have led you this far. You led yourself on. It was always already only the vomit of things: goods heaped up on the floor of an abandoned warehouse which shakes as the trains pass by. It was a world of items listed, priced and labelled for dispatch. You may of course – please don't let me stop you – project onto the things your half-realized desire for some magical revival, be it only the least little paltry thrill, the merest shimmer within the frame, but I don't hold out much hope for you: spells, like codes or distant stars, tend to vanish at the moment you become aware of them.

In the end we must be quite clear that the only animate moments in the life of things are in movements between hands, the hurried transactions of sellers and buyers.

20
Missing

A WEEK or so after my shipment of pigments and perfumes left Egyptian shores, I was filing away a number of official forms when I became aware of the presence of some papers inside the front cover of my ledger for that year. They were neatly pinned together and I assumed that they must somehow have slipped out of one of my other files. Although I had carefully examined all extant Siriso documents upon my arrival in Egypt, in order, among other things, to take note of the discrepancies which Signor Feste had failed to set right, I could not for the life of me recall having seen these papers before. Perhaps a dozen in number, the pages recorded a disagreement between Stephanides and Mehmet Ali which had broken out in January of 1896 and had perhaps, to judge from the tone of both correspondents, been under the surface for years. I had been told nothing of this affair either by Sir Rodney or Giovanni Feste. The letters gave only a fragmentary account of the quarrel but it was tolerably clear that Stephanides had threatened to prosecute Mehmet Ali for incompetence, obstructiveness and even, it was hinted, corruption.

All this shed a different light on Stephanides than that cast by Signor Feste. I now understood far better the difficulties that Stephanides had faced; to some extent, I shared them.

That afternoon, I mentioned the matter to Mr Nopheles as we sipped our coffee in the lounge of the Colonial Club. He folded his newspaper in which he had been reading of the recent discovery of radium and put it to one side. The quarrel between Stephanides and Mehmet Ali; the accusations levelled by the former against the latter; my failures of understanding: these, I said, were yet more examples of the way in which I seemed to work without information.

'With no clues, you mean?' Mr Nopheles smiled easily enough but I noticed that there was something strange in his manner.

'Yes. In the dark, as it were.'

Mr Nopheles paused for a moment. 'Is it your impression, then, that you are being deprived of information?'

I laughed. 'Starved of information or smothered by it: it's the same thing. I had been led to believe that there were irregularities in the way Stephanides conducted Siriso business. Now I am not so sure. I am wondering whether somebody else pilfered the cargoes.'

'Who, for example?'

'Well – Mehmet Ali, perhaps. He's the harbour master.' I clicked my fingers with irritation. 'No: I'm being absurd. It must have been Stephanides, mustn't it?'

'I'm sorry that I can't enlighten you,' said Mr Nopheles. He seemed hurt. 'I – I knew Constantin Stephanides well, of course – '

'Did you?' I was genuinely surprised. 'I didn't know that, I'm sorry. I didn't mean to –' I trailed off into an embarrassed silence.

'Didn't mean to hang him without trial?' Mr Nopheles's eyes glittered.

I tried to extricate myself from my difficulties. 'I was reliably informed that there were suspicions. The case, I realize, was never proved; nothing was proved. Signor Feste suggested that any irregularities might well have been caused by the onset of the illness which finally killed Stephanides.'

'The illness?' Mr Nopheles kept up his pressure.

'Whatever it was – you knew him. What was it that Mehmet Ali said when I arrived? Yes: the sickness. Mehmet Ali said it was the sickness.'

Suddenly Mr Nopheles seemed to relax. He leaned back in his chair. 'I don't know what it was, Mr Spellman. I was abroad at the time. I know only that, for months before his death, Constantin was in a state of great nervousness and tension. Mehmet Ali called it the sickness, did he?'

'He did. He wasn't very specific.' I finished my coffee. 'So I have it from you, then, that Stephanides was an honest man?'

Mr Nopheles turned his head to look out of the window. A corvette was speeding along the coast from the direction of Aboukir. A gull with a fish in its bright bill landed on the railings outside the window.

'Honest?' Mr Nopheles replied at last. 'Yes, I suppose so. Honest.' He turned to me with an odd expression on his face. 'He was a good friend to me, Mr Spellman. That was back in the 'seventies, when things were happier. I never knew a kinder man. He – ah – he gave me the fruit knife which I sometimes use. That's a mere detail, of course, and –'

Mr Nopheles toyed with his coffee spoon. He seemed to make up his mind. 'I should like to tell you about Constantin Stephanides, Mr Spellman. I should like to tell you about him one day soon.'

I was touched and intrigued. Stephanides had always been a somewhat vague figure to me. Only now, oddly, was his face becoming clearer. I arranged to meet Mr Nopheles the day after next: the fourteenth of November.

Later that afternoon, in my rooms at the Pension de l'Est, Mistral brought me a letter on his tarnished tray: Mehmet Ali cordially invited me to dinner at eight o'clock the following evening. He hoped that I would be able to attend despite the unavoidably short notice I had been given and was sure that I would look forward to meeting Mr Krzstof Pustynia, whose presence had been fortuitously secured by the last-minute cancellation of another engagement. Mehmet Ali thought that I would welcome the chance to discuss economic affairs on a personal basis.

I had little desire to meet Krzstof Pustynia and my morning's reading had hardly increased the scant relish I felt at the prospect of Mehmet Ali's company. I was lying on my bed idly flicking the pasteboard rectangle which Mistral had delivered and mentally composing a polite refusal when I suddenly realized with annoyance that my 'exhaustion through overwork' could constitute no reasonable excuse: the dinner was to be held at the Pension de l'Est in the rooms below mine – the rooms which had once been occupied by Stephanides.

I knocked on the door therefore, that thirteenth of November, with considerable disinclination. The stained glass skylight filtered coloured rays across the landing walls. Mehmet Ali opened the door.

'Welcome, Mr Spellman, to the feast! A feast for a festival! You know Mr Feaver, of course' – he sat colourlessly on a couch – 'but let me introduce you – it's remarkable, isn't it, that you haven't met already? – to Mr Krzystof Pustynia.'

A corpulent maggot of a man rose to met me. It was an uncanny moment and a veil, somewhere, seemed to tremble.

The man who took my hand was Christopher Desert: I could be quite certain of that. He and Amelia between them had been responsible for my flight from London eighteen years previously, and that had led to everything else. Desert was one of the authors of my life. But . . . but . . .

'Please sit down, Mr Spellman,' said Mehmet Ali. 'A drink?'

'Thank you. Mareotic.'

'Of course,' smiled Mehmet Ali, 'when in Rome –' He gestured sharply to Mistral, who, dressed in the dusty uniform of a waiter, poured out the wine in a distant corner of the room.

After I had sat down, Pustynia still seemed to be examining me closely. 'Haven't we met somewhere before, Mr Spellman?'

Mr Feaver was triumphant. 'I knew it! Jack Spellman has been fibbing all along! How would it be possible for a businessman in this city not to know Mr Pustynia?'

'No, no, Feaver. It was a long time ago.' Mr Pustynia scrutinized me carefully once again. 'Was it Djibouti, Mr Spellman, or Aden?'

I replied firmly. 'No, Mr Pustynia: I don't think so.'

'Oh come now!' chortled Mr Feaver. 'This is taking a joke too far.'

At that moment I had no desire to acknowledge the way in which, despite all our efforts to forget, the present occasionally retrieves the distant past and lifts from the waters an earlier section of our umbilicus. I did not want this coincidence: it was thrust upon me. The past was nothing: I was different now. To admit that I knew Krzystof Pustynia would somehow be to expose myself to even greater suspicion. Christopher Desert too, for that matter, was different. I watched him as he began a conversation with Mr Feaver. Once he had been a thug. Now, in his tailored suit, he seemed the perfect businessman, attentive and discreet. He was smaller than I remembered, although perhaps this was the change in my own perspective, but he still smoked the vilest dark tobacco.

There was laughter and, taking a sip of my drink, I leaned forward to listen. Some allusion had been made to Mehmet Ali's near-namesake: the Mehemet Ali who, in 1819, had donated Cleopatra's Needle to the British government.

'Can't understand it at all,' said Mr Feaver. 'It's like putting Stonehenge up in the Place Mohammed.'

'I expect,' said Mehmet Ali blandly, 'that Mehemet Ali thought the gift might smooth the way towards an agreement which would be advantageous to him.'

Mr Feaver laughed raucously. Then he clapped me on the shoulder and gestured towards the assembled company: 'You are looking at the directorate of the most rapidly expanding company in Lower Egypt, Mr Spellman.'

He bent his head confidentially in the direction of Christopher Desert. 'A couple of months ago, sir, Mr Spellman claimed never to have heard of the Eastern Trading Society.'

Mehmet Ali smiled colourlessly and Christopher Desert's drooping eyelid flickered for a moment. 'Is this true, Mr Spellman?'

'I am afraid so, Mr Pustynia. Until this moment I was completely unaware of the fact that Mr Feaver and Mehmet Ali were engaged in any form of private enterprise.'

'You – a businessman – a merchant? You surprise me.'

I was about to reply when Mr Feaver intervened on my behalf. 'Sir: I think we must bear in mind that Siriso is a rather unusual company. Perhaps Mr Spellman might describe himself as a scholar and not a merchant. I hear that he has spent whole nights in the Colonial Club library researching his cargoes.' He looked over at me for confirmation.

I did not want to be myself examined so I prompted others to speak: 'Tell me, in any case, about the Eastern Trading Society.'

Mr Feaver and Mehmet Ali turned deferentially towards Christopher

Desert, who glanced at his pocket watch and wiped his moist lips before beginning.

'The Eastern Trading Society is the major exporter in Alexandria of native Egyptian products: rice, maize, wheat, cotton, flax and so on. I control the company and own a sixty-six per cent share of it; the remaining thirty-four per cent are divided equally between my two colleagues – Mehmet Ali and Mr Feaver.'

When their names were mentioned, both Mr Feaver and Mehmet Ali looked at each other smugly.

'We own a large, seaworthy vessel,' continued Christopher Desert: 'the *Typhon*. Our trading partners include most of the European nations. And one of these days' – he wagged a thick forefinger at me – 'we might be interested in purchasing the Siriso Trading Company.'

I felt unaccountably chauvinistic. 'I very much doubt, Mr Pustynia, whether the Siriso Trading Company will ever be for sale.'

'We shall see.' He smiled as he rose to his feet. 'We shall see.' And he bade us farewell in turn, apologizing for his early departure: he had urgent correspondence to attend to. Before he left, he turned on his heels and addressed me once again. 'Are you sure we haven't met before, Mr Spellman? You have no association with Kew Gardens, have you?'

'None.'

Christopher Desert closed the door behind him and as we took our seats for dinner I was stranded between the iciness of Mehmet Ali and Mr Feaver's dyspeptic belches.

'How will it feel to be an employee of the Eastern Trading Society, Mr Spellman?' asked Mehmet Ali, unrolling his napkin.

I repeated that such a possibility seemed remote to me. 'In any case,' I said 'the character of your business ventures is the very opposite of my own.'

'Rarities! Exotica!' Mr Feaver could not conceal his disdain. 'I think we could manage.'

'Talking of rarities, by the way,' said Mehmet Ali, rising from the table and crossing the room to pick up a small object which stood on his bureau, 'have I shown you this? I picked it up in the bazaar the other day.'

He passed a little box to me. Peering through a dusty pane of glass which was mounted in the lid, I saw a china doll with painted features and glass eyes. Her hair had fallen out and her clothes had mouldered. I felt Mehmet Ali's breath on my cheek. 'Charming, isn't it, Mr Spellman? I bought it as a sort of *memento mori*.'

He straightened, returned to his chair and clapped his hands. 'Now for the feast! Do you have a good appetite, Mr Spellman?' Before I could reply, Mistral emerged from a communicating room and proceeded to serve the first course.

Until the previous evening I had been unaware that Mehmet Ali now occupied the rooms which had once belonged to Stephanides. On my only previous visit there had been dust, some armchairs, a pot of anchovy paste, a stick of sealing-wax and a scarab signet ring. In contrast, the doors to the balcony now stood open and long draperies stirred in the breeze from the street. The walls were covered with patterned hangings, great figured damasks and tapestries. Yet still, as before, the centre of the room was occupied by a small table on which stood a vase containing dried flowers. Around the base of the vase, blemishless wax fruits were scattered.

'Don't you think the room is a great improvement from when Stephanides was here?' Mehmet Ali casually gestured towards the wall hangings and furniture.

'Oh, certainly. Mr Stephanides was not a very tidy man.' It was then that a thought struck me: 'Why is it that I never see you in the building, Mr Mehmet? Surely our paths would have crossed before now?'

Mehmet Ali ignored me. 'I enjoy collecting beautiful things, you see. It is a weakness of mine. The tapestries, the doll . . . '

I spoke without thinking. 'I remember! I once heard a noise from your rooms when I was on my way to bed. It was a long time ago – have you been here that long? It must have been in June 1897, because I remember that I had just sent off my third cargo.'

Mehmet Ali was irritated but unruffled. 'I am afraid to say, Mr Spellman, that I only took up residence here – to be precise since the matter is so unaccountably at issue – in the August of that year.'

'I am sorry. I did not mean –' I had not meant to seem inquisitive.

Mehmet Ali crushed the insect of my remark: 'No. You did not "mean" anything.'

'Perhaps,' suggested Mr Feaver cheerfully, 'you heard a burglar.'

'Oh, I doubt it,' I said. 'I don't think so for a minute.'

'Really?' Mr Feaver smiled stonily. 'It is not unusual in Alexandria. Only three nights ago, for instance, somebody broke into Mehmet Ali's office in the docks.'

'I'm sorry to hear that,' I said.

'It was nothing, Mr Spellman,' said Mehmet Ali. 'The petty cash was stolen. A few files have gone missing. Nothing of any importance.'

Mistral collected the plates and brought on the main dish. As we began to eat, I sensed that I had somehow managed to put myself in a position where I seemed to be concealing information from all those in the room. Yet I had no wish to describe the unmistakably orgastic character of the cries which had penetrated as far as the landing on the evening in question.

Mr Feaver broke the silence. 'Well, if it wasn't a burglar you heard all those months ago, then perhaps it was a ghost.' He raised his glass in a toast. 'To the ghost of Stephanides!'

I laughed and drank. As Mehmet Ali refilled my glass, he began to speak with the rapidity which I had noticed once before and which was so difficult to reconcile with his usually languid manner. 'Do you believe in ghosts, Mr Spellman? Spectres, revenants, the spirit world? Do you think that the shade of Stephanides haunts the Pension de l'Est, that his reprieved voice whispers in the corridors along refracted sunbeams? Does he leave messages between the leaves of books?'

I felt uncomfortable. 'I hardly know. I should think, perhaps, that if Stephanides was a superstitious man then he might return as a ghost.'

Mistral placed a dish of chutney on the table. 'He was a very superstitious man, Mr Spellman. He worship the Christian god and fear the evil eye. He throw the salt over his shoulder like the English do.' Mistral bowed to excuse his interruption and left the room.

'I expect Stephanides learnt the trick with the salt from Signor Feste,' said Mr Feaver.

'Or perhaps from Lord Tramont,' suggested Mehmet Ali.

For some reason I felt sad. 'Everybody knows each other,' I said, 'but I know nobody. I feel like a stranger in this country.'

Mr Feaver reached across the table and patted my hand. 'There, Mr Spellman: please don't be miserable. After all, this is a celebration! And you know us: aren't we intimate, personal, friendly?'

Whilst Mr Feaver was speaking I had become aware of a familiar smell which I could not place. I located its source, however, the moment I began to eat. The plum chutney on my plate had the identical aroma to that which had met me once before, as I entered this room on the first and only prior occasion. Despite its spicy edge it was a delicious garnish. I consumed my meal with a speed that surprised me, for I had not felt hungry upon arrival. Looking on and eating more slowly, Mehmet Ali and Mr Feaver seemed to enjoy my rising good humour. I began to feel that the anxieties of the previous months were behind me. I called for more wine, feeling completely in control of my faculties, and began to tell jokes.

'Was your quarrel with Stephanides ever satisfactorily resolved, Mr Mehmet?' I remember that I asked this question at one point.

Mehmet Ali laughed fastidiously, showing pointed white teeth. 'Every quarrel is resolved by death,' he said. Mr Feaver roared with animal glee.

We had finished our sorbets and Mistral stood over us with the coffee pot when I thought to take another dig at Mehmet Ali:

'I suppose your friend Stephanides gave you those almonds you are eating?'

At that moment Mehmet Ali was poised to place one of these delicacies in his mouth. It had a purple sugar coating which, with infinite care, he proceeded to examine.

There was complete silence.

I suddenly noticed that Mistral, who was distributing the coffee cups, seemed to be pitching from side to side as though he was walking on the deck of a ship. A lamp flickered at the corner of my eye and a trail of incense smoke passed across my vision. I lifted my hand a little and let it fall, suddenly, utterly exhausted.

Mehmet Ali's face seemed to expand as at last he spoke. 'No, Mr Spellman. I stole the almonds from Stephanides after hanging him from that hook on the ceiling.' He pointed upwards, over my head, but I was unable to follow the direction of his hand.

I smiled. I remember that; for some reason I smiled.

Wearing his flowing jibbah, Mehmet Ali approached me. He had no edges and seemed part of the tapestry on the wall. Bending over me so that his sleeve brushed across my face – it felt soft, like a feather – he clicked his fingers in front of my eyes.

I did not blink. I could hear – nothing . . .

At the risk of bewildering you, Mr Secretary, I must now interrupt my narrative and leap forward three weeks to the late afternoon of 2 December 1898.

I am compelled to do this for the very good reason that I was not myself present during this lapse of days. Yet they were the most vital of my life, without doubt. I was closer to death then, at any rate, than I have ever been. I must admit to some exasperation that, at this crucial point, I am unable to be the hero of my own story and must become – a corpse? – something less than a character in my memoirs. It is like a rent in the fabric through which a section of my life has been lifted as they lift a pallet from the hold of a ship. And then? Then, unaccountably, it has been lost.

Unfortunately, I cannot even identify with the voice that speaks in Lindhorst's transcriptions. That is to say, I cannot visualize the scenes described as if I framed the point of view. I am neither protagonist nor percipient; these things happened to another, the words belong to someone else.

I must apologize: in my impatience I have overtaken myself and forgotten to introduce you to Dr Lindhorst, chief medical officer of the Queen Victoria Hospital in Cairo. At the time of which I speak, Dr Lindhorst was approximately seventy years of age. He had trained as a surgeon in Heidelberg, his native city, under the great Hungarian physician Ignaz Semmelweis. Together, they had been the first to recommend and enforce antisepsis in the battle against puerperal fever. Despite such early promise, however, Lindhorst's career had failed to flower and, seeking to ameliorate a chronic lung condition, he had arrived in the dry heat of Cairo in 1886 a more or less broken, if brilliant man who at intervals fell prey to a morbid craving for alcohol. I was fortunate enough, however, to be admitted to the Queen Victoria Hospital during one of Lindhorst's comparatively sober periods and he, intrigued by the riddle I posed, attended to me personally and ordered that transcripts should be made of my fevered sleep-talk.

So let me, Mr Secretary, jump into the skin of the good doctor and speak of myself as an object. I will quote from the transcripts of my ramblings and from Dr Lindhorst's own case notes, both of which he was good enough to present to me before I left Egypt.

See: I stand before you with grey hair and pince-nez. My hand is shaking for a morning whisky as I button my white surgical gown.

5pm, 2 Dec 98. Case 1400
European male. Perhaps thirty-five years of age. Medium build. Average appearance. Unconscious. No papers, no ring, no evidence of origin or identity.

I asked the goitred fisherman who brought him in to wait whilst I conducted an examination.

Coma or catatonia? Physiological or psychological? He is underweight and his muscles are wasted. It is as if he had been ill in bed for weeks. Yet there is no obvious illness or injury. Pupils slightly dilated and do not respond to light. No reaction to pinpricks. Some water in the lungs. Chafing under the armpits.

Fisherman says he found patient on an abandoned sandbank out in the delta. His body was covered by shore crabs and he was dressed in some sort of flaxen winding-sheet.

10pm
A fuller examination has been performed. The only peculiarity about 1400 occurs in the genital region. The area is covered by a symmetrical and brightly-coloured birthmark. There are several scars along the membrum virile *and on the glans. Most peculiarly of all, 1400 appears to have been newly – and I must add, amateurishly – circumcised.*

The fisherman's story seems unlikely. A European, dressed only as the dead are dressed, lying unconscious on a spit of sand? But the cloth that 1400 arrived in was indeed damp and muddy. And there was certainly water in his lungs.

If, conscious or unconscious, he had been in the water for any length of time, he must have escaped drowning by a hair's breadth. If the Nile had been in flood; had it been a month, two months ago, then he would now, like the Mahdi, be floating face down along the Damietta channel.

am, 3 Dec
His skin is mottled this morning.
   Another speculation: has he been poisoned? Certain snake bites produce similar symptoms but, as far as I recall, they are not native to Egypt. Perhaps copaiba — or even belladonna? Both, taken in excess, could do this. But what about the immobility? It almost amounts to paralysis. Curare? Upas sap? Doubtful.

5pm
The petechiae or stigmata upon his body suggest the early stages of purpura. Quinine could be both cause and cure in such a case. Weinz suggests astringent dressings to reduce capillary action. Gallic acid solution?

8pm
The eyelids have begun to flicker. Dr Wigfield says he has seen patient's hand twitch spasmodically.

am, 4 Dec
It is not purpura — nothing so exotic — but typhus, contracted in all probability from contaminated river water.
   Usual procedures: isolation, asepsis.

pm
He has started rambling. Since it may provide some clue to his identity, I have posted Wigfield at 1400's bedside to make a transcription.

8am, 5 Dec
Worse: a high temperature. Vibices. But he is talking nineteen to the dozen.

' . . . Eater, eater Stephanides . . . ghost evoked . . . saltsprinkler . . . picklegobbler . . . consommateur, gastronome, peachsucker . . . food slipping past moist lips into soft belly . . . hanging from your hook with your moon face and bursting waistcoat and flowers popping up . . . '

2pm
Stephanides! Surely not. Surely, surely not.

' . . . Etsetsets . . . etsetsets . . . etsetsets . . . '

6pm
He has been repeating this gibberish for two hours. Wigfield has rendered it phonetically but it makes sense in none of the languages we are familiar with. At least we now know that he is capable of speaking English.

'. . . Etsetsets . . . why isn't he moving, why has everything stopped, why aren't you laughing at my little joke, it was only a joke, why can't I drink my coffee and go to bed. I am so tired. Why are you throwing that rope up there, why is that hook there, I noticed it the first time and many times before that. Why does it smell funny in here, funny that I should end up here . . . '

'. . . Humpty Dumpty sat on a wall . . . Humpty Dumpty had a great fall . . . All the king's horses and . . . London Bridge is falling . . . '

'. . . Couldn't put Humpty . . . together . . . again . . . '

'. . . Why couldn't they put him together? You ought to know, Mr Nopheles. Sealing wax and ships. Or bits of string. Vinegar and brown paper. Glue from the knacker's yard. Stick him up. Disjecta membra, says my learned friend. I'll have to look that up in a dictionary. Disjecta membra with a knight in his big pink hand and he plants it in my vitals but it's not the knight after all, that was only a disguise. I know I've lost but I don't know how . . . '

am, 6 Dec
Nopheles! He knows Nopheles! In the name of all coincidences! So perhaps he was talking about Constantin Stephanides after all. . . I have telegraphed Nopheles in Alexandria.

pm
My old friend has replied: he will be here tomorrow morning. Perhaps he can enlighten me.

'. . . Sirisosirisosiriso . . . round and round and round in the room in my head or somewhere in between like music is sometimes in the room and in your head in the same moment . . . everything stops, he's holding a sugared almond . . . he's clicking his fingers but they barely move and the draperies are quite still, hanging limply . . . '

'. . . Sirisosirisosiriso . . . round and round Sir Rodney head Magenta heart the baroness bowels and Spellman scarred genitalia given up for lost and who's she with her supernumerary nipples coming down on the plain and folding the great curtains of her wings to water the earth with her tears? . . . '

'. . . All those children around who are they? And then two tall people and the nurses and a thin lady takes my hand and she's holding some red beads and the other one smells funny. Is that nice or nasty? I can't remember. His stomach is soft, he shows me his watch, he opens it up and I see the face but this is all in no-time and then both of them hold my hand and there aren't any more children, but two more tall ones standing in the rain as we walk past. My hand hurts, she holds it so tightly. He takes off his hat and smiles with a white face like a clown. The other one has red hair and they aren't there any more and *she's talking to me in funny buzzing words and there are bits of wood in my hair . . . '*

' . . . Mehmet Ali's face. I stole the almonds from Stephanides after hanging him from that hook on the ceiling . . . '

Noon, 7 Dec
The fever has broken; his sleep is less disturbed. He has stopped raving.

Nopheles arrived this morning: demystification at last. I have to admit that I was somewhat disappointed: our babbling prophet from the delta turns out to be a businessman. His name is Jack Spellman and he is the Alexandrian agent for the Siriso Trading Company.

I showed the transcripts to Nopheles, who read them carefully. He suggested that the 'etsetsets' repeated throughout 5 Dec. might refer to the Eastern Trading Society, ETS. I had not thought of that and, in my office, we looked across at each other, suddenly aware that Spellman's testimony might have some bearing on the scandal whose development in the newspapers we have both been following. Nopheles asked whether he could take the transcripts back to his hotel and go through them once again. I agreed.

am, 8 Dec
His temperature is lower today. He is out of danger. The rash is less inflamed. Nopheles met me in my office an hour ago. I asked him to stop being secretive and to tell me all he knew about this Spellman. He drummed his fingers on my desk and asked if my request was a medical one.

'Of course it's not a medical one,' I replied. 'I know full well that all of this has got something to do with Constantin. Come on, out with it: what's going on?'

To my surprise, Nopheles said that he wasn't sure what was going on. He had last seen Spellman on the afternoon of 12 November. They had discussed Stephanides but Spellman had shown no knowledge of the coroner's verdict. At that time, Nopheles had been convinced of Spellman's ignorance and, therefore, innocence. Now, however, having read the transcripts, he is not so sure.

'Look at this, Lindhorst,' he said, putting one of the pages in front of me, 'Look: he knew that Stephanides had been hanged. The hook, the moon face and so on. And here, again: "we stole the almonds from Stephanides", et cetera, et cetera.'

'But if Spellman was the victim of an attack by persons unknown,' I said, 'surely that indicates that your faith in him was not misplaced?'

Mr Nopheles did not agree. 'Not at all. Only if he was the victim of an attack by certain persons could we even begin to exonerate him.'

I saw his point. 'Anyway, what happened after the twelfth of November?' I asked. 'When did you realize that he had disappeared?'

'He didn't keep a meeting we had arranged on the fourteenth. I only became worried a few days later.'

'Worried?'

'For his safety.'

'For his safety — when you suspected him?'

'Ah, that's the point,' said Nopheles. 'I didn't suspect him — not then. I thought I had evidence, you see. That's why I was going to tell him about Stephanides. I suspected him before that, of course — suspected him for the two years I had known him. But I couldn't help liking him, all the same.'

I asked Nopheles what he was planning to do. He said he was going to book himself a room at Les Deux Continents until Mr Spellman regained consciousness. It was almost as if he considered himself in loco parentis.

9 Dec

He has come to life, our sleeping prince! Wigfield came to my office in great excitement this morning. He seemed relieved that his stint as amanuensis had reached a natural conclusion.

Mr Spellman was weak but hungry. I gave him a little maize porridge. Then he fell into a calm sleep; the strange death-in-life stillness of the catatonic had gone.

am, 10 Dec

Spellman seems confused by the dressings which still swathe most of his body. He accepted my explanations, however, readily enough. He was, in fact, remarkably incurious. Most men, I think, would have had questions to ask (where am I? — what has happened to me?) but he had none. His passivity worries me; it is as if he is refusing to think through something that disturbs him.

6pm

Met Nopheles in my office. He was eager to begin some sort of interrogation of Spellman as soon as possible but I immediately put my foot down. 'Don't be ridiculous. He's as weak as a kitten. He needs at least six or seven days to recuperate.'

Nopheles reluctantly agreed that there was little advantage to be gained from forcing the issue. There was also the further consideration that another week would perhaps bring to light more information concerning the Occidental-ETS-Assuan affair.

Nopheles decided to go back to Alexandria. Unless Mr Spellman's condition deteriorates, he will return to Cairo on 17 December.

8pm
I was passing Spellman's bed when I noticed that he was awake. I decided to try a small experiment: I asked him what day of the month it was. After a while, he hazarded a guess at 15 November but it was clear that it was virtually a shot in the dark. When I told him the correct date, he was utterly unable to account for the lapse.

am, 18 Dec
Spellman is much recovered and has even been walking about the hospital grounds. He can count himself lucky that he received so mild a dose. The vibices have almost vanished, leaving only the faintest traceries. He still complains of stiffness in the joints but I told him that this was probably as much the result of enforced inactivity and perhaps confinement as of his illness. Privately, I wondered again whether some poison had been involved.

He greeted Nopheles with great pleasure. When we asked him about his recent experiences, he readily admitted that he could remember very little. He recalled meeting Krzystof Pustynia on 13 November; afterwards, at dinner, somebody had handed round a painted china doll. Beyond this, his mind was a blank.

I asked him whether he would consider undergoing hypnosis and he was agreeable to the proposal.

pm
Nopheles, Spellman, Wigfield and myself crowded into my office. I asked Spellman to sit in a comfortable armchair which had been pushed into a corner by the window. Then I drew the blinds so that the room was in shadow. Wigfield was ready with his pad and pencil; Nopheles sat quietly but alertly to one side.

I made several passes across Mr Spellman. At length he entered that curious limbo known to all practitioners of the art – the science – the magic, if you will, of hypnosis.

The narrative that follows is, I believe, an accurate transcription. I have chosen only, for the sake of clarity, to elide my own questions and promptings. Mr Spellman spoke in a faint but level and clearly enunciated voice:

'. . . He snaps his fingers in front of my eyes several times but his movements are so slow . . . and I can hear nothing, everything takes place in the silence. Mr Feaver is drinking his coffee and watching me. I cannot move my eyes but somehow I can tell that Mehmet Ali is taking down the draperies at the window. Then I feel the rough curtains against my skin because they have taken my clothes off. I am lying on the floor and they are wrapping me up in a curtain. Soon I am completely cocooned, except for my face. They are tearing up other draperies and twisting them to form a rope. Above my head, an iron hook is set into the cypress beam. They have moved the table a little to one side and I am looking up through the flowers in the vase to the hook in the ceiling. After hours, perhaps, a dried petal floats slowly down and lands on my left eye. It is cool and the light is filtered through it but I cannot even blink it away. Mr Feaver holds me up and the petal falls away and I feel a throb as though I am parting from a companion. Mehmet Ali throws the rope over the hook and Mistral, holding the other end, approaches me. I am suddenly aware that I am to be hanged and I wonder whether they did this to Stephanides too. But no: Mistral ties the rope around my chest and not my neck. There is to be a stay of execution. All this takes an age. They move so slowly and so quietly. I cannot tell whether this is me or their fear of making a disturbance and arousing suspicion; I think it is mostly me. As they drag me to the window, Mr Feaver stumbles against the sideboard and an object falls onto the floor: a glass paperweight with a roundabout spinning inside. There are tiny horses on poles and garishly painted children on their backs. They tip me head foremost over the balcony. It is all faintly ridiculous. I feel like a – like a mummy stolen from a museum – and then the rope tightens around my chest so that I can hardly breathe. I had forgotten I was breathing. I am spinning round in the air. I see the Orpheus in the bay – some lights – houses – the deserted street – the first floor windows of the Pension de l'Est – then the dark sea again. Hands seize me: there are two men standing on a cart. They guide me down and place me in a coffer. I see the lid come down on top of me, blocking out the stars. Then I feel the movement of the cart, heat and an awful, reminiscent darkness. I think that they have put a hood on me. Later I smell oil and a different movement begins: a train? After that – long after – I find that I can hear again: the river steamer's empty whistle, steam escaping through a vent, a rending, homesick noise as if the ship was calling out to the yard which built it. More noises: feet on the deck, whistles, shouts, the note of the engine, the squeal of the hawser. The vessel heels a little to one side in the current. And then . . . then I am at the edge of the river in dim light with people I do not know. Somebody mimes . . . recites . . . lisps . . . incants . . . words. I do not understand the words but I know that they are solemn and mournful. Something is sprinkled on my face. It smells so old but it is beautiful and they throw rice on me as if I had just been married and somebody puts something pungent between my legs and with a push I am floating away on the river . . . the voices fall back and I am lonely . . . there is water spilling over the rim of the coffer . . . in midstream where the current flows strongest . . . cool water . . . my head goes under . . . breaks the surface again . . . again . . . I want to breathe the water but for some reason I cannot . . . there is something else close by, will-o'-the-wisp, jack-o'-lantern, I don't know what . . . something like a breath which vanishes so that . . . I am lying on a muddy bank in my shroud and I wake only to fall asleep to *the soft twittering of the birds which nest in the low cliff: sand-martins which I have seen somewhere before. Later, I begin to feel tiny movements on the surface of my body as if a thousand creatures are trying to pinch me awake. Or perhaps they think that I am already dead. I am so tired. I want to sleep for such a long, long time . . . '*

21

Locking the Stable Door

I OPEN the blinds and take off my white coat. Look! I am no longer Dr Lindhorst but myself again: Jack Spellman.

And that, Mr Secretary, is how I came to be unable to narrate my own autobiography and to be found, dressed as no Englishman should be, on a bank in the delta with every spare inch of my skin not covered by my swaddling clothes being prospectively picked over by oxyrhynchids: river crabs, delta crabs. You might say, I suppose, that my caul had saved me from death by water. In most respects, however, I felt hardly fortunate in my birth.

That evening, Dr Lindhorst gave me a copy of his case notes and the transcripts made by Wigfield of my delirious chatterings. When I had read them I was in the unenviable position of having to decide whether to believe my own voice. Over the passing years, my memories of Mehmet Ali's dinner party on 13 November have gradually returned. My memories of what happened in the following days are still blurred. Afterwards, lying in my bed at the Queen Victoria Hospital, I could recall nothing of the evening in question beyond the departure of Krzystof Pustynia, except that at some point a china doll had been passed around. The lineaments of reality returned only when I woke in a strange bed with crisp white sheets to find myself swaddled in dressings which smelt of the chemicals I had once handled. No mercury had visited my darkness and my recollections were an undeveloped plate.

Had somebody poisoned or tried to murder me? Somebody? If it was anybody, it had to be Mehmet Ali and Mr Feaver. But why? And why, in addition, had I been circumcised? The act was peculiarly appropriate, for all the injuries of my life had left their traces here. My sick ramblings had seemed to continue the theme of dismemberment. All the time, as I lay sleeplessly in bed, the face of Stephanides was drawing nearer. What had happened to him? Why had it been kept from me?

All my life I had shrunk from involvement. Now, in the grossly exaggerated way which life often has, it had been thrust upon me.

At last, towards dawn, clueless, I slept.

The next morning in Lindhorst's office, the questions began. After a while, to my surprise, there were even to be a few answers.

'How did you know that Stephanides had been murdered?' Mr Nopheles was incisive; he had completely dropped his usual scholarly vagueness.

I thought for a few seconds. 'I'm not sure that I do "know" any such thing.'

'The transcripts tell a different story, don't they?'

'Yes, they do. Admittedly so.' I picked them up from the table and looked them over once again. 'I am not sure, though, that it is my story. Of course, I accept that I talked about, for example, "Stephanides . . . hanging from your hook with your moon face and bursting waistcoat," and later, under hypnosis, I wondered "whether they did this to Stephanides too". Nevertheless, I can't identify with this voice. Its memories are not my memories.'

It was then that a happy thought occurred to me: 'I have an idea that I might have got Stephanides confused with somebody else.'

Mr Nopheles was quietly curious. 'Who, for instance?'

'Well – partly with my father, and partly with a man I once knew called Mortimer Croop, a circus owner.'

'How did you know that Stephanides had been murdered?' repeated Mr Nopheles.

I stared at him. 'You mean it's true?'

Nopheles looked at Lindhorst and then back to me. 'Not only is it true, Mr Spellman, it is also suspect.'

'Why? I don't understand.'

Mr Nopheles examined his nails as he spoke. 'To know that he was murdered, you see, is to show evidence of involvement, knowledge of something more than the official version.'

'What was the official version?'

Mr Nopheles took a sheet of paper from his briefcase and began to read from it:

' "Constantin Stephanides, aged fifty-six years, died of asphyxia after hanging himself in his rooms at the Pension de l'Est, Alexandria, on the twenty-fourth day of March, eighteen hundred and ninety-six. His body was discovered the following morning by the hotel *boab*, one Mistral Mussanah." '

Mr Nopheles handed the paper across to me. 'That death certificate, Mr Spellman, is a lie.'

'You mean it *wasn't* suicide? Can you be sure?'

He smiled. 'I had thought you might ask that. Yes, I think so.' He shuffled once again through the contents of his briefcase. 'As you know,

Mr Spellman, I was away from Alexandria between May 1895 and October 1896. In the April of 1896, Dr Lindhorst – who had been one of Constantin's closest friends as he is one of mine – wrote to me in London. He informed me that our old friend had died. The funeral had already taken place, of course, and being unable to alter my many engagements and commitments, I decided not to return to Alexandria. When I did get back, however, I found this note waiting for me at the Colonial Club.'

Mr Nopheles handed an envelope to me and I took out the single page it contained.

Colonial Club   March 7, 1896
Re: CYANE

My dear Nopheles,

    I came across this character in my reading. Was she a nymph or something? Can you find out about her from one of the encyclopaedias at the Club?

    I wonder whether Cyane gave her name to the condition cyanosis. Wasn't that what poor Tramont's child – Magenta – died of as a baby?

    I know that you enjoy this sort of work and besides, I am alas very busy with other affairs at the moment.

    Perhaps we could meet in a week or so.
                             Yours,
                                 Constantin.

'An unusual request,' I commented. 'Did Stephanides know Lord Tramont well?'

Mr Nopheles looked up sharply. 'Ah, you're very quick, Mr Spellman. Yes: both Constantin and I knew Lord Tramont well. Well enough, of course, to be perfectly aware that his unfortunate daughter, who died in 1869, was called Alizarin and not Magenta.'

I still thought that Stephanides's letter could hardly be said to have predicted his impending murder and added that Stephanides was supposed to have been behaving in a rather erratic manner for a couple of months prior to his death.

'Certainly,' said Mr Nopheles. 'Everybody was saying that Constantin had gone mad. It was not until the January of 1897 that it struck me – I had been a fool not to realize it before – that Constantin had not written to me for the reason he claimed. He couldn't have done, you see, because he knew I was to be abroad for months to come. There was another thing which made me even more suspicious. Constantin's letter of 7 March appeared to have been tampered with.'

'Opened?'

'I thought so, but I couldn't be sure. It might have been the porter's carelessness. In any case, I decided to follow up Constantin's odd reference to Cyane.'

Mr Nopheles took a book from his briefcase: Lascelle's *Dictionary of Mythology*. 'Perhaps you could turn to the entry for "Cyane", Mr Spellman.'

I did as I was told. 'I can't find anything,' I said after a moment or two. I had been expecting to find a piece of paper slipped between Lascelle's leaves.

'Look more closely. Can you see lines under some of the letters?'

I held the book closer. 'Yes: pencil marks.'

'Do you think that you could call them out in their order?'

I did.

'm, y, d, e . . . '

There were perhaps four hundred characters spread across twenty pages underlined in this manner; Mr Nopheles copied them all down in his notebook.

'i, d, e, s,' I finished. 'That appears to be all. They stop after that.'

'You're quite right. That's the end of the cryptogram. Here it is.'

Mr Nopheles handed over the little notebook, where the reconstituted message now stared me in the face:

> my dear nopheles i have nobody here to help or advise me i
> know that my correspondence is being intercepted and so pick
> this out of lascelles words hoping that you will find me suspect
> feaver mehmet ali the englishman last has hangmans hands
> they wanted me to join their cabal blackmailed me you know
> why i couldnt do anything now they want to guarantee my
> silence complaints from siriso in london mehmet ali has
> confiscated my papers everybody suspects me i cannot leave
> alexandria dont know what theyre up to its not just stealing
> almonds they want money for something very big very secret
> feaver is not the anglophile he seems other elements too some
> preordained ritual draws closer a fate they make yours
> stephanides

When I looked up again, with a growing sense of a deep disorder, Mr Nopheles was standing at the window and gazing bleakly across the road at the Hôtel Les Deux Continents. 'This makes your theory of Stephanides's murder considerably more plausible,' I said. 'Why, in that case, did the coroner record a verdict of suicide? Investigations must surely have been carried out.'

I think that Mr Nopheles was irritated by my slowness in grasping the implications of what he had already said. 'You have seen a copy of the death certificate, haven't you Mr Spellman?'

'Yes: you read it to me.'

'Who was it signed by?'

I examined the bottom of the page in question; my heart sank. 'It is signed by Lewis John Feaver, Senior Coroner for the central districts of Alexandria.'

'He was, don't you think, in a perfect position to conceal his crime – always assuming, of course, that he had committed one?'

Mr Nopheles sounded his words as if he were driving nails into a coffin. The coffin, I think, contained all my desires not to be associated with these matters. I didn't want Stephanides to have been murdered; I wanted, impossibly, his letters to have an innocent explanation. More than anything I wished that there was no plot and no conspiracy. Even as I thought these things, however, I knew that they were fantasies which came too late. I had one last line of resistance to fall back upon. 'If, by the January of 1897,' I said, 'you were convinced that Stephanides had been murdered and that Mr Feaver had simply concocted the death certificate, then why didn't you go to the proper authorities?'

'The "proper authorities"!' Mr Nopheles almost scoffed at me. 'With Constantin's name under a cloud? A suspected man? With no evidence in his own writing – only letters underlined in an obscure book? With "authority" evidently having such a vested interest in his madness, in the story of his suicide?'

I was forced to admit that he was right. Mr Nopheles paced up and down the small room, leafing through Wigfield's transcripts. At length he stopped in front of me:

'My original question remains to be answered, Mr Spellman. How did you know that Stephanides had been murdered? And why, more importantly, did you associate yourself with the crime? You have not mentioned the other allusion you made to Stephanides during your fever. Let me remind you of it: "I stole the almonds from Stephanides," you said, "after hanging him from that hook on the ceiling."'

The face of Mr Nopheles loomed inexorably above me in the dim office. All at once, for a moment, my memory seemed to clear. I saw the distended face of Mehmet Ali and heard, with something approaching my first shock, the words he had spoken that evening.

'No!' I said. 'I remember now. Mehmet Ali said that at the dinner party. It wasn't me; I don't know why I said "I."'

At that moment, one of the hospital runners knocked on the door of Dr Lindhorst's office. He brought with him a telegram for Mr Nopheles which had been delivered by a messenger from the Hôtel Les Deux Continents. Mr Nopheles tore open the message, read it and collapsed into a chair. He seemed relieved.

Dr Lindhorst looked at me from his corner. 'Are you quite certain, Mr Spellman, that you remember Mehmet Ali speaking those words?'

'Yes, it's very clear to me now. It's just come back.'

'Is there anything else at all that you remember?'

I shifted in my seat. 'Well, as I said, I have no sense of personal association with what is described in the transcripts – except for one other part, and that is the very faintest of recollections. I must admit that I do recall something about a hospital or an institution . . . nurses . . . tall people.'

'You cannot place the memory?'

'Not at all, I'm afraid. It seems to come from nowhere.'

'It's a difficult area,' said Dr Lindhorst, raising his shoulders in a sort of shrug. 'That memory, you see, may well have sprung from a different, an earlier source.'

'Maybe so.'

It was then that Mr Nopheles leaned forward and took my hand. 'I must apologize, Mr Spellman, from the bottom of my heart. You are completely exonerated.'

I was startled. 'Why? Because of what I just remembered about Mehmet Ali?'

'Partly. But there is another reason.' Mr Nopheles put his fingers to his lips and collected his thoughts. 'I expect you can understand why I originally suspected you?'

'I'm not sure I can.'

'I thought, you see, that you were the Englishman mentioned in Stephanides's cryptogram.'

'I see. The one with' – I scanned the paper on the desk – '"hangman's hands"?'

'Yes,' said Mr Nopheles. 'You were the most likely candidate. You must understand that I was determined to discover the truth about Stephanides. Towards the end of January 1897, therefore, I engineered – perhaps clumsily – a meeting with you. I made your acquaintance. My original theory was that you had wanted to supplant Constantin.'

'That's impossible!' I broke in. 'I never even met Constantin Stephanides. I arrived in Alexandria six months after his death, in September 1896. I told you that – oh, ages ago; it must have been in 1897.'

'You told me that on 7 April 1897,' said Mr Nopheles after he had consulted his notebook. 'But I have to say that I was convinced that you were lying. I – ah – I had written to your superiors in London, you see, Mr Spellman. Sir Rodney Rouncewell claimed that you had been sent out to Alexandria on the *Nepthys* in September 1895.'

'*1895*? Impossible. He made a mistake.'

'He must have done.' Mr Nopheles flourished his telegram. 'I have just received a message from Captain Shore of the *Nepthys*. He has looked through his records and I am glad to say that he confirms your version of the story.'

'So am I.' I think I must have sounded aggrieved. 'In any case, I can think of two other candidates for Stephanides's mysterious Englishman: Giovanni Feste, who was in Egypt on Siriso business at the time of Stephanides's death, and Krzystof Pustynia.'

Somewhat to my disappointment, Mr Nopheles was not surprised by this information. 'Yes: they were also high on my list. Just after your disappearance, they were higher on my list than you. But for reasons which will soon emerge, they have put themselves above suspicion.'

The reasons mentioned by Mr Nopheles were not, however, to emerge that day. Dr Lindhorst was called away on his rounds and, while the nurse waited at the door, we agreed to meet the next morning in the lounge of the Hôtel Les Deux Continents. Lindhorst said that the walk would do me good.

Next day, having had another sleepless night to ponder what I had learned, I was quick to put the first question: 'I am curious to know why, Mr Nopheles, you stopped suspecting me shortly before my disappearance?'

Mr Nopheles looked up and down the great, high-ceilinged room before he replied. Distant groups of people were deep in conversation; near the lifts, like a nervous blackbird, the manager of the hotel hopped about behind his desk.

Mr Nopheles coughed. 'I have to make a somewhat embarrassing and indeed incriminating confession. By the beginning of November this year, my investigations had led nowhere. Although I was convinced that Stephanides had been murdered, I had nothing amounting to positive proof, and I must admit that I was having particular difficulty with you, Mr Spellman. Either your apparently continuous state of – how shall I put it? Blinkered bafflement? Either your bafflement, as I say, was cosmetic or, alternatively, you were entirely innocent. All those worries about codes and secrets: you seemed to be hinting at something you were pretending to be unaware of. I thought that you were playing with me.'

I laughed incredulously. 'That,' I said, 'would have been utterly beyond me.'

'In any case,' continued Mr Nopheles, 'I decided to take a more active step. I – ah – broke into Mehmet Ali's office on the wharf.'

'*You!*' I exclaimed, as another recollection flashed before me. 'Mr Feaver mentioned that at the dinner party.'

'Yes, it was me.' Mr Nopheles seemed distinctly ill at ease. 'I – ah – took the petty cash to make it seem like a conventional burglary. I spent most of the night going through the files and came across some letters between Stephanides and Mehmet Ali. They stood as further evidence that Constantin was innocent of the accusations which had been circulated concerning him and they also contained further implications and hints of Mehmet Ali's guilt.'

'Go on,' I said to Mr Nopheles, 'go on.'

I had never seen him so awkward before. 'It's a difficult admission, Mr Spellman. I decided to set a trap for you. I thought that I might as well be hanged for a sheep as a lamb and – well – I broke into your rooms in the Pension de l'Est and concealed the papers in one of your ledgers.'

I was frankly puzzled. 'What purpose did that serve?'

In spite of himself, Mr Nopheles was proud of the subtlety of his plan. 'It was a trap, you see. My observations of your character led me to believe that you would confide the matter to me if you were what you seemed.'

'And if I wasn't? If I was the "Englishman"?'

'Well then, of course, if you were implicated, you would be bound to keep quiet. Of course, in the event you spoke. That was on the twelfth of November. As a result I decided to tell you everything.'

'I see.' Then the enormity of it broke upon me with all its force. Not only had I been suspected by Mr Nopheles, I had also, for some reason, been under investigation by Feaver and Mehmet Ali and my knowledge of the quarrel between Mehmet Ali and Stephanides had somehow sealed my fate.

'Did you realize, Mr Nopheles, that by placing the correspondence in my room you were exposing me to great danger if I was innocent?'

'I –? No. I –'

'I mentioned the letters, you see, at Mehmet Ali's dinner party.'

This gave my friend a pause for thought. 'If you were innocent – something I wasn't sure about – then I can understand their suspicions. From their point of view, you would have looked guilty. But I'm afraid to say that at the time that possibility did not occur to me. I – ah – I didn't know, of course, about your arrangement to meet Mr Feaver and Mehmet Ali that night.'

'Would you have warned me?'

There was an even longer pause. 'I'm very sorry, Mr Spellman. I suppose that I – that perhaps I myself was responsible for the attempt on your life. My single-minded desire to discover the truth about one man's death came near to causing the death of another friend. That,' said Mr Nopheles humbly, 'was very foolish of me. I am most sincerely sorry.'

I accepted his apology as gracefully as I could but I must confess that I was shaken enough to order a large brandy from a passing waiter.

'At any rate,' I said, 'surely Mr Feaver, Mehmet Ali and Mistral can now be arrested. Even if the evidence of their plot against Stephanides remains in doubt, their guilt in my case could surely be demonstrated.'

'I am afraid, Mr Spellman,' said Mr Nopheles, 'that litigation would unfortunately be to bolt the stable door after the horse has – ah – locked.'

'I think,' intervened Dr Lindhorst, 'that this is where we come to the Occidental-ETS-Assuan case.'

'Ah yes,' I said, 'I was curious about that: you mentioned it in your case notes.'

Some businessmen had started a loud discussion at the next table and Mr Nopheles was beginning to look uneasy. He suggested that we went outside into the garden, where we succeeded in finding a secluded bench.

Mr Nopheles stooped to open his briefcase. He took out a bundle of clippings from the *Egyptian Times* which, whilst he was talking and to support what he had said, he handed to me one by one. He had been following the case with interest since April 1898. It was in that month that the Comptroller-General, in an attempt, perhaps, to restore his public standing after the Hrocka furore in February of that year, had ordered the establishment of a commission to investigate the affairs of the Assuan Dam Construction Company. It was only when the commission met for the first time on 14 November 1898, however, that further details began to emerge. Two days after my body was recovered and only a week after the body of the Mahdi, a latterday, inverted Orpheus, had been disinterred by Kitchener's troops, decapitated, and thrown into the Nile, warrants had been issued for the detention of Mr Feaver and Mehmet Ali on charges of fraud and embezzlement. Eight days later, on 12 December it was finally established that on the day preceding the issue of the warrants, the pair had fled Alexandria for Djibouti aboard the Eastern Trading Society vessel, the *Typhon*. As everybody now knows, the English gun-boats gave chase but, with nine days to spare, Mehmet Ali and Mr Feaver had been allowed ample opportunity to disappear.

'They escaped?' I was scandalized. 'You mean to say that they are at liberty?'

'I am afraid so, Mr Spellman. The matter was badly mishandled.' Mr Nopheles smiled ruefully at my exasperation.

That afternoon was drawing to a close and Dr Lindhorst voiced concern for my health. He was right: I was desperately tired. Since my illness, each waking hour had been a great effort and, although I knew that there was more to come in the way of secrets and revelations, I was glad to save it for another day.

As we left the gardens of the hotel, we passed an old man with a patch over one eye. He was standing in the shade of a date palm; sitting at his feet was a small dog on a silken leash.

'Well, Mr Spellman: Lindhorst and I discussed the matter from every possible direction last night and we think that we have arrived at a plausible version of recent events. We are also convinced that we know why Mr Feaver and Mehmet Ali suspected you. Nevertheless, there are still a number of mysteries.'

We had gathered once again in Dr Lindhorst's office. A nurse had brought us a tray of coffee and, after Lindhorst had taken it from her, he locked the door. Slowly and quietly, Mr Nopheles began to unravel the story, as he put it, of the story:

'It seems likely that by April 1898, with the announcement of the impending commission into the Assuan Dam Construction Company, Mehmet Ali and Mr Feaver would have been fully aware of the instability of their position.

'They had behind them a history of crime which might, perhaps, have begun before their attempts to embezzle the Siriso Trading Company. I think it likely that, finding Stephanides's blackmail payments too small, they did away with him and set their sights on bigger game.'

'One moment,' I interrupted. 'How were they able to blackmail Stephanides in the first place?'

'Ah –' Mr Nopheles hesitated; it was a delicate issue. 'He was a homosexual, you see, Mr Spellman. He would have died – he did in fact die – to prevent this being generally known.'

'I see.'

Mr Nopheles took up his thread once again. 'After Constantin's death in the spring of 1896, Feaver and Mehmet Ali must have felt fairly confident. They did their best to make sure that the Stephanides case remained closed. The damage to the affairs of the Siriso Trading Company was so slight and they had displaced it so successfully onto the shoulders of their unfortunate victim that rumours circulated only of petty theft and minor corruption. They probably had plenty of opportunity to go through Stephanides's papers and remove all evidence relating to the quarrel: this evidence is what I eventually rediscovered in Mehmet Ali's office. Finally, with your arrival, Mr Spellman, any lingering doubts would, they hoped, be laid to rest.

'It was then, we think, that Feaver and Mehmet Ali turned their attention to the Occidental Bank. In May 1897 they acquired the account of the Assuan Dam Construction Company. It must have seemed like a godsend: the money of investors both private and public, in England, France and Germany as well as in Egypt, concentrated in their hands.

'This is where the Eastern Trading Society comes in. Mr Feaver and Mehmet Ali had been directors and shareholders in the company for almost a decade but it was only now that they began to buy shares in the ETS with funds transferred from the Assuan Dam account. Previously, the ETS had been thought of as a solid but unremarkable enterprise. Within a year, however, it had become – on paper – one of the largest asset holders in Egypt.

'Suddenly, in the midst of success, Mehmet Ali and Mr Feaver were pulled up short. Why was there to be a commission? Or, more to the point, who had spied, who had informed on them? It would have been most logical to think first of Krzystof Pustynia. For various reasons, however, they discounted him: perhaps they thought that they had succeeded in pulling the wool over his eyes. Next on the list would have been your Signor Feste, Mr Spellman. He had, as we know, been sent out to Egypt to investigate inconsistencies arising from their earlier activities. Again, for one reason and another, they decided to disregard him. Perhaps they thought that he was too far away to do any damage.'

I put some sugar into my coffee and began to stir it. 'So their thoughts turned to me? They suspected me although I was the only person with no knowledge whatsoever?'

'Precisely. But it was a logical step. You were Feste's agent in the field. It was you who were trying to revive the Stephanides case; it was you, they thought, who had begun to ask questions about their other business activities.'

'Do you think they followed me?' I asked.

'Almost certainly; they prepared their ground carefully. Why? Were you aware of it?'

'Yes, I always had that feeling.'

'Always?'

'Well, from time to time. Afterwards, I thought I was imagining things.'

Mr Nopheles finished his coffee. 'In any case,' he continued, 'they must have rejected the possibility of blackmail or bribery. They plotted your death. Revenge? Certainly. Perhaps they also hoped that, if the commission was deprived of the evidence they thought you possessed, then they might be able to escape arraignment.'

'But I hadn't been called as a witness by the commission; I told them that.'

'Did they believe you?'

'No: Mr Feaver kept on about it. I repeated again and again that I knew nothing.'

Mr Nopheles smiled. 'Nothing, in their eyes, could have seemed more suspicious.'

I had to accept this; it made sense. I walked to the window and looked out at the gardens of the Hôtel Les Deux Continents. The old man we had seen yesterday was sitting on a bench with his dog in his lap. In the bright morning light, everything – such as it was – seemed at last before me. It appeared that there was another, completely different story beneath the story that I had been living. In this reconstituted tale, a scholarly shipping magnate was a detective, a burglar and a thief. A banker, a harbour-master and a hotel receptionist were poisoners, fraudsters and murderers. All the time, amongst my scattered shipments, I had been a dupe. It was, as Mr Feaver had once said, a hydraulic history. Beneath my own clear but rippled current had flowed a darker and a colder one, another one destined in the end to surface before plunging into the deep.

'Very well, then,' I sighed. 'We know why they killed Stephanides and tried to kill me. Where, then, are the mysteries you mentioned?'

Mr Nopheles scrutinized me. 'Can you not see any problems at all, Mr Spellman?'

I considered the matter for a minute, after which time I thought that I had caught the tail of at least one:

'I wonder why, if ruin stared Mr Feaver and Mehmet Ali in the face and my death was of paramount importance, did they delay it from 13 November, when I was drugged, to 1 December, when I was thrown into the Nile?'

It was Dr Lindhorst who spoke next: 'Can you think of any reasons for that?'

I turned my coffee cup in its saucer and watched the dark grounds flow from side to side.

'Perhaps,' I speculated at last, 'they hoped to extract the truth under narcosis.'

'Perhaps,' said Dr Lindhorst. 'But why, then, were they so fussy about the details? Why did they bring you upriver to Cairo? And why, in the end, did they fail to make sure of your death?'

'It could all have been done along a dark alley in Alexandria,' said Mr Nopheles.

'And why,' I added, 'why on earth did they circumcise me?'

Dr Lindhorst scanned his case notes. 'The problem is, Mr Spellman, that the transcripts provide no clue to what happened during your abduction. You speak only of the events of 13 November and then of 1 December. It is all a parenthesis: you seem to have no recollection of what happened to you in the time between.'

I looked across the room at Mr Nopheles, who was lighting a small cigar. 'That is the first problem,' he said as he blew out the match. 'This is the second: what were Feaver and Mehmet Ali actually up to? What was their plan, their end, their goal? In the cryptogram, Stephanides said that they wanted the money for something "very big, very secret".'

'Are you implying that they didn't do all this merely to line their own pockets?'

'Yes. I don't think they did it for personal profit. Nor did the commission.'

'What did they say?'

Mr Nopheles raised his hands, palms upward. 'Well: it could all be feverish jingoism of course, propaganda meant for the English Parliament. The commission found no irrefutable evidence. They concluded that Feaver and Mehmet Ali were probably siphoning money out of the Assuan Dam account at Occidental in order to fund the Mahdist insurgents. This would still have been possible after Omdurman. The Mahdist organization is not broken even yet.'

'But Mr Feaver was delighted by Omdurman,' I objected. 'He was the most narrow-minded of patriots.'

'He protested,' said Mr Nopheles, with a gentleness that laid bare my own *naïveté*, 'perhaps too much. He was not, said Stephanides, "the Anglophile he seemed".'

'In any case,' said Lindhorst after a few moments, 'they have vanished with the elusiveness of forged banknotes. Whatever we know, they may never come to book.'

I spent two more weeks – over Christmas and into the New Year – recuperating at the Queen Victoria Hospital in Cairo. During this time, I underwent further hypnotic sessions with Dr Lindhorst. My memory of the time between when I was drugged and when I was set adrift on the Nile, however, seemed to have been irretrievably effaced. I had hoped that the whirlpool might have regurgitated its sucked jujubes but I was disappointed. I made a statement, witnessed by Dr Lindhorst and Mr

Nopheles, to the Cairo police. The Head of Police was singularly indifferent to my story. 'Feaver, Mehmet Ali and Mistral Mussanah have escaped,' his eyes seemed to say. 'You may make a statement if you wish – I have no objection to that – but in the absence of the accused no further action can be taken. What more can I do?'

I was forced to admit – both Nopheles and Lindhorst had suspected that it might be so – that the ravings of a patient suffering from typhus and his unconscious ramblings could not count for much in the already great weight of evidence against the triumvirate.

The Stephanides case was not to be re-opened.

On 12 January 1899, Mr Nopheles accompanied me back to Alexandria by railway.

We chatted for a while and then, in the warm carriage, I began to drowse. When I awoke, we were beginning to enter the suburbs of the city. Mr Nopheles was watching me intently.

'What's the matter?' I asked. 'Is something wrong?'

He roused himself from his thoughts. 'No, not at all. It is just that for the last couple of weeks I have been wondering why you have stopped asking questions.'

'Questions? Why? It's all over: is there anything else to ask?'

Mr Nopheles had taken an orange out of his pocket. He carefully began to peel it with the knife which, long ago, his friend Stephanides had given him: 'I would have thought that there is at least one.'

I thought for some minutes but eventually admitted defeat. Mr Nopheles wiped the blade of his knife on his handkerchief: 'Who was the other?'

'The other?'

'The third one: the Englishman with hangman's hands. If we believe Constantin's letter – as I think we do – then there has to be another member of the conspiracy. Constantin knew enough not to be wrong.'

I admitted with some embarrassment that I had not thought of that; there were so many details, it was so hard to see things clearly. 'I remember that I suggested it might have been Feste or Pustynia, although you and Dr Lindhorst said they were beyond suspicion; I never found out why.'

'That's right,' agreed Mr Nopheles, consuming the last segment of his orange. 'I don't suppose you have been reading the papers since your recovery?'

I had not.

'You won't know, then, that Feste and Pustynia played important roles in the formation of the initial idea for the Assuan Dam commission.

Pustynia, you see, grew suspicious of the success of his own company, the Eastern Trading Society. It has only recently emerged that he approached the Comptroller-General about it.'

'And Feste?'

'It was Feste who, back in England, encouraged Mr Poynter, the Member of Parliament for South Kensington, to table question after question to the Foreign Secretary and the Egypt Office.'

'I see.'

'Do you?' In the flickering light of bridges and tunnels I saw doubt on Mr Nopheles's face. 'Are you certain you understand the implications?'

I was working hard and, as the train entered the central station, I thought I had the answer. 'If either of them had been involved in the murder of Stephanides, then it wouldn't have been in their interest to cast suspicions on Feaver or Mehmet Ali.'

'Precisely. Then who was the other person?' Mr Nopheles alighted on the platform. I passed his briefcase down to him.

'I thought that we knew everything,' I said, disappointed. 'I thought we could at least be sure of the basic facts.'

Mr Nopheles looked up at me with his earnest, scholarly face. 'The details have been lost,' he shouted over the noise. 'We know nothing.'

He was right. It was an exemplary story: it had led us on. It was full of echoes which sounded off nothing and clues which led or came from nowhere. I had convinced myself for a while that I had solved everything. To enter the streets of this exemplary city once again, however, was to be faced with the knowledge that my hopes of a clear ending – which was as much as to say a clear beginning – were the most fragile of fantasies. All geography had vanished and it was as if the Amazon had flowed like honey into the Nile, as if a forest had sprung up overnight on the pellucid waters of Lake Victoria.

I no longer, understandably, had much relish for the shadowed corridors and beamed ceilings of the Pension de l'Est and Mr Nopheles kindly offered me a room in his house on the other side of the city.

We went to collect my possessions. Turning into the old street (washing was hung above our heads and in the distance, at the bottom of the hill, the sea was a sheet of the darkest blue) we found to our surprise that the Pension de l'Est was under new management. Even as we entered the hallway, workmen were putting the new name above the door. With its fans, its ormolu mirrors, its potted palm trees and richly upholstered settees, it seemed that the Hotel Assuan would cater more to the tourist than the resident.

Towards the end of January I received a letter from Giovanni Feste. He was able to confirm and elaborate on Mr Nopheles's report of his part in the establishment of the commission. Through his business contacts, he had been accumulating evidence against Mr Feaver for years. It seemed that in the early 1880s, Mr Feaver had been drummed out of the Colonial Service in Malaya after it had been demonstrated in court that he had been manipulating native land rights for his own profit. Feaver had tried to bury his past and he had at first, apparently, done good service for the Occidental Bank. He was not a particularly subtle defrauder, however, and, with Krzystof Pustynia's information, the first link in his new chain of dishonesty had come to light. Feste had known Pustynia from his days in Alexandria. They had co-ordinated their investigations and used the Member of Parliament for South Kensington as their public voice. As I would perhaps recall, Signor Feste reminded me, Mr Poynter was well-known for his opinions on the Egyptian situation. He advocated firm – pale liberals would say repressive – measures. His patriotic passion, in fact, had led on one famous occasion to a fist-fight with a Whig during a performance of *La Traviata* at Covent Garden.

Although Feaver and Mehmet Ali had escaped, their machinations had caused surprisingly little damage. All the diverted funds were recoverable, having been separately amassed but not, as yet, used. Confidence in the Assuan Dam project had been damaged, but not fatally so; the minor crisis would do nothing to impede the formation of the Anglo-Egyptian Condominium of the Sudan.

Feaver and Mehmet Ali had left Alexandria rich men, having managed to convert their personal shares in the ETS into specie. This manoeuvre, through dubious, was not in itself illegal; the money belonged to them.

Feste commiserated with me on the unfortunate and completely unpredictable attempt on my life. He hoped I had made a full recovery and expected I would be pleased to hear that, after I had negotiated the thirteenth shipment, Siriso was planning to recall me to London.

The letter contained no apology for the fact that, if Feste had suspected corruption all along, he had used me as a stalking horse whilst he drafted memoranda in the safety of London offices. It had not been thought appropriate, said Signor Feste, that I be fully informed. Nor had it been felt that it would add to my happiness to tell me of my predecessor's suicide whilst under house arrest. It was clear that Feste, at least, was happy with the official version.

As I finished the letter, I found myself regretting for the hundredth time my disappearance. It had happened at the vital moment and I had never had the thrill of the chase or experienced the sense of an ending that might have accompanied the apprehension of a criminal. All that had happened, after it was over, was a series of leisurely discussions. Lindhorst, Nopheles and I might as well have been talking about share prices or trade prospects.

The mysteries multiplied and to have seemed to have solved some was hardly to have arrived at knowledge. The only thing I was certain of was that I was not the detective I might have hoped to be, nor the policeman the situation seemed to demand. What was right? I no longer knew. Murder? Certainly, that was wrong. Nor, on the other hand, could I dredge up much sympathy for the British business interests that Mr Nopheles and myself now seemed to be supporting. Me? On the side of Christopher Desert, Her Majesty's Government and the Comptroller-General? I could make no sense of the situation. Perhaps I, and not Mehmet Ali or Mr Feaver, was the criminal.

I realized then that all along, without knowing it, I could not but have been on the English side: I was swallowed by its ways and habits; I was in debt to it for all my consciousness. Were Mehmet Ali and Mr Feaver on the side of Egypt? Not at all; they had merely chosen to support the French campaign of destabilization. All that I had seen was the way in which one empire tried to undermine the other as they writhed and twisted in the dark. Like a blank cheque, a mere matter of potential figures and signs, Mr Feaver's inscrutable face came into my mind. Wars, battles, conspiracies; Omdurman, Fashoda, the Assuan incident. These enigmas, as Mr Feaver had himself implied, were generated by the things we wished to seize, the desire in us which gave them life.

All this: the guilt, the bafflement and the sense of anti-climax that accompanied it, was on my mind when I travelled in mid-February to Heliopolis, that city older than Cairo which stands to the north-east of the modern metropolis. I was to collect and to arrange for the transportation of the thirteenth and final cargo: that for Giovanni Feste.

I do not know whether it is there still, but there used to be a gambling house a short way out of town on the way to the scattered fragments of the ancient necropolis. This faded casino had been selected as my final rendezvous.

I was shown by the manager, a wheezing and somewhat pitiful man who had become sentimentally obsessed by his plans to live in a little place on the coast after his retirement, to an upper, private room. An enormous selection of games was displayed on trestle tables along one wall. There were dozens of packs of cards, all of different compositions and designs; dice in a score of materials; chess sets whose pieces were made of stone, bone, wood, even of compacted dough and boot polish (the last from a famous prison). There were ornate shōgi sets, roulette wheels, counters and boards for mah-jong and backgammon, instruction books and manuals for bridge, poker, bezique, canasta and snip-snap-snorum. There were coloured juggler's balls, whirligigs, tops and dibs, a hundred pucks, chips and tiles. I could have played jack straws or trick-track, fantan or écarté, gobang, diabolo or tiddly-winks.

'Great numbers of birds come through the sky at dawn to feed in the marshes,' wheezed the manager softly.

Laid out on another series of trestle tables along the opposite wall was a hoard of money both current and ancient: moidores, ducats and maravedis, rose-nobles, wampum beads and toman; picayunes and scissel; sequins, staters, napoleons, solidi, sestertii and doubloons.

'And the sky is pink, very pale and very pink. All is quiet.'

In March 1899, when the final cargo had been dispatched, I considered myself at liberty. I was invited by Mr Nopheles to spend some time at his lodge on the southern shore of Mareotis.

We read; we walked through the marshes; in the evenings, on the verandah, we played chess. On one of these occasions, I remember, we had been talking about my 'death'. Mr Nopheles had developed some interesting theories and he began to elaborate them from his armchair. I leaned over the balcony and looked down into the water. In the distance an egret speared a fish. In the shallows of the lake, the lilies closed their petals in the failing light.

'It's a latterday version of an old Alexandrian theme,' said Mr Nopheles.

'What's that?'

'Body smuggling. Cleopatra in her carpet; the body of Saint Mark hidden in a pork barrel and taken back to Venice. There are echoes of other rituals too: the Galli's self-administration of a sanctifying wound, the castration that fertilizes.'

I lit a lantern as Mr Nopheles continued. 'Porpyrius records that King Amôsis ordered the substitution of waxen images for human sacrifices. Herodotus talks of celebrations where the host would pass around the wooden figure of a dead body in a coffin. "When thou lookest upon this," he was supposed to say, "then drink and be merry, for thou shalt be such as this when thou art dead." You were lucky, Mr Spellman, losing only your foreskin. The Mahdi had his skull turned into a drinking vessel by Lord Kitchener.'

One evening towards the end of the harvest, an injured *fellah* was brought to the lodge on a stretcher carried by his brothers. He had cut himself with his own sickle and was bleeding profusely. I took rolls of bandage from my little travelling medical chest and bound these around his leg after Mr Nopheles had cleaned the wound. As the man limped away into the darkness, Mr Nopheles called out after him: 'The fields will thank you for your blood!' Then he turned to me. 'The old man is not so dead after all. He keeps coming back.'

During June we sat outside until dawn. Occasionally a moth would fly, with a sharp tap, into the glass cover of the lantern; otherwise everything was silent. Then Sirius, brightest of all the fixed stars, called Sothis by the Egyptians, would rise in the east. It was the time of the festival of Isis; this was her star. She had risen to mourn the dead Osiris; soon, her tears would cause the Nile to swell once more.

In August I returned to Alexandria and booked my passage to Marseilles. A few days later, at the bottom of the gangplank, I put my hand for the last time into Mr Nopheles's pink and fleshy palm. The ship was to leave that evening. Once aboard, I stood at the railings and looked down onto the wharf, searching amongst the crowds for the face of my friend. I could not see where he stood; perhaps he disliked farewells. The ship slipped away from the dockside and the *Orpheus* escorted us out to sea. The exemplary city shimmered in the late afternoon haze; an hour later, in the dusk, it was lost to view.

I was preparing to leave the custom-house at Marseilles when an official beckoned me to his desk. He examined my ticket.

'You are continuing your journey by sea?'

'Yes: tomorrow. On the *Duke of Devonshire*. I am staying here tonight.'

'You must re-register your shipment to London.'

'I thought I had already done so: one trunk to Spellman, London. To be collected.'

The official shook his head and indicated that I should follow him. 'No, no: the shipment, not your luggage. There are forms to sign.'

I was led into an enormous warehouse which stood to one side of the custom-house, near the railway sidings.

'I don't know what you mean,' I kept saying. 'There must have been a mistake.'

The official clicked his tongue, shook his head and brandished papers at me. The hollow noise of colliding goods wagons could be heard.

In a corner of the echoing depot was a large wooden crate. It was labelled in a hand I did not recognize.

SIRISO
Cargo 14
c/o J Spellman

'It came from Alexandria,' said the official brusquely. 'No mistake. You want it to London?'

'I —'

'It's yours. Sign here.'

Hardly knowing what I did, I signed my name and paid the fee which was owing. It was only then that I thought to ask what the crate contained. The official sighed impatiently. 'Don't you know? It's your cargo.' He took a screwdriver from his pocket, however, and levered one side of the chest away. Inside, padded with straw, was a large wooden box. Unlike the crate, however, it was polished and beautifully veneered; its design was ineffably familiar to me. I carefully lifted the box from the crate and opened its lid. Inside was another box which closely fitted the first and was likewise patterned in a manner which, even yet, I could not quite place. Inside the second box was another and in that, another one. The marquetry work differed slightly from each to each, but I would have been prepared to wager that it all came from the same hand.

A few minutes later, fourteen boxes stood before me in descending order of size. The official was watching me uncomprehendingly. I opened the lid of the fourteenth box, which was small enough to fit in the palm of my hand. Seeds were sprouting inside and pale stems twisted in the darkness.

The uncanny feeling of familiarity was taking on, moment by moment, a tangible form. Using the screwdriver, I began to prize the cork base away from the last box. Burnt into the wood exactly where I had known it would be, I saw at last the maker's brand:

ADAM SPELLMAN
14 Regis Street
Canonbury
For Rouncewell
SIRISO

22

A Hundred and Forty Pounds

THUS ENDED my strange stay in Egypt. I have never returned and I suppose that now I never will, being so near to the end of the twisted cable of my narrative. Yes: it is all downhill from now on, thank goodness. I feel sucked dry by my words and you, Mr Secretary, must be bloated with them.

I went to the window this evening. For the first time in months I looked out over Bartholomew Square as I thought about what I was going to say to you tonight. It was fairly quiet: a few maids hurried past on late errands and, in the distance, the tune of a barrel-organ could faintly be heard.

A few minutes later I spotted the Pencil hurrying into the square from the direction of Alexandra Gate. He was carrying a package which, I was sure, contained the typescript of my fourth and final Egyptian chapter.

On the morning of 3 September 1899, I stood on the deck of the *Duke of Devonshire* and, leaning over the rail, stared across the few miles of English channel which separated me from the English shore. Within the next hour we had entered the mouth of the Thames. I could see Tilbury on my right hand and Gravesend on my left. Up ahead, the river turned to the north and was lost amongst the mudflats. I think that I wanted the Thames to have some majesty about it – a propitious, a distinctive air – but everything around me seemed familiar and completely ordinary. Perhaps I was hoping for some kind of revelation: a flash of understanding as to why I had gone away and why I now returned. But the dark mud of low tide, the little jetties of the eel fishers, the lines of posts half-submerged in the water and the current which ran feebly against us: none of these things produced any new consciousness at all – beyond the consciousness that there were no reasons and no meanings apart from the jetties, the posts, the mud and the slackly resistant tide.

I had little appetite, after these somewhat gloomy reflections, for any immediate encounters with my old friends. Instead, I took a room at the General Gordon Hotel in Limehouse, where I decided to await the arrival of my trunk and my father's boxes. The window of my room overlooked the river. For several hours that day and the next, I stared out over the Thames at the slowly moving barges, the wherries and the steamers. I thought what a sad farce this city was, sprawling incontinently in every direction, being fed, like an invalid, by grimly solicitous boats.

A shoddy waiter brought me my meals in my room. I slept and ate. On the second day I strolled around the neighbourhood for a couple of hours. I felt that the exercise did me some good and so, on the morning of my third day, I went out again. I had been wandering around for some time when I found myself in Canonbury. I was suddenly seized by an impulse to seek out the house in Regis Street where I had lived until my twelfth year. It was not my birthplace, of course: the reader will remember that I was born, as it were, in transit. It was in this grimy soil, however, that my roots had first sprouted, in this place that I had come to consciousness.

I turned the corner that I had turned so many hundreds of times before and the street – was not there. I think I must have blinked with astonishment. At any rate, after a few seconds, I laughed at myself. Such was the consonance, then, I thought, between nostalgia and actuality! I had followed my imagination and lost my way.

I paused at the familiar corner. Surely this was it: the post-box, the little shop across the road, the blackened walls of the surrounding houses – everything had the correct configuration. In front of me, a line of wrought iron railings which had once protected the scrappy gardens stretched to the end of the road, where a high wall and a sign announced the premises of the London Water Company.

I had begun to walk slowly along the street when I noticed that the regularly spaced gates still had their numbers on them. The gate of number 14 Regis Street was chained and padlocked. Behind it, a stretch of wasteland thickly overgrown with the past summer's weeds descended to a railway cutting. As I waited there, uncertain what to do, a train passed through the cutting and a small child looked up at me expressionlessly through the window of a carriage.

It was only then that I saw the notice-board a few feet away from me, black letters on a white ground:

TO BE DESTROYED
BY ORDER
CONTRACTORS: THE SIRISO BUILDING CO.
(SIR RODNEY ROUNCEWELL)

I cried then; I admit that. I took out my handkerchief and wept into it. Later, I lay on the bed in my room at the General Gordon. In the dwindling light the ships still came and went in the poisoned channel.

Next morning I paid my bill at the hotel before collecting my trunk from the docks. My father's boxes had not arrived; I was informed that they would come by a later boat.

I took a cab to Blackfriars, intending to put up at the Plough and Stars before finding myself more permanent accommodation. As I drew near my destination I began to notice new shops and businesses in the neighbourhood. I missed the names and signs I looked for and found only a profusion of ones I did not know.

The cab turned into Blackfriars Lane, where I asked the driver to stop and unload my trunk. I paid him and, as he made his horse move away, I stood on the pavement and looked across at the Plough and Stars. Something here, too, was greatly amiss. The windows – it was early and I had been prepared for drawn curtains – were whitewashed. The inn sign, which depicted a plough-boy on his furrow with a bright star (perhaps Sirius) in the dawn sky, was peeled and faded. The blue had turned to grey and, where the gold leaf star had once shone, bare board now showed. I crossed the street and found a note pinned to the front door:

CLOSED UNTIL FURTHER NOTICE
BY ORDER

Making sure that I was not observed, I slipped through a gate into the courtyard which separated the inn from the hay loft. Even here I found, to my disappointment, no signs of habitation. A mangy cat squatted on a beer barrel which had had its bung drawn. I tried the latch of a door but it did not give. I began to experience the peculiar impression that I had somehow arrived in the wrong city: I had made an unaccountable mistake in my booking. How could a city so paralysed with inertia seem at the same time so altered? In the end it was a mere thing which persuaded me that not all links with the past were severed. Pushed into a corner near the door which gave onto the street was the wax head of Charles I.

My only resort now was Lady Magenta. It was she, after all, who I had most longed to see. I had not wanted, however, to appear unannounced with my suitcase literally in my hand. It would have been far better to have found another temporary lodging in which to prepare myself for the meeting I had dreamed of. I had run out of patience now and besides, the city had unnerved me. If I could not soon find somebody to answer me I would begin to suspect that I had vanished.

After some difficulty – the neighbourhood was devoid of cabs – I succeeded in arranging transportation and, at about eleven o'clock in the morning, arrived at Bartholomew Square. The leaves on the plane trees were beginning to turn; flimsy clouds raced across the sky; a nanny carefully tucked a child into its pram before disappearing around a corner.

I rang the bell and Lady Magenta's maid opened the door. I could have hugged her in my delight at finding a familiar face. Once more, however, there was perturbing news of absence and removal.

Lady Magenta was not at home, had not been at home since January. Poor thing, she had not been well; no, she had not. The doctor had said she shouldn't be living in the city, not with the fog and the smoke. When the baroness died, her ladyship had moved out to Hampstead. The air was fresher up there, more bracing.

I stood in the hall and looked up the dim stairs. The faint notes of a violin reached my ears.

'Who is the occupant at the moment?' I asked.

'Mr Perkin, sir. He took the house for a year, having so much business in town these days.'

'He's not at Greenford Green any more?'

'No, although the housekeeper says he still owns a house out there. Can I announce you, sir? He is practising upstairs.'

'Ah – the violin. I remember he liked music. I once sent him some instruments.' I found myself hesitating between the hat stand and the door. At length, however, I excused myself: 'No, no. I won't interrupt him.'

Promising to collect it later I entrusted my trunk to the maid.   As I left Bartholomew Square I reflected how appropriate it was that Mr Perkin – Lord Tramont's Leonardo of dye – now lived in a house decorated in colours he had himself invented. Perhaps, as their creator, he would remain unaffected by the sombre echoes they seemed to start off in the hallway and in the long, quiet rooms.

I ate some lunch and strolled across Kensington Gardens in the direction of Lancaster Gate. On one of the neat pathways along the west side of the Long Water a swan was preening itself. As I passed, it shook its dark and gleaming feet one at a time. Then it spread its wings in the sun; I was close enough to see each translucent feather.

A little further on, I gave the attendant my fee and sat in a deck-chair. For some reason I had lost all sense of urgency. Nothing I could do would change anything. I would see Lady Magenta soon enough. In the meantime, dogs barked in the distance; children were playing under the trees.

I looked at my watch and startled myself: it was half past six. The dogs and the children had gone; a bank of clouds obscured the sinking sun. It was beginning to grow dark.

I decided not to take a cab over to Hampstead. Instead, as I had always done before, I would walk. Under my tread the city assumed once again a human dimension. Not everything, I reassured myself, had gone; the great urban roar was only the sum of a million individual noises and not the stertorous breathing of a vast animal.

The baroness's house was better cared for than it used to be and a streetlamp cast its light into the once shadowed garden. New tiles had been laid along the path; the laurels around the portico were neatly cut back. The gate swung easily on its oiled hinges and the clanking doorbell had been replaced by an electrically operated one. Despite these changes, however, the baroness's maid remained and we performed, on the doorstep, the usual rituals of Polishness:

'You're thinner, Mr Spellman. And older. But it's good to see you.'

I laughed. 'You haven't changed much. I'm glad to see you too.'

She led me into the hallway and then, seizing my lapel in an unusual gesture of intimacy, she looked up into my face.

'You heard about the baroness?'

'Yes. I'm very sorry.'

She took my hat and gloves. 'Don't be sorry, Mr Spellman. The baroness was never sad.'

'No,' I said meditatively, 'no, I suppose she never was.'

As we walked along the hallway to the drawing-room at the back of the house she turned to speak to me over her shoulder:

'How was Egypt, Mr Spellman? Was it full of minarets, and monkeys in the trees?'

I smiled and found it hard to reply. My heart was beating faster with the anticipation of meeting Lady Magenta at last.

'No, no: it was not like that at all.'

The double doors swung wide and, as I stepped into the room, I was startled and half-blinded by a blaze of light: the crystal chandeliers had been lit; candelabra and lamps shone from every available space. At first glance the room seemed unoccupied. I immediately noticed that the baroness's French furniture and her draperies were gone. In their places were chairs and wall hangings of Japanese design. To the left of the roaring fire was a large and over-figured paper screen, from behind which came a familiar voice:

'Ah, it's you, my dear. Come and sit down. Take some tea. Rest yourself and watch Giovanni trounce me at whist.'

The logs crackled in the fire and after a moment or two the voice spoke again. 'He's a dab hand, I assure you, but I must say that I suspect some roguish chicanery.'

If I had not sensed, behind the closed door through which I had just passed, the waiting and hovering maid, I think that I would have quietly crept away.

'It's Jack Spellman,' I called out at last. 'Home from Egypt.'

There was a pause during which I thought I heard a low and rapid colloquy. And then Sir Rodney Rouncewell emerged from behind the screen.

'Why, my dear Jacques! May I still call you Jacques? It is so much more euphonious than plain old proletarian Jack.'

He crossed the room with vigorous strides and I was still amazed that his lean shanks could bear his weight.

'How charming of you to call!' he said as he held out his hand. 'What a rare pleasure!'

I was forced to repress a shudder of repulsion at contact with his cold flesh. He must have been sixty years of age but, with his ghastly face and his dyed hair, he looked like a galvanized centenarian.

'Do I find you well?' he enquired urbanely, as though we had met only yesterday and I had taken it into my head to stroll around the corner and pay him a brief visit. 'I gather from Signor Feste that you got yourself into a bit of a muddle out in Alexandria.'

'There were some problems,' I confessed. 'Were you unhappy with my work?'

'Unhappy – I, Jacques? I hardly knew about your work. I paid as little attention to it as possible. However, the problems are over now, aren't they? All over and done with?' He lit a cigarette and stationed himself in front of me with an ironic smile: 'I expect you're glad to be home. You must have missed your old friends.'

'I am not glad to be home, sir, but I did miss my friends.'

'Good, good.' Sir Rodney affected his customary vagueness.

'Is – is Lady Magenta at home, Sir Rodney?'

'Ah! – speaking of friends. She'll be delighted to see you, of course, but she's not well, poor thing.' He wagged a warning finger at me. 'Garth-Thompson tells us we must be gentle with her. She's a little weak these days, but as pretty as ever. I keep telling her that her upholstery hasn't sagged.'

'Is she at home, Sir Rodney?'

He ignored my question and, extinguishing his cigarette, looked me straight in the eye.

'She has tuberculosis, you know.'

'Ah. I – I somehow suspected that. It's – it's very sad.'

Sir Rodney nodded his head wisely: 'Yes, I know: a tragedy, unutterable. Especially with all the other dead piling up in the plague cart: Zabel and Dinmont, Mr Bellowes and the dear old baroness.' For a moment Sir Rodney gleamed with pride at having seen his old lover into the grave.

I looked at the carpet. 'Is Lady Magenta very seriously ill?'

Sir Rodney's voice came at me with the same jolly cruelty as the lights in the brilliant room. 'Oh, it's bad enough, Monsieur Jacques. Fairly serious. She's had it for a long time, of course. Never told anybody – typical of her self-sacrificing nature. Rather admirable desire not to be a burden and a worry – all that sort of thing. Still, she's got a year or so if she's careful,' he finished brightly.

'A *year*?'

'Mm: tragic, isn't it?'

'May I – may I see her?'

He raised his arms theatrically: 'So sorry, Monsieur Jacques. She's not here at the moment. Went off to Bethnal Green this afternoon.'

'She's at the studio?'

'Yes. Busy with her whatnots: her photographs, her chemicals and so on. Claims to be happy. Inexplicable woman!' As Sir Rodney spoke he toyed with a ring on one of the fingers of his left hand and put on an expression of disinterested concern. 'We don't think the studio is good for her, Monsieur Jacques. It's a strain, really, don't you think? She should take more rest and learn to be still. She easily becomes obsessive and hysterical; it's most distressing.' He waved an admonitory finger under my nose. 'You should warn her about it, you know. Tell her not to go to Bethnal Green – she'll accept a bit of brotherly advice from you.'

Sir Rodney took me by the arm and began to lead me towards the fire. For a moment, almost angrily, I resisted him:

'Sir Rodney: why did you demolish Regis Street?'

He looked down at me with surprised amusement. 'Regis Street? Can't quite place it.'

'In Canonbury.'

'Ah, that little alley!' He laughed out loud. 'You'll never be a business-man, Jacques. I sold it to the railway. The land, you see, was more valuable as track since the rents had always been pitiful as well as irregular.'

I was about to speak when Sir Rodney indicated the Japanese screen, from which protruded a besuited and cufflinked wrist and a hand which clasped a large cigar. 'Signor Feste and I have been reduced, in Lady Magenta's absence, to gambling on rubbers of whist.'

Throughout our conversation, sporadic sounds of merriment had been heard. With Sir Rodney's last comment, these muffled giggles broke for the first time into full-throated laughter. The hand which held the cigar seemed to have been overcome with mirth: it jerked and twitched

317

convulsively. Sir Rodney and I looked towards the concealed source of this disturbance, he with indulgence and I with increasing unease. My interlocutor turned once again towards me:

'At any rate, my dear Jacques, if it is only whist tonight then who knows what pleasures await us on the morrow? I think you will agree that we must have our fasts in order to make our feasts the more enjoyable.'

A howl of uncontrolled laughter came from behind the screen. Sir Rodney seemed suddenly irritated with himself and began to apologize: 'But Good Lord, I play the host damnably! You haven't been introduced to Signor Feste have you, Monsieur Jacques?'

He led me behind the screen, where a table stood before the fire laden with money, cards, glasses of spirits and half-consumed food. The small hand tossed its cigar into the flames and, seizing the arm of its chair, raised its owner to his feet.

Standing before me with the same diminutive stature and an undiminished fever of energy, monocled and dressed to the nines, my correspondent of the past three years greeted me in the shape of Luigi Pesto. Doubled up with laughter, he flung himself on me with delight, clutched and kissed me.

'Mr Jack!' he chortled as he pinched my cheeks. 'I knew we would be reunited!' As tears of laughter began to course down his cheeks, he dug me violently in the ribs: 'Haven't I given you a shock? I've been waiting three years for this moment! No – longer! I've been waiting ever since I left two golden guineas in the eye sockets and chuckled to think of your face when you found out!'

Sir Rodney Rouncewell stood to one side, looking on with amused approval at the meeting he had just staged.

I awoke the next morning in a small guest bedroom to the unpleasant sensation of a refreshed Pesto, cigar already ignited, positively bouncing on my bed and grinning with delight.

'Well, you old astute thing, you! What a life you've been leading! My, you are the calculating one. Mixing with the nobs. Putting yourself in the way of a pile – oh, such a pile! – a golden pot of money.'

As Pesto chattered in his rapid, disconnected way, I observed him from beneath my covers. His hair was grey now and one side of his face was badly scarred, presumably from the fire which Aramind had started in his caravan. Strangely, his scorched features operated as expressively as do the lines more usually etched by character and the accumulations of time.

I attempted to sit up in bed but a sinewy arm held me down and, at the end of it, Pesto's cicatrized face twisted into a dozen shapes a second. 'Just a moment, Mr Jack. I've a few bones to pick with you.' He held a single finger in front of my nose. 'Number one: where's that horse suit of mine which you purloined? It was worth a bob or two.'

'I –'

'Don't be nervous, old fellow. Feste's not angry; it's just that Pesto wants his money.'

'I gave the horse suit to Lady Magenta,' I managed to bring out at last. 'She wanted to use it in the studio.'

He puffed at his cigar for a moment. 'Oh, so she's got it has she? It doesn't surprise me. Sir Rodney told me that you two were as thick as thieves. She'll give a decent price, I don't doubt.'

'No!' I exclaimed. 'I'll pay. How much do you want?'

He looked at me appraisingly: 'Twenty-five quid?'

'Ridiculous! I'll give you ten –' Pesto shook his head furiously '– Twelve pounds ten?'

Pesto put his head on one side and considered my offer. 'Half a pony? That's very apt. Call it done – I don't bear grudges. Where's your money?'

'There,' I pointed, 'on the dressing-table.'

Pesto hopped across the room and extracted the coins from my purse. I was attempting to reach for my trousers when, before I knew it, Pesto leapt onto the bed and knelt on my legs. 'Not so quickly, Mr Jack! Number two: where's the money for that girasol ring you stole from me?'

'Ring? What do you mean?'

'You know perfectly well what I mean! Hagsproat gave it to you and you gave it to Aramind and Aramind gave it to me. Then you stole it back, you greedy thing!'

It was a difficult moment and I did not know what to say.

'Cat got his tongue? Given it away, has he? Given it to a loved one?'

Pesto was horribly perceptive. Next moment, however, he was laughing with glee and rocking from one side of the bed to the other:

'Mr Jack doesn't know he's already paid! Mr Jack never thought about the hundred and forty quid he sent me when I made up that error in the insurance premiums!'

'But you said it was worth seventy!' I objected, recalling our conversation about the opal ring ten years previously in the circus meadow.

'Seventy, eh?' he glared at me. 'That was a long, long time ago. Price of opal has doubled since then.'

I watched him light another cigar and puff a plume of smoke into the air. Despite his injuries, it was impossible to believe that anything could kill him. He seemed invulnerable; he had too much life.

'Come now, Mr Jack, don't be so solemn. Let's have a nice little chat. Tell me about the paperweight.'

'I beg your pardon?'

319

'Oh, don't disappoint me! I planned it all so carefully.'

'Planned – what?' I never suspected the blow that was about to fall.

'Croop's paperweight in Mehmet Ali's room, of course. Don't you remember? It was made of glass and had a roundabout spinning inside. There were tiny horses on poles and painted children on their backs. It was very pretty: Croop threw it at me once.'

'Croop's paperweight – *where*?'

'In Mehmet Ali's room the night they drugged you! Don't tell me you didn't notice it – I asked them to make sure. It was such a nice touch, I thought. Subtle.'

'Paperweight? I –'

He pounded my pillow in his irritation. 'Confound it! I spend all that time setting a trap and then you're too stupid to notice!'

'You mean –?'

He fixed me with his fearsome merriment. 'Exactly, Mr Jack. That is exactly what I mean.'

As it had done once before, the room seemed to expand and contract as if the walls were made only of the finest fabrics. Pesto's grossly distorted face loomed into view and I felt like an anaesthetized patient watching a surgeon at work.

'But why?' I whispered inanely, 'why?'

Pesto stubbed his cigar out on the floor. 'Oh really, Mr Jack, you disappoint me! A failure of acuity, most definitely.' He put his face up to mine and I, a man of thirty-five, felt all the terror I had at fifteen. 'You and Aramind,' he hissed. 'It was a nasty trick to play. You spoilt my lovely face.' He gingerly touched his ear and cheek as though his injury still troubled him. 'An eye for an eye, Spellman, a scar for a scar. It was tit for tat: all's fair in love and war.'

'Me?' I felt like shrieking but my voice was very faint. 'It wasn't me!'

He pouted and stuck out his tongue. 'Don't believe you. You're fibbing!'

'It's true!'

'It's a lie! I know about you and the ladies. You took my sweet pure Aramind behind the joiner's shed and fucked her in the dark. And then you tried to burn me up.'

'Me? – no!'

'Don't deny it, Mr Jack! Fibbing's a sin. I know your lecherous habits. Sir Rodney's told me all about you and Lady Magenta.'

'What has he told you?'

Pesto's mood suddenly changed; he patted my hand in an attempt to placate me. 'Now then, Mr Jack, you're not going to be ill-tempered are you? I can understand your passion, you poor, love-lorn thing. Yes, she's a fine, full woman – though she's forty. She's as pretty as one of Joey Grimaldi's Dartford Blue butterflies and I wish I could pin a few like her. I'm sorry you lost your chance, my lad. We can console each other.'

'What are you insinuating?'

He put a finger to his lips. 'Quietly now, Mr Jack. I'm not getting at you. You're a nice enough young man – I wish I had your looks – but Sir Rodney, now he's a real old goat.'

'What are you talking about?' I almost shouted at Pesto in my impatience for knowledge.

He answered me with equanimity. 'Haven't you heard about her imminent marriage? Surely somebody must have told you?'

'No – I – I knew nothing.'

'Oh dear me,' sighed Pesto regretfully. 'I seem to have put my foot in it. Don't be down-hearted. Yes, Sir Rodney and Lady Magenta have been engaged for ten months. The wedding is at the end of October.'

I stared at the ceiling, imagining how Pesto had enjoyed the prospect of telling me this piece of news. He knew me intuitively, from the inside out. His gaze lanced my tenderness; his leers brought into the open the things I wanted to hide.

Pesto watched me for a while out of the corner of his eye. 'Lovely name, Magenta,' he said at last with studied carelessness. 'It's my home town, you know. They make silk and matches. My mother is buried in an ossuary there.'

With relief, I saw that he had got up to go. Before he left the room he shot his final bolt:

'Know how I knew, Mr Jack?'

'Knew what?'

'I smelt a Spellman before I ever joined Siriso, you know. I smelt you close by, burrowing away, digging for gold. That's my instinct, of course. But when Sir Rodney introduced me to Lady Magenta, I was sure at last. Guess how!'

'I don't know. How?' I looked up and saw that Pesto was licking his lips as he peeped around the door.

'I took her lovely pale hand,' he said, 'I looked down at it and there was an ember burning on her finger. And then I said to myself: "Luigi Pesto – Giovanni Feste, whatever you call yourself – stick tight and you'll have your old friend back again!" '

23

Behind the Screen

L ATER THAT day (I made good my escape from Hampstead as soon as possible) I found Lady Magenta asleep beneath the skylight in the studio at Bethnal Green. As usual, the windows had been opened to allow the fumes of chemicals to escape; she had been forced to employ the pantomime horse as a blanket against the cold.

It shocked me beyond measure to discover that she was of the belief – as was Dr Garth-Thompson – that she had not long to live, so hard had I tried that morning to persuade myself that Sir Rodney had exaggerated the gravity of her condition for his own purposes. As she sat up in the camp bed to drink the coffee I had made her, she looked scarcely thirty years of age. Her eyes were very bright.

'But you look so well,' I said, unable to believe the death sentence she had just passed on herself.

'Don't let it mislead you,' she replied quietly. Dr Garth-Thompson had told her that a healthy complexion (pale, but lifted by areas of colour) was frequently met with in tubercular cases.

We had been talking for about ten minutes when, getting up, she crossed the room to a small bookcase which stood in a corner. 'You must see this, you must see this,' she muttered as she attempted to extract a large volume from one of the lower shelves.

'Let me help you,' I said quickly, noticing that she barely had the strength to lift it. She refused my assistance.

'Close your eyes,' she commanded. 'It's a surprise.' I obeyed and she pressed the opened book into my hands: 'You can look now.'

I found myself gazing down on the frontispiece to the first copy of *Photographic Impressions of the Circus and the City*, where I saw myself riding a wooden horse on a steam roundabout. I did not tell Lady Magenta that, in August 1897, at the Selima Oasis in the Sudan, I had bought a copy of this work from a dealer in erotica.

Over the next few days we talked, Lady Magenta and I, of her marriage. I did not attempt to dissuade her; nor did I tell her of my own experiences at the hands of Sir Rodney – the patrimony seized, the misleading date given to Mr Nopheles, the demolition of 14 Regis Street. I did not want her to think that I was acting purely in my own interests. Besides – it would have made no difference. A part of Lady Magenta was desperately struggling against something that frightened and even disgusted her, but another part of her – a stronger part, a part that I would never know – seemed to long for pain and humiliation.

She conceded that she did not love Sir Rodney and that she doubted his love for her. She said that he was neither good nor sympathetic. Yes, there was a streak of cruelty in him. Yes, he had taken delight in our photographs of misery. Yes, he loved power and, yes, he used it without compunction for his own ends.

It was clear that she was held by some other logic. I remembered how Sir Rodney had once stroked the inside of her thigh whilst she leant against his chair like a hypnotized animal. Did this form a part of her reasoning? I hesitated to ask so blunt a question and tried to put it a different way. I began to reminisce. I reminded her of our night walk through London all those years ago and of the desperate questions she had asked as we stood on Southwark Bridge. 'You were concerned, I remember, about the limited possibilities of change.'

'Yes,' she agreed. 'But even then I was losing hope. I thought that change could come only as a miracle.'

'And you do not, any longer, believe in that?'

She toyed with a cushion. 'I do not believe in miracles.'

The more resigned she seemed, the more I tried to struggle for her. A great weight oppressed me and I almost felt that the peeping children who played along the interminable corridors and echoing stairways were demons who had some hold on my friend. They resisted me, these imps, with all the force of their hundred piping voices. On the top floor of the creaking, windswept house it seemed that afternoon as if I was fighting for a human soul.

'You used to hate the way society was organized. You wanted to tear it down and start again.'

'Did I?' she smiled wanly. 'I suppose I still do. But I have so little energy these days and – and it seems to me now that to hate the city is to pretend to be free of it.'

'Why? I don't understand.'

The corners of her mouth had turned downwards with self-disgust. 'I was rich. I was independent. Once upon a time I could afford to hate the city.'

'You still can,' I protested.

'No. I don't want to be free of it, like a philanthropist or a doctor. I don't want to look down on the city as if it were a – a formicary.'

She spoke thoughtfully, but it was as if she had been mesmerized. 'The city is only things, Lady Magenta,' I said gently, 'only dead things.'

'I want them,' she returned with decision. 'I want them to run through me; I want them to seize my absurd virginity; I want – I don't know –'

'You want –?'

'Oh, something: I don't know.' She lapsed into vagueness, picked up a jar of iodine crystals and gazed into their violet depths.

'Something?' I probed. She turned the stopper in the little bottle. It made a faint grating noise. 'Somebody else?'

She looked up sharply:

'Other than who?'

'Than – me, for example.'

She looked at me long and hard. 'I don't want you, if that's what you mean.'

My heart was beating very quickly and my throat was tight.

'Perhaps,' she continued, 'perhaps before you went to Egypt. For a while there was the ghost of a chance, but I woke up one morning soon after you left and the ghost had vanished.'

'I –'

'Jack,' she interrupted, making an attempt at a smile, 'you are a nice man.'

I had never, I think, felt so insulted. Suddenly I knew that everything I had become could only separate me from Lady Magenta. Tenderness would have been a failure and an evasion for her. My desire made everything impossible and absurd and I almost laughed at myself for my dreams.

'Nice?' I said at last. 'Is that all?'

She shrugged. 'Of course not. There are other things.'

'But they are not enough, those things?'

Once again I brought down on myself the fixity of her gaze and the clarity of her rejection. 'No. They are not enough. You are not enough.'

'Never?'

'I thought you were once, but I made a mistake. And you never will be. But I love you.'

She looked at me sadly and I saw her through a thin veil of tears. Our whole relation over the past decade hung palpably before us and, before I spoke, I knew that I was taking my last chance. 'Leave the city to its own devices,' I said. 'Forget all the lines that progress has foisted upon us. Forget the history of warehouses. It would be like crossing a great desert in a train. We could stand at the window and watch the world whirled past us. Great monuments and ruins would appear in front of us and then fall back in the distance. We could follow a pathless path.' There was a long pause, during which I almost thought that I had offered her the only temptation that would succeed.

'You are speaking of the circus,' said Lady Magenta at last, placing the bottle of iodine crystals on the floor. 'Yet you yourself said years ago that the circus was only costumes, nothing else. In the end we must stop being children and admit that the circus is the city.'

The words to finish hers – 'and more besides' – floated into my mind but I could not utter them, although I wanted desperately to believe them. As the evening came down, it seemed to me as if a juggler somewhere had made a final slip. The audience began to laugh; the coloured balls rolled away into corners and stopped moving. I had lost and the world was that much smaller: it had shrunk, in fact, to the cramped space of a cluttered attic.

'You mean that you believed me, all those years ago, on the bridge?'

Lady Magenta seemed surprised. 'Of course I did. It was true.'

I was baffled. I had never known anything: how could my doubts have been her certainties?

'What do you want?' I asked again.

She shrugged.

'What *is* it?' I was almost violent; I forced her to look me in the face; I took her chin in my hand and forced her. 'Are you seduced by death?' I shouted. 'Do you want it to violate you with its bitter force?'

She would not reply.

Two weeks later, Sir Rodney and Lady Magenta invited me to a celebration which was intended to mark the beginning of the last month of their engagement. I arrived at the Baroness Hrocka's old residence unconscionably early. An appointment had fallen through in town and, instead of returning to my lodgings, I decided to drive over to Hampstead and await the commencement of the festivities.

On the doorstep, the baroness's maid told me that nobody was at home. 'I was rather afraid of that,' I said. 'May I wait for them?'

She showed me into the drawing-room at the back of the house. The lamps and candelabra which had dazzled me on my previous visit were now gone; much of the Japanese furniture had been removed and the room seemed as stark as a dance-hall although here and there, as if to relieve the austerity, stood vases of dried flowers. To one side, an odd variety of garments hung from hat stands: a dark cloak, a length of silk and several shimmering gauzes. A bronze helmet in the fashion of Greek antiquity had been placed on a table. In the centre of the room was an

325

enormous pile of cushions covered in black bombazine. In a corner, an Eastman roll-film camera of the most recent design was mounted on a tripod. The curtains had been parted to admit as much light as possible. I stood at the window and noticed that the trees in the garden were beginning to shed their leaves; only the laurels were as green as ever. Turning away, I realized that the maid was still waiting in the centre of the room.

'Tell me about Egypt, sir,' she said imploringly. 'Was it very romantic?'

I must have looked as if I did not understand.

'I have only read about it in books,' the maid continued, 'but you have seen it for yourself. It must have been wonderful.'

'Wonderful? Not really.'

My companion was not to be discouraged. 'Did you go out into the desert, sir?'

'Yes, a couple of times.'

'Did you meet the tribesmen with their robes and moustaches?'

'Yes, I did.' I resisted the impulse to say what Egypt was really like, to tell her that all places were much the same. I was not cruel enough.

The maid took a step towards me and across her face I saw the gaping need for dreams of the exotic. 'What were the markets like?' she asked. 'Were there piles of strange fruits all in different colours?'

'Yes, Martha,' I said, trying to infuse my voice with conviction. 'There were stalls where traders sold many different perfumes and there were other places where you could buy song-birds in cages. Near the Pyramids (I slept one night between the paws of the Great Sphinx) sounds carry for mile upon mile in the inky dark.'

'Oh, sir,' she breathed. 'It sounds just like a story.'

Before she left the room, I had a sudden impulse to stop her. 'Martha?'

'Sir?'

'Do you listen outside the doors? Once or twice – I can't be sure – I thought you were at the keyhole.'

She stared shamefacedly at her shoes. 'Yes, sir,' she admitted after a long pause. She looked up at me with her bright face: 'I can't help it. I love to hear the gentlemen and ladies talk.'

I sat down to wait in a chair behind the Japanese screen. I was grateful for the fire, since the afternoon was chilly. But I must have become too comfortable and fallen asleep, for I woke to the sound of voices in the room. I had started to get up in order to announce myself when I was restrained by a sudden realization that the occupants of the room, presumably unaware of my presence, were talking about me.

'What did you start to say about Jack Spellman?' asked Lady Magenta's voice. 'I didn't understand what you meant.'

Her question was met with a laugh which I immediately recognized as Sir Rodney's. 'I said, Lady Magenta, that we are hot-house flowers, bred with care in the dark. Mr Feste, if he will forgive me' – there was a murmur of assent from the ingratiating clown – 'is the proverbial Bradford millionaire: a bark, no doubt, of baser kind but as plain and forthright as a dandelion. I mean no offence, Mr Feste: you are an honourable plant. And unlike us, you are an adaptable one. Mr Spellman, on the other hand, is a somewhat repellent mixture: brute horseflesh, I think, with the most delicately piquant of sauces.'

'Why do you say that?' asked Lady Magenta.

'Because he has cultivated himself and tried to erase all trace of his birth. He is a mimic, you see, and now performs the part of a gentleman with ease. My only reservation is that we gave him his chance; perhaps it would have been better to keep him in the cellar where he belongs.'

This was an unfortunate situation and I felt extremely uncomfortable. Although Sir Rodney and I cordially disliked each other I had no wish to bring our mutual antipathy into the open. Strangely enough, I was not afraid of being discovered; behind the Japanese screen I felt inviolate and invisible.

Turning my head to pick up the quieter tones of the softly protesting Lady Magenta, I discovered, a foot in front of my face, a small aperture in the surface of the screen. The figured design represented a jungle which was being stalked by a tiger. Somebody had neatly cut out the eye of the tiger to make a tiny peep-hole. I bent carefully towards it and found myself looking into the room. The hat stands were empty now; arrayed in the finest fabrics, Lady Magenta stood by the door. Facing her across the pile of cushions, Sir Rodney had put on his cloak and was even now adjusting a strap on his Grecian helmet. Pesto convulsed and silently cavorted in the space between the sideboard and the camera.

Sir Rodney burst into laughter. 'Come now, Lady Magenta! As good as any of us? You are not serious – you, a Tramont, with Langley and Mowbray and Percy running in your veins! Your blood is the distillation of centuries. His? Half of London pissed into a pot to impregnate his dam!'

Lady Magenta fell silent. After a minute, she raised her head and turned to Pesto:

'Mr Feste: do you have the pomegranates we purchased?'

Pesto conjured these items, to Sir Rodney's delight, from beneath his clothing and juggled with them for a few seconds. Then he went to the sideboard, where he halved the fruits with a long knife and carefully arranged them on a large white plate.

There was a pause during which they all exchanged glances. At last Sir Rodney spoke:

'In the absence of Mr Spellman, perhaps you could play Ascalaphus with a camera, Mr Feste.'

Giggling softly, Pesto retreated behind the camera. I began to feel as though I were watching a back-stage rehearsal from the front of the house through the hole in the theatrical curtain.

Sir Rodney whirled around Lady Magenta like a great black swan. She seemed demure, ashamed, frightened. He offered her flowers; he touched her hair; he knelt before her and looked up into her face. At length, resorting to force, he pulled her down upon the cushions. As she turned her head away from him, he took her throat, her chin with his hand and forced her lips to his.

Each of these actions contained a frozen pause during which the mechanical click of the camera could be heard. The whole thing was like a game of charades in which it was my duty to guess at the word represented by the tableaux before me.

In the light of late afternoon, Sir Rodney dragged a claw-like hand from Lady Magenta's throat to her hip. Her delicate wraps snagged and puckered under his touch, gathered themselves into his grasp. Her skin was beautifully, radiantly white, almost waxen in its smooth sheen.

I was rooted to my chair, fascinated beyond the possibility of intervention. All that took place now was accompanied by the drum-beat of a pulse that raced with anger, desire and tenderness, with a horrible sense of loss and of all life's impossibility. The room seemed to have been filled with water, through which everything took place in slow-motion. The pomegranates shone on the white plate, where a ray of the setting sun picked them out.

The click of a camera.

Sir Rodney kneaded Lady Magenta's nipples with his gaunt blue fingers. Mid-way between her breasts and her navel, two smaller supernumerary nipples seemed also aroused by his chafing.

The camera's click.

Across the surface of Lady Magenta's face, like the shadows cast by clouds, played hints of many expressions. There was pain and disgust and humiliation but also a mounting ecstasy, a yielding pleasure and, behind it all, indifference.

Click.

Sir Rodney slowly pulled aside the final piece of gauze to reveal Lady Magenta's softly shaded veneric mound. I glanced at Pesto as the camera clicked again. Upon his face was a mask-like leer; he was licking his lips.

Sir Rodney did not remove his cloak; it lay across the united bodies of himself and Lady Magenta like a bed sheet. Her legs loosened to his urgency. She no longer seemed to have any will or muscular force. I could not see Sir Rodney's face. His movements had a sinuous grace, but despite this, Lady Magenta did not embrace him: she allowed him. He did not make love: he perpetrated it.

Lady Magenta's breathing came faster and sounded increasingly tortured. A few seconds after her final, soft exhalation, Sir Rodney penetrated her once more with several savage thrusts of undisguised contempt. She screamed with pain.

Sir Rodney began to chuckle and, raising himself from the makeshift bed, stood above her and watched with interest the darkly emergent blood of her ruptured hymen and his own white ink.

Lady Magenta lay helplessly stretched out, subjected to the gaze of six complicit eyes. She began to cough. Sir Rodney crouched near her face. 'There is your utmost intensity of verity, Lady Magenta. Blood to blood, aristocrat to aristocrat: all within the family to which – despite yourself – you belong. Anything, your ladyship, in the service of your art; there is no disgrace I should not perform.'

Still laughing, Sir Rodney turned to leave the room and, like a falling blow, I saw that his half-erect penis was complemented by a birthmark which, in extent and character, precisely paralleled my own. Sir Rodney was shortly followed by Pesto, who could not restrain a last salacious glance at the barely conscious Lady Magenta.

I crossed the room, knelt at her side, held her hand. She did not seem aware of me and, within a few moments, began to cough bright arterial blood from her mouth. I fixed my eyes upon the plate, where the rosy pomegranates looked like vulgar painted toys. And I felt like a beast, for running even now down my leg was my own useless seed.

I rang the bell for the maid, squeezed Lady Magenta's hand and escaped through the French windows into the garden.

24

Consumption

L OVE, Mr Secretary.
If it is the duty of the memoirist to survey all the multifarious movements of a single heart then I should suffer the penalties of failure.

I –

Perhaps I have inadvertently hidden things from you. It was not my task, I thought. I did not need to speak of everything. I had only to follow the logic and the magic of things, to describe in the minutest detail what happened when my skin brushed against the inert surfaces of the world. To live, it seemed to me, was to stagger ridiculously on some peculiar frontier between the circus and the city. To write was to commemorate this lurching life in which, bewildered, I turned my head this way and that to watch the traffic crossing the border.

Desire?

I had not concealed that, for desire has the same logic as this ceaseless commerce and even occasionally includes the transient fulfilment of a concluded transaction.

Magic?

This was here too, for magic consists in believing that desire is love and that what you want to be, quite simply, *is*.

But love? 'Love' itself?

I believed that it existed – elsewhere. When I fled from the Baroness Hrocka's garden that evening, when I lowered myself from the wall and, panting, gained the street, I was aware only of the criminality of my desires. The violence of the game of charades had disgusted me; everything disgusted me. I disgusted myself because I had been so profoundly aroused. When I passed a policeman on his evening beat, I was tempted to give myself up. Instead, as usual, I said nothing. I went onto the Heath and walked for hours in circles. I called up once again the images my mind had just photographed and I knew that they would never fade. I could only hope that with time I would become accustomed to my own insistent ache.

When I returned to my lodgings late that night, it was as if I had become aware of a new organ in my body. My need for love was a fiercely protesting stomach, a searing gut. I felt that I was possessed by something that was not me, that I had been colonized by a hollow space.

Me? I was only clothing. Half an inch beneath the skin there was nothing. If I turned my eyes inward, I could almost see the inner vault of myself.

In the dusty corner of an enormous warehouse, the lover is imprisoned in a sealed crate. The lover beats against the walls, shouts, weeps, attempts to peer out through the chinks between the planks. But we do not hear the lover; we pass by. Only the most observant amongst us will notice that the crate rocks slightly from side to side.

Perhaps too late but with surprise and some pleasure I find that I can speak of these things without excessive difficulty.

The words –

They are efficient enough detectives. It is not their fault that the crime was committed outside their jurisdiction, that they have no warrant to search the speechless house of the lover.

The writer, of course, wants to believe that the song of Orpheus can bring Eurydice back from the ghostlands, that his incantations can make her pallid face flush once more with life. He hopes that his words are not bound by everyday laws and that they will not fade away like the shadows cast by clouds. But then there is always a lover who turns round in the urgency of his passion and on the threshold, with a wail, the object of his feelings is sucked back into the dark.

Is love light? If so, this autobiography was composed in the underworld. I tried all the techniques that were known to me but despite the sensitivity of my paper I found no trace of love. I could not capture the passage of a single ray.

I returned to the Baroness Hrocka's former residence early the next morning. Brushing against the laurels along the pathway, I pressed the door bell with great impatience. After some time, Tom (the baroness's old serving-boy and the hero of the encounter with the Italian organ-grinder) poked his head around the corner and beckoned to me. I followed him down a passageway which stretched along one side of the house and in a few seconds we reached the scullery door.

Tom squatted on the step and whistled as he began to polish a pair of shoes. I could see the steam of his breath. Bundles of kindling were piled neatly against the wall; a cat was attempting to drink from a frozen saucer of milk.

'How are you, Tom? Keeping well?'

'Not so good, Mr Spellman. I'll be moving on soon.'

Shivering in the morning cold, I was unsure of his meaning. 'Shall I – shall we – go inside?'

Tom put Lady Magenta's shoes on the ground and stood up. 'Of course, Mr Spellman. You're not busy: you must be cold.'

Along one wall of the scullery, I noticed a line of bells. In a corner, several buckets had been stacked one inside the other. Ewers, stoups and urns gleamed dully from their hooks.

'You said you were moving on, Tom?'

'That's right, Mr Spellman. It hasn't been the same since the baroness died. There's no visitors: it's so still. And I want to be in a warm house where people are living. I want to run after the maids and tickle them in corners.'

I traced the edge of a floor tile with the point of my stick. 'What about Martha? Won't she let you "tickle" her?'

I began to move away but before I left the scullery I caught Tom's quick scowl. 'Martha! She's as old as you are, Mr Spellman.'

As I dragged my hand along the surface of a stone table my laughter echoed in the chilly kitchen. I wandered into the deserted hall and looked about me. Where was everybody? Slowly I began to climb the stairs. I was met on the first landing by Martha. She had an odd expression on her face. 'What's happening, Martha? Is everything all right?'

Her frown deepened accusingly. 'She's very bad sir – since yesterday. It was too much for her.'

I instinctively grasped the handrail of the stair. 'Have you called a doctor?'

She glanced at the door to Lady Magenta's room. 'Dr Garth-Thompson is with her now.'

I hurriedly brushed past Martha and knocked at the door. A nurse in a starched white apron showed me into the room. The curtains were drawn; a lamp burned on the bedside table. Lady Magenta's face was pale against the sheets. She was so thin that I could barely trace her outline beneath the counterpane. Dr Garth-Thompson sat at the head of the bed. He was plumper than I remembered and he no longer sported his pitiful moustache. He had rolled up one of his sleeves and was in the process of administering a direct blood transfusion. The nurse handed him an implement from a sterilized tray. He bent forward, opened a valve in the pipe which led from his arm and allowed his blood to pass into a collecting vessel. I took a step towards him and he looked up at me:

'She's not in pain, Spellman: I've given her morphine.'

I stood at the bedside and surveyed the scene with rising panic. The nurse released another valve and Dr Garth-Thompson's blood began to flow into Lady Magenta's extended arm.

'Is – is she going to die?'

The doctor shook his head. 'I don't think so, not yet. I have succeeded in staunching the vaginal haemorrhage which began yesterday evening.'

'*Haemorrhage?*'

Dr Garth-Thompson shrugged. 'It happens: sometimes a hymen is more than usually resilient.' He removed the syringe from his arm and dabbed at himself with a piece of lint. 'The pulmonary haemorrhage, however, was more serious. Much more serious.'

I waited at the window whilst the doctor tidied away his equipment. Peering through the curtains, I noticed that frost still remained in the shadow cast by the house. In the distance a church spire gleamed above the mist.

'Lady Magenta possesses only a small area of healthy tissue in one lung,' commented Dr Garth-Thompson a few minutes later as we stood outside in the corridor.

'And the rest?'

'Beyond recovery.' He answered me curtly but I could see that he was worried. 'There is only the slightest of chances that she will survive the winter.'

I gripped the handle of my cane very tightly. 'Couldn't we move her? Take her abroad?'

The doctor laughed as he left. 'It's too late for that – far too late. It would kill her.'

I sat outside Lady Magenta's bedroom door all day. In the evening the nurse emerged to fetch some dressings. I detained her and with difficulty extracted the news that Lady Magenta had awoken. Showing great reluctance, the nurse allowed me into the sickroom. I was to stay only for a minute; talk should be kept to an absolute minimum.

I quietly sat down next to Lady Magenta's bed. She smiled and indicated that I should lean towards her. Her eyes seemed darker than ever before.

'Don't blame Sir Rodney,' she said faintly. 'It was my fault.'

I looked at her with disbelief. How could she mean this? Why was she mesmerized by the violent force of another life?

Sir Rodney and Lady Magenta were married a month later, on 21 October 1899, in her room at the house in Hampstead. With the constant attention of Dr Garth-Thompson, Lady Magenta's health had greatly improved but although she was out of immediate danger she was still confined to her bed.

There were three other wedding guests beside the doctor and myself:

Luigi Pesto, Sir Stafford Singleton and Mr W.H. Perkin. Pesto stared at me fiercely when the priest took his position at the foot of the bed and began to read the service. The vows were made and the rings were exchanged. I felt numb, inert. There was an inevitability to events now; each repetition came with added force and I felt as if I was being pulled down a slope by the dead hand of the past. I myself was only a recapitulation of another, earlier man.

After the ceremony we all gathered in the hall. The priest removed his cassock and placed it in a small hand bag. At the door, Sir Rodney helped him into his overcoat.

'You bore yourself well, Sir Rodney,' said the priest. 'Only the strongest love can assert itself in the face of death.'

Sir Rodney smiled beautifully down at the old man. 'Her youth and her physical charms, sir, are such that I thought it only right to seize her, to retain her in life. More than any other, her death would truly be the canker to the rose.'

The priest nodded wisely and went on his way.

A few days later, at the end of October, Sir Rodney left for Italy. He had, he informed us all, no wish to deprive himself of the suave pleasures of an autumn honeymoon. Nothing, he thought, could be worse for his own health – ravaged as it was – than to remain as an attendant upon sickness. Lady Magenta regretted his decision, without a doubt, but she would patiently await his return. What a beautiful woman she was! Why should he watch her grow ugly?

Sir Rodney left instructions to contact him if his wife's condition became grave. In the meantime, he was to travel with Pesto to a point approximately mid-way between Novara and Milan in the Piedmont area. There, at Magenta, he would visit the commemorative ossuary and handle the urn which contained the remains of Luigi Pesto's mother, the witch who, one day in 1859, had chosen an inauspicious moment to gather herbs.

As soon as Sir Rodney had left England, Lady Magenta summoned up the remnants of her strength and began to make preparations to return to Bartholomew Square. She said that she disliked the silence of Hampstead. She did not want to die in a void but in the midst of life, as if she had fallen asleep during a conversation amongst friends. Dr Garth-Thompson ardently but unsuccessfully attempted to dissuade her. He refused to bear responsibility for the consequences. Lady Magenta replied that he had no need to: the decision was her own. Calling upon the services of Sir

Stafford Singleton, she arranged for the baroness's house to be put up for auction.

With much careful preparation, the move was eventually accomplished in a sealed and heated carriage. Lady Magenta was accompanied by Martha and the nurse. Tom had been dismissed with a month's wages. As Dr Garth-Thompson had predicted and in spite of all the precautions which had been taken, the brief journey completely prostrated Lady Magenta and brought on a further series of haemorrhages.

I called morning and evening at Bartholomew Square for several days. On each occasion the dour nurse turned me away. I learnt from Martha that Dr Garth-Thompson had been forced to administer another blood transfusion. On All Souls' Night, feeling dreadfully lonely, I sat up late in Lady Magenta's study. It was the room where I had first met her. I could still remember her coughing into her handkerchief on that occasion, could still see her taking a purse from the bureau to give me money.

I drank a glass of wine and, awaking from my reverie, found myself staring into a large mirror which stood against one wall. Then, as I had done ten years before in the charcoal-burner's cottage, I waited to see the ghosts in the mirror. But the glass remained blank and in the faint light of dawn it seemed to me that the ghosts were no longer over there. They were all around me now, closing fast around me.

On Guy Fawkes's Night, as boys collected pennies in the streets and effigies flared on every scrap of common land, I at last gained admittance to Lady Magenta's room. She was very calm and quiet but there was an expectancy in her resignation. One might almost have thought that she was waiting to give birth. When I touched her translucent hand she looked up at me and began to speak:

'I was too afraid. I was afraid of everything: of the world, of my sensations. I wanted to hold myself apart: to be free, to be certain.'

'You – didn't want to be corrupted,' I suggested hesitantly.

She nodded. 'Yes, I didn't want to be corrupted. How absurd.'

I frowned. 'Absurd? Why so?'

'Purity!' she exclaimed contemptuously. 'The very notion is hateful to me.'

'I – I don't know what you mean.'

'You do. Oh yes, you do!' Lady Magenta fell silent for a while. I found myself hoping that the nurse would not return to interrupt us.

'I only wanted you to be free,' I said.

'Then your desire sprang from your fear!' she answered angrily. 'You wanted me to be a dream, safe and clean as a dream.'

'I wanted you to be safe,' I conceded after a moment.

'But don't you *see*?' asked Lady Magenta with great intensity. 'Don't you see the lie in that?' She smoothed her blanket and relented a little: 'Perhaps you don't understand after all. You are incapable of anger.'

'But –' I protested, 'I swing this way and that like a pendulum!'

'Really?' It was plain that she did not believe me. 'Then why do you never say anything? What do you really think?'

I turned the lamp down and thought for a few moments. 'I don't know. I just feel stupid.'

Lady Magenta lay back on her pillows and began to speak in a distant voice. 'Corruption . . . resignation . . . submission. These things are better than a taxonomist's purity, an eccentric's freedom.'

It was my turn to be irritated. 'I don't understand you! Why do you lie down like this and turn your face to the wall? Why do you submit?'

There was a long pause. I went to the window and parted the curtains. Fireworks were exploding in the night. I realized suddenly that Lady Magenta was right: I had never been truly angry. All that I had ever known was a frozen fury.

Lady Magenta beckoned me back to her side. She had the coal-black eyes of a snowman. 'I tried very hard not to –'

'– Not to submit?'

'I tried to keep the illusions dancing, but they fell to the ground. I couldn't keep it up. I never knew –'

She began to cough. I held her up until the fit had passed and I suppose that I should then have called the nurse and left her alone. I could not help myself, however; I encouraged her to continue:

'Never knew what?'

'That there – there are stronger things than mere love.'

With the weight of my own emotion, I was naturally unable to imagine what these might be. 'What do you mean?'

Lady Magenta took her arm from beneath the covers and showed me her finger. 'I mean this,' she said. 'This is stronger than love.'

The opal ring glinted in the shadows.

A month later I was standing in the hot-house watching the gardener raking up the leaves outside. A small fire smouldered near the compost heap. In the red room it was still the height of summer. Dionysus basked amongst the orchids. On a table near the door into the scullery, a hundred hyacinth stems sprouted from clay pots. I did not hear the soft-footed nurse behind me until she spoke: 'Lady Magenta can see you now, sir.'

I followed the nurse upstairs and we passed Martha on one of the landings. She seemed to want to speak to me but I pretended to ignore her as I hurried along the corridor which led to the sick-room.

The thick but curiously chilly vapour of fumigatory pastilles met me as I crossed the threshold. 'You look like a picture,' I said to Lady Magenta in a weak attempt at jollity.

'In that case I was painted very thin,' she replied drily. 'The canvas shows through.'

I pretended to give her an appraising look: 'Oh, I don't know. The sponge, the varnish bottle: you're not beyond redemption.' I noticed a letter on her coverlet. 'Has Sir Rodney written to you?'

She stared at me. 'He has not.'

'Oh – I'm sorry. But I hope the letter has made you happy.'

She considered. 'It was interesting. It's the letter you sent me from Egypt.'

'Ah,' I breathed. 'I expect I was very miserable.'

Lady Magenta took the letter from the envelope and began to read it aloud:

'"At first there was the seamless sheath of perception. It was a profusion of vision. All things were there – all the dangers and delights. Later, everything became too complicated. Dust blew in from the desert and fragments of old statues accumulated in my rooms. In the end, more than anything, it seemed like a trifling dream which diverted me for a few seconds before I awoke and saw, simply, the bleakness of it all, the nudity of the surrounding artefacts."'

Lady Magenta allowed the letter to fall from her hand. 'The same things,' she said, 'always the same things, even though we change so utterly that our past selves are forgotten like half-read stories. All the parts of my life seem separate, like differently coloured fragments, like a broken plate.'

'Everything is jumbled up,' I said glumly.

'Day after day of bits and pieces,' she mused. 'I never settled to anything, you know. I suppose I deserve this. What do they call it, the scientists? "The survival of the fittest." I was not fit.'

I looked at her across the few feet which separated us. 'Who is?'

'Sir Rodney is,' she said with conviction. 'Sir Rodney will survive. He wants to live so much.'

'He gets what he wants. What about you?'

'Me?' She seemed surprised by my interest. 'I remember I said once that I wanted different parts of me to exist in different places.' It was as if Lady Magenta had swept the string of an instrument I had lost. Through an opened door, forgotten images came at me in a rush, like a wind. 'I wanted to be free of the body's organization.' She continued, 'What do we inherit, after all? Only a temporary collocation of moving parts.'

'And now?' I asked. 'What do you want now?'

'Now, I want only to be enslaved by matter; to be insensate; only to be dust which is washed away.'

A few days later Lady Magenta suffered a further and sudden relapse. She was forbidden to talk by Dr Garth-Thompson. Sir Stafford Singleton, who had been with her for several hours that morning, telegraphed Sir Rodney in Florence. I sat with Lady Magenta night and day. Neither the nurse nor Dr Garth-Thompson objected to my continual presence and for once I experienced the positive benefits of my own invisibility.

What did we do, Lady Magenta and I, during this time? We watched the room; we watched each other; we watched ourselves. It would be a mistake, I think, to say that the silence between us was set aside from language and that nothing broke through the surface. No: words are never thrown out, like a die, upon blank surfaces. Our wordlessness was richly figured, expressive, turbid with particles of memory –

Or so I hope. Twenty years later, I cannot tell. I want to say 'our' silence, 'our' words, 'our' memories. Yet I cannot be sure that we shared these things.

The grimly efficient nurse arose one day and put away her sewing. At the door she indicated that I should follow her and I imagined she wanted to tell me something in confidence. Instead, without uttering a word, she led me downstairs to the scullery and handed me a basket of laundry. Together, over the sink, we began to wash Lady Magenta's bloodstained garments. When the nurse returned to the sick room to give Lady Magenta her morphine injection, Martha and I hung the clothes to dry in an airing cupboard.

'Sir?' She was watching me intently.

'Not now, Martha.'

Later, in the silent hours when the house slept, I opened the cupboard door with a palpitating heart. I began to run my fingers over Lady Magenta's fabrics. I held them to my face. I wrapped her thin-spun silk night-dress about me like a scarf and, turning, noticed that Martha was watching me from the shadows. All my old shame returned, and I averted my face.

'Sir?'

I could not speak for several moments.

'Sir?'

'What – what is it, Martha?'

'Can I talk to you, sir?'

'What do you want?'

She took a step towards me. 'Keep me, sir,' she said in a pleading voice. 'When her ladyship dies I have nowhere to go. I can cook for you, sir, and keep house.'

I felt hugely embarrassed. Who was I to offer this patronage? But I could not bear to refuse her. 'You can be my housekeeper,' I said at last, 'on the understanding that you never ask me to remember – to recall – to repeat –'

She covered my confusion with her curtsy. 'Thank you, sir. I never will. Even though –'

'– Hush,' I interrupted. 'Enough.'

Martha beamed at me in great delight and returned to her room.

Lady Magenta entered a new and final phase. She was barely conscious; her lips were cracked and stained with particles of blood. She was disappearing. It was like watching her recede into whiteness. All her life – everything coloured – was coming out. Soon there would be only white skin and white bone.

Dr Garth-Thompson called two and even three times a day but it was, as he said, only for the sake of friendship. There was nothing he could do in his professional capacity.

At dawn on the fourteenth of December Lady Magenta opened her eyes and looked at me with a strange expression on her face.

'I can taste the blood,' she said, wrinkling her nose with displeasure. 'Odd: I never tasted it before, when I had so much more than now.'

I was rather mystified and glanced at the nurse, who was asleep in a chair by the window. Lady Magenta seemed unusually clear in her mind. The morphine appeared to have had no effect on her. She was in complete possession of her faculties.

'Are you in pain?' I asked.

She looked puzzled. 'No. Why?'

'It doesn't matter. Try to sleep. It will soon be morning.'

Lady Magenta turned her face slightly towards me. 'I don't want to taste blood. Could you bring me some sweet fruit?'

'In a minute.' I straightened out her sheets and plumped up her pillows. Before I left the room she called out after me:

'When I slept – I was very far away, but I knew you were there.'

'Hush. Try to be quiet.'

I picked up a lamp and went down into the kitchen, where I found a pear in a cupboard. I was about to leave when I noticed, in a corner, on a plate, slices of rose-red pomegranate.

As I climbed the stairs, I began to hear low, urgent whispering. When I reached the landing, Martha emerged from Lady Magenta's room bearing a surgical tray of bloodstained dressings which she hurriedly deposited on top of a bookcase.

The nurse would not let me into the sick room. I caught a glimpse of figures moving to and fro. The only sounds I could hear were those of Lady Magenta's laboured breathing. Supporting myself on the bookcase I began to mutter – I don't know what – mere gibberish to keep me company, to stop me thinking. I picked up one of the steaming dressings and walked into another room. Throwing upon the curtains, I held the piece of cloth up to the early morning light. The scarlet stain was still spreading, slowly being taken up by the fibres of the cloth. My mouth fell open; tears obscured my vision.

Later, Martha found me. She helped me to my feet and, holding my hand, led me into Lady Magenta's room. Candles burned at each corner of the bed. I could almost hear the echo of the last blocked breath.

Sir Rodney arrived that evening. Lady Magenta's body had been washed and laid out during the day. Having been told the unhappy news, he asked at once to see his wife. He went up to her room and remained alone with her for a few minutes.

I sat in the corridor and toyed with a kaleidoscope which I had come across in the library that afternoon. I was told by Sir Stafford that Lord Tramont had once used it in a short-lived attempt to design printed fabrics for Mr Perkin, but the mechanism had failed; perhaps the mirrors had fallen out or been broken. In any case, as I twisted it this way and that in the lamplight, the coloured crystals refused to assemble themselves into any pattern.

Sir Rodney emerged from Lady Magenta's room and began to pace up and down.

'I thought she seemed rather fine,' he said after a while. 'She was like a saint in rapture. I had worried that once the flesh was gone she wouldn't manage it with the bone structure alone, but I have to say that she has carried it off with considerable charm and grace.'

Lady Magenta's funeral took place on 17 December 1899 at the Tramont Mausoleum in Kensal Green Cemetery. I stood on the steps of the great grey building watching the drizzle slant through the arches and fall softly onto the lid of the coffin. Many people were present but everybody seemed very far away. As we stood between the massive pillars, all sensations of touch came with a peculiar gentleness. Here and there amongst the crowd I clasped a hand and tried to smile. I did not look at the people I greeted.

The cemetery stretched away into the distance; the horizon was obscured by mist. From a short way off, with our dark coats and our umbrellas, we must have melted one into the other. The gravestones looked like scattered teeth; their stark shapes were muted by the rain.

After the ceremony a small group of us gathered beneath a commemorative plaque which had been set into one of the pillars:

MAGENTA
1859 – 1899

'Where thou perhaps under the whelming tide
Visit'st the bottom of the monstrous world'

'Can't understand it,' growled Sir Rodney beneath his breath. 'It's most inappropriate. Anybody would think the poor woman had drowned.'

I decided to make my way back to the cemetery gatehouse. Pesto scampered after me. We reached a point where a smaller path intersected with the main avenue.

'Well blow me!' exclaimed Pesto, tugging at my sleeve and indicating with his other hand a small and undistinguished gravestone which stood in an overgrown plot. 'Any relations of yours, Mr Jack?'

I followed the line of his pointing finger and then, with deepening curiosity and mounting distress, approached the stone, which bore the following inscription:

Janina Spellman
1835 – 1875

Adam Spellman
1821 – 1876

'What ho!' Sir Rodney had caught us up. He strode through the long grass to join us and examined the mossy headstone with interest. 'Have you found the tomb of your fathers, Monsieur Jacques, the ancestral sepulchre? Might one surmise that the prodigal has returned too late?'

Without replying I pulled on my gloves and moved off along the avenue. I could see the main gates in the distance and, beyond them, traffic passing in the street. Sir Rodney was not at all put out by my silence. As he and Pesto sauntered along behind me they began to debate their possible return to Italy. Sir Rodney suggested that in the circumstances, travel abroad might not be appropriate. It would be much better to have fun closer to home.

'Will you marry again?' panted Pesto. 'Go on: for a dare!'

'Ah!' sighed Sir Rodney sadly. 'To sport with Amaryllis in the shade! If only, Giovanni! If only!'

Fifty yards in front of me the procession of mourners had reached the gates and were beginning to file through into the street. They looked like a giant millipede.

When I next overheard their conversation, Sir Rodney seemed considerably more optimistic concerning his future marital prospects.

'I take your point, Signor Feste. Marriage then! – Dionysus willing. And if I can pay you back the money I owe you!'

Pesto giggled furiously.

'Yes, why not?' continued Sir Rodney. 'If life and the fifth member remain, it would be a fine thing. Sixty is a good age, is it not?' He paused for a moment and then continued slyly: 'Take that little Elizabeth Tramont, for example.'

'Lady Magenta's niece?'

'Yes – I thought I caught a glimpse of her a moment ago but it's so hard to be sure with all these veils.'

'She's very nubile,' said Pesto lasciviously. 'Don't you have to love her?'

'Love, my dear Feste?' exclaimed Sir Rodney incredulously. 'An emotion for clerks and scullery maids! In any case,' he added a moment later, 'little Bess is repulsively good.'

'What's the use in the good, Sir Rodney?' cried Pesto. 'Leave 'em alone. She's married to Lord What's-His-Name anyway.'

'I agree with you entirely, Giovanni, although marriage is not usually an impediment I recognize. Good people are so *dull*.'

I had reached the carriage, where I waited for my companions. After a short delay we all climbed in and moved off along the Harrow Road. We were silent for some time. Pesto twitched and scratched himself furiously: he was bored. When we reached Marble Arch he suddenly pulled a photograph from the breast pocket of his jacket and thrust it into my hands:

'Take a look at this, Mr Jack. It'll make your eyes water.'

It was one of the obscene photographs of Lady Magenta stretched out on the black bombazine cushions. I tried to give it back to Pesto but he would not take it. I turned away and saw, through the open window, a rag and bone cart in an alleyway.

'She had a beautiful cunt,' observed Sir Rodney over my shoulder. 'Smooth as a piece of gut.'

The sheer horror, as well as the perverse humour, of Sir Rodney's deliberately cold-blooded remark has remained with me for twenty years. I flattered myself that I had achieved some understanding of the people I had met and would have claimed some insight even into the character of Luigi Pesto. But Sir Rodney? He was a mystery to me, an alien form of life. Perhaps I should admit that my failures of understanding have become increasingly frequent of late. Almost everybody is a mystery to me today.

I wish I could shock you, Mr Secretary, as Sir Rodney did me but I must be so familiar to you now. The words in my mouth can come as no surprise.

It was twenty years ago and that world is over now . . . almost. I can take the story only a little further. With our veils, our umbrellas and our long black coats we might as well have buried it that day at Kensal Green. I wish that we had. But it didn't stop there – not quite.

It's so difficult to explain why it continued, especially now that I have started to speak so slowly. I find that I need to choose each word, you see. A few months ago we were rattling along at such a pace that it almost felt like living. Now, with so few things left to say, each word is as heavy as a brick. A sentence? I put my shoulder against it as if against a wall, but I cannot push it into place.

I wonder, Mr Secretary, whether you would be so good as to fetch my medicine from the bureau over there? Martha has been somewhat remiss tonight; that is unusual for her.

Thank you. And the spoon? Most grateful.

For my lungs?

No, I am not another Lady Magenta. I wheeze, of course. I have bronchitis in the winter, when Martha covers me with a blanket. But my problems are not pulmonary. Since you ask, the medicine is a purgative. I have been having . . . trouble. The bowels, you understand . . .

Do we choose our illnesses? I am certain that mine is the autobiographer's ailment. Poets, in contrast, never suffer from diseases of the bowel.

One day soon, when I have finished these memoirs I might begin another story: *The Life of my Entrails*. I could talk about the end of another twisted cable. Perhaps it would only be the same thing all over again.

I'm playing for time, I know, and there is so little left. The Pencil looks restless. Let us plunge in once more.

On Christmas Eve I walked along the Brompton Road, turned into Bartholomew Square and took out my watch. I was late: Sir Stafford had emphasized, in a note which I had received the previous day, that we would take our seats at three o'clock in the afternoon. Lady Magenta's will would then be read out to the surviving members of Siriso.

I hurried to the door of number 14 and rang the bell. Before I was admitted, I caught a brief glimpse of an old man sitting on a bench in the middle of the square. He had a patch over one eye and at his feet sat a dog on a silken leash.

I was shown into the red room where I found, as I had expected, that I was the last arrival. Apologizing for my lateness, I took my place at a table which stood on the low stage. The red room had been a good enough place for a pantomime but it lent a most peculiar atmosphere to the reading of a will.

Martha served tea. As she gave me my cup she winked as if she wanted to remind me of the promise I had given her several weeks previously. I looked away into a corner of the hothouse, where the hyacinths had now produced their sanguine flowers. The orchids seemed to listen to us and the statuary looked down, reserving judgement.

Lady Magenta's directions for the disposal of her assets followed to the letter the requirements of the Siriso tontine: the sum she had originally invested was to be divided amongst the surviving members. There were, however, two additional clauses contained in a codicil which she had dictated to Sir Stafford Singleton on 8 December. The first of these concerned myself. Lady Magenta drew the attention of the members of Siriso to the fact that my private means were considerably smaller than their own. She stipulated, therefore, that Bartholomew Square should be given to me for the remainder of my natural life. At my death, providing I left no dependents, the house was to be sold by auction. The proceeds would be divided amongst the institutions maintained by the Siriso Charitable Foundation.

As you might imagine, I was stunned by this unexpected piece of news. A chorus of surprise went up in the red room and was followed, after a few moments, by several murmurs of dissent. Sir Rodney was the first to voice his objections. He said, as I recall, that I had already been amply rewarded for the trivial inconveniences I had undergone in the service of Siriso by three years' salary, life membership of the tontine and an inalienable right to its annuities. He pointed out that as a cabinet-maker who had not even yet completed his apprenticeship, I should count myself a remarkably fortunate man.

Sir Stafford Singleton interrupted him. 'I appreciate your views, Sir Rodney. But I must make it clear that this clause is a requirement, not a request. To disobey it would be to dishonour the dead.'

Sir Rodney said that he had no objections to that. 'None at all, Sir Stafford, I do assure you.'

'Oh come, come,' murmured Mr Perkin appeasingly.

Sir Rodney stared the dyemaker down and continued. 'I am an habitually generous man, Sir Stafford.' Pesto looked round at us all and nodded furiously. 'Yet even I have wondered whether there might be

344

grounds for the suspicion that Monsieur Jacques deliberately and with intent – how can I put it? – *inveigled* himself into the affections of Lady Magenta. I have never for a moment, of course, doubted that his conscious motives were altruistic in the extreme. I mererly wonder whether the reasonable man might speculate that the tiniest particle of pecuniary greed lurked somewhere in his – ah – proletarian mind.'

Whilst Sir Rodney rolled out his elegant phrases, Pesto's muttering was audible to all:

'Oh yes, quite right, Sir Rodney. Nail on the head. He was after the yellow-boys, sure enough. Sharp young chap. Eye for the ladies. Poor old Lady Magenta – very vulnerable. Needed protection.'

Sir Rodney eventually conceded that my legacy was an unalterable fact and Sir Stafford began to read out the second part of the codicil:

'"Dr Garth-Thompson told me this morning that I shall be dead within the week. I am determined to make the following arrangements for the disposal of certain parts of my body and the doctor is prepared to testify to my sanity."'

Sir Stafford looked up. 'Is this true, Andrew?'

Garth-Thompson nodded. 'Her ladyship dictated the codicil in her normal state. She was firmly set in her purpose –'

'Astonishing!' interrupted Sir Rodney. 'I would not have been prepared to testify to any purpose in the sex exceeding the duration of two minutes!'

'I can assure you, Sir Rodney,' said the doctor, 'that Lady Magenta was unaffected by delirium, delusion or hallucination.'

As the doctor spoke, Sir Stafford fixed him with watery eyes and fell visibly victim to his hopeless passion. When Garth-Thompson finished speaking, however, he managed to collect himself and continue with his reading:

'"My instructions will be carried out on New Year's Eve. On the night that I have mentioned I will be exhumed from the Tramont mausoleum in Kensal Green Cemetery . . ."'

The words did not sink in at first. The heavy scent of flowers wafted through the room. Water dripped into the mossy tanks. I noticed that Pesto was amusing himself by poking his finger into the burning tip of his cigar. He appeared to feel no pain.

As Sir Stafford continued, it became . . .

She – she wanted . . .

I'm sorry, Mr Secretary, I can't . . .

25

Icicles and Thunderbolts

. . . GO ON.

But I must go on, mustn't I? Shouldn't lie down in darkness – not yet. If I stopped now, I might as well never have started. I simply cannot bear, however, to recount the words that Sir Stafford Singleton read out to the assembled company on Christmas Eve, 1899. You will allow me to pass over this single day, won't you? I tried my best and, in the last resort, I am entitled to my lapses.

My inheritance, what do you think about that? 'Closes another circle,' you say. Closes another door as well. You must have been wondering all along how I came to end up in Bartholomew Square. Did you think I married her? I wanted you to think that.

I wanted to think it myself.

Don't think I toyed with you, though; I wasn't playing. The inheritance, I readily admit, is a somewhat melodramatic peripeteia. 'Where have I heard this one before?' I almost hear you ask. 'Such dénouements can be found between the pages of a hundred silly novels.'

I agree. I felt a complete fraud.

I remained in Bartholomew Square after they had all gone: Pesto, Dr Garth-Thompson, Sir Stafford Singleton, Mr Perkin and Sir Rodney. It was then, that very evening, that I began to take possession of the house – the home that did not belong to me. I lit a lamp and wandered through the gloomy rooms; I began to take up the threads of my false lineage. Finding a complete set of keys, I threw open all the cupboards. Lord Tramont's fossils gleamed out at me, imponderably ancient, complacently unaware of their miraculous escape from decay. I picked one up and found that it had been labelled in his lordship's neat hand:

Murex purpureum tramonti
Hunstanton
1849

Trays of minerals, chunks of ore. Statues and paintings: from room to room the house unfolded around me. I gazed into the amethystine hearts of halved geodes. I saw for the first time the portraits of my adopted family and looking about me, felt their presence as a sudden, almost unbearable pressure. They had left their books, with marked pages, on these tables; written their letters, perhaps, as they sat at this mahogany escritoire. I would never know them. They were extinct, although their things survived them. As I handled them, the things seemed nervously to assess their new proprietor. The fact that I owned them made them seem stranger than before.

I passed into the kitchen and found that Martha was preparing my evening meal. She looked up at me oddly as I went into the scullery where, rattling about amongst the old saucepans, I came upon a pasha's hookah enamelled in vermilion. Later, in another room, I was comforted to find the camera which Lord Tramont had once taken to the Crimea. I examined the purpleheart and yew veneers and found that my own work had lasted well. I could barely trace the suture which divided the restored surface from the original one.

In memory, it seems as if I wandered through the house all week. I thought of Lady Magenta and of how she too must have lingered and paused in her mourning. I tried to calculate the amount of death required to produce and amass so many things. Lord and Lady Tramont, Ronald Indigo. In a room at the back of the house I opened a drawer and came upon a stained sheet which had once, I was sure, served as Mauve's baptismal gown. Lord Tramont's housekeeper must have clung to it with a secretive nostalgia despite the contempt she had affected for the young Perkin's desecration of the family linen.

In the place of Alizarin Tramont, who had died after only ten days of life, I found on a shelf a flask of red dye. The death of Mortimer Croop had brought a swirl of other objects into the orbit of the house. In an attic I came across the circus properties which Alf and Wilf had purloined for our performance of *Piramus and Thisbe* in 1890. There were ropes and wires, a rolled up curtain with a tiny aperture in it. There were tools, coloured balls and lengths of canvas. There was a tambourine. I struck it in the silence. The noise fled and was lost in a moment.

One day the removal men arrived in the square with their wagon. They had brought the contents of Lady Magenta's studio in Bethnal Green. The pantomime horse suit had been flung over the rattling goods to protect them from the rain. One of the men carried it into the house, holding his nose. It seemed that the olfactory ghost of Bill Stephens still haunted the costume. I put my hand at random into a crate and brought out a stoppered bottle containing half a pint of gallic acid.

347

'*Gealla*,' Lady Magenta had said. '*Gealla*: a sore on a horse.'

In an ebony box which had been inlaid with ivory I found Lady Magenta's writing equipment. I handled the pens and the pot of ink, leafed through the blank sheets of paper. At the bottom of the box there was a photograph in a frame. I turned it over and found – to my surprise – myself, looking like a blind man, in her daguerreotype of December 1892.

New Year's Eve approached. I will never forget the awful darkness of that cemetery nor the noises made by our crowbars as we lifted the lid of the sarcophagus in the echoing mausoleum. Nor will I forget that later that night there were bright electric lights in Dr Garth-Thompson's private theatre at the back of his house in Chelsea. We opened the coffin with chisels, we took her out and laid her on the slab.

Everything is forgetfulness. It all fades, dissolves and breaks apart.

Another painful day, Mr Secretary: as painful to recall as it was to live through. Once again I am afraid that I must pass this over in silence. Perhaps – perhaps one day I will speak of it. Perhaps one day I will try to cut out some sort of shape to fit the last section of the quilt. At the moment it is impossible. I have no need to be downhearted, however: this is the only rent in my surface.

The other one? What do you mean?

In Egypt?

Ah, my 'death', you mean. Yes, there is always the 'death'. We will never know about that one.

What else is there?

My poisoned legacy has made me a rich man. I have ended up where I started out and spoken myself to the point where I started speaking. Everything seems satisfactory – to a point.

No: I see it now. I must make this chapter a repository for the assorted frozen fragments which accumulated in the years between 1900 and 1919. In my next chapter, I shall arrive at the end of my – of our – journey: the present moment. I will no longer be living in the past. You will see me as I am. I will step out of the frame, out of history, and take your hand.

The circus: you will want to know about that. I went back, you know, on 22 March 1918. It was my last venture into the outside world. Some houses had been built on the meadow and the view over the Stour to the cathedral had been lost to my anxious gaze. I found no remnants of my own past – neither a ribbon nor a garter – until, about to leave, I suddenly came across the unfinished foundations of Pesto's mansion. At first –

What? Mentioned this already? When was that?

You're quite right: I had forgotten. How stupid of me to repeat myself. But I didn't tell you what happened when I got back did I? No, I thought not.

I caught an early train from Canterbury the next morning and arrived in Victoria Station at about ten o'clock. Soldiers were being packed onto the Dover train. Wounded men, just back from the front, lay about on stretchers or wandered here and there with bandages over their eyes. Although a thousand people were speaking in the great space, it seemed empty, muted. I made my way through the crowd to the exit on Wilton Road. A band was playing; people were handing out leaflets advertising their god. A newspaper vendor shouted out the news of the German offensive on the Somme. It was most peculiar. Everywhere you could see the effects of war but in the cab, on the way back to Bartholomew Square, daffodils had begun to bloom in the gardens. The crowd which flowed past me on the pavement, composed of a million routes and pathways, still seemed to me like a giant, soft web.

When I got back to Bartholomew Square, I took the pantomime horse into the garden, thrust it into the rusty brazier and burnt it. I watched the flaring squirrel skins and I waited until nothing was left. So now you know about the circus.

You already know about the city.

My father's boxes, registered from Marseilles as the fourteenth Siriso shipment from Alexandria, never arrived in London. I made a few enquiries but eventually I was forced to give them up for lost. It seemed ironic that having found them again after twenty-three years, I should nevertheless have been ultimately deprived of my father's only autograph. I should have liked to run my hand occasionally over the shining geometric patterns. It would have been interesting to plant the seeds I had found in the fourteenth box and wait for something to come of it.

Nothing definite was ever seen or heard of Mr Lewis John Feaver, erstwhile manager of the Occidental Bank in Alexandria and Senior Coroner for the central districts of the city, or of Mehmet Ali, harbour-master. But in July of 1902 the wreck of the *Typhon* was reported to have been discovered on a sandbank along a deserted stretch of the Chinese coast. There were rumours inland that two foreign gentlemen had passed through a couple of years previously on their way to the interior. In the hold of the ship, manacled to a girder, was found the skeleton of a man whose gold teeth suggested that he might have been Mistral Mussanah, once *boab* at the Pension de l'Est.

I never succeeded in tracing Gertrude Desmoulins. Towards the end of 1902, however, I happened one day to be passing a tailor's in Stepney when I noticed one of her wax figures in the window. I think that it must originally have been Charles Darwin. It was now being employed as a window dummy to model a type of waistcoat that was already several years out of date. *The History of Wax* has never, so far as I can ascertain, been published.

What happened to Gertrude? I was never to know. Fiction ties up the ends so nicely. Life, in contrast, tends in its endings towards the merely messy.

There are so many others I should have liked to tell you about – and would have done – except that they are gone. What happened, for example, to the tall stilts walkers? Did they make off, one day, at a furious pace? And are their striped trousers still flapping in the breeze? What of the charcoal-burner and the woman who lived with him? The rheumy-eyed old man? The elderly child who copied her texts in the night? And whatever became of Sergeant Pail, who once shot a tiger at dawn on Christmas morning?

Did the hired woman at Fairfields ever drag her eyes from the cupids which intertwined on the ceiling of the chapel? Did her bruises heal? I would never know. Is the bargee still sleeping and the peripatetic agricultural labourer still shading his eyes? Information is pitifully lacking. Do the Eduardini brothers still travel between provincial theatres and eat their lunch in barren fields? And what became of the stevedore? The match girl? Or the bereaved mother we violated with our lens? Is Dr Chawl still working in the sunlight, dictating case notes into his phonograph?

I wonder whether the cloth merchant at Eleusis still scolds his grand-children? What happened to the Berber? Are they still laying out their mats in the desert? There was once a little girl who took my hand and asked if the gentleman wanted a companion. What became of her? She will be in her early thirties by now, perhaps with children of her own. Is the cicerone at Cairo still asking tourists for baksheesh? Does Mr Crute, the plumassier at Zagazig, still carry feathers pinned on boards? Has the Chief of the Cairo police remained indifferent to the stories which are told to him? Does the asthmatic manager of the casino at Heliopolis still dream of living in a lodge on the shores of Lake Mareotis and of watching flocks of birds land in the marshes at dawn? And has the fellah recovered from his wounds?

I have been wondering whether there is an official in the custom-house at Marseilles who clicks his tongue and carries a screwdriver. Last of all and perhaps most mysterious of all, what happened to the blind soldier with a stick? He took the money we sent out to him and simply wandered off. As we watched from the upstairs windows, he turned a corner and was gone.

This is not nostalgia – don't think I want to bring things back, Mr Secretary. No: it is bafflement, pure and simple. The past lies on my mind like a great, smothering weight. But to reach out towards its beauty, to touch, to hold, to seize it – then – then the past is without weight or substance and the faster we follow the faster it flees before us.

There are a few certainties.

In 1901 Aramind stopped eating and died.

In 1903 I heard from Mimi and Bessie that Alf Hagsproat had died in a mining accident in Australia. When the props inside the opal mine began to collapse, he rushed into the working, presumably in an attempt to rescue or warn his colleagues. Seconds later he was buried beneath tons of rubble.

In 1905 Dr Lindhorst judged that he had finally recovered from the lung condition which had troubled him for many years. He resigned his post at the Queen Victoria Hospital in Cairo where, despite his age, he was still a consultant and returned to Dresden to live with his daughter. He died barely a year later, an embittered and disappointed man, of cirrhosis of the liver.

Mr W.H. Perkin was knighted in 1906. Dr Garth-Thompson advised him to take a less active role in the administration of the dye works and to retire altogether from scientific research. Sir William found retirement unendurable, particularly since arthritis had made it impossible for him to play the violin. In early 1907 he started on his ill-fated tour of Italy. He returned to England at the end of June having contracted hepatitis in Rome and died on 14 July. His home at Greenford Green was put up for auction and another company took over the running of Imperial Dyes, Ltd. Poor fellow! He had spent a life of red and blue and he ended it a jaundiced yellow.

In 1908, after a brawl in a public house at Greenwich, Christopher Desert (who was, I gathered, more correctly known as Krzystof Pustynia) was convicted of manslaughter and sentenced to ten years' imprisonment in Wormwood Scrubs. The businessman had reverted to the thug. He died in 1912.

Mimi and Bessie still own a sweetshop in Chalk Farm. They are elderly spinsters now. Mimi is in her early sixties. When schoolboys enter the shop to buy their penn'orth of sweets they never notice Mimi and Bessie holding hands beneath the counter.

Wilf Patchkey is still alive. He is fifty-eight years old. He has nine children and twenty-three grandchildren. Two of his sons died in the war. We exchange Christmas cards every year. I have never met Laura, his wife.

Mr Nopheles, too, lives on, a venerable gentleman who makes the journey every day from his apartment to the Colonial Club on foot. He smokes and writes letters in the morning, reads his books in the afternoon and has never been known to lose at chess over his evening coffee.

On 27 July 1909 I had returned to Bartholomew Square from a trip abroad and, having bathed and changed my clothes, I picked up a copy of that day's paper. I had just finished reading of Blériot's crossing of the English Channel by aeroplane when my attention was caught by an article at the bottom of the page, which contained an interview with a police officer who had witnessed an accident in Jermyn Street that morning. His testimony read as follows:

> I was walking northwards along St James's street when I heard a disturbance in Jermyn Street. I attended the scene expeditiously, where I found a gentleman stretched out in the gutter. He had already expired from his injuries, which were grievous. The driver of an omnibus told me that the aforesaid gentleman had rushed headlong into the street from the steps of his club and that he (the driver) had been unable to rein in his horses. A crowd had gathered and I attempted to dispel it, vigorously blowing my whistle for assistance. At this point a second gentleman in the crowd withdrew from an interior pocket of his coat a small pearl-handled revolver which he placed to his right temple and discharged in my presence, thus causing his life to cease immediately and forthwith.

The Secretary wishes to know the name of the first gentleman. Dr Garth-Thompson. The second? Sir Stafford Singleton.

The first weeks of 1910 were extremely cold ones, particularly at night. During the day, temperatures rose a little above freezing. These conditions, as the newspapers pointed out, were ideal for the formation of icicles. There was one report, from Devon, of an icicle reaching the unheard-of length of fourteen feet. Conditions were not so perfect in London. Nevertheless, by the middle of the third week of January it was not uncommon to see aqueous stalactites of three or four feet in length.

On the morning of 20 January a warm wind of Mediterranean origin sprang up throughout the south of England. Overnight in London the temperature had sunk many degrees below freezing point. By eleven o'clock that morning it was a warm, almost spring-like day. As you can imagine, a most hazardous situation was rapidly developing.

The accelerated rise in temperature was not least acute outside a toyshop on Bayswater Road where Luigi Pesto, oblivious of the thaw outside, was busily negotiating a price for a model train set and a human skeleton. Smiling beatifically, he emerged from the shop at about half past eleven, having arranged for his purchases to be delivered to his home in Kensington. It was then, as he stood on the steps of the shop and surveyed the morning scene, that he was struck on the suture of his cranium by an icicle which had fallen from a balcony on the fourth floor. Pesto put his hands to his head, staggered and then collapsed. The owner of the toyshop, not having noticed the rapidly descending object, rushed to Pesto's assistance, assuming at first that his customer had fallen victim to a seizure.

It was some time before a doctor could be found; a time during which, as the shopkeeper reported later at the inquest, Pesto jerked spasmodically and even, as a result of his convulsions, moved several yards along the pavement. The doctor doubted this account. The extent of the damage to Pesto's cerebral cortex, he said, was such that he would have been killed instantly. The coroner recorded a verdict of death by misadventure. As the assembled crowd began to leave the hall, however, the owner of the toyshop – piqued perhaps by the doctor's peremptory dismissal of his version of events – loudly reaffirmed the truth of his story to any who cared to listen:

'He was flailing about like a lunatic!'

'And his head all split open with the icicle sticking out,' said a woman at his side who I took for his wife. 'It was horrible.'

I attempted to rise from my seat but was restrained by a powerful hand. Twisting round in the chair I found myself looking up into the spectral face of Sir Rodney, whose mouth was open in an expression somewhere between a laugh, a yawn and a wail.

'Poor little monster,' he whispered into my ear. 'His life was gone but the animus still jumped and cavorted within him. Even after the universal ringmaster's frigid thunderbolt had laid him low, he struggled to rise above the earth; he wanted to be free, to be sportive in the blue realms of the infinite.'

I did not attend Pesto's funeral.

Two weeks later, at the beginning of February, I received a note from Sir Robert Haslett, a colleague of Sir Stafford's who had agreed several months previously to take responsibility for the legal affairs of Siriso. He informed me that an auction would shortly be held at Pesto's house in Kensington.

I had forgotten all about the matter until one day, as I was returning to Bartholomew Square after a stroll in the park, I happened to pass along the street where Pesto had once lived. As I turned into the crescent I had to lean against a fierce gust of wind and shield my face against the stinging rain. I did not attempt to look up until, as I reached the mid-point of the cobbled arc, my way was blocked by a group of young men who were unsuccessfully attempting to carry a stuffed camel down the street. Somebody shouted out a warning: the mangy dromedary, caught by another gust of wind, seemed to be about to fall from its plinth. I was forced to skip to one side as men in shirt sleeves rushed forward to support the creature.

I was seized with a sudden pang of familiarity but I think that I would almost certainly have walked on had I not noticed another product of the taxidermist's art abandoned in the street.

A llama.

Without stopping to think I pushed my way through a knot of onlookers and entered the spacious hall of Pesto's house. I was immediately caught up in a frenzied throng of people who were rushing eagerly from room to room. The parlour, which was immediately to the right of the front door, contained a large and most uncanny collection of machines. Broken bicycles hung from the walls; mangles stood in the corners. The centre of the room was occupied by a huge loom. With great effort, a small boy began to turn the handle of this engine as I watched. After a moment the shuttle shot part way across the sley before sticking fast.

Children darted here and there amongst the sewing machines, butter churns and barrel-organs. They turned all the handles and pressed all the levers. Squealing mechanisms added their note to the hum of the crowd. As I left the room, the barrel-organ burst into life with a cracked and tinkling version of Handel's *Messiah*.

I moved on through the rooms on the ground floor. There were wardrobes bursting with clothes which nobody but a clown could wear. There were teetering piles of hat boxes, cupboards filled with cheap china and vulgar trinkets. Cabinets spilled financial papers and promissory notes across the floors. In one room I found the train set and the human skeleton which the owner of the toyshop had delivered in spite of his client's death.

It was tempting to forget the outside world in here. The place was a seething museum which bore no relation to anything else. The crowd hungrily inspected this world of strange ingredients, examined the labels, paid the prices and bore their goods away.

I emerged once more into the hall but a determined group of people immediately swept me into the drawing-room which opened off the hallway immediately opposite to the parlour. Greater order prevailed here. At the far end of the room a gentleman in a checked suit stood on a raised dais and held up his hands for silence.

'Item number one, ladies and gentlemen: a japanned black box with brass hinges and hasps.'

An overalled assistant lifted up the box to show it to the crowd. In an instant I recognized the chest which Pesto had buried, one day during early November 1899, in a cave near Wormshill.

'What am I offered, ladies and gentlemen, for this sturdy receptacle?'

Unsteadily, I attempted to move towards the door. But my way was blocked by a malevolent butcher, still in his bloodstained apron, who stood with crossed arms on the threshold.

'Item number two: one fob watch in perfect working order, with an engraved dedication on the inside of the case which reads: "To my darling Mortimer, from his loving mother."'

Startled, I looked up. Some cynical children started to giggle. The bidding began and the auctioneer's assistant lifted Mortimer Croop's watch high into the air. It swung from its chain; it gleamed in the light of a lamp.

Over the next half hour, whilst I was still trapped in the drawing-room, Mortimer Croop's wig, leather boots and top hat also went under the hammer. At length the butcher made a successful bid and moved aside. I staggered out of the door and found myself in the hall. The afternoon was drawing on. A chilly breeze came in from the street and fluttered the price tags. A young man was attempting to carry a bicycle out through the front door at the same time as a large and noisy family sought an entrance. An argument began to develop, during which the young man was recommended to get out of the way. Swallowing like a fish in his irritation, he retreated into the parlour and gazed at the ceiling with bulging eyes. The noisy family surged into the house and bore down on me with greedy faces. I found myself lifted up and moved into the kitchen at the back of the house, where people were struggling with each other over the contents of Pesto's larder.

'These biscuits are stale!' a loud voice complained.

A child with a handful of sugared almonds passed by me. She looked up into my face; her lips were stained purple.

'That's my anchovy paste!' an indignant voice proclaimed.

'Garn! I'll swap you for the plum chutney.'

With an enormous effort I forced my way back into the hall. I could still hear the wheezing barrel-organ, which had given up on the *Messiah* and started out on music-hall tunes. The auctioneer was still in full cry. Just as I thought I had secured my egress, I saw the gaunt figure of Sir Rodney at the door. He stood head and shoulders above everybody else and he seemed to pass through the crowd with ease. Hoping that he had not noticed me, I managed to slip aside into the auction room.

'Item fourteen: one scarab signet ring and stick of sealing wax. Do I have a shilling?'

An old woman with a wart raised her hand.

'One shilling then. What more do I have? One and six? Any offers at one and six?'

There were no offers at one and six.

'A shilling then to the elderly lady!'

I stood beside the old woman as she received her purchase from the auctioneer's assistant. Her face lit up with a strange joy and she looked, for a moment, like a girl. For a moment, before she put them into her pocket, I recognized two of the objects I had once seen in Stephanides's bureau. For a moment, in the jostling crowd, I stood alone in a room at the Pension de l'Est. The door was open and I caught a glimpse of refracted sunbeams passing across the wall.

I was somewhere else and somebody else was speaking to me; I had only just woken up. In the hum of voices, I came out from the tunnel into the light – for an instant, only for an instant. There were so many details; it was all so confusing. I saw Mr Nopheles below me. I handed him his brief-case and he looked up at me with his scholarly face. We knew nothing; in its end and its beginning it was a mystery to us.

'One album of artistic photographs. Ten shillings? Do I have ten shillings?'

'Come to pick over the carcass, Monsieur Jacques?'

I started violently. Sir Rodney took my hand and seemed to gloat over me. He draped an arm affectionately over my shoulder and enquired after my health.

'Fifteen shillings? Fifteen? To the gentleman in the bowler. Going, going –'

'Ten pounds!' shouted Sir Rodney.

The auctioneer was plainly stunned. Whispers began to circulate around the room and Sir Rodney was the focus of many admiring glances.

'Ten pounds, then, to the tall gentleman.' And the auctioneer's hammer descended.

'I rather imagine,' said Sir Rodney lazily, 'that my purchase contains a few photographs which Signor Feste, in the kindness of his heart, once made for me.'

The assistant passed Sir Rodney the album and he began to flick through it unhurriedly. 'Yes, indeed: as I expected.' He turned to me and winked. 'It would have been most regrettable if these had fallen into the hands of some sweaty clerk, to be fingered by candlelight.'

Sir Rodney kept me by him and for the first time, with the crowd around me, I felt almost safe in his company. I think that I envied him his easy, aristocratic elegance. I was unnerved by his wit, the odd attractiveness of his cruel boredom.

'Item sixteen!' cried the auctioneer. 'One paperweight with a spinning roundabout inside. Who'll give me five bob?'

'I will,' said Sir Rodney, his quiet voice easily penetrating the hubbub. He turned to me. 'Our friend was quite a magpie, wasn't he? His house is like a bazaar.'

With my growing sense of disorientation I could not for the moment reply. Sir Rodney took my silence for lack of interest or disgust and was greatly amused: 'Monsieur Jacques: the frown! the sneer of cold contempt!' He caught the immediately deferential attention of the auctioneer. 'I'll give you five pounds and have done with it.'

'Gone again to the tall gentleman!'

Sir Rodney received his paperweight and once more flung his arm across my shoulder. He had never been so intimate with me; I could smell him. 'Cheer up, Monsieur Jacques! Giovanni would not have wanted you to be unhappy.'

I shook him off. 'I am not mourning for – for Giovanni, Sir Rodney.'

My companion raised his eyebrow. 'What? But you must have loved him, in spite of all his faults – surely?'

I stepped back. 'I did not love Pesto, Sir Rodney.'

Sir Rodney leaned over me and spoke in an almost imploring tone. 'Come now, Monsieur Jacques! We should love the little man. We should treasure his memory.'

'Why do you say that?'

Sir Rodney snapped his fingers in front of my face. 'Ingrate! We owe him such a great deal, you and I.' He shook a fistful of debt slips at me. 'I, for instance, have been released from my losses at whist!'

357

'And I, Sir Rodney? What can I possibly owe to Signor Feste?'

He looked at me with pity. 'Don't you realize? Is it possible that you don't know? Signor Feste made you a rich man. It was he who put you up for Siriso.'

This was a new and entirely unexpected blow. 'How? I don't understand.'

'He never told you?'

'Never.'

Sir Rodney glowed with triumph. 'What a saint! Selflessly, he never advertised his good deed. What a martyr!'

'I thought –'

'You thought that it was Lady Magenta and the Baroness Hrocka who secured your place? Not so: they would have left you to rot in the street. It was Feste and Feste alone who cared for you. He wanted you to belong. He wanted you to be a part of our little family. He said that you were like a son to him. And behind my back he managed to persuade Sir Stafford and Dr Garth-Thompson. They all said – the fools! – that they wanted a proletarian presence in Siriso. It was one nation not two, rich and poor fighting the same fight – all that sort of thing. Democratic rubbish and toss-pot radicalism! I was the only one to vote against you. "Giovanni," I said, "think of our responsibility in raising this wretch from the gutter. We will enfranchise him, we will liberate him. He will worm his way into our noble body and when we die, he will inherit!"'

It never occurred to me to doubt Sir Rodney's word as I scrambled for the only clarity that was available to me: 'Pesto was corrupt,' I said with a trembling voice. 'He illegally built up the financial reserves of the Eastern Trading Society.'

To my utter confusion, Sir Rodney merely laughed. 'I take it that you refer to the jape he played with Mr Feaver and Mehmet Ali. But were they not entitled to their games? After all, the Eastern Trading Society has always belonged to Siriso.'

'What?' I could feel my heart beating erratically. 'Nobody told me. Pustynia never mentioned that.'

Sir Rodney sighed regretfully. 'Christopher? A wonderful rogue. I knew him of old, back in the 'seventies. Still visit him in prison. Poor chap: he could never control his temper. Yes, Monsieur Jacques, we used the Eastern Trading Society as a wooden horse from which to watch and be amused by the antics of our triumvirate of scallywags. It was our secret.'

'And – and you were prepared to allow them to defraud the Occidental Bank for your own amusement?'

My blankness delighted Sir Rodney: he laughed until the tears ran down his cheeks. 'I – I also, of course, Monsieur Jacques, took the precaution of owning the Occidental Bank!' He gestured weakly towards me. 'How upset you look! Be merciful, Monsieur Jacques! Forgive the little man: his was a playful viciousness. I wanted him to glory in his magpie naughtiness. All the money was going round and round but nobody except me knew that it was never changing hands!'

I felt very sick. Sir Rodney took me by the arm and led me into the hall. 'Let's have a foot around upstairs, old fellow.' As he nimbly began his ascent, he turned his head to speak to me: 'Of course, in the end, I made Feste drop the other two. The joke had gone on long enough.'

I steadied myself against the stair rail and feebly began to object. 'I don't understand. Siriso is such a small organization.'

It was then that Sir Rodney sat me on the landing and began to tell me about Siriso:

'It's the policeman and the thief, Monsieur Jacques! It's the poacher and the gamekeeper. You knew only the tiniest part of our activities, the merest embellishments. Exotica! Rarities! We sell the icing, sure enough, but we also sell the cake. Coal and iron, houses and railways, wheat and cotton. We make ships and we launch them into the deep waters. They sail far away and they return with their bellies full of goods. We print the money and we make the forges that glow in the night. We also produce the little photograph that hangs over the engineer's bed and the piece of porcelain – the gift of his wife – which stands on the captain's mantelpiece.'

I listened to Sir Rodney and I was completely fascinated. A few minutes earlier I had been convinced that Pesto had cut his own path through Siriso and successfully misled his master. We learn the patterns, I suppose, and then we expect them to repeat themselves. I had wanted Sir Rodney to be another Mortimer Croop, another figurehead whose authority had been captured and held to ransom. But as Sir Rodney spoke to me that afternoon on the gloomy landing, I quickly realized how wrong I had been. He sprang surprise after surprise; one by one he reviewed each area of Siriso's activities. His eyes gleamed with an intelligence beyond my own. He seemed to have known everything, always: he had never put a foot wrong. Trading under many names in every part of the world, the banks and warehouses, the mines and farms, the cities, the railways and the steamships all did his bidding. Added together, the many-tentacled Siriso would have been one of the largest companies in England. It employed thousands of people and its maritime trade accounted for a significant percentage of the traffic through the Port of London.

Sir Rodney rose to his feet and began to open a door into one of the upstairs rooms. I restrained him for a moment and looking up into the pale blur of his face made a last attempt to be angry:

'Why did you tell Mr Nopheles that I had been sent out to Egypt in 1895? Why did you lie?'

Sir Rodney laughed soundlessly as he went into the dark room. 'I knew it would add to the fun. And it gave my dear Giovanni a little time to put his affairs in order. There was a problem, if I remember correctly, relating to a miscalculated remittance and he wanted to sort it out before he covered his tracks.'

Hesitating for a moment, I attempted to revise my life in the light of Sir Rodney's revelations. I could not even begin. Looking up, I saw that the door was still open in front of me and I followed Sir Rodney inside.

It was much darker in the room than it had been on the landing. Until Sir Rodney struck a match I could see nothing: in the flickering light, I found myself in a stark little attic. On a camp bed near the window, combing grey hair that had once been red, sat Amelia.

'Ah, it's you my dear!' exclaimed Sir Rodney with delight. 'I hoped that I would find you. Have you taken refuge from the unruly throng?'

I felt as if I was drunk, as if I had downed glass after glass through the long day. Only a few feet away from me, Sir Rodney and Amelia sat next to each other on the bed. It seemed to me that I was watching them through the wrong end of a telescope. He lit a lamp and combed her hair; they talked quietly and companionably to each other. 'Did you hate it down there, my dear?' asked Sir Rodney. 'Did it make your head spin?' He delved in his pocket and took out the paperweight: 'A little present for you.'

Amelia took it from him and examined it carefully. She watched the little figures spinning on the merry-go-round and then she looked up at Sir Rodney with grateful eyes.

Sir Rodney suddenly noticed my presence and began to apologize. 'I'm so sorry, Jacques. Allow me to introduce you to a dear old friend of mine – Amelia: this is Mr Jack Spellman. I call him Jacques.'

Getting up from the bed, they came towards me across the room and for a moment I could not see their faces. They were two tall people silhouetted against the lamplight.

Surely now I knew.

Barely able to stand, I took Amelia's hand. Once it had been so delicate; now it was rough and red. 'We knew each other before,' I said. Amelia turned away from me. Sir Rodney thought for a moment and then struck his forehead:

'Of course! You are old friends – I had completely forgotten! How delightful!'

I leaned against the door and covered my eyes.

Sir Rodney was most concerned for my well-being. 'You don't look at all well, Jack. Is anything the matter? These occasions can be so trying. Let me take you out into the air.'

It was the first time he had ever called me by my proper name. He took my hand and led me onto the landing. People laughed and chattered on the stairs. As we descended I was jostled and thrown from side to side; if it had not been for the people around me, I would have stumbled and fallen.

In the hall the auctioneer's voice rang out once again:

'Item fifty-three: a painted china tiger with one of its eyes missing. What am I offered for this fine old piece?'

It was only then that I fully realized that I had known nothing. Everything in my life – my structures and my patterns – everything had been built upon a false premiss. Sir Rodney took me into the little garden near the front door. The windows of the drawing-room had been opened and tradesmen sat on the sills. We could hear the progress of the bidding. In the street, a man was lighting the lamps.

I turned to Sir Rodney for the final time. 'You knew?'

Sir Rodney's face worked with various emotions. Suddenly I realized that I was not frightened of him any more, that he had lost all his horror for me. He was just a tired old man. For a moment he seemed almost kind.

'I knew,' he softly said.

'But what? What did you know?' I stepped towards him and he fell back. He crumpled; it was as if he were afraid of me.

'How far back does it go, Sir Rodney? And why me, of all people?'

'Oh, Mr Spellman,' he said with sympathy, 'leave it alone. Why such an urgency, such a longing to know?'

'I can't help it,' I whispered.

'Can't help it?' he repeated. He seemed to want to protect me, to spread his arms over and around me. 'Even if you make all the stories cohere, you still face the impossible world of things.'

'It's not impossible,' I said with the stubbornness of a child. 'I have won, you see.'

His forehead creased. 'How so?'

'You predicted it, Sir Rodney. You are seventy; I am only forty-six. When you die, I am the worm which will inherit.'

His face was as pale as paper and when he smiled at me it seemed that his fragile body had been folded up out of scraps and clippings, pages torn from old magazines.

'Even if I die you will not have won, Jack.'

'Why not?'

He turned to leave me. 'You could never spend your inheritance. You would want to avoid its corruption.'

The sky was very large and the trees were black against the sky. People began to spill out of the house. Everything was being taken away and the auction was almost over. A little way down the street, despite the efforts of its new owners, the camel had fallen from its plinth. Sawdust spilled from a rent in its side.

'One last item, ladies and gentlemen!' cried the auctioneer. 'A painted wooden horse, possibly Russian.'

Nobody heard him. All the money had been spent and there was nobody left to buy.

'What did you know, Sir Rodney?' I repeated.

He glanced back at me as he went into the house. 'Poor Jack,' he said. 'I knew more than you did yourself.'

Tom, the Baroness Hrocka's serving-boy, died on 25 May 1915, on the last day of the second battle of Ypres.

1917 saw the death of Count Ferdinand von Zeppelin, inventor of the dirigible which bears his name. During the war just ended, these airships made 53 raids on British territory, during which 556 civilians were killed.

On the night of 19 October 1917 the seventy-seven year old Sir Rodney Rouncewell defied the warnings posted in the streets and visited a manicurist's and brothel in Stepney. He was returning to his home in Westminster at about one o'clock in the morning when an incendiary bomb exploded directly above his motor car. He died a few hours later, almost completely excoriated. Despite extensive disfigurement, however, he went to his grave with the most beautiful set of nails a corpse could have wished for. I suspect that he would have found this conjunction a most amusing circumstance.

Many other things happened in the great big world during these years. The Empress of the Indies was interred at Frogmore. A railway opened across Siberia. People took to the skies in aeroplanes. An earthquake destroyed San Francisco. A tunnel was driven beneath the Alps. A man stood at the North Pole. A man in America produced more motor cars than anybody had done before. A man stood at the South Pole. A great ship struck an iceberg. There were triumphs and disasters . . . and then, of course, there was the war.

Martha and I lived in Bartholomew Square like strangers. When she muttered her Polish prayers, and counted the beads of her rosary, she reminded me of my mother. The Secretary wants to know whether she kept her promise. Well – sometimes I thought I detected the trace of a question on her lips but in the end she always managed to restrain herself, she never encouraged me to talk. I did not talk: these years were a long silence. I spent my time eating in expensive restaurants. I travelled south for the winter and made my round of the consecrated sites: the Coliseum, the Circus Maxentius. I looked up into the Roman sky through the roof of the Pantheon. I went to Pompeii and climbed Vesuvius. One afternoon, when the spring air seemed filled with the past, I walked along the beach at Sorrento. I did not visit the little town of Magenta, where they make silk and matches.

Siriso? I expect that you are wondering what happened to that organization. Sir Rodney was right. I wanted no part of it and after his death I completely resigned my role. But don't think that I was worried about my purity. I knew that I had already been corrupted. The directors and the managers, the bankers and the clerks took over. It goes under another name these days.

All this counted for nothing. I was not living. I began to feel that the point at which I had succeeded to my inheritance was the point at which I ceased to exist from the point of view of autobiography. Worse even than not oneself being in life, I knew that I was preventing others from living. My survival meant only that my wealth concentrated itself upon me like a deadweight, like a smothering blanket. I immobilized the things around me and prevented their redistribution.

One thing only persuaded me of the survival of the past. Each year, on the anniversary of her death, I received a letter from Lady Magenta. They were love letters, after a fashion. But I could not reply to them. From what hand, from what source they came I shall never know. I thought for years that they were sent by Pesto to torment me, then he died. My suspicions turned towards Sir Rodney until, two months after his death, I received another letter. Lady Magenta's last communication arrived the following year as Europe sank exhausted into an uneasy silence and waited for the beginning of some aftermath.

'Write something down,' Lady Magenta said. 'Write about something before it is too late.'

It was then that I started talking to Martha. I told her about Egypt but she still insisted that it was like a fairy-tale. And all the time I was searching for a subject to write about.

I became ill and lost myself in a nightmarish theatre. But I was given a stay of execution. There was so much work ahead of me although I did not know what it was. There was so much to do. I travelled in my mind and conjured up places I had never visited. I tried to find some way of talking about this strange magic that we glimpse around us. Although I knew that it was vital, its secret eluded me and I let my books fall from my hand. I sat idly by the fire and watched the flames. Would I ever do anything? I doubted it.

Only then did it seem to me that I could fall back on the old familiarities. I might catch something in my net, and at the very least I would make Martha's mouth fall open in delight. Yes: I would write about my life as the back end of a pantomime horse.

The next day I got up early and sent a letter. I placed my advertisement in *The Times*:

GENTLEMAN
SEEKS SERVICES OF A
COMPETENT AMANUENSIS
Apply to Mr Jack Spellman
Bartholomew Square

26

Catharsis

THE SECRETARY came to me one night like the ghost I had wanted. We shut ourselves off from the world and set to work like monks beginning a stained glass window. For a while – for months – I experienced a great improvement in my health. My voice had never been stronger and I almost laughed at the pitiful scratchings made by the Pencil as he tried to keep up with me.

We were comfortable, were we not? I admit, of course, that we had our disagreements and that there were moments of tension between us, but in the end it was easy enough. After all, we drank our wine three solid floors above the mud. Outside in the square things were much worse: blind men were tapping their sticks and, as I chattered on in my sick room, treaties were negotiated between nations. Something died whilst I spoke. I say this, I think, without Zanzare's nostalgia.

Wonder? The uncanny? They have survived in spite of all my traps. We still take ideal connections for real ones and so people our prisons. I can see a certain sense in this now. Magic is a voice within us that dares to assert the impossible and which therefore feeds our lives with a little, lingering hope.

I am trying to put my finger on the thing that died.

The vast expansion of the market has been accompanied by a movement of an equal and opposite nature. We shrink into our shells; we run for cover. When people talk to each other these days you can hear the clattering of their carapaces. Protagoras has been surpassed and man is no longer the measure of things. We are spectators of our own toys. Our nervously flickering eyes betray the knowledge that we are accidents born of huge but senseless indiscretions, lost between atoms and stars.

Lost but not orphaned. Once upon a time we could bewail our birthright, bemoan the fact that our bodies were torn asunder by aristocrats and prostitutes. It is all a matter of matter now and physics has no morality.

In the cities we stagger from heap to heap. We stuff ourselves and the old ruins exercise no fascination. God knows it was a tired beast, the circus: paint peeling, a place of stale delights. And now the giant commerce has swallowed all our thoughts.

I am beginning to sound like John Bunyan.

The Secretary's pen sputters its last gobs of ink into his notebook and I find myself gabbling out these final thoughts with precious little story left to make them live. This is the frayed end of the cable: the threads unravel themselves and disappear. There are many regrets, of course, as there always are in such cases. One cannot avoid a gnawing desire for the magnesium flash which illuminates everything from start to finish. But my beginning seems so far away and the old words have hidden themselves in cupboards or run off into the woods.

Despite these losses, I know that I am still playing with the toy horseman and the china tiger. I know that I am still a fly trapped in amber. I could not be more certain that I am still inside the pantomime horse, struggling to get out.

Everything moves. Nothing changes. Order is an accident of chaos.

The end, Mr Ghost: soon the last full stop. The end of writing – is it not? – is to stop and never say another word. I shall be glad of that silence. In any case, the sound of my voice was never enough. My voice? It seems so unrelated to the way in which it has been recorded. Over there, Mr Ghost, on the escritoire: page after page and chapter after chapter stretched out in a long segmented line. I have no sense of – what is it called? – of authorship. It could all have happened at a *séance* and you must do what you will with the ectoplasm.

I suppose that I am no exception. We all live on the dead and it is their tongues which have waggled in our heads down through the ages.

The Secretary wishes me to tell him the final chapter in *The Life of my Entrails*.

I had for many years been disturbed by a sudden wriggling or kicking inside me. It came suddenly, went as quickly and I never mentioned it to anybody. From the winter of 1918 onwards, however, the sensations increased in frequency and became painful. In June I noticed with anxiety that there was blood in my stools and also pale rectangles which faintly resembled pieces of pasta. Despite my discomfort and increasing exhaustion, however, I forged ahead with the writing. I knew that something was living inside me but instead of acting on my knowledge I chose to dream. At the beginning of November – we were reaching the end of Chapter 23 – I at last plucked up the courage to seek medical advice. Dr Wilding, who had succeeded Dr Garth-Thompson as the senior member of the Chelsea practice, took away a faecal sample for examination. He called the next day and informed me that he had succeeded in identifying the pale rectangles as egg-bearing proglottides, or segments, belonging to the cestode *Taenia solium*, commonly known as the pork tapeworm.

Dr Wilding prescribed santonin, the anthelmintic extracted from the dried buds of a species of wormwood. I took the powder in hot water later that day and shortly afterwards began to feel most unwell. In the middle of the night, shivering uncontrollably and vomiting black bile from time to time, I discharged a longer than usual section of the uncanny creature.

But the doctor was not satisfied that my digestive tract was free from infestation. He was also concerned by my weakness and generally poor state of health:

'We can continue the purges, Mr Spellman,' he told me, 'but I should make it clear that what poisons a tapeworm will also poison you. I have to say that in your case I am not convinced of the superior hardiness of the host in relation to his parasite. One might even invert the Aristotelian terms and say that a strong cathartic might, so to speak, be your nemesis.'

I was nonplussed. 'Are you saying that you can do nothing for me?'

The doctor shrugged. 'It's up to you. I can only point out the risks.'

I thought for some time. 'I can't accept your view,' I said at last. 'I want a second opinion.'

Dr Wilding reluctantly agreed to make me an appointment with the eminent Viennese parasitologist Dr Weinz, who was shortly to arrive in London for a conference on nematodes at Guy's Hospital. He had met Dr Weinz several years previously when the Austrian scientist had been recovering in St Bartholomew's Hospital from an accident involving a tram which had unfortunately necessitated the amputation of one leg above the knee. Wilding had himself supervised the fitting of an artificial leg and, despite the brevity of their contact, he had been greatly impressed by Weinz's intelligence and had followed his career with interest.

Weinz had devoted his life to studying the many denizens of the gut and all the strange creatures which make their homes in human bodies. He had been the first scientist to have studied in detail the life cycle of the beef tapeworm, *Taenia saginata*. His stained slides had enabled every stage of the creature's double life to be examined under the microscope. Swallowed by a specific host, the egg split apart and developed into an oncosphere which drilled through the wall of the gut and found its way into the eyes, brain or liver of the creature which entertained it. The oncosphere there established itself as a cystocercus and became a tapeworm in waiting. Its invaginated scolex, or head, was clearly visible in Weinz's sections. When the living cystocercus was eaten it grew rapidly into a sexually mature hermaphrodite.

Weinz's article in the Spring *Lancet* of 1894, 'A Case of a Parasitic Cyst in a Human Foetus' was, Dr Wilding told me, a classic of parasitological literature. Weinz had been fortunate enough to be working temporarily in a hospital in Berlin when the daughter of a Wittenberg farmer was admitted to the Kaiser Wilhelm ward in the last stages of a difficult pregnancy. Two days later she had been delivered of a child which had been infected, either through the blood supply of the umbilicus or through the lining of the womb, by an oncosphere of *Echinococcus multilocularis*. The poor dead baby was, as Weinz had elegantly put it in his monograph, 'merely an habitation for a form of life with a greater energy than its own'. To the horror of both the young woman and her doctor, the robust cystocercus had grown to over a foot in diameter.

Amongst Weinz's many achievements was *Dark Secret Love*, a collection of classical writings on the strange spontaneous generation of parasitic worms. It seemed that the Wittenberg farmer's daughter treated by Weinz in Berlin was but a latter-day version of the case of Deimas's child as recorded by Hippocrates in his *Epidemics*. In the seventh month of pregnancy this girl suffered a wound 'from which there remained a fistula; sometimes a large worm came out of it'.

When Dr Wilding left me that afternoon I began to wonder again whether I was not suffering from the quintessential ailment of the autobiographer. Was it the madman's maggot which fomented visions?

Dr Weinz called on me a couple of days later. He limped across the room, took my hand with a gentle grasp and beamed down at me. I asked Martha to leave us. Dr Weinz gave me a thorough physical examination which lasted about half an hour. He took a professional interest in my genital birthmark and asked me a number of questions about it. I think that he was leading up to the suggestion that I should have it photographed for medical science. I managed to change the subject, somewhat awkwardly I suspect, by enquiring about his wooden limb. Without a trace of self-consciousness he rolled up his trouser leg to allow me to inspect the mahogany appendage. On a brass plate which had been neatly set into the shin, I read with delight the following inscription:

J.W. STRIDE
Surgical appliances
Manufacturers
of Prostheses
Harley Street

'I was the model for that leg!' I exclaimed. Dr Weinz looked somewhat surprised. 'It must have been almost thirty years ago,' I continued. 'Stride employed me for a week because he said that I had the perfectly average organ of locomotion.'

'What a remarkable coincidence,' mused Dr Weinz as he rearranged his trousers. It was clear that he did not quite know what to say.

'Have – have you been pleased with it?' I asked.

'Oh yes,' he replied, 'most satisfied.'

He began to rummage through his pockets. 'Now then: dear me where did I put it? I'm sure I had it somewhere. Ah – '

He brought out a glass Petri dish and showed me its contents. 'This is one of the proglottides which you excreted after taking wormwood,' he said.

'I see.' A soft pale scrap of flesh floated in a gelatinous substance which somewhat resembled aspic.

'Dr Wilding was quite right: *Taenia solium*, without a doubt. It's a good specimen.'

'Good?'

'Healthy: big.' The doctor grinned at me. 'You must forgive my enthusiasm for the objects of my research. I tend to become over-excited, you know. Each one is a real find and they're all so different. But I expect that you consider your situation to be uniquely miserable.'

'No –' I wanted to qualify his statement. 'I do not share your ardent interest but I must admit to a degree of fascination. The tapeworm has such an unprecedented intimacy with its host.'

Dr Weinz patted my hand approvingly. 'Rest assured, Mr Spellman, it has been closer to you than any other living being.'

'It has led its whole career inside me, Dr Weinz.'

'It has copulated with itself inside you, Mr Spellman. It will be producing three quarters of a million eggs each day by now.'

'Good God!' I was stunned. 'How long has it been doing that?'

'How long have you been experiencing the symptoms?'

I thought for a moment before replying. 'They have persisted over many years, although they have only become unbearable in the last few months.'

'I see,' said Dr Weinz as he stroked his beard. 'And none of the previous treatments have been efficacious?'

'It's not that. I didn't go to a doctor, you see.'

'Why not?'

I was unsure how to reply. 'Because – I suppose – I thought it was just me.'

'You thought it was in your *mind*?' The doctor's tone rose in astonishment.

'Yes – my imagination. I thought it was that.'

Weinz gestured uncomprehendingly into the air. 'But how, Mr Spellman, in the face of such obvious evidence, could you possibly have believed that your ailment was imaginary?'

I smiled. 'Sometimes our wishes come true, Dr Weinz. It's a sort of phantom pregnancy.'

The doctor gazed down into his Petri dish. 'It's hard to tell how long you have had the worm. They can last a lifetime and Dr Wilding mentioned that you had had an earlier encounter with *Taenia solium*. It is entirely possible that you never freed yourself of that original infestation.'

'But that was in my early days in the circus!' I cried. 'That was forty years ago!'

The doctor shrugged. 'Who can tell? They are secretive and solitary creatures. They are wonderfully adapted for life in the viscera. The parasitic cestode was one of God's most subtle works. It tends to manifest itself in the autumn, you know: a fruit of the harvest. Hippocrates was the first to observe this fact.'

I found Dr Weinz's almost benevolent interest in my uninvited guest faintly perturbing. 'But what can you do about it?' I asked. 'How can I get rid of it?'

The doctor sighed and looked up at me. 'Are you sure you want to get rid of it? To dethrone the monarch of your alimentary tract?'

'Fetch me the guillotine,' I replied. 'It's been with me too long.'

Weinz tapped his Petri dish regretfully and the proglottis trembled with a moment's artificial life. 'I can suggest only a surgical solution, Mr Spellman. The scolex has found too good a purchase for purgative removal; medicine cannot untie the Gordian knot.'

At last, Mr Ghost! I coincide with myself and have reached the present day. Dr Weinz visited me last week and I am going into hospital tomorrow. We are no longer living in the past and at each stage of this the remainder of my narrative, I do not know what is going to happen next. It is a vertiginous feeling. Throughout my dictation I could comfort myself with the vague pleasures of retrospection, the knowledge that I was playing in the shadows. Now I feel as if I am being flung bodily forward into the future, into the white spaces of unknown hospital wards. Is this mortality? The flush of life? I do not know why I have pursued my story this far. I remember wanting to join up with myself. Having done that, however, why go on?

I go on because, ironically, something has started happening to me. Twenty years of dullness and then, at the end of it, just when I had hoped to quietly fade away, another story is littered in my gut. It's very disruptive and I cannot say that I am happy about it. When we had finished the manuscript, I was planning to show the Secretary round the house. He has only ever seen the hall, the stairway and this room. We could have gone out through that other door in the corner. Over there, Mr Secretary: beyond the escritoire. We could have walked along the passage which stretches the width of the house and then descended to the kitchen by the back stairway. Martha would have been sleeping in front of the fire. I would have forced open another door and invited the Secretary to precede me through it. In the bleak chill light of the red room he would have seen the passage of time: the fallen heating ducts, the dry tanks, the scattered glass. I would have pointed out the remains of a stage and perhaps he would have picked up part of a broken terracotta pot. Dionysus looks soullessly down on the sepulchre. The grapes have fallen from his hand. The frost has cracked the statue and the porphyry tomb.

And over here, Mr Secretary, brushed carelessly into a corner so many years ago: the fragile and faded petal of an orchid.

My peculiar virgin birth was brought off successfully four days ago. Dr Weinz cut into my intestine through the right-hand side of the abdominal lining. As blood began to flow from my wound he succeeded in clasping the writhing scolex with a pair of forceps and began to draw it from my gut. 'Come, *Katharma*! Come, *Katharma*!' he chanted mysteriously but with gusto. It was like watching a conjuror pull a rope of coloured scarves from his pocket. I wondered how it felt to be so brutally exposed. Tapeworms have muscles and nerves and brain. Fortunately for them, perhaps, they do not possess sense organs. Cut off from the world they are so deeply buried in, they know nothing even of the food supply in which they swim.

Dr Weinz managed to remove about four feet of the ancient invader that afternoon. Another ten feet, having lost its anchorage, followed by a more ignominious route within the next two days. Once I had overcome my horror that five pounds of alien life had lived inside me for years, I regretted having overthrown the *imperium in imperio*. If it had not in its tetchy dotage set itself against me (in this at least it showed signs of a family resemblance) I think that I would have allowed it to remain. The stitches in my side will be removed in a few days. All in all it was a strange Caesarian. My eviscerated guest has now been bottled in alcohol and stands on my bedside table.

I feel cleaner. But I also feel weaker.

Thank you for your visit, Mr Secretary. Yes: Dr Weinz has returned to Vienna. No: I am not at all well. I shall not be coming home just yet.

It is certainly purpura this time. The doctors are running frantically back and forth. And as before in Alexandria, the minute stigmata dapple my body, grow rapidly into vibices and expand still further into ecchymotic patches. It is worse than it was before. The specialists speculate whilst I bleed into my own tissues. They brought a group of students to look at me today. 'Is it toxic?' one of them asked. Was I trying to commit suicide by ingesting some obscure poison? Absurdly they search my bedside cabinet, hoping perhaps to find copaiba, extract of belladonna, or even cinchona – misspelt, stolen drug!

Erasmus Bond's Aerated Tonic cannot help me now.

One of the students suggested that I was concealing a poisonous snake. I told him that they had themselves removed the only serpent in the garden of my body and that, far from being poisonous, it had been the only umbilicus which connected me to life. After I had delivered myself of this speech, the junior doctor and the Principal exchanged glances.

I am completely purple. Mr Perkin would have been proud of me: mine will be an aniline death.

Well then: they have their theory. It was delivered to me this morning by the Principal. I have, he thinks, a severe case of surgical shock. Doubtless this had been aggravated by my mental instability. It is what is called post-operative trauma. He intends to treat me with unguents based on arnica.

The unguents have not worked. They try astringent dressings: gallic acid again (I make a pretty picture) and phlebotomy. But I am not responding to fleam or scalpel.

The surface of my skin is crawling. This, they tell me, is a pruriginous symptom which is also traceable to my hysteria.

And now priapism too. 'Phallic infarction,' they call it. Where will it end? I am an engorgement, a monstrous purple bruise. I am drowning in an inner tide which gurgles in my moats and sweeps away my little sand-castles.

'Post-operative trauma!' That's what the doctors think, Mr Secretary. Because old Weinz has been sticking a scalpel into me. We know better, don't we?

We know it's the writing.

It began as a pastime. I looked on it as an entertainment: it was a sort of hobby-horse. And then, over the weeks, without my realizing it, the writing became a necessary tonic. I thought that it would heal my wounds and help new skin to grow. How mistaken I was ! For the writing changed into something else again. Addiction? Possession?

In the end, in a hospital which is far too familiar to me for my own peace of mind, it is a way of putting off the end, a means of postponing judgment. The Secretary watches me curiously. With tenderness? Perhaps. He was a mystery to me. I never asked him much about himself, his life. Soon he will be looking for another job.

Doubled up and split apart.

Everything is twinned and we stand on a peculiar Bridge of Sighs, stranded between a palace and a prison. The fog comes down, and we forget where we have placed our feet. We can only just see our hand as it reaches out to touch the balustrade. We cannot see the water.

Is this the philosphy of the worm? Possessed, infected . . . infested with monstrous living beings. None of this was ever to do with me. It was not me but molecules. It was rays and waves. It was atomies. I never managed to steer by the small star which lights our lives. On the one hand and on the other: either way, gigantic or minuscule, I did not understand. So I turned inside and, following the straitened passageways, tried to reach the microscopic galleries and caverns of my vesicular soul. I rooted about in the cerebral mushroom like a hog snouting truffles in the autumn. Tapeworm or silkworm, at every turn I met only new stageries, costumeries, vast and unshiftable accumulations of silt. A thing amongst things: a batik, a sudarium on which shadows dance from a distant source of light.

There are two tall people. There is sawdust in my hair and strange words are spoken. None of this convinces me of myself. I was only a colloquy of moving parts, and in the curiosity shop of my heart the fragments crop up like random bits of teeth.

The only refuge left was to speak the outside, to be its mouthpiece. I was a journalist of the world of things. I was a cartographer who tried to map the labyrinth of external objects, the falling jungles of the heart. But all my tools, which once rested so inertly in my hand, seemed to rise up against me and speak to each other through me. Perhaps I was seduced by things. They led me on too much. Nevertheless, in some way I shall never now be able to define, delight lurks in the crushed heart and not everything is entirely lost.

It is not so much that we remember the past as that, on bridges in the air, we glimpse for a few seconds the obscure forms of its survival.

And then dumbness.

Wordlessness.

27

At Gravesend

Jack Spellman died on 31 December 1919 in Guy's Hospital of purpura haemorrhagica and its resultant complications in the liver, bowels and kidneys. The words with which he ended the previous chapter were more or less the last he spoke. The following passage was found amongst his papers. The Secretary regrets that it has proved impossible to include a photograph of Mr Spellman as the frontispiece to this volume. The representation in question has faded beyond recognition, become the shadow of a shadow.

A T TWO O'CLOCK on the morning of 31 December 1899, Dr Garth-Thompson turned the brilliance of his electric lamp onto Lady Magenta's body and commenced his examination. A few minutes were sufficient for him to form an opinion:

'We must be thankful for the time of year and the sealed coffin. Decomposition is not too advanced – the belly only slightly distended with gases and very little discharge.'

I mopped my forehead in the quietness of the operating theatre. Dr Garth-Thompson and I washed our hands. We looked at each other for a second before we began our task.

We clothed the dead woman in a white gown and, lifting her from the slab, carried her to a nearby chair where, with the aid of steel clamps, we arranged her in a lifelike pose. Fortunately her limbs had not stiffened and we had no need to break them, as she had instructed us to do if necessary.

For the last time in my life I stood behind a camera and threw the black cape over my head. I saw an inverted image of Lady Magenta and, before I pressed the shutter, I wondered why it was necessary to give somebody up so finally, to say such an utter farewell.

For an instant the room was bathed in a magnesium flash. Dr Garth-Thompson then took a pair of scissors and removed a lock of Lady Magenta's hair. When this had been done I helped him to take off Lady Magenta's gown. We shaved her hair away and covered her body with finely powdered talc. We placed her face upwards in a shallow bath, the base of which was covered to the depth of several inches with softened wax poured over oil cloth. Gently pressing her body into the receiving surface of the wax, we ensured a perfect impression. I helped Dr Garth-Thompson to roll into a position directly over the bath a gigantic zinc vat which hung from a stand and contained 750 lbs of melted wax. Slowly and very carefully we tilted the vat and began to pour the soft warm liquid around Lady Magenta's form. From time to time we would stop and allow the wax to harden.

When half of Lady Magenta's body had been immersed in wax, we took strips of oil cloth and laid them over the wax to separate the lower half of the cast from the half which we had yet to pour. We placed iron rods through this second cast to enable us to lift it when it had cooled.

It was dawn when we finished this part of our labours. The lights burned on in Garth-Thompson's operating theatre and the curtains were drawn. Later, in the early months of 1900, there was to be a plaster and then a bronze statue cast from our moulds. The bronze was to be placed on a porpyry block in the hot-house at Bartholomew Square. I would cease to water the orchids, close the valves on the heating ducts and allow the red room to decay.

When we had lifted away the second mould, we removed Lady Magenta's silk-white body from the bath and washed it once again. No blood flowed from the wound when Dr Garth-Thompson cut my half-brother from her womb. We placed the little foetus in a crucible and cremated it in Garth-Thompson's furnace. When the ashes had cooled, I poured them into a cinerary urn which had the following inscription on the side:

Jack Tramont
21 September 1899 – 14 December 1899

We rested awhile and Dr Garth-Thompson took a glass of whisky. Then, under lamps which cast no shadows, I helped him to cut out and cremate Lady Magenta's brain, her heart, her ovaries, her eyes, her ears, her nose and her tongue. We placed the residual dust in an unmarked urn and sealed the lid.

We cut the girasol ring from her finger. I washed it and slipped into my waistcoat pocket. Dr Garth-Thompson then took a fresh blade and carefully cut the skin off Lady Magenta's back. It was to be cured and one day in the future, as Lady Magenta had commanded, the skin was to be used to bind the first copy of the book I was to publish.

Dr Garth-Thompson, of course, was more used to these things than I. But at eleven o'clock on the morning of New Year's Eve, as we washed

375

ourselves after our atrocities, we both looked at each other like branded men.

That night, under cover of darkness, Dr Garth-Thompson was to return the coffin containing the remains of Lady Magenta's body and the urn which held the residue of her son to the Tramont Mausoleum in Kensal Green Cemetery.

A different task had been allotted to me. At noon I took up the urn which contained the ashes of Lady Magenta's sense and feeling and thinking and travelled by hired carriage to Gravesend, where I put up for the day at the Pegasus's Arms and sat down in the snug to wait. I placed the urn on the table in front of me and tried to drink some wine. Parting the curtains, I held the glass up to the light. Outside, in the bare garden, the black bough of a tree rose above me and tattered leaves drifted in little eddies across the path. Beyond the garden was a low wall. Beyond the wall, the street. Across the street, a lumber yard which was shut. Along the street, the wharf. There were few people about. Frost lay on the ground and over the whole scene hung a sky of the brightest blue.

I slept through the afternoon and awoke in darkness at about half past six. I think that I had wanted, with a gasp, the glimpse of a face disappearing into gloom. But I was alone.

At about seven o'clock I went down to the wharf, where I hired a skiff and consulted the tide table. The river would begin to ebb at three minutes after midnight: three minutes into the new century.

My memories and my thoughts had exhausted me. The only way to escape them was to drink my way through the evening, to cut a swath of numb forgetfulness. I held the urn safe under my arm and felt the other customers jostle against me.

At half past eleven I staggered back to the wharf and found my skiff tied to the seventh post on Gravesend quay. I climbed down into the little boat and stowed the urn securely in the prow. And then, as I took my watch out of the pocket of my waistcoat, something – some small object which must have become entangled in my watch chain – fell through the air and bounced, once, off the gunwale. I caught a last quick glimpse of the opal ring before it disappeared, like a quenched ember, into the greasy water.

Untying a rope which was already stiff with frost, I cast off into the stream. The boat heeled a little and some water came in over the side. For some time there was only the slow drip of water from the lifted blades of my oars.

In mid-stream, then, at the confluence of two currents and at the moment of the turning of the tide, whilst the boat was held motionless for a few minutes in the quiet embrace of the river, I reached into the bottom of the boat and, taking up the urn, began to release the ashes of Lady

Magenta into the night-black waters. They fell through my hand, and I watched the pale dust float slowly away.

I waited for some time, but as the tide ran out more quickly, gathered its pace for the sea, the boat inexorably drifted in the current. A wind sprang up on the water from the Tilbury side, and the night tightened its grip. I lifted my oars, set my back to the Gravesend lights, and pulled for the shore.